Unexpected Path

Path Series

by:
Neri Lopez

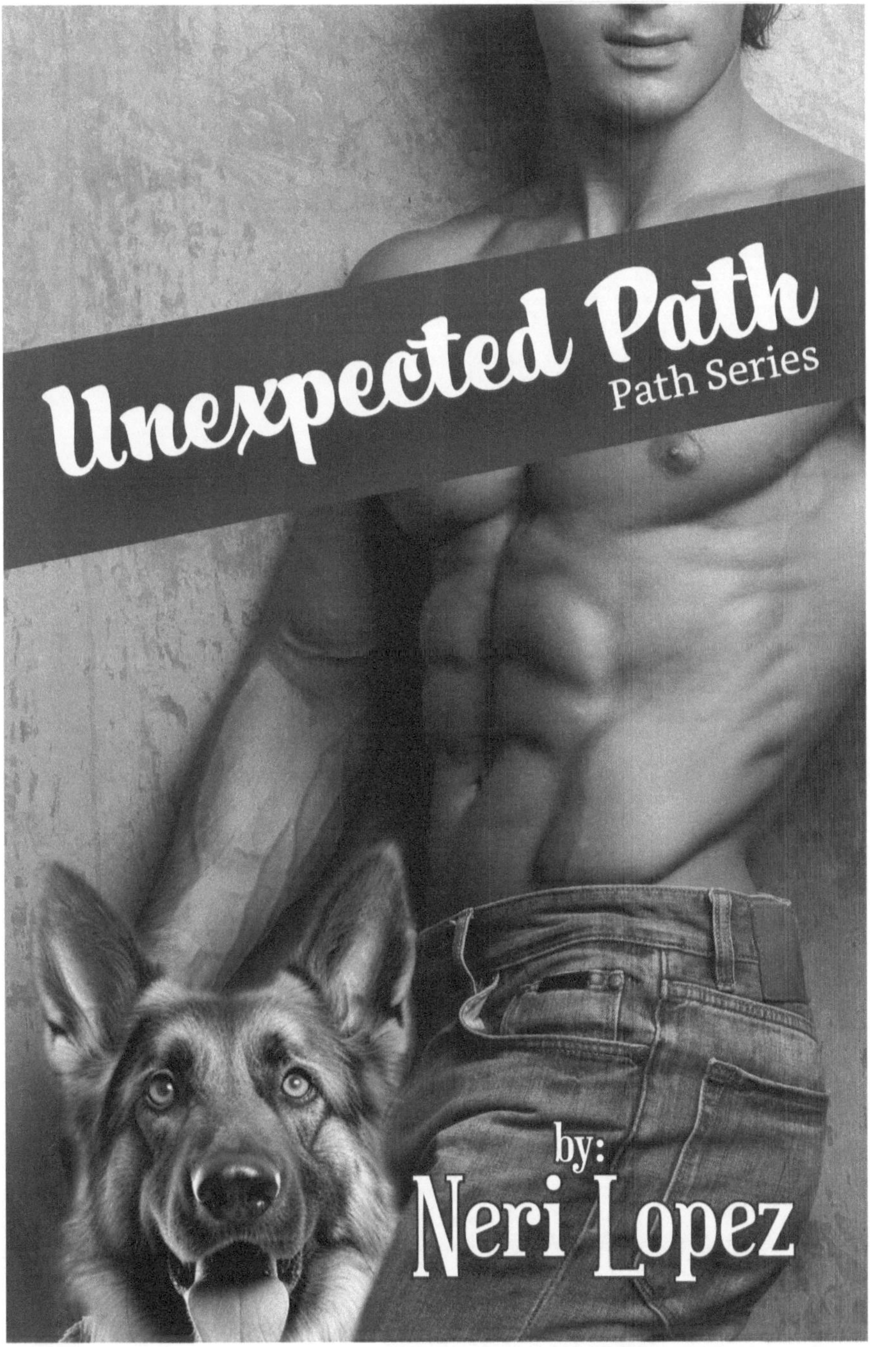

Unexpected Path

The Path Series: Book 4

Neri Lopez

Siren Book & Craft LLC

Copyright © 2024 by Neri Lopez
Publisher: Siren Book & Craft LLC
Editors: McKenzie Gibel, Tenesha L. Curtis, Whitney Morsillo, Michelle Rosquillo, and Deb Krickovich
Cover designer: Neri Lopez
Cover image: Depositphotos
Maps are fictional and designed by Neri Lopez

Disclaimer

This work includes themes of sexual assault and rape that some readers may find disturbing or triggering. Viewer discretion is advised.

If you or someone you know experienced sexual assault, please know you are not alone and that resources exist to help you during this difficult time. If you are or have been a victim of sexual assault, you can contact your local police department or call the number below.

National Sexual Assault Hotline: 800-656-4673
Or chat online at: http://www.rainn.org

RAINN (Rape, Abuse & Incest National Network) is the nation's largest anti-sexual violence organization. RAINN created and operated the National Sexual Assault Hotline in partnership with over 1,000 sexual assault service providers across the country.

For victims of a roofie assault, please contact: 844-960-2939
    http://www.theedgetreatment.com
Help is available 24/7 on the Suicide and Crisis Lifeline. You can call or text in English or Spanish.

The number is: 988 or reach out to them online at http://988lifeline.org

American Indian Cultural Center

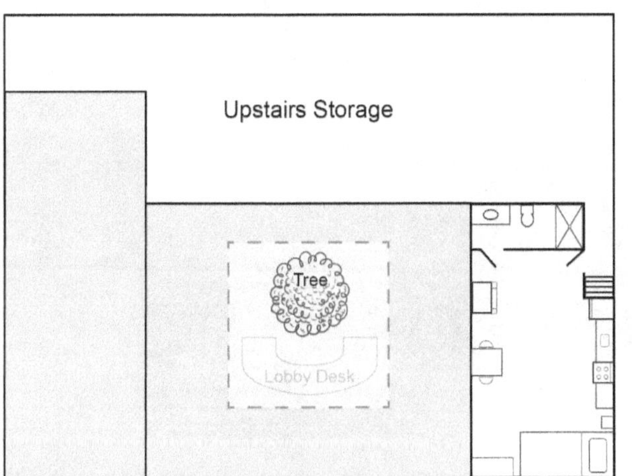

Second Floor

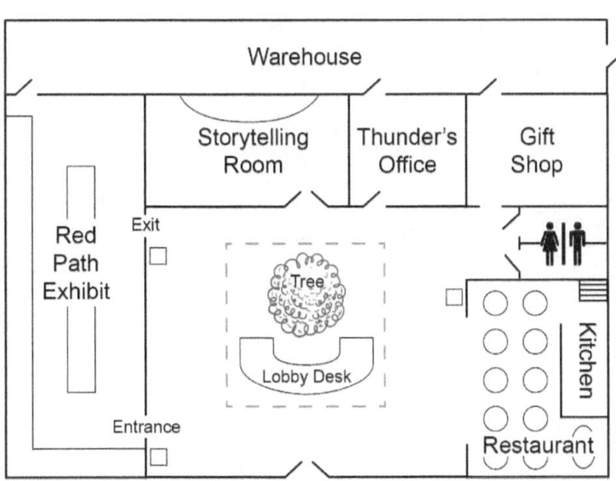

First Floor

Rock 'n' Roll Resort & Casino

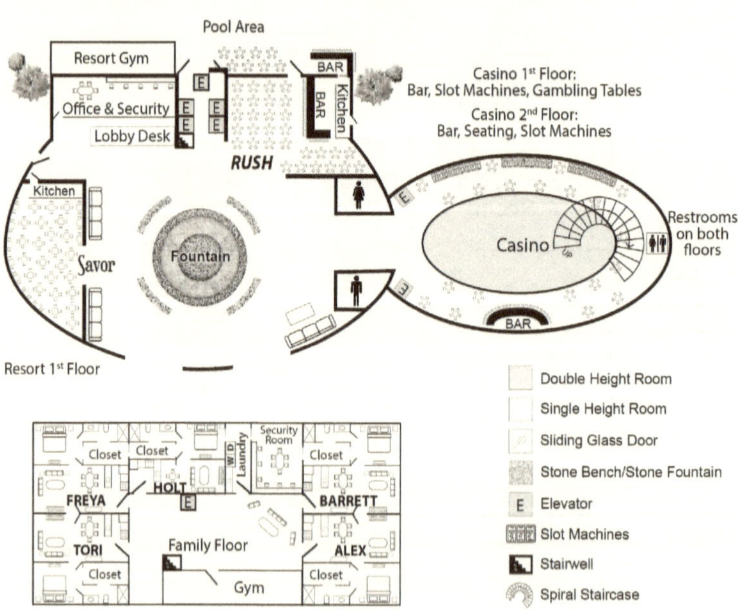

Path Series Family Trees

d.-deceased ❧ div.-divorced ❧ a.-adopted ❧ shaded box is their significant other

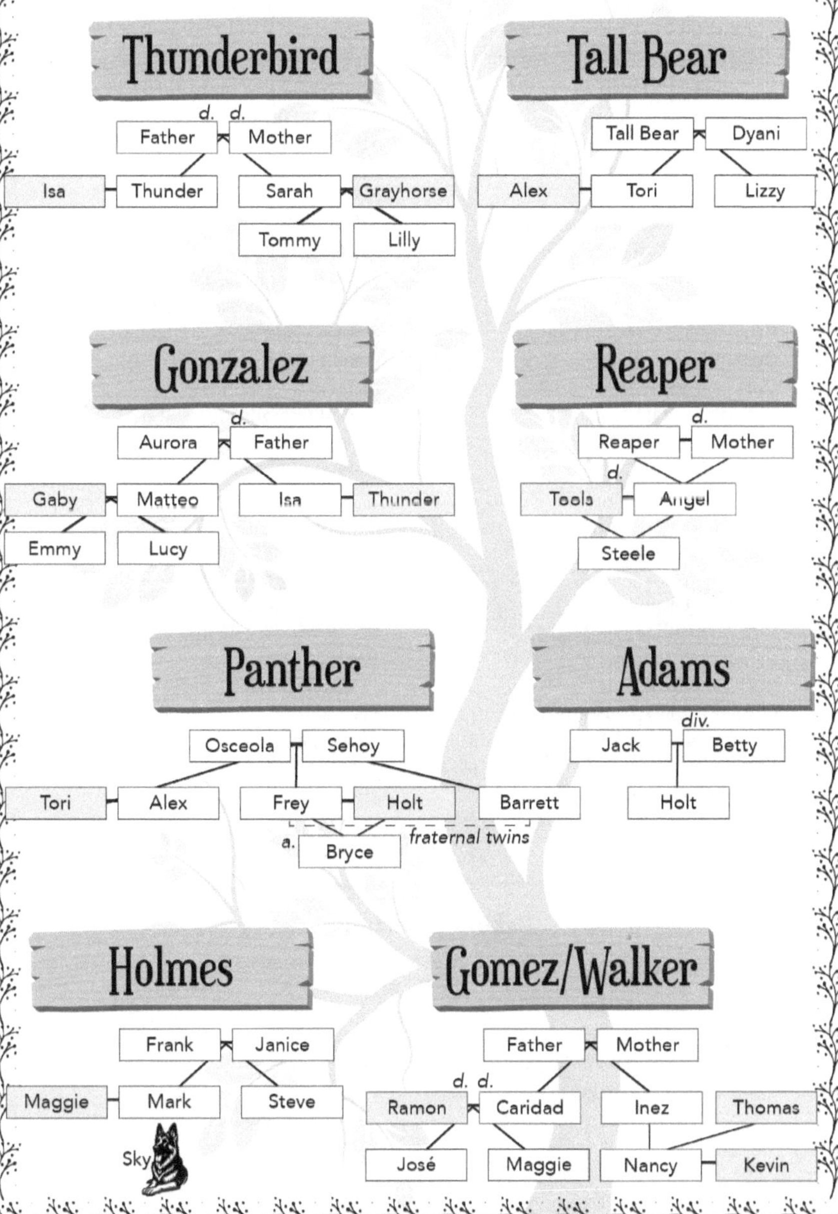

Spanish Translations

Aléjate de la ventana – get away from the window
Apúrate – hurry
Arroz blanco con frijoles – black beans with rice
Ay, Dios mío – oh my God
Ay, qué lindos – oh, how pretty/cute
Bájense – get down
Cállate – quiet
Capuchino – Cuban sweet dessert shaped like a cone drenched in sugary sauce
Coge – get
Cómo estás – how are you
Coño – fuck
Correcamino – road runner
Croqueta – ham croquet
Cuídate – take care of yourself
Dime – tell me
Empanada de pollo – chicken empanada
Escondete – hide
Espera – wait
Familia – family
Feliz Noche Buena – Merry Christmas Eve
Gracias – thank you
Gringo – non-spanish speaking person
Jefe – boss
Hermanita – little sister
Hijo de putas – sons of bitches
Hola – hello
Lechon asado – roasted pork
Levántate – get up
Mami – mom
Mi hermanita – my little sister
Mi niña – my girl
Mi sobrino – my nephew
Mija – my daughter
No me dejen – don't leave me
Papi – dad
Pastelito de guayaba – guava pastry
Pastelito de guayaba y queso – guava & cream cheese pastry
Perdon – sorry
Pistola – gun
Platanitos – plantains
Platanitos maduros – soft fried plantains
Platanitos tostones – crunchy double fried plantains
Por todo – for everything
Qué paso – what happened
Quédate aquí – stay here
Rápido – quick
Sí, soy yo – yes, it's me
También – also
Te quiero mucho – I love you a lot
Tía – aunt
Tío – uncle
Ya voy, pendejo – I'm coming asshole

Lakota Translations

até – father
ciŋkší - son
haŋ – yes
lekší – uncle
wíŋyaŋ mitáwa – my woman

Contents

Chapter 1

11 Years Earlier

Maggie

"*¡Bájense!*"

On the floor, sprawled on her stomach in front of the television, Maggie blinked up at her father. He was standing at the window, yanking at the cord to the blinds. Outside the house, she heard the roar of motorcycles.

Maggie sat up, but before she could follow *mami* to the window, *papi* shoved *mami* away.

"No!" he hissed, glaring first at *mami*, then her before he turned away from the window. "*¡Cállate! Aléjate de la Ventana.*"

"*Papi?*" Maggie whispered, spooked by the look on *papi's* face. Suddenly, she heard what sounded like the roar of fireworks before the windows exploded in front of *papi*, sending shards of glass into the house. Maggie scrambled back against the wall and curled up with her arms covering her head attempting to protect herself. She heard her parents crying out in pain. What was happening? Was someone aiming fireworks at her house instead of the sky? Why?

Maggie glanced up in time to see her parent's bodies fall in slow motion. Her body trembled as a bolt of ice raced down her spine while she watched *papi's* white shirt turn red, *mami's* favorite yellow scarf stained crimson. It took Maggie a second to process what was happening and realize her parents had been shot. Those weren't fireworks, they were bullets.

By the time *papi* landed on *mami* on the floor in front of the couch, Maggie realized *mami's* chest wasn't moving and *papi* had blood bubbling out of his mouth. As the bullets continued to fly into the room in rapid succession, Maggie army crawled to her parents. Her elbows and thighs stinging from the glass cutting into her skin.

"*Mami*, no!" There was a growing red puddle on the floor under *mami's* head. That's when Maggie saw the gunshot wound on her forehead. Praying for a miracle, Maggie pressed a trembling hand against *mami's* neck to check for a pulse like she'd seen people do on television when someone was hurt. *Mami's* neck was still against her fingers. Her beautiful *mami* with the kindest soul she'd ever known had left this earth. What was she going to do?

"Mija." *Papi's* gurgling voice was hoarse. *"Coge...pistola... escondete...te quiero...Margari..."* *Papi* closed his eyes, dropped his head onto *mami's* shoulder, and took his last breath holding onto the love of his life.

"No," she croaked. "No. *¡No me dejen!*" Her fists scraped against the glass-strewn floor. "No, no, no!" Maggie wasn't sure if she was screaming out loud or just in her head, staring at her parents' blood-splattered bodies. Her head was spinning out of control as she looked down into *mami's* soulless eyes.

"Te quiero mucho tambien, Mami y Papi," Maggie whispered, ignoring the blood and dropping on top of them for one last hug. With tears streaming down her face, Maggie reached out with a trembling hand and closed *mami's* eyes. *Mami* was a good soul who needed to rest in peace and not see *papi* bleeding on her.

She couldn't hear the bullets anymore over the pounding of her pulse and her own choked breath. This wasn't happening. It wasn't real. A strange silence fell in the wake of her cries, like the calm in the eye of a hurricane. The bullets had stopped, she realized. Then she heard the murmur of voices.

What was happening? The voices were getting closer. *Papi* told her to get the gun and hide. She didn't want to leave them, but she wasn't ready to die. *Papi* had taught her and *mami* how to shoot his gun and where he hid it. She needed that gun.

Maggie scrambled back toward the wall. Her hands hurt, but she pushed through the pain. Getting into a crouched position, she glanced out the window and saw a man wearing a Lucifer's Renegades Motorcycle Club vest talking to another man. José, her brother and prospect for Los Lobos de Muerte MC, had showed her a picture of that logo and told her to stay away from anyone wearing a vest with that emblem.

Closing her eyes, she cupped her mouth with her blood-soaked hands to cover up her cries for help. If they saw or heard her, they would kill her. She took a couple deep breaths to calm down, but her eyes shot open when she heard footsteps approaching the front of the house. Her time had run out.

On hands and knees while slipping on her parents' blood mixed with her own, she crawled out of the living room. The shards of glass sprinkled all over the floor continued to cut into her skin, causing searing pain to shoot up her arms and legs. But Maggie knew she couldn't stop. If they found her–she'd be dead. Gritting her teeth, she used every bit of inner strength she had and continued to her parents' bedroom. Once inside, Maggie used her dad's dresser to help her stand before she limped into her parents' closet.

Papi kept his gun on the top shelf in a shoe box. He didn't keep it in a safe because he couldn't afford one. Right now, she was glad because she wasn't sure she could remember a code. He'd bought the gun and taught Maggie and *Mami* how to shoot it shortly after José joined Los Lobos. She and her parents had all lived in fear of exactly what was happening right now. José always said Lucifer's Renegades wouldn't dare attack family members, but guess what–they dared.

Maggie had to decide–run or hide? She'd seen so many bikers in her front lawn during her brief glimpse out the window. What if they had the house surrounded? If she tried to escape out the back, they might catch her. *Papi* had told her to get the gun and hide–she would hide. José was supposed to come home for dinner. Which was why when *mami* and *papi* heard the motorcycles, they had gotten up to answer the door. Many times, José brought club brothers over for dinner. Part of her wished he'd been there with her when the LR's arrived, but the other part was afraid he would have died alongside their parents. Where was José?

She'd thought *Papi* was crazy having her and *Mami* practice those stupid hide or escape drills, but now she was glad he'd been strict about it. Maggie knew she wouldn't be able to kill all the bikers—heck she'd never even shot a person, just a target—but she could at least take some out before they killed her.

Maggie grabbed the rope hanging from the attic stairs and pulled. Once the stairs dropped, she snatched the long rope on the inside of the door, grabbed the shoe box, and climbed into the attic. Maggie weighed about eighty pounds soaking wet, and she knew, from previous practice, that closing the attic door was harder than opening it. With her body shaking and her nerves fried, she panicked that she wouldn't be able to close it in time. The stairs felt like they weighed a ton when she tried to pull them up with one hand. That wasn't going to work. She needed both hands. Putting the shoe box down, she braced one hand on a sturdy two-by-four post, wrapped the rope around her other fist and pulled with all her might, finally enclosing herself in the attic.

"Oh my God," Maggie mumbled between tears. With trembling hands, she grabbed the gun, turned the safety off, and scooted back to lean against another wooden post with her knees up. The gun wobbled in her hand so bad, she used her knees to steady it while gripping onto the rope. Murdering someone was not one of her life goals, but if they came for her, she was not going to be taken. Her friends at school had told her female rival MC members were not treated well if they were kidnapped. Not only were they beaten and tortured, but they were also passed around and raped by all the members. Maggie checked the bullet rounds in the gun, she wanted to make sure she left one for herself if the police didn't arrive in time.

Maggie stopped breathing when she heard the biker's mumbled voices. She couldn't make out what they were saying, but she didn't like how close they were. Putting down the gun, she held the rope tight. If they couldn't get into the attic, they couldn't shoot her. Their voices became fainter until all she heard was silence. *They must be leaving the bedroom.*

Suddenly, she felt a tug on the rope. They were trying to open the attic door. *No, God. Please no!* Maggie held tight and prayed they didn't try again. Then she heard the faint sounds of police sirens, and the tugging stopped.

A few seconds later, she heard the roar of the motorcycles leaving, and that eerie silence again. Maggie took a couple deep breaths. Had they all left? Maggie got to her knees and cracked open the attic door, peeking through a small slit. She was terrified to leave the attic in case one of them was still there.

"Fuck! Margarita!"

When Maggie heard her brother's voice from down the hall, she pushed the attic door down with enough force to drop the stairs to the floor with a bang.

"José?" Maggie was relieved to hear her brother's voice.

"Where are you?" José yelled.

Maggie climbed down and ran toward his voice, smacking right into him.

"What the fuck happened?" José held her shoulders. "I saw a shit load of LR's racing away down the block before I pulled up and saw the front of our house. Are you okay? Were you shot? You're bleeding."

"This is all your fault," Maggie screamed at him, slapping his chest while she cried hysterically.

"*Margarita. Perdon, mi hermanita,*" José choked out. "I never meant for this to happen." José grabbed her and held her so tightly she could feel his body trembling.

"Look what they did!" Maggie shoved José away and pointed to *Mami* and *Papi*. "They didn't deserve this. Why would the LR's do this? We've never done anything to them."

"No, *coño!*" Jose ran his hands over his head, gripping the back of his hair. "*Dime. ¿Que paso?*" José looked around the room.

"They killed our parents!" Maggie wailed. Running to their parents, she dropped to the ground and laid her head on her father's back. Wrapping her arms around them, she ignored the blood and gore on the floor. She found some solace knowing they died together, holding each other, but she would have preferred for them to stay with her.

"Please, God, bring them back to me." Maggie begged and pleaded with God to create a miracle and bring them back to life. How was she going to live her life without them? They would never see her graduate, get married, and have kids. "Oh God, please."

"Shit. Are you sure it was the LR's?" José stood near them, tears rolling down his cheeks, his hands clenched in white-knuckled fists at his sides.

"*Sí,*" Maggie was blubbering, "I...I s..saw their vests." Maggie sighed into her parent's bodies when she heard the police sirens getting louder. Help was on the way.

"I gotta go. I'm gonna get those motherfuckers." José turned away and headed for the bullet riddled front door. "Wait for the police."

Maggie bolted up and grabbed his arm. José spun around. She could see the anger and evil in his eyes. She had to stop him. If he killed anyone, he could wind up in jail. What would happen to her then?

"No, José." Maggie frantically grabbed both arms. "Stay with me."

"No, *hermanita.*" José pulled out of her grip. "I'm gonna take care of this...motorcycle club style."

"What does that mean?" Maggie tried to grab his shoulder, but he moved out of her way. "Wait, José! Let's tell the police together. They can help us. Please, don't go after them."

"I'm gonna kill them for *mami* and *papi*." José wiped his tears with the back of his hand and turned to Maggie. "I'll be back. I love you."

"José, no! Please, don't go after them. Don't leave me. Let the police handle it. Please!" Maggie screamed, trying to pull him back. But he was filled with anger, stronger than her, and in a hurry. Breaking her hold again, he fled, jumped on his motorcycle, and peeled out around the back yard seconds before the police cars screeched to a halt in front of the house. Maggie looked down and saw all the blood on her hands and body. It was a miracle she hadn't been shot. Maggie dropped to her knees next to her parents and prayed. She heard the police shouting outside but remained inside.

"*Mami, papi,* please look after him. I need him now that you are both gone. I know you didn't like him joining the MC, but please keep him safe for me." Maggie heard the officers enter the house.

"Hello, police. Is anyone here?" an officer called out.

"Young lady are you hurt?" another officer said before a hand rested on her shoulder. "We already called an ambulance. Please, come with me."

"I don't need an ambulance." Maggie kissed the inside of her hand and first placed it over *mami's* cheek, then *papi's.* Her heart hurt, but she had not been shot. A female officer helped her stand.

"My name is Deputy Vanessa Davidson." The female officer led her outside the house to the ambulance. "You can call me Deputy Vanessa. Can you tell me what happened?"

Maggie sat on the back fender of the ambulance with Deputy Vanessa while the paramedics checked her over and cleaned her up. She recounted how the LR's came to her house and opened fire. Not sure how much to say because she wanted to keep her brother safe, so she told them she didn't know why they had shot up her house. She played the part of the dumb little girl, which was easy to do as a fourteen-year-old.

"You're shaking." Deputy Vanessa wrapped her hands around Maggie's. "Can we get her a blanket, please?" She asked one paramedic.

"Yes, ma'am." The paramedic jumped into the ambulance and dropped a blanket over her shoulders.

Deputy Vanessa wrapped it around her. The warmth of the blanket soothed her. Until that moment, Maggie hadn't realized she was shivering. When she finished telling them her side of the story, she gripped the blanket tightly around her and looked down, not making eye contact in case Deputy Vanessa wanted to ask more questions.

"Is there someone you want to talk to?" Deputy Vanessa held her phone out to her.

Maggie looked up just as two paramedics wheeled out a stretcher with a body bag and gasped.

Deputy Vanessa glanced in that direction and stood in front of Maggie. It was nice of her to block her view, but it was too late. Not only had she seen one stretcher, but the other soon followed. Maggie reached out toward the stretchers and would've fallen to the ground had Deputy Vanessa not grabbed her and hugged her as she cried.

"Who can I call for you?" Deputy Vanessa stroked her hair.

"No one," Maggie croaked. She didn't know who to call. If she called her brother and he was with his club, he wouldn't answer his phone. She was scared to involve her aunt, *mami's* sister, and uncle. They hated that José was a prospect for Los Lobos and had warned her parents about motorcycle clubs. She wouldn't put it past them to tell the police about José being in Los Lobos and their rivalry with the LR's.

"Okay." The female officer held her until she calmed down, then led her to her car. "Come with me to the station so we can finish our conversation. Are you hungry?"

Maggie shook her head and was grateful when Deputy Vanessa let her sit in the front passenger seat. Deputy Vanessa went to Maggie's favorite fast-food restaurant drive-thru and bought her a burger, fries, and a drink. Maggie waited and ate her meal when they got to the deputy's desk.

"Are you sure there's no one we can call?" Deputy Vanessa stopped typing and looked her way.

"Can I please call my brother?" Maggie crossed her fingers and hoped he would answer.

"Of course." Deputy Vanessa turned the phone around on her desk, facing Maggie.

"Can I have some privacy?" Maggie winced. She wasn't sure if Deputy Vanessa would walk away.

"Sure. I'll be right back."

As soon as Deputy Vanessa walked away from her desk, she dialed José's cell number. He didn't answer, so she left a message telling him she was at the police station and to please come get her.

José picked her up an hour later. He wasn't wearing his MC vest and drove his truck instead of his bike. Maggie also noticed he'd showered, reminding her she needed a shower to wash off all the blood. Her parents' blood. Her blood.

Chapter 2

11 Years Later...Office Bullying was Getting Old

Maggie

"**G**ood morning," Maggie smiled brightly at Ana as she walked in. Maggie had worked as the receptionist at Teramar Studios Advertising Agency in Ft. Lauderdale, Florida for the past five years. Everything was going fine until she made the fatal mistake of dating Ryan in accounting. That's when she learned you don't shit where you eat, as that old saying goes..

Maggie liked her men to be good looking, fit, alpha, spontaneous, and fun. Ryan was nothing like that, but since her usual type had not been working for her, she tried dating a nice, rational, average guy with a steady job. Ryan was cute in a clean-cut, professional way; he just wasn't doing it for her anymore. She liked bad boys and Ryan was an accountant—not bad boy material. In the beginning, Ryan had followed her lead, and they went out a lot. But after about a month, he just wanted to stay home and watch movies. Maggie got bored with staying in. She liked the nightlife action in bars. Really, she enjoyed dancing. After what happened to her parents, she never truly felt safe at home. She loved to be spontaneous and unpredictable.

Unfortunately, breaking up with Ryan turned the entire accounting department—and anyone who was friends with him within the company—against her. Most of Ryan's friends ignored her, which was fine. But others made snide remarks or treated her like a pariah.

"Hi." Ana smirked, then coughed 'bitch' into her hand as she walked by her desk. Maggie was dying to put Ana in her place. Anyone who knew her knew she never backed down from a fight, but she forced herself to remain professional.

Maggie wished Ana would just ignore her. The bitch cough bit was getting old. She knew she was the villain in this story, but it wasn't like she left Ryan at the altar. She thought they'd had a pleasant break up conversation over pizza—no tears were shed—so, what was everyone's problem? She had asked her best friend Isa if Thunder, her husband, needed help at the American Indian Cultural Center (AICC) and was waiting to hear back because one of these days she was going to explode and get herself fired. And she couldn't afford to be fired, and quitting wasn't an option unless she had something else lined up. Annoying as it was to find another job, she wasn't heartbroken about having to leave and would be thrilled to work at the AICC.

Thunder had built the ideal cultural center, which not only taught Native American history but helped kids in the community. Maggie would love to be a part of such an amazing place. Working at Teramar wasn't the be-all end-all. She had taken the job because it paid better than a fast-food restaurant. Plus, the daytime hours allowed her to finish college night classes and pay her bills.

The swish of the door opening jolted her from her memories. Maggie looked up to see none other than Ryan stroll through the door.

"Good morning." Maggie smiled at Ryan. Even though it was uncomfortable to talk to him, she remained professional. Ryan stared at her for about a second without saying a word and walked away. That had been his reaction ever since their relationship ended. Once his office co-workers found out and if they were all in the same room at a meeting, he added an angry look to the cold shoulder. So much for their amicable breakup.

"Good morning," Maggie said to another one of Ryan's friends from accounting who walked in after him. Mornings were the worst part of her day because that's when she saw everyone as they entered the building.

"Yeah, for some of us." He glared at her on his way to the elevators.

She didn't know why she tried. They only answered her nicely when a client or one of their bosses was present. Hearing the door again, Maggie looked up and was grateful to see her best friend, Isa. They had become fast friends on Maggie's first day at Teramar. They hung out together all the time until Isa met Thunder. Now, Maggie was a part of Thunder and Isa's friend group.

"Good morning, Isa," Maggie sighed. "Am I glad to see you."

"Good morning. Are you okay, Mags?" Isa walked to her desk.

"No." Maggie rubbed her forehead. "Isa, have you talked to Thunder about me working there?" Maggie whispered. She didn't want to be overheard.

"Shit, I'm sorry Mags. I totally forgot. Pregnancy brain and all. I promise I'll talk to him tonight. Shoot, this baby is sitting on my bladder. I've got to run to the bathroom again. I'll be right back."

Maggie grinned when Isa dropped her purse and laptop bag behind Maggie's desk and bolted to the restroom. She was so happy for Isa. She deserved to find a great man. Still smiling from watching Isa waddle to the bathroom, Maggie turned her head to the door when she heard it open.

"Good morning." Maggie smiled at Martin.

"Why are you so happy?" Martin grumbled.

"It's a beautiful day." Maggie's smile lost its genuine tilt, but she kept a fake smile pasted on her face.

"For some of us. But not for others who had their hearts crushed by a shitty girl that chased him for weeks." He scoffed and raised a skeptical eyebrow at Maggie. "You" –Martin pointed at her– "pulled us all into your schemes to get him only to dump him after a couple months. That makes you the shitty girl, in case you didn't know who I was talking about."

Maggie remembered that saying 'kill them with kindness,' so she refrained from saying something mean and just continued to smile at him. "Oh, believe me, I knew who you were talking about and I'm sorry."

"Yeah, right." Martin snorted and walked around the corner to the elevators.

"Good morning, Martin." Maggie heard Isa. She must've seen him and stopped outside the bathroom.

"Good morning, Isa. How are you feeling today?"

Wow, Maggie thought. She couldn't believe he talked to Isa so nicely, knowing they were friends. Why couldn't people just act like adults? She told Ryan and everyone else she was sorry. Maggie closed her eyes and sighed. This was going to be another shitty day for the shitty girl.

"I was doing great until I overheard your conversation with Maggie. What happened between Ryan and Maggie was between them. You all need to stop the office shaming. It's not nice."

Maggie's eyes popped open, and she tried to look around the corner to watch the drama unfold. Go Isa! Unfortunately, she couldn't see either of them, so she turned back around and pretended to work, but was still listening. Isa's comments humbled her, Maggie welcomed her friend's support. Everyone at Teramar loved and respected Isa, just like they loved and respected her before the Ryan breakup. Maybe now Martin would tell everyone what Isa said, and Ryan's posse would leave her alone.

"I didn't mean for you to hear that." Martin sounded apologetic.

"Of course you didn't. Which makes what you said so much worse. Leave her alone."

"Will do. Sorry."

"Mags," Maggie jumped in her seat. "Is that what you were talking about?" Isa whispered in her ear.

Maggie thought Isa had gone to the bathroom after the conversation with Martin. She sure as hell wasn't expecting her to be right next to her. Wasn't she in a hurry to pee? "I thought you were going potty?" Maggie turned in her seat and quirked an eyebrow at her.

"I was until Martin talked to me like a human being right after he dissed you." Isa pointed toward the elevator where Martin had just been standing.

"Yeah, it's like this every day and it's wearing on me. I've already said I'm sorry, but it's not enough. I know I chased Ryan. I know I broke his heart. But what was I supposed to do? Stay with someone who doesn't make me happy?" Maggie looked at Isa teary eyed. Sometimes it all got to her and made her feel like a horrible person.

"I'm so sorry, Mags. With my pregnancy brain, I totally forgot to ask Thunder if he had a job for you at the cultural center. I'll call him as soon as I get to my office. I didn't realize you were being bullied at work." Isa pulled Maggie out of her chair and into a hug.

Damn, Isa was strong for a pregnant lady.

"I'll let you know what he says. Now, I really gotta go or you're gonna have 'clean up at the receptionist's desk.'" Isa bolted to the bathroom.

Maggie laughed at Isa's imitation of a person saying 'clean up on aisle seven' on a bullhorn. As more employees came in, she continued to greet them with her professional façade in place. Her day was looking brighter. Soon Ryan's posse would know she had Isa's support, and they would leave her alone.

"Let's also get out of here for lunch."

Maggie jumped again and placed a hand over her heart. "Would you stop sneaking up on me? Is Thunder teaching you how to do that?" Isa was always telling her how quiet Thunder walked.

"Sorry, I thought you heard me." Isa winced. "Can you hand me my stuff so I don't have to bend down?" Isa pointed to her purse and bag.

"Of course." Maggie gave it to her. "Going out for lunch sounds good. Come get me." Maggie lifted the corner of her mouth in a half smile. Leaving the office, even if only for an hour, was better than nothing.

*** Isa ***

Isa was angry at herself for forgetting to talk to Thunder. Maggie had approached her a week ago when they were in the pool with their friends at the Rock 'n' Roll Resort & Casino after Thanksgiving dinner. Thunder managed the American Indian Cultural Center and Isa was supposed to ask him if he had a job for Maggie. Her pregnancy brain was getting out of control.

After seeing how Martin treated Maggie, Isa knew she had to help her friend. Being frozen out by your colleagues made for a terrible work environment. She hated when people acted like assholes instead of mature adults. Nobody had said anything to her about Maggie, but that was because they knew Maggie was her best friend. Then again, nowadays, Isa worked from home a lot because of her morning sickness, so she wasn't as aware of workplace drama as she was in the past.

Isa entered her office, shut the door, and locked it, not wanting anyone to come in and overhear her conversation with Thunder. Slamming her purse on her desk, she drilled her finger multiple times on the keyboard to turn on her computer.

Isa took a couple of deep breaths before calling her hubby. If Thunder heard the anger in her voice, he would be here within minutes to take care of the problem. He was very protective of her and her friends. When she had her temper under control, Isa took out her phone and dialed his cell.

"Hi honey, miss me already?" Isa heard the smile in Thunder's voice.

"I always miss you, but I need to ask you something." Isa sat at her desk.

"Okay, this sounds ominous. What's up?"

"Maggie is being bullied at work by Ryan and his friends. I just watched one of them be mean to her. She told me it was happening, but I didn't know how bad it was." Isa leaned her head on her hand.

"That sucks. Maggie's a nice person. She doesn't deserve that. What can I do to help? Do I need to come up there and set some people straight? Nobody messes with my wife and her friend."

Isa smiled. She loved that Thunder always had her and her friend's backs. "You don't need to come here, but can you hire Maggie as a receptionist for the center? I can't take my best friend doubting her self-worth, wondering if she is a bad person." Isa held her breath, hoping Thunder would say yes. He'd never said no to her before, but she wasn't sure he could afford this request. "I know Mark isn't always there because of his training and Tori is running ragged."

"I can. You're right, Tori needs help. I can't pay her a lot, but once we get the grant we applied for, I can raise her pay."

"I can't thank you enough for doing this for me. Do you know how much I love you?" Isa released her breath.

"I do, and I can think of many ways for you to repay me for my kindness," Thunder growled into the phone.

Isa loved hearing that sexy voice when he was turned on. It would be her pleasure to do anything he wanted. "Well, I'll make you a very happy man tonight."

"Mm, you always make me a happy man, but I can't wait for tonight. This day feels longer by the minute," Thunder sighed. "Do you want me to call her or are you going to tell her?"

"I'll tell her to call you so you guys can work it out. Besides, I want to get to my meeting and get the hell out of here before I say something I might regret. Some of these people are really pissing me off." Isa collected her papers and checked her watch. Her meeting started in five minutes.

"I can get to you in ten. Call me if you need me."

"I will. I know I made the right choice when I married you." Isa smiled. He would always be her white knight. "Thank you for always wanting to help me. I'll call Maggie before I go to my meeting. I love you."

"Love you too, *wíŋyaŋ mitáwa*. Till tonight," Thunder whispered before he hung up.

Isa couldn't wait until tonight. Making love with her husband was a true pleasure, which she enjoyed every day, especially since she was very horny during this pregnancy. Okay, well, she was always horny around him—pregnant or not. Isa called Maggie.

"Hey, Isa. What's up?" Maggie answered on the first ring. Her office phone had caller ID.

"Hey, Mags. I'm gonna text you Thunder's cell. Call him. He wants to talk to you." Isa wanted to be vague in case their calls were recorded and monitored.

"Is this about what we were just discussing?"

"Yes." Isa nodded, even though Maggie couldn't see her.

"I can't thank you enough. Thanks, Isa," Maggie replied.

"My pleasure." Isa grabbed her cell and shared Thunder's contact information with Maggie. "What are best friends for? Let me know how it goes."

"I will. I'm gonna call him as soon as we hang up."

"Okay, see you at lunch."

Isa was glad Thunder could help Maggie. Nobody deserved to work in a job where they were being harassed. Isa grabbed her materials for the meeting and headed out her door.

Chapter 3

Thank You, Thunder

Maggie

Maggie wanted to strike while the iron was hot. She couldn't leave her desk, but she could turn her chair and watch for any incoming clients or co-workers. Switching on her personal cell, she called Thunder immediately after getting the number from Isa.

"Hello, this is Thunder," he answered.

"Hi, Thunder, it's Maggie." Maggie was nervous. Isa said Thunder wanted to talk to her. Fingers crossed, she hoped he could hire her. "I hope it's okay that Isa gave me your cell number?" Maggie placed her hand over her queasy stomach.

"Hey, Maggie. Yeah, it's fine. Isa said you need a new job. I can hire you as our receptionist. Mark has been busy with his training and Tori has a lot on her plate. I'm assuming you want to come on board as soon as possible?"

A giant weight lifted from Maggie's shoulders, and she sighed with relief. "Yes, but I would still like to give my two weeks' notice. I don't want to burn any bridges." Maggie looked around and took a couple of deep breaths. The last thing she needed was one of Ryan's friends seeing her on her cell phone during work hours. "I can't thank you enough, Thunder. I really appreciate this."

"Anything for you Maggie. There's no way I could let my wife's best friend suffer at her job. Can you come by after work and fill out an application form? Then we can discuss your hours and pay."

"I'll come by today." Maggie's business phone started ringing. "I gotta go, but I'll see you later. Oh wait, I work until five."

"That's okay. I'll wait for you."

"Okay, thank you." Maggie felt guilty that he had to work late, but was so very grateful.

"No problem. See you when you get here."

"Okay, bye." Maggie heard Thunder say bye and hung up the phone quickly, trading it for her desk phone.

"Good morning, Teramar Studios. How may I help you?" Maggie directed the call and texted Isa.

> Maggie: Called Thunder. He will give me a job! Can you believe it? I'm so excited! I can't wait to start working there! Totally understand why you love him. He's a keeper.

> Isa: He sure is. I'm glad he could help you.

> Maggie: I'm gonna go by after work. He said he'd wait for me. Sorry, he'll be home late because of me.

> Isa: No worries. It will give me a chance to put on something sexy for him. After all, he should be rewarded for helping me…LOL.

> Maggie: I'm sure you would 'put on something sexy for him' with or without him helping you.

> Isa: True. See you at lunch.

> Maggie: Yep.

Maggie took a deep breath and smiled. She couldn't wait to leave Teramar and work at the cultural center surrounded by her friends.

Thunder

Thunder hung up and went in search of Mark and Tori. He wanted to talk to them before Maggie showed up this afternoon. Lucky for him, they were both sitting at the lobby desk.

"Hey, guys." Thunder interrupted their conversation and stood in front of the desk, facing them. "Do you have a minute?"

"Sure, shoot." Mark spun his chair around.

"What's up?" Tori turned and smiled.

"Maggie is being bullied by some co-workers because she broke up with Ryan, a guy she was dating at Teramar, and needs to find another job. Mark, since you are busy with training, I thought she could help you here instead of Tori. It will help Tori focus on her other duties and lessen her load. What do you think?" Thunder leaned against the counter, waiting for their input.

"I overheard her talking to Isa about some issues at work at the pool party on Thanksgiving, but I didn't know how bad it was. I love the idea of Maggie working with us." —Tori clapped her hands in excitement— "It'll be nice to have another girl around here and I could get caught up with all our paperwork."

"Mark, are you okay with this?" Thunder turned to him. Maggie and Mark had a unique, borderline combative relationship. They loved to tease each other. He'd say it was like siblings, but Thunder had noticed a little of something else.

"Sure, Maggie's cool." Mark smiled. "Plus, I can do my last couple of online courses and finish quicker."

"Great. She will come by today after work to fill out an application and go over the job description. I'll stay until she gets here and close." Thunder pushed off the counter.

"Do you want me to stay late?" Mark asked.

"Not necessary." Thunder shook his head. "You can go over everything once she is on board."

"When is she going to start?" Tori asked.

"She wants to give Teramar two weeks' notice. So, unless something happens, she'll start then." Thunder pivoted to go back to his office when he heard Mark.

"Hey, Thunder," Mark called out. "I need to practice running background checks for my class. Can I run a background check on you, Tori, and now Maggie?"

"Tori, are you good with that?" Thunder asked her because she was his assistant.

"Yes, I think it's a good idea to run background checks on anyone who works here. While you're at it do one on Alex and let me know if you find anything interesting?" Tori winked at Mark.

"Now you want me to get beaten up?" Mark dramatically placed his hand over his heart. "I thought you liked me?"

"Who do you like, Sweetheart?" Alex came up behind Tori and joined the conversation.

"You, I like you." Tori smiled sweetly at Alex.

"What are you up to?" Alex quirked an eyebrow at her.

"Mark is learning how to run background checks, and I told him to run one on you and tell me if he finds anything interesting." Tori softened the blow by hugging Alex and kissing his cheek.

"Of course you did." Alex bent down and whispered something in Tori's ear that made her blush.

"Okay, time for me to get back to work. Mark, run the checks. I agree with Tori that anyone who works here or helps us out needs to be vetted. Let me know how it goes." Thunder left them in the lobby, heading to his office when the cell phone in his pocket buzzed with an incoming text.

> Isa: Just talked to Mags. Thank you. I'll have a little something special for you Mr. Thunderbird when you get home.

> Thunder: Looking forward to it Mrs. Thunderbird.

> Isa: Love you.

> Thunder: Love you too, honey.

With a wide smile on his face, he entered his office to gather the paperwork for Maggie. He didn't need a reward from his wife for hiring Maggie. Being married to Isa was reward enough for him, but he was going to enjoy every minute of whatever she had in mind.

Chapter 4

Must She Always Bust My Balls?

Mark

"It will be nice to have Maggie here," Tori told Mark after Alex went back to work. Mark popped in one earphone to review his video instructions for running background checks on his computer. It was necessary for him to only wear one so he could hear when someone came into the cultural center. After all, a good security officer was always aware of his surroundings.

"Yeah, although she's always giving me shit." Mark smirked. "But she is fun."

"She sure is." Tori smiled at him. "You guys are funny together. Is there something going on I should know about?"

Mark wasn't touching that comment with a ten-foot pole. He didn't realize everyone paid attention to their back-and-forth banter. He liked Maggie and when he first met her, he would've asked her out, but she was dating Ryan. Mark was not into stealing another guy's girl, so they became friends. But were they friends? Every time she spoke to him, she was busting his balls. Mark wasn't sure if she liked or hated him.

"Uh, no. Why?" Mark frowned.

"Just curious." Tori faced her computer and grinned.

Mark didn't like the grin on her face. Maggie and Mark were always being thrown together since all their friends were coupled off. Although he enjoyed bantering with Maggie, he never got the impression that she saw him as boyfriend material. Probably because he was always dating a different girl. Besides, dating Maggie when they shared the same friends was a recipe for disaster.

If it wasn't for the friendship thing, Maggie would be the perfect person to date. She wasn't whiny and sensitive like some of his exes. Being raised on a farm with so much work to do, Mark and his brother, Steve, had been taught to say what you mean and not beat around the bush. His dad would always tell them, 'Too much talking takes away from working. So, either learn how to work and talk or be quiet and get your chores done'.

His tendency toward sarcasm and short answers made him a lousy boyfriend to some girls—probably why he had so many one-night stands and short relationships. He wasn't a commitment-phoebe but liked strong females and unfortunately, he hadn't met his match. Although Maggie would give him a run for his money. Not something he could tell any of the guys, or the girls for that matter, or they would push them together every chance they got.

"You just want more time to flirt with Alex." Mark wiggled his eyebrows at her.

"You are so right." Tori pointed at him and laughed. "But I do think it will be fun to work with her."

"Agreed." Mark shook his head. "With her here, I can finally finish my last couple of classes."

"I know you'll be happy to be done." Tori grabbed her files and stood.

"You got that right." Mark couldn't wait to transition into his new job. As a security officer, he could get up and wander around instead of being tied to the lobby desk. Thunder offered to increase his pay, but Mark didn't need the money. Now, knowing Thunder had enough money to hire Maggie full-time, he was glad he made that decision.

"Are you good here?" Tori asked. "I need to do some filing in the office."

"Yep, I'm good." Mark logged into his online course. "See ya later."

"Call the office if you need me."

"Will do." Mark opened his instructional video. "Oh hey, Tori."

"Yeah?" Tori stopped and turned toward him.

"Can you bring me our application forms from the office so I can run the background checks?"

"Absolutely, I'll bring them to you."

Mark never set out to be a receptionist. He'd taken some business courses at a local college back home, but they didn't appeal to him. Wanting a change, he took his savings and moved to Florida. When he saw the American Indian Cultural Center being built, he stopped and went in, curiosity getting the better of him. That's when he met Thunder. After Thunder told him about his dreams of integrating the American Indian culture into South Florida, he wanted to help any way he could. His great-great-grandmother was Piegan Blackfoot, which was part of the Blackfoot Confederacy, one of the largest American Indian tribes in Montana. Mark's mom loved telling him stories passed down from generation to generation about their Blackfoot ancestors.

Mark's favorite story was about how their people came to be after the Great Flood.

After a flood, Old Man gathered the people on a mountain and gave them water of different colors. He told them to drink the water and speak, and everyone spoke a different language except those who drank the black water. These people were the bands of the Blackfoot, the Piegan, the Siksika, and the Blood.

Working the lobby desk, he enjoyed meeting new people and telling them about the different American Indian cultures. After what happened between Rachel Doe Eyes and Tori, he asked Thunder if he could become the center's security officer. First, he took the 40-hour security officer training course, but that wasn't enough, so he took online criminal justice courses and a course that trained him in firearms and allowed him to get his Class "G" Statewide Firearm License. The license allowed him to carry a firearm at work. This career choice fascinated him, and he couldn't seem to learn enough.

He debated becoming a police officer after talking to Deputy George and Deputy Sean, but decided against it since he wouldn't be able to only protect the cultural center. He also took Taekwondo and Jui Jitsu classes at a nearby self-defense school. Besides deputies, George and Sean, Barrett and Holt also took him under their wings and gave him some on-the-job training at the casino.

Feeling good about his training and certifications, he was glad Maggie was coming on board so he could focus on the safety and security of the cultural center. They had a lot of guests and field trips. Mark planned on running background checks on everyone who came through their door. Safety first.

Mark began with himself to see what was out there under his name. He found his previous home addresses, school information, work information, and a previous speeding ticket. Criminal history, drug information, driving history, financial records, sex offender lists, social security number, and incarceration records are also things he could see with a background check. It took a lot longer than he thought it would to do a thorough background check on every employee because he checked all the information provided. He looked at his watch when he heard the front door open.

"Hey, Maggie." Mark looked up and smiled at her. Maggie looked sexy as hell in her floral wrap around dress and fuck me pumps. Shit, he wondered if he pulled the bow on the side of her dress, would the entire dress fall open? Maggie was brimming with excitement as she walked up to him with a little pep in her step. Mark stayed professional—she didn't need to know about the dirty thoughts in his head.

"Hi, Mark. How's it going?" Maggie walked up to the lobby desk.

"It's going. I hear you'll be working here with me—I mean us."

"I hope so. I told Thunder I'd come over after work to fill out the forms and talk to him." Maggie nodded. "Is he in the office?"

"Yep." Mark pointed behind him. "You can go on back."

Mark glanced back at his computer, not to ignore Maggie intentionally, but to avoid saying anything foolish if he kept looking at her. Wondering what she would look like with her dress open was wreaking havoc on his dick, which was now standing up, ready to take notice. Shit. Mark scooted his chair further under the desk.

"You're working late." Maggie came around the desk. "Are you sucking up to the boss?"

"Must you always bust my balls?" Mark sighed. "For your information, I was working on my online class and lost track of time. I'll head out after I shut down my computer."

"Oh, are you taking a class on how to be a good boyfriend and not date every girl in town?" Maggie smiled a sweet, fake smile at him.

"Funny. Clearly, I haven't dated every girl in town, because I haven't dated you yet." Mark wondered why the hell he just said a sentence that combined her and dating. Idiot. Now he was thinking about fucking her. Maggie needed to leave—her comments were turning him on.

"You should be so lucky." Maggie winked at him, softening the blow.

Mark shook his head. "Tell Thunder I'm locking the front door when I leave."

"So" —Maggie smirked at him— "now I'm your secretary?"

What the hell? Did she not realize her sexy smirk accentuated by her bright red lips were a turn on? Was she flirting with him? Bet she wouldn't be smirking like that if his cock was in her mouth and his hands gripped the back of her head, holding her still until it reached the back of her throat.

"Fuck, are you sure you want to work here?" Mark shut down the computer while he spoke to her and stood facing away from her. "With me?"

"I can't wait to work with you. Every day will feel like Christmas!" Maggie jumped up and down, clapping her hands.

"Fuck me." Mark sighed, propped his hands on his hips, and dropped his head.

"Not today, potty mouth. Maybe tomorrow." Maggie winked at him. "You're lucky Thunder doesn't have Lucy's swear jar, yet."

Mark turned his head toward her and groaned. Maggie laughed. When they were in the pool at the resort after Thanksgiving Dinner, Lucy, Thunder's niece, had called him a potty mouth. Then she asked her Uncle Thunder to buy her a swear jar. Mark owed her money as soon as Thunder got her the jar. Then again, Maggie owed her money too.

"Have a good night." Maggie waved at him before she walked away.

"Good night, Mags," Mark grumbled as he watched her ass sway from side to side.

Well, one thing was for sure, his job was going to be a hell of a lot more interesting with Maggie around. Between her smart mouth, sarcasm, and flirting, there would never be a dull moment. Mark placed the application forms in his drawer and locked the front door on his way out.

*** Maggie ***

"Knock, knock," Maggie announced her presence at Thunder's office door.

"Hey, Maggie." Thunder looked up from his desk and smiled. "Good to see you. Come in and have a seat. I have your paperwork ready for you."

"I can't thank you enough for helping me, Thunder. I really appreciate it." Maggie sat and reached for the paperwork Thunder slid across the desk.

"I'm glad to have you onboard. I spoke to Mark and Tori. They're happy to have you here as well." Thunder grabbed a pen off his desk and laid it on top of the paperwork. "Fill all this out and then we'll talk about the job, hours, and pay."

Maggie read through everything and filled out all the papers Thunder gave her. She was excited to be able to leave Teramar. These next two weeks were going to go by so slowly.

"Here you go." Maggie handed all the papers back to him.

"I have one more." Thunder grabbed it off the printer. "This is your consent to let us do a background check on you. Because of all the problems we've had in the past, we've decided to run a check on anyone that either works here or volunteers for us."

"Uh, okay." Maggie could feel the blood draining from her face. At Teramar they never said anything about a background check. Would she have to list all her names? Nobody knew about her brother and his involvement with the motorcycle club, not even Isa. Hell, Isa didn't even know she spoke Spanish fluently.

"Maggie, are you okay? You look really pale." Thunder got up and came around his desk, kneeling in front of her. "I'm gonna get you a bottle of water. Stay put."

Maggie watched Thunder leave the office. Shit! What if Thunder found out about José? The cultural center had an encounter with Lucifer's Renegades just a few months ago when their president and their drug dealer, Winston, kidnapped Tori. Would that stop Thunder from hiring her? Was he leery of all motorcycle clubs? Maggie felt her new job slipping away. She was about to get up and leave, but Thunder was walking toward her with a water bottle. Should she confess? She hadn't done anything wrong. Was she guilty by association? Or was it a lie of omission?

"Here, drink this." Thunder handed her the water.

Maggie opened it and gulped about half of it down. "Thank you, I feel much better."

"Are you sure? Do you need anything else? Food?" Thunder sat in his chair and watched Maggie.

"No, no." Maggie replaced the cap on the water bottle and set it by her feet. "I'm good. Thank you." She reached over, grabbed the sheet of paper, signed it giving consent for a background check, and handed it to Thunder. Isa knew her, so if Thunder questioned anything, she would at least have Isa on her side. Besides, her brother was in an MC not her. She rarely saw José anymore after that fateful day when her parents were killed. She loved him, but he insisted he had to stay away to keep her safe. They updated each other via text and a rare visit whenever he said he needed to see her.

Shaking those thoughts away, she tuned in to what Thunder was telling her about her pay and hours. Lucky for her, the pay was about the same.

"I'm one semester away from graduating with my marketing degree." Maggie said while Thunder checked her paperwork. "After that, I can help you or Tori with marketing or social media." Maggie would love to put her degree in action. She had a lot of ideas that would help their membership grow.

Thunder looked up and smiled. Relief written all over his face. "That would be great. We could use someone with those skills around here to make our lives a little easier. We'll reevaluate your pay at that time."

Those words were music to Maggie's ears. Extra money would get her out of her cousin's apartment and into her own. "Thanks Thunder. I really appreciate everything you're doing for me."

"I would never let my wife and her bestie down." Thunder smiled. "We care about you Maggie."

"Isa is lucky to have you." Maggie grinned. "You know" –Maggie pointed at him– "you are the best guy she ever dated. I'm so glad she married you. Though I do miss going out dancing with her especially now that you got her pregnant and all she wants to do is stay home to put her feet up. I can't really compete with your 'wonderful foot massages.'"

Thunder busted out laughing. "I'm the lucky one." Thunder placed his hand over his heart. "She is my soulmate and I'm so grateful to have found her. As for the going out part, she won't be pregnant forever and I know she loves hanging out with you. You know you can come by anytime, right?"

"Thanks, I appreciate that. And we'll see about the pregnant part." Maggie quirked her eyebrow at him. "I have a feeling this won't be her only pregnancy."

Thunder grinned. "You're probably right." Leaning forward, Thunder placed her papers in a tray at the corner on his desk. "So, when do you want to start? Tomorrow, one week, two weeks? You give me a date and we'll make it happen."

"I'd like to give them two weeks' notice, even though I will count the days." Maggie placed her hands on his desk, fidgeting with her fingers. "It's the right thing to do."

"That's very kind of you. However, if it gets unbearable, let them know you are being harassed and leave. I'm sure they'll understand. No one deserves to be treated like that at work, or anywhere, for that matter." Thunder placed his hands on top of hers and squeezed. "You are more than welcome to start here as soon as you want."

"I can't thank you enough. I'll let you know if anything changes."

Thunder released her hands, got up from his chair, and walked around his desk to hug her. "It's gonna be okay. Let me or Isa know if you need anything."

"I will." Maggie released Thunder and nodded. "Thank you again."

Thunder walked Maggie out. She felt as if a weight had been lifted from her shoulders. What she needed now was a Girls' Night Out. When she got into her car, she texted her girls.

Maggie: Ladies, GNO tomorrow night? 7pm? I need my tribe!

Isa: I'm in. We can do it at my house.

Freya: Woo-hoo! Can't wait.

Sarah: I'll be there. Grayhorse can watch the kids.

Tori: Yes, I'll be there.

Gaby: Sounds good. Matteo can watch my kids too.

Sarah: You know the boys will all get together and keep all the kids.

Gaby: Oh, Lucy would love that!

Freya: Can you make sure the guys invite Holt?

Sarah: Absolutely, I'll tell Grayhorse. The boys and kids can come here since Lilly goes to bed early.

Maggie: I love you guys. Thank You. See you then.

Maggie was relieved and getting excited to talk to her friends when another text came through from Isa.

Isa: Hey, come over early tomorrow and we'll walk to the beach and enjoy our day before our GNO.

Maggie: I would absolutely love that.

Isa: Great, see ya around ten?

Maggie: Ten is great, I can sleep in.

Isa: Perfect.

Her day just got a hundred percent better. Maggie drove to her apartment to tell Nancy her good news.

Chapter 5

Where the Fuck is My Lawyer?

Reaper

B eing in jail sucked because Reaper couldn't ride his Harley. Reaper loved the feel of the open road–the wind whipping his face, the roar of the engine, and the freedom to ride wherever the hell he wanted. Trips on his motorcycle helped him to relieve stress. Being enclosed within these four walls for the past two months was driving him crazy. He had allies in jail who didn't want to fuck with his Lucifer's Renegades MC, but he also had enemies from the Los Lobos de Muerte MC. Always watching his back was getting old and he wanted out–now.

"Reaper, you have a visitor." A correctional officer came to open his cell.

"Who is it?" Reaper sat up and stood facing the officer.

"I don't know." The officer shrugged. "All I was told was to get you and take you there."

Reaper followed the officer to a visiting room.

The guard stopped and faced Reaper before opening the door. "When you're done, bang on the door and I'll take you back to your cell."

"Sure." Reaper nodded. When he entered, he saw Numbers, the MC's accountant. He stayed silent until the officer shut the door.

"Numbers, where the fuck is Mr. Stone?" Reaper said before he sat. "I haven't fucking seen him since the morning after my arrest when the man swore he would get me out quick."

"Working on trying to reduce your sentence since you didn't hold the gun. He's working his magic, trying to convince the judge that you didn't know anything about the kidnapping since Winston was the one that everyone saw taking the girl." Numbers crossed his arms and rested them on the table.

"What the fuck is he saying?" Reaper paid their lawyer a shit ton of money, so he better come up with a good plan to get him out sooner rather than later.

"The truth." Numbers smirked. "That you were a puppet to Winston's plan. You were just trying to score some drugs for yourself when Winston shoved jewelry in your pocket, threatened your life with his gun, and forced you to drive away with the girl."

"Do they believe him?" Reaper stared at Numbers. Reaper knew that a conversation between a client and his attorney couldn't be recorded. That was why they said Numbers was a part of his legal team. But just in case the police found out it wasn't true, they tried not to say anything that could convict him. "I didn't know anything about Winston's plan. How was I supposed to know he wanted that girl all to himself? He never told me."

"Mr. Stone is doing the best he can."

"Have you seen my daughter?" Reaper wanted to know where she was. Angel was going to be madder than a wet hen when she found out he was in jail for attempted kidnapping. She hated when Lucifer's Renegades committed crimes against women, which was why Reaper kept so much from her. It was bad enough that Angel knew he was still trying to find that asshole "El Loco's" sister.

"No." Numbers winced. "I have not."

"Fuck! Not only can't she be bothered to be my primary lawyer, she can't visit her father either?" Reaper placed his elbows on the table and rubbed his face with his hands. His daughter, Angel, was a hell of a lawyer. If she had taken his case, he would be out by now. "Find her. I want to see my grandchild. And I want to know what she's thinking."

"She might not want him to see you in jail," Numbers suggested.

"I don't give a fuck." Reaper slammed his hand on the table. "I usually see him every two weeks and it's been two months. Tell her to bring him to me. I need to see him. I don't want him to forget about me. I love that kid."

"I'll locate her and talk to her," Numbers mumbled.

"Do it today. I know you have a sweet spot for her so take care of the problem. Anything else?" Reaper knew Numbers would know what he was talking about.

"Got it. Nope, everything is still the same." Numbers met his stare.

Reaper and Numbers had been in Lucifer's Renegade's MC for the past twenty-five years. They formed their bond when they prospected together. Most of their brothers swore they could read each other's minds. They could have a full conversation in a single look. For the past eleven years, they had both been on a mission to find the sister of "El Loco", a member of the Los Lobos de Muerte Motorcycle Club.

Reaper had killed El Loco's parents in retaliation for a drug shipment that El Loco had stolen. As a fucking prospect, that fucker had intercepted his ten-million-dollar shipment of meth. Reaper had been so fucking mad, he went out with his brothers and shot up El Loco's home, killing his mother and father. When the shooting stopped and there was no movement from inside the house, Reaper walked in with Numbers to check the body count. They never found the sister. He would've searched longer, but the wailing of the police sirens was a sign to get the hell out. Nevertheless, in his mind, it wasn't over until he killed the sister. They would never stop looking for that bitch.

In retribution for Reaper's act of vengeance, El Loco rode past their garage and killed his son-in-law, Tools, along with two other brothers, wounding a fourth. Tools was the one who pressured Angel to keep Reaper in their lives. Once Tools was gone, it caused a rift in his relationship with his daughter. Angel started to withdraw and tried to keep Steele, his grandson, away from him.

Reaper was not going to stand for that. Angel was going to have to shape up and play along by his rules now.

Reaper knew Numbers had been circling around her like a wolf hunting his prey ever since Tools died. Even though Numbers was closer to his age and more of a father figure to Angel, Reaper would love for them to get together. Numbers had a firm hand, just like Reaper. Plus, Numbers would convince Angel that Reaper had a right to be in his grandson's life and straighten her ass out.

"Okay, send me my lawyer and tell my daughter to get her ass here with my grandchild." Reaper was done talking.

"I'm on it." Numbers stood and nodded.

Reaper banged on the door. The guard opened it and took him back to his cell.

Chapter 6

Beach Time with My Bestie

Maggie

Maggie went over to Isa's in the morning. Thunder had already left for work but had loaded up a beach cart for the ladies. Isa only lived a couple of blocks from the beach. Maggie made sure they had plenty of water and snacks. Thunder would be pissed at her if she didn't take care of his pregnant wife.

"I think we have it all." Isa checked the cart.

"Looks like it." Maggie placed the last water bottle in the small cooler. "I'll push this bad boy. Thunder would kill me if I let you strain yourself."

"He is very protective." Isa rolled her eyes and opened the front door for Maggie.

"I think it's cute. It's easy to see how much he loves you." Maggie waited for Isa to lock her front door.

"I'll be honest, he makes me feel special and loved. I've never had that in any of my other relationships." Isa caught up to Maggie as they began their walk to the beach. "I hope you find that same special love."

"I hope so too but I keep picking the wrong guys." Maggie rolled her eyes.

"How about Mark?"

"Mark, who?" Maggie knew who Isa was talking about, but didn't know how to answer.

"Uh, Mark Holmes. He works at your new place of employment." Isa shoulder bumped her. "'Mark, who?' Don't play dumb with me. I see the way you guys banter and flirt with each other. I think it's a form of foreplay."

"You're funny." Maggie didn't think Mark was interested in her. She teased him about it, 'but he really did date just about anybody. He was hot, with his eight pack abs, veined forearms, sexy as hell ass, strong legs, piercing hazel eyes...

"Earth to Maggie." Isa snapped her fingers in front of her face. "You were daydreaming about him, weren't you?"

"What? No!" Maggie shook her head. She would deny Isa's comment until her last dying breath. Wait, why hadn't he asked her out? She was pretty. She turned heads.

"Yes, you were." Isa shoved a finger in her face. "Your cheeks got all pink when I said that. You like him."

"I don't think of him like that." Maggie slapped Isa's finger out of her face. "Besides, I already screwed up one job by screwing a co-worker. I'm not about to make that mistake again."

"We'll see." Isa looked around. Maggie assumed she was looking for a place for them to set up, giving her the perfect chance to change the subject.

"Ooh, maybe I should join one of those dating apps?" Maggie stared at Isa questioningly. It was all the rage now for meeting guys. She hadn't done it before because it seemed scary, but meeting at bars wasn't working.

"Well, I know a lot of people are doing it. I guess it's worth a shot, but you need to be careful when you meet someone. Make sure they're not a catfisher or serial killer." Isa pointed toward an area of the beach. "Let's go over there. Less people."

"I'll go wherever you want." Maggie followed Isa to a spot near the water. Isa took things off the cart, but Maggie stopped her.

"I got this." Maggie took out a chair for her. "Sit here."

"I'm only five months pregnant. I'm not an invalid." Isa sat and smirked at Maggie. "Don't turn into Thunder two-point-oh."

"Sorry, but I have my orders." Maggie took out the umbrella and dug it into the sand to give them shade. Then placed her chair outside the umbrella's shade and lathered up with her coconut scented sunscreen. She enjoyed feeling the sun bake her skin. She rarely burned. Usually, she tanned right away. Closing her eyes, she focused on listening to the waves crash against the shore. The sounds of the beach always gave her a sense of peace. "Now, this is the life. I wish I lived this close to the beach. It's so calming."

"I agree. Watching the waves is so relaxing." Isa spread her legs out and took a deep breath. "Just breathe in the salty air."

"I'm glad you suggested this. I needed it." Maggie's toes played in the sand. "I wrote my letter of resignation last night and I'm gonna give it to HR on Monday."

"Thunder told me you wanted to give two weeks. Mags, if they continue to harass you, tell HR and leave. Promise me you won't stay there." Isa reached out to grab Maggie's hand. "I worry about you."

"I promise." Maggie squeezed Isa's hand. "Do you want your book? I brought my Kindle."

"That sounds perfect – and a bottle of water." Isa smiled.

"Got it." Maggie grabbed two bottles from the cooler, placing them in their cup holders. Handing Isa her book, she found her Kindle. They both settled into their chairs and read until Maggie heard Isa's stomach rumble.

"Are you hungry?" Maggie closed her Kindle.

"I'm starving." Isa placed her bookmark in her book before shutting it.

"It sounded like it." Maggie chuckled.

"You heard that, huh?"

"Yup." Maggie nodded.

Isa rubbed her tummy. "This love bundle is always hungry. I swear you'd think I was carrying multiple children in here."

"Are you sure you're not?" Maggie walked to the cooler.

"Yep." Isa sighed. "Saw the ultrasound a couple days ago. It's a boy, and it is one."

"Then let's feed this little man, shall we?" Maggie dove into the cooler, taking out the lunch Thunder packed for them. He'd given them all the food Isa was craving: PB&J sandwiches, grapes, and chips. Maggie wished she had a Thunder.

After eating, they read some more and went for a walk as the sun set. When they returned to their chairs, they saw Thunder sitting on Isa's chair reading her romance novel.

"Whatcha doin'?" Isa asked when she got closer to him.

"This is good." Thunder raised the book with his hands and quirked an eyebrow at her. "It gives me some great ideas."

"I'm sure it does." Maggie rolled her eyes before plopping down in her chair.

"Like you need any." Isa leaned down for a kiss. "What are you doing here?"

"Mark said he would close for me, so I came out here to help you guys bring the cart back." Thunder stood, hugged her, and handed her the book. "Looks like I got here just in time. Hey Maggie."

"Hi Thunder." Maggie tried to give them some privacy while she packed up their items. When she grabbed the umbrella, Thunder stopped her.

"I'll get that. Why don't you guys start heading back?" Thunder pushed his finger on Isa's shoulder. "I think you've gotten enough sun. I'll rub some lotion on you after your shower."

"Ugh, you guys are so damn sweet, gag me." Maggie pretended to use her finger to throw up. She heard Thunder chuckle. Yep, she wanted a Thunder.

"Stop." Isa smacked her arm. "Wait until you find your soulmate. I'm gonna give you so much shit."

"I would expect nothing less." Maggie turned around and walked away.

"Are you sure you can work with her sarcastic ass?" Maggie heard Isa ask Thunder.

"Love you too, bestie." Maggie said, giving her the finger behind her back.

"Aww, I love you too." Isa came up behind Maggie and side hugged her as they walked home.

Chapter 7

Hanging Out with My Tribe

Maggie

Maggie used the spare bathroom to take a shower and get ready for their Girls' Night Out. She should've talked to Isa about her background check. When they first met, Maggie didn't want to tell Isa she was in hiding. Then, over the years, she feared for Isa's safety if she knew too much. But now Isa had stuck her neck out for her with Thunder and she really needed to come clean. It was bad enough she had hidden the truth from her best friend for over three years. Would Isa be mad at her? Maggie strongly suspected Isa would be hurt.

Maggie stared at her reflection in the mirror, not proud of the girl she saw. If their roles were reversed, Maggie knew she would be angry that her best friend hadn't trusted her. She should've talked to Isa when they were at the beach. Now she had to rush through the conversation before the other girls got here, unless she wanted them to know her secrets.

Damn, how had she gotten herself into this mess and why the hell were her shoulders pink? She never burned from the sun. It's a good thing Isa always kept aloe in her bathrooms for sunburns. She applied some, wishing she had a significant other to apply it for her. Someday, she would meet the right guy, and not only would he rub lotion on her, but he would also make her food, keep her safe, and love her all night long. Maggie sighed and said to mirror Maggie. "Snap out of it, girl. You're not gonna meet him tonight. Tonight is for the ladies and for you to talk to your best friend."

At the beach, Isa and Maggie had agreed to order pizzas for everyone after they arrived. Ready to face Isa, Maggie walked into the kitchen. Isa placed the red wine on the counter next to the wine glasses.

"Isa, can I talk to you before everyone gets here?" Maggie sat on a stool.

"Sure." Isa opened the red wine. "Why do you look so serious? Tonight is all about celebrating your new job."

"I..." Maggie started but never finished because Thunder came into the kitchen.

"Ladies, I'm gonna head out to meet with the guys at Sarah's. I'm their pizza delivery guy." Thunder wrapped his arms around Isa from behind and kissed her cheek. Isa turned in his arms for a proper kiss.

"Tell everyone I said hi. You guys invited Holt, right?" Isa asked after her kiss.

"We did, and he will be there." Thunder gave her another peck on the lips and let her go.

"Thank you." Isa was all smiles. "Hey, make sure Tommy takes photos of Lucy's hair styles tonight."

Thunder stopped in his tracks, sighed, and bowed his head. "I forgot Lucy was going to do her hair salon tonight."

"Yep, she's very excited." Isa laughed as Thunder grabbed his keys and headed out. "I want to see either the hair style or photos!" Isa screamed.

"Yeah, yeah, yeah. Got it!" Thunder hollered back.

"I want to see those photos, too." Maggie covered her mouth while laughing.

"Right? Lucy is very creative. I love how she does their nails if they don't have long hair." Isa grabbed a water bottle. "No one is leaving her hair salon untouched."

"That little girl is so darn cute." Maggie took a sip of wine. She loved Lucy and she owed her money for her swear jar.

"And sassy. I love that girl. She keeps those men on their toes," Isa giggled. "So, what did you want to talk about?"

Ding-Dong

"We'll talk later." Maggie stood from her stool when the doorbell rang. "I'll get it."

"Okay." Isa shrugged.

Maggie swore she would tell Isa soon. For now, she wondered if she dated someone with long hair if Lucy would do their hair too. Of course she would. Lucy loved doing hair and anyone Maggie dated would be brought into the fold. Well, if it was serious. She didn't want to bring guys around if she wasn't in a committed relationship. That clenched it. She wasn't bringing anyone to Lucy's Hair Salon anytime soon.

"Hi, Maggie." Gaby, Isa's sister-in-law, brought Aurora, Isa's mom, with her. Maggie loved talking to Aurora. No one could replace her mom, but Aunt Inez and Aurora, both helped her when she needed them. They were great moms. Sometimes, Maggie would get teary eyed watching Isa with Aurora, wishing she still had her mom.

"Hola, Maggie." Aurora hugged her and whispered in her ear. "*¿Cómo estás?*"

Aurora knew about her past. She'd caught her at a weak moment a few weeks ago at another Girls' Night Out. She saw Maggie leave a room teary-eyed and followed her. Aurora had led her into a bedroom where Maggie broke down and told Aurora all the secrets surrounding her parent's death. No one could ever replace her mom, but from that day on, she knew she had another adoptive mom to talk to.

"I've been better." Maggie looked at Aurora with watery eyes. Maggie would never understand why talking to Aurora always brought on the tears. She never cried around anyone else.

"Then I'm glad we're here." Aurora wrapped her arm around Maggie's shoulders. "I'm gonna get some water. I'm driving us home so Gaby can drink and relax."

"Thank you for that, *Mami*." Gaby side hugged Aurora and kissed her cheek. Maggie was in awe of their mother- and daughter-in-law relationship. So, to go along with her future boyfriend, she also hoped to have a nice mother-in-law. She'd heard some horror stories from other friends, but not from Gaby. Anyone looking in would think Gaby was Aurora's daughter.

"Hola, *Mami*. Hey, Gabs." Isa came out to greet them.

Ding-Dong.

"I'll get it." Maggie turned and opened the front door.

"Hi bitches! We're here. Let the party begin!" Frey shouted as soon as Maggie opened the door.

"Frey." Tori smacked her.

"Sorry, I forgot about Tori's sensitive ears. Hi ladies" –Frey turned to Tori– "better?"

"Yes." Tori nodded. "Hi, Maggie."

"Hey, bitches." Maggie laughed as Tori's eyes widened. "Sorry, I couldn't help myself. Come in."

"You're just as bad as she is." Tori humphed, leaving Frey and Maggie hugging each other while they laughed.

They followed Tori into the kitchen for drinks.

"Hi, Tori. Where's Frey?" Isa looked around.

"Behind me. Goofing off with Maggie." Tori hugged Isa and walked to the kitchen.

Maggie and Frey walked past Isa, giggling. Maggie heard Isa say. "Maybe you two shouldn't hang out together all the time. You're a bad influence on each other."

"Frey's definitely a bad influence on me." Tori pointed at Frey. Frey, being her funny self, ran to Tori and hugged her tight from behind.

"Aw, you know you love me." Frey hollered, and they both started laughing.

Maggie watched them all hugging and laughing. She was blessed to have a great girl tribe.

"Where's Sarah?" Gaby asked.

"She was going to wait until Thunder got there and then head over. She should be here soon. What kind of pizzas should we order?" Isa got a pad and pencil. "What do you guys like?"

"Mushroom and Pepperoni," Maggie said.

"Ooh, I like that too," Gaby interjected. "I never get to eat that because the girls don't like mushrooms."

"Ham and pineapple," Tori announced.

"I like ham and pineapple too," Isa agreed.

"I vote for the ham and pineapple." Aurora pointed at Tori.

"Can we get a veggie pizza?" Freya asked.

"Yep." Isa nodded and wrote it down. "I know Sarah will eat any of the above."

"Yeah, those all sound good." Maggie grabbed her purse to get her wallet. "I'll pay since I invited everyone to this GNO."

"Absolutely not." Isa grabbed her wallet out of her hands. "It's at my house. I'm paying when I order. Besides, we need to celebrate your new job!"

Leave it to Isa to announce it to everyone.

"You have a new job? Where?" Gaby asked.

"I'm glad you are going to be helping me." Tori hugged her.

"Thunder hired me yesterday." Maggie smiled at everyone.

"Why are you leaving Teramar?" Aurora looked puzzled.

"Because assholes are bullying her," Isa blurted.

"You were being bullied?" Freya crossed her arms and stared at her. "By whom?"

"Frey doesn't like bullies," Tori explained.

Ding-Dong.

Saved by the bell. "I'll get it." Maggie bolted off the bar stool and headed for the door.

"Hey, Maggie." Sarah, Thunder's sister, hugged her.

"Hi, Sarah. I take it Thunder is at your house with the pizza."

"Yup, along with all the other guys." Sarah followed Maggie to the kitchen.

Everyone yelled 'hey' as Sarah walked in to get a drink.

"All the men are at my house eating with the kids, including Holt and Mark." Sarah poured her wine.

"Well, I hope Mark doesn't cuss or Lucy is going to make a lot of money." Maggie knew Lucy would make bank tonight. Mark was always cussing.

"She took her swear jar along with her hair ties, barrettes, and nail polish." Gaby winked at them.

"You'll have to let us know how much money she makes from Mark," Tori said.

"Okay, I'm gonna go upstairs and order our food from my laptop." Isa tore the sheet off the pad. "Sarah, I'm going to order one Mushroom and Pepperoni, one Ham and Pineapple, and one Veggie Lovers. Are you good with one of those?"

"Yep." Sarah nodded.

"Does anyone want anything else or dessert?" Isa looked at all of them.

"Choose one of their desserts for my sweet tooth." Aurora grinned.

"You got it," Isa laughed. "I'll be back. Go into the living room and make yourselves comfortable."

They all went into the living room to watch a reality television show they could talk about. Agreeing on one took some time, but they decided to watch the one where the one man picks from several women to marry. Everyone had an opinion on their antics.

Chapter 8

Potty Mouth

Mark

Mark had moved to Florida to get away from the family ranch in Montana. The Holmes family had migrated to the United States from Ireland a long time ago, and his family's ranch had been there for five generations. He loved his family but was tired of the harsh winters. Plus, he didn't want to be a rancher for the rest of his life like his younger brother, Steve. Mark missed hanging out with Steve and was glad when Thunder invited him to join them for their boy's night.

Mark had never been to one of these boy's nights, but he'd heard about them from Thunder and Alex but hadn't had the privilege of being invited. He drove to Sarah's house with some trepidation. He'd heard Lucy would paint their nails if their hair wasn't long enough for braids. The top of Mark's hair was long enough for small braids, but the rest was not. If Lucy gave him a funky style, he would have to keep the pictures away from Maggie. She would never let him live it down, especially now that they would be working together.

Mark knocked on the door and heard someone say, "Come in".

"Hey, hey," Mark announced before entering the living room. All the guys were on the couch eating pizza and drinking beer while the kids sat on a blanket on the floor eating their food with water. "Are you guys having a picnic?" Mark asked the kids.

"Yep," Tommy answered first. "We love our indoor picnics."

"Cool." Mark walked up to him for a fist bump, setting off an accidental chain reaction. After fist bumping all the kids, Tommy twice, he moved toward the kitchen.

"Pizzas are on the island and the beer is in the fridge," Grayhorse hollered. "Help yourself."

"Thanks, man." Mark helped himself to a couple of slices of Meat Lovers and a beer. Then sat on the other side of the love seat, next to Alex.

"Long time, no see." Alex smirked at him.

"Yeah, right," Mark chuckled. They had both worked today at the cultural center.

"Are you ready for Lucy's Hair Salon?" Alex mumbled.

"As ready as I'm gonna be." Mark looked at him. "Do you think she'll remember?" Mark couldn't believe he was afraid of a little girl. Well, he wasn't afraid of her, just what her little hands would create with his hair.

"Oh, yeah." Alex laughed. "She lives for this shit."

"Mr. Alex." Lucy jerked her head toward him. "Did you just cuss?"

Everyone looked at Alex. He looked like a deer caught in headlights. Now Mark was not only afraid of her little hands, but her ears too. Apparently, she had supersonic hearing.

"How the hell did she hear that?" Mark mumbled to Alex.

"Now you just cussed, Mr. Mark." Lucy stood up and walked toward them, sticking her hand out. "You both owe me a dollar. "Right *lekší*?" Lucy looked at Thunder. After Thunder married her aunt, she started calling him the Lakota word for uncle just like Tommy (Thunder's nephew - his sister, Sarah's son).

Mark quirked an eyebrow at Thunder who was trying to hide his laughter.

"Yup." Thunder grinned at Alex and Mark.

"Shit," Mark said before he caught himself. This little girl was going to get rich from him before the night was over. Damn, he didn't think he had a lot of ones in his wallet. Although if he kept this up, he would be changing ones for twenties before the night was over. *Shit.*

"That's two dollars, Mr. Mark." Lucy looked at him sweetly.

Mark reached for his wallet and pulled out two one-dollar bills. He was right, he only had a couple other ones and then fives and tens.

"Thank you, Mr. Mark. Mr. Alex, you still owe me one dollar." Lucy moved the two dollars from one hand to the other, holding the empty hand out to Alex.

"Sorry, Lucy." Alex took a dollar out of his wallet and handed it over. Meanwhile, Thunder, Matteo, Barrett, Holt, Grayhorse and the kids laughed at him. Grayhorse had just fed Lilly and was patting her back when a loud burp came out of her mouth.

"Wow." Matteo quickly turned to Lilly. "Nice burp, baby girl." The kids continued to laugh while Lucy got her money and ran out of the room.

"Is she okay? Where did she go?" Mark asked Matteo.

"Probably to get her swear jar from Tommy's room." Matteo said between his laughter. "I won't have to worry about paying for her college at the rate you guys are going."

"Ha, ha, funny," Mark said before chuckling. He was grateful Emmy, Lucy's older sister, didn't have her own swear jar or he would put them both through college if he didn't clean his language around them.

Lucy strolled back in with her swear jar labelled "Oops, now pay up." The money was already inside.

"I like your label, Lucy." Thunder pointed at her jar.

"Thank you, *lekší*." Lucy beamed at her uncle. "Emmy helped me make it."

"Well, you girls did a great job." Thunder winked at them.

"I'll be back." Grayhorse stood with Lilly. "I'm gonna change her and put her to bed. *Ciŋkší*, if I'm not back when you guys are done eating, make sure you help the girls clean up."

"*Haŋ, até.*" Tommy nodded.

"So, how do you feel about Maggie working with us?" Alex asked Mark.

"Shit, now she gets to bust my balls every day." Mark answered between bites.

"Mr. Mark." Lucy walked over to him again with the swear jar.

"Damn," Mark mumbled and pulled out his wallet again.

"You might as well leave your wallet out," Thunder chuckled. "I think you're going to need it."

"Mr. Mark, that's two dollars. You shouldn't say the 'D' word either." Lucy stood before him with the jar.

"Can you give me the two dollars back and I'll give you a five since I owe you four total?" Mark asked Lucy while everyone else looked on.

"No, because I glued the lid on." Lucy pursed her lips and frowned. "But I can take the five and then you have a three-dollar credit. Right, daddy?" Lucy turned toward Matteo.

"Yes, baby." Matteo tried to cover his laugh with a cough into his fist. "Good math."

"Fine." Mark slipped the five-dollar bill in the slot at the top of the swear jar. The boys were not helping him out at all. It was sink or swim at this boy's night. He'd be broke before the night was over, but damn if she wasn't a cute little girl. Mark wanted to have a family when he found the right girl. It just hadn't happened yet. As the eldest son, he knew his parents were getting antsy about grandchildren. Mark knew he would make his parents happy one day, just not today. He was not about to have kids out of wedlock–he was old school that way. First, he had to find the right girl and then he would have at least two kids. He wanted his kids to grow up with a sibling. Someone to share the good and bad times.

"Thank you, Mr. Mark. It's nice doing business with you." Lucy held her hand out for a handshake.

"You're welcome, Lucy." Mark smiled and shook her hand. If he had a little girl, he would want her to be just like Lucy. She was confident, creative, and had such a sweet little smile. His mother would love to have a little Lucy that she could teach to cook and go shopping with. Mark and his brother always felt loved by their mom, but she was known to make little comments about how it would be nice to have another girl on the ranch to help her since the boys always went out to help their dad.

"Can we do hair now, Daddy?" Lucy turned to Matteo. "I have a perfect hairstyle for Mr. Mark."

"Of course you do." Mark smiled and mumbled low enough that only Alex heard him.

"Let's wait until Grayhorse comes back so he can tell you where to set up." Thunder answered before Matteo. "Are you done eating?"

"Yes, *lekší*." Lucy nodded. "I'll go clean up my plate." Lucy headed to where she was sitting, placed her jar on the blanket and picked up her trash, taking it into the kitchen.

"She can do everyone's hair in my room *lekší*," Tommy said while he cleaned up his area. "Emmy, are you done?" Emmy nodded and Mark watched as Tommy picked up her plate to take it with him into the kitchen. A budding romance. Emmy already had Tommy wrapped around her little finger. After all the kids cleaned up their mess, they left.

"I think Emmy has a suitor," Mark said to Matteo.

"Nah," Matteo sighed. "They're just friends."

"You never know, man." Mark finished his pizza.

"They'd be lucky to have each other." Thunder elbowed Matteo.

"You're right, but let's not marry them off yet. They're only eight." Matteo elbowed him back.

Chapter 9

Lucy's Hair Salon...OPEN for Business

Mark

"U ncle Thunder," Emmy announced from the hallway. "Lucy says you're first."

"Okie, dokie." Thunder stood up, grabbing his trash. "Let me throw this away and I'll be right there."

Mark watched Thunder follow Emmy, wondering if he was next.

"I see Thunder is first." Grayhorse grinned and sat to finish his pizza and beer.

"Are you nervous?" Alex glanced at Mark.

"No?" Mark answered.

"Is that a question or a statement?" Alex slapped him on the back. "You'll be fine man. It's only for a few minutes. Tommy will take your photo and then you can take all the braids out. Well unless you're me, those fuckers..." –Alex pointed at Grayhorse and in the direction Thunder went– "told me I had to wear it home. I even went to a fast-food restaurant with a princess Leia hairdo."

"That was awesome." Grayhorse and Matteo slapped their thighs and laughed at Alex.

"You're lucky Lucy wasn't in here or you would owe her another dollar." Matteo pointed at Alex.

"Okay, everyone." Emmy ran into the room. "Lucy wants you all to keep your hairstyles until Tommy can take a group photo." Emmy ran out just as quick as she ran in with her news.

The guys just looked at each other. *Great,* Mark thought. *At least Maggie wasn't there.*

"Well, we may as well get comfortable." Grayhorse grabbed the remote and turned on the TV, putting it on the sports channel.

Mark didn't care what game they watched; he loved sports. As they were watching and commenting, Thunder came out with a hairstyle that belonged in the movie 'The Grinch Who Stole Christmas'.

"How the hell did she get your hair to look like Cindy Lou Who in the human version of the grinch movie?" Mark stared at Thunder, dumbfounded. Wow, his hair had height. Mark was so stunned he didn't realize he'd cussed until Lucy spoke up.

"You only have two credits now, Mr. Mark," Lucy said behind Thunder. "I used a Styrofoam cone. I came prepared for tonight." Lucy beamed at them.

Mark pursed his lips and raised an eyebrow, she had come prepared. There was no way Thunder's long hair would have done that without artificial help.

"Mr. Alex, it's your turn." Lucy turned to leave as soon as Alex stood.

"Good Luck, man," Mark whispered.

"What are we watching?" Thunder sat and grabbed his beer.

Mark was stunned at how well he was taking it. "Doesn't that hurt?" Mark pointed at Thunder's hair.

"Well, it's not the most comfortable hairstyle she's given me. I have to keep my head straight because if I tilt it, I might ruin Lucy's hairstyle." Thunder stared at the bottle. He tried to tilt it instead of his head, but it wasn't working.

"So, how the hell, are you supposed to drink your beer?" Mark smirked at him, amused at his effort to drink his beer.

Thunder snapped his fingers. "I'll get a straw."

"Straws are in the pantry, second shelf," Grayhorse told him.

Alex entered the room, his hair in a back bun with black things sticking out from the back.

"What did you get?" Mark asked. "It just looks like a bun."

Alex turned around and showed them his spider bun. The head and eyes were in the middle of the bun and the pipe cleaners were the legs.

"That's fantastic." Mark shook his head. The girl had talent for being as young as she was.

"I like it. She did a good job. Grayhorse, your turn." Alex turned toward the kitchen. "Anyone need another beer?"

Everyone said yes. Thunder helped Alex carry them in since he was still there getting his straw.

It seemed like only a few minutes before Grayhorse came walking out with what looked like a Palm Tree on top of his head with a ball and chair made from pipe cleaners on either side of the tree.

"Palm Tree." Grayhorse pointed to his head. "I lucked out. She forgot her colored hair spray. Mark, you're up."

"Okayy." Mark stood and walked down the hallway slowly, as if he was walking toward the gallows. "Lucy, where are you?" Mark had never been to Sarah and Grayhorse's house.

"We're in here, Mr. Mark," Lucy called out. Mark followed her voice and was glad when Tommy stepped out of the room with a camera around his neck. Mark followed him inside.

"Where should I sit?" Mark looked at Lucy.

"You can sit here." Lucy pointed to the corner of Tommy's bed.

Mark sat down. "So, what are you going to do?"

"Why?" Tommy elbowed him in the shoulder. "You nervous?"

Mark was nervous, but he would never let Tommy know. Snarky little dude.

"No," Mark humphed and shrugged his shoulders. "Just wondering." *Show no fear or these kids will eat you alive.*

"Tommy, where's that little surfer toy you use when we play in the pool?" Lucy asked while she grabbed a bottle of Got2b Glued. Mark knew of the product and knew he would have to wash his hair several times to get that stuff out. He watched Lucy from the dresser mirror.

Lucy got to work, giving him a mohawk that wasn't quite in the center of his head. When she got the hair to stand up on top, she let the tips swoop down like a wave. *It looked really cool.* Then she pulled all his hair from the sides back and created another mohawk to the back. Okay, that looked weird, but she was having a good time, focusing on her work like a professional.

Digging into her bag, she pulled out a spray can with a photo of a woman with blue hair. *Oh Shit!* He thought Grayhorse said she hadn't brought hair color? Clearly, she brought the blue hair color. Lucy pulled the cap off and sprayed his hair.

"Close your eyes." Lucy said when she got to the front. "Emmy, cover his face so I don't get any more blue on it."

Mark felt little hands on his face while he heard Lucy's spray bottle and Tommy clicking photos on his camera. At least his face wouldn't look like a Smurf—well most of it. He'd already felt it on his forehead before Emmy covered his face.

"Okay, you can open your eyes," Lucy said. "Tommy, can you hand me your toy?"

Mark stared at himself. *Holy shit, that blue really worked.* He didn't think it would since he had dark brown hair, but he was wrong. Lucy cut a pipe cleaner, wrapped it around the surfer and stuck it in his stiff hair.

"Done." Lucy beamed at him through the mirror. "What do you think, Mr. Mark?"

"Wow, Lucy." Mark wasn't crazy about how many times he would have to wash his hair, but he would not break this little girl's heart. He had to admit, she did a good job. *Hell, the surfer in the wave was a nice touch.* "I'm stunned."

"You don't like it?" Lucy's eyes watered.

Oh Shit! "No, no, Lucy. I love it." Mark reached out and pulled her into his arms. "You did a great job, honey. Very creative." *What had he done?* The last thing he wanted to do was make Lucy insecure and sad. He could not break this little girl's heart like his dad sometimes broke his while he was growing up. Living on a ranch was a lot of hard work and having a dad that was always pointing out his flaws was not fun. His father was a man of few words, but a 'good job' or 'well done' would have been nice to hear.

Lucy broke away and kept him at arm's length, staring into his eyes with lips trembling, she asked, "You really like it?"

"I love it." Mark stood and held her hand. "Let's go show the boys. They're gonna be jealous they don't have a cool wave and surfer dude in their hair."

"Okay." Lucy swung their arms back and forth while she skipped down the hallway, pulling him along since he wasn't skipping. At least she was smiling. If she had gone in there crying, not only would he feel like shit, but the guys would have kicked his ass.

"Everybody, look!" Mark almost tripped over Lucy when she came to an abrupt stop as they entered the living room. "Doesn't he look great?"

The living room echoed with "Yeahs," "Yeps," and "Good job." Mark walked back to his seat and leaned toward Alex to whisper. "She found the blue hair spray."

"I see that," Alex chuckled. "Do you need another beer? I'm heading to the kitchen."

"Sure." Mark looked at Thunder, still drinking through a straw, and realized his surfer guy might fall out if he tilted his head back. Fuck! He did not want to make Lucy cry if his hairstyle fell apart before the photo op. "Bring me a straw too."

"You got it, princess." Mark scowled at Alex before he stood.

"Pedicure time!" Lucy pulled two nail polish bottles, a neon pink and a neon yellow. "Emmy and Tommy, can you help me?"

"Sure. Dad, Holt, and Barrett sit on this couch because it'll be easier for us." Emmy directed them to shift around.

"Uh, Lucy, Em, I don't know how to paint nails?" Tommy looked at the bottles of nail polish like they were foreign objects he'd never seen before.

Mark smiled because he'd never painted nails before either. He wouldn't know what to do. Lucky for Tommy, he had Lucy and Emmy to show him. Or was that unlucky for Tommy?

"Watch us. You can paint Mr. Barrett's nails." Emmy gave him neon green. "You gotta make sure you paint the nail and not the skin around it." All the men focused their attention on Emmy while she sat in front of Holt.

"Uh...I don't know what that means, but show me when it's my turn." Tommy sat crossed legged on the floor, looking petrified as his eyes bounced between all the guys before landing on Emmy.

"You guys have to take your shoes and socks off unless you want us to do your nails instead of toenails." Lucy spoke while she shook her nail polish bottle.

Mark was enjoying the show. He'd never seen three grown men take off their socks and shoes so fast.

"Phew, your feet stink." Lucy pinched her nose. "Maybe we should have them soak their feet in water?" Lucy turned to Emmy.

"Let's just do it fast. Next time, we'll make them soak and clean their feet while the others are getting their hair done." Emmy and Lucy grabbed toe spreaders and stuck them on their toes.

Holt grunted, "that feels weird. What's that for?"

"So we can paint your toenails right and your toes don't ruin the nail polish when they're all squished together." Emmy opened her bottle and applied neon pink to Holt's toes.

"You get used to it," Matteo whispered to Holt.

"I don't know that I want to get used to it," Holt murmured.

"Mr. Holt." Lucy looked at him with sad puppy eyes. "You won't let me paint your toenails again?"

"Now you did it." Alex stopped mid-stride behind Holt and slapped him on the back of his head.

Mark was laughing until he realized Lucy looked ready to cry. That little girl was good. He felt sorry for whatever man married her. Mark looked at the guys and they were all glaring at Holt.

Holt turned to glare at Alex before he turned to face Lucy. "I'm sorry, Lucy. You can spread my toes to kingdom come whenever you want."

"Really?" Lucy immediately stopped crying and dried her tears.

"Sure." Holt smiled.

Mark had gotten up to get his own damn beer when he saw Alex bend down and heard Alex murmur in Holt's ear, "You're fucked now." Mark stopped. *Well, hell. Why hadn't Lucy heard that?* He turned and saw Lucy was talking to Emmy about the polish they were going to use and wasn't paying attention to Alex or Holt. *Figures.*

"I'm sorry, did you say something, Alex?" Holt smirked. "Lucy, Alex has something he wants to say to you."

"Sure. Do you need something, Mr. Alex?" Lucy stopped her conversation with Emmy and stared at Alex. Shit, Mark thought, this was getting good.

"Nope. I just think you are doing such a great job, that you should do Holt's nails too." Alex smiled and rocked on his heels back and forth. "He would really like that. Right, Holt?"

"Nice one, big bro." Barrett reached back with his hand for a fist bump with Alex.

Holt first glared at Barrett, then turned his head and mouthed to Alex 'fucker' before facing Lucy. Sweet as can be, he told her she could do his nails.

Lucy beamed. "Okay. Thank you, Mr. Holt." Lucy was bouncing in her seat with excitement. Mark was pretty sure she would be getting nail polish on his skin. Emmy was faster, so when she finished with Barrett, she shifted over to paint her dad's toes.

"Tommy, you saw how I did that?" Emmy looked at Tommy and handed him the topcoat after he shifted in front of Barrett. "You can do the clear coat after we put the color on."

"Okaayy. I just brush this on the nail?" Tommy held the topcoat bottle up and looked at Emmy.

"Yep." Emmy smiled.

Tommy held his hand steady and focused on painting Barrett's big toe. Mark was amused by Tommy doing Emmy's bidding. He wondered what was going through that little man's head. If Matteo didn't think these two would someday date, he was living in a dream world. Hell, they were following in Frey and Holt's footsteps. Those two had liked each other since elementary school.

"You got it." Emmy patted his back.

"Thanks." Tommy puffed out his chest and smiled.

"Besides, if you mess up, it's clear so you don't have to worry too much." Emmy began her dad's foot.

"Wait, Emmy." Lucy cried after she finished Holt's feet. "I want to do daddy's nails too."

"Okay, I'll do one foot, and you can do the other when you finish with Mr. Holt's nails." Emma compromised with her.

"Okay." Lucy smiled and quickly put one coat of nail polish on Holt's feet before she pulled Matteo's foot toward her.

"Great," Matteo grinned. "Mommy will love that you shared."

When Tommy finished with Barrett, he moved to Holt and finished with Matteo. Tommy's attitude amazed Mark. Most boys would've said 'no way' and left the room. Tommy focused and followed Emmy's lead.

"Okay, let's take a photo." Lucy announced. "Tommy and Emmy, pose everyone."

"Mr. Mark, *lekší*, Mr. Alex, and *até* stand behind the couch." Tommy grabbed his camera. "We don't need to see your feet."

"Mr. Holt, Dad, and Mr. Barrett, lift up your feet and prop them on the couch so we can see your awesome pedicure. Oh, and Mr. Holt, hold up your hands too." Emmy directed them.

Mark was glad he was standing instead of having his knees up to his chin on the couch. That didn't look comfortable.

"Wait. Mr. Alex, turn around so we can take a photo of your spider bun. Ooh, yes, that's good." Lucy jumped up and down clapping her hands while Tommy lifted the camera and began taking several photos.

"Look, we came just in time!" Mark heard Sarah's voice from behind him. *Shit, maybe it was just Sarah coming home. Wait, she said 'we'. Oh, fuck me!*

Chapter 10

Surfer Smurf

Mark

"Awwww, photo time!" Maggie screamed. "I love photos!"

Shit, Fuck, Motherfucker! Mark closed his eyes and sighed. He was so screwed. He was never going to live this down.

"Hey, sweetheart." Mark noticed Alex left his side. He must've walked to Tori when she came in. Alex was the only one facing the door. Out of the corner of his eye, Mark saw Tori hug Alex and turn him around so she could see Lucy's hairstyle. "I like it." Tori poked the spider legs.

Maggie walked around the couch. "Oh, shit! Hey, Surfer Smurf. Lookin' good."

And there Mark was, thinking he didn't look like a Smurf since his entire face wasn't blue...just his forehead. Leave it to Maggie to make the connection to those little blue men.

"Thanks." Mark pointed at her. "You owe Lucy a dollar for her swear jar."

"What?" Maggie looked between Mark and Lucy.

"I have a swear jar, Miss Maggie." Lucy grabbed it and held it out in front of Maggie. "You cussed so you owe me a dollar. Mr. Mark has already paid his debts and has a two-dollar credit."

"Oh, well, then Mr. Mark can pay for me." Maggie glanced between them.

"Ah, yeah, no." Mark shook his head.

"Mr. Mark, that's not very gentlemanly." Lucy wrinkled her brow at him. "My daddy always pays for my mommy."

Mark had just taken a gulp of his beer and it went down the wrong way, choking him. Maggie thumped his back hard. *What the hell, why am I the bad guy? It's not like we're dating. Damn, the girl can hit. Maggie was stronger than she looked.*

"Yeah, Mr. Mark. Help a girl out." Maggie winked at him.

"Fine. But I'm not her husband, boyfriend or date, Lucy." Mark glared back at Maggie. Getting his coughing under control, he got down on one knee in front of Lucy. "I'm her friend, so she can use one of my credits. You can keep the last one. My extra gift to you."

"Thank you, Mr. Mark." Lucy hugged him.

"You're welcome, sweetie." Mark got up and turned to Tommy. "Did you get all the photos Lucy wanted?"

"I sure did," Tommy smiled.

Thank fuck. Mark couldn't wait to get home and shower.

"Cool." Mark knelt in front of Lucy. "Lucy, I'm gonna take the surfer out of my hair and give him back to Tommy before I go. Is that okay?"

"Yes, Mr. Mark." Lucy nodded.

"Oh, honey." Isa covered her mouth with her hand and looked at Thunder's Grinch style hair. "You look so sexy. I promise not to take away your toys this Christmas."

Mark watched Thunder pull Isa into a hug and whisper something into her ear that caused her to blush.

"I feel like I want to go to the beach." Sarah placed her arm around Tommy as she regarded her husband's new 'do. "Lucy, no green paint?"

"I forgot to bring it." Lucy crossed her arms and sighed.

The boys on the couch had lowered their feet when they heard the girls come in.

"Okay, boys." Frey waved her fingers toward her, in a come-hither motion. "Lift up those feet. Let's see your pedicure."

Matteo, Holt, and Barrett looked at each other and lifted their feet back onto the edge of the couch.

"I love it!" Gaby hugged Lucy. "You did a great job, baby."

"Emmy helped me." Lucy beamed at their work. "She did Mr. Barrett and one of daddy's feet. I did the other and Mr. Holt. Oh, and Mommy, Mr. Holt let me do his fingernails too." Lucy stood tall with her shoulders back and turned to Holt. "Show them Mr. Holt. Oh, and Tommy put the clear on top."

Mark watched Holt smile at Frey and pull his hands out from behind his back to show everyone that his neon pink mani/pedi matched. Mark didn't miss the wink Frey gave him. Oh yeah, he was getting lucky tonight, even with his nails painted.

"*¡Ay! ¡Que lindos!*" Aurora was the last one around the couch.

"Well, you all did a great job." Gaby bent down and kissed her cheek. "Go clean up your stuff so we can head home."

Everyone gave Lucy, Emmy, and Tommy a hug and thanked them for their hard work.

Mark saw Maggie sneak a photo of him while he was down on his knees, talking to Lucy. Maybe she would show some mercy and not post it all over social media. It was bad enough she saw it live and in person.

"Maggie?" Mark called her over. "Can you please get this out of my hair? I don't know how Lucy put it in."

Maggie walked over and told him to sit on the couch since he was over a foot taller than her. It didn't take Maggie long to figure out how the pipe cleaner was holding the surfer in his hair. It must be a girl thing. The kids came back in with Lucy's stuff all packed up.

"Thanks." Mark stood and gave it to Tommy. "Thanks for letting me borrow this, dude." Mark made the sign for hang ten with his pinkie and thumb. Tommy shook his head and laughed at him. Mark walked to Sarah and Grayhorse.

"I appreciate the invite. It was a lot of fun." Mark hugged Sarah and shook Grayhorse's hand.

"Anytime." Grayhorse put his arm around his wife's back. "You're always welcome here."

Mark lifted his arm to say bye and hollered. "I gotta go. Thanks everybody. Lucy, you did a great job. See you all next time. Tori and Thunder, I'll see you on Tuesday."

Everyone said goodbye or waved, and he walked to his car. Working for Thunder had not only given him friends, but a family. Now with Tori, Alex, and Maggie, their family was growing, and he loved it.

Chapter 11

Enough is Enough!

Maggie

On Monday, Maggie went to work, ready to give her two-week's notice. Ryan came in as usual and ignored her. No surprise there. Some of his other colleagues came in and nodded, but didn't speak to her. Maggie was glad she didn't have to endure the silent treatment much longer. As soon as she saw her boss, she was going to buzz his office and bring him one of the resignation letters she printed this morning. She printed out two letters, one for her boss and one for HR.

Through Teramar's glass front door, Maggie saw Ana approaching. Bracing herself for another rude comment, she smiled and greeted her.

"Good morning, Ana."

Ana looked around the lobby, then blurted venomously, "It was until I saw you."

"Ana, what have I ever done to deserve your wrath?" Maggie turned her chair toward her. She'd had enough and was tired of backing down. Maggie wasn't good at being a punching bag.

"You begged us all to help you date Ryan." Ana leaned over Maggie's desk and got in her face. "Then you got him. But nooo...bitch that you are, you treat him like shit and throw him away."

"I'm sorry you feel that way, but I never treated him like shit. He said he was okay when we broke up." Maggie remained professional even though she wanted to say was 'bitch stay out of my business. You don't even know what happened'. "Was I supposed to stay with someone that I didn't have things in common with? He deserves someone who shares his hobbies and that's just not me. In the long run, I was doing him a favor."

"You didn't even give it a month, Maggie. That's shitty." Ana sneered at her and threw her breakfast sandwich wrapper at Maggie's head.

"Hey," Maggie said after it hit her in the face. "Now you're the one being shitty. That's not nice." *What the hell was wrong with her? If she liked Ryan, why didn't she go out with him?*

"You're lucky that's all I had in my hand," Ana growled at her.

"Is there a problem here?" Isa asked from behind Ana.

"Nope. I was aiming for the trash can and missed." Ana turned to face Isa, wiping the angry look off her face as she shrugged.

Wow, Maggie didn't know anyone could turn anger on and off so easily.

"Mags? Are you okay?" Isa ignored Ana and watched Maggie's face.

"Well, I have work to do. See you later, girls." Ana pivoted and headed toward the elevators as if nothing had happened.

Wow, what a bitch. Good riddance, Maggie thought. When she turned back around, she saw Isa staring at her.

"I'm good." Maggie grabbed her two resignation letters, crumpled them up, and threw them in the trash. "Just need to write two new letters of resignation. I had written that I was giving two weeks, but now I just want to leave this hellhole. Fuck it. I'm done."

"Oh, Mags. I'm so sorry. I'll miss you." Isa sighed. "But if I were you, I would leave too. No one deserves to be treated like Ana just treated you."

"Thanks." Maggie turned to her computer, opened her letters and edited them, printing them out once again to the small printer behind her desk.

"If you need anything, let me know. I saw Ana throw that paper at you and I'm more than happy to tell HR and get her written up for her unprofessional behavior and harassment."

"I'll let you know." Maggie grabbed her two sheets of paper. "But I don't want to put you in a weird position. You still work here."

"Yeah, but most of the time I work from home and don't have to deal with anyone." Isa came around the desk and hugged Maggie. "Besides, what she did was wrong."

"True." Maggie squeezed Isa before letting go. "Thank you for being my best friend. Maybe we can still do lunch sometime?"

"You can count on it." Isa heard the door and saw Maggie's boss coming in.

"Good morning, Mr. Hopkins." Maggie greeted him when he came near her desk.

"Good morning, Maggie...Isa." Mr. Hopkins nodded and continued to the elevator.

Maggie looked at Isa who tilted her head toward Mr. Hopkins as she mouthed 'Do it now'. Maggie shook her head and widened her eyes, pleading for Isa not to say anything.

"Why didn't you talk to him?" Isa said as soon as Mr. Hopkins got on the elevator and the doors closed.

"I'm gonna wait until he gets into his office. I'd like to have some privacy." Maggie looked at Isa with a duh look. Really, she was being a coward, but she needed a minute to gather her wits after that encounter with Ana.

"Okay." Isa took a deep breath and rubbed her baby belly. "Let me know how it goes. I'm not staying all day and I can leave after I talk to John about the new ad campaign for a sneaker company."

"I'll stop by your office and if you're not there, I'll text you." Maggie faced her phone, ready to call Mr. Hopkins. "I'm sure he'll want me to leave as soon as I talk to HR. Wish me luck."

"You got this." Isa gave her a thumbs up and left.

Maggie took a deep breath and dialed Mr. Hopkins' extension. He should be at his desk by now.

"Maggie, did you need something?" Mr. Hopkins answered on the second ring.

"Yes, sir." Maggie placed her hand on her stomach to stop the butterflies that were fluttering in there. "Can I please come speak with you?"

"Of course, come on up. Please set the phone to voicemail mode."

"Great, I'll be up there in just a few minutes." Maggie programmed the phone, grabbed her two letters, and took the elevator to Mr. Hopkins floor which was also the accounting floor. Holding her head up and not making eye contact, she walked directly to his office. He'd left his office door open, but Maggie knocked anyway as a courtesy.

"Maggie, come on in." Mr. Hopkins waved her in.

"May I shut the door?" Maggie wanted privacy in case Ryan or any of his cronies walked by.

"Yes, of course." Mr. Hopkins put his pen down and held his hands over his desk. "This sounds serious Maggie. Is something wrong? Do you need some time off?"

"Sir." Maggie had loved working for Mr. Hopkins. He never treated her like a lowly receptionist. He always respected her and included her in all their company outings and celebrations, but enough was enough. Standing tall, Maggie gave him her letter. "I'd like to turn in my resignation."

"Resignation letter? Why?" Mr. Hopkins held it up, glancing at it. "I thought you liked it here. Please sit down, let's talk."

Maggie sat on the edge of the chair facing his desk. "I did sir, until recently." Maggie fidgeted with her hands.

"What happened recently?" Mr. Hopkins' eyebrows drew together.

"I broke up with a fellow employee and I've been getting backlash from his friends who work here." Maggie looked down. "I realize it might not have been a good idea to date a co-worker, but hindsight is an incredible thing. I'm sorry."

"That is a difficult situation, but we don't have a fraternizing policy so it shouldn't be an issue. If you are being harassed, let me know who it is, and I'll take care of it. We have zero tolerance for any type of harassment. Is there anything I can do to get you to stay with us?"

"No, sir. I'm sorry. Originally, I was going to give you two weeks" –Maggie pointed toward her letter– "but after this morning's incident, I'd rather leave today."

"By whom?" Mr. Hopkin's jaw clenched.

"I'd rather not say." Maggie winced. She had not intended to say she was being bullied. He was being so kind and caring, it just slipped out.

"I'd rather you did say. Maggie..." Mr. Hopkins dropped her letter, braced his hands on his desk and stared into her eyes. "It doesn't sound like I can change your mind, but I will not allow someone in my employment to bully anyone here. I'd like to know who it was so I can have a discussion with them. As far as you wanting to leave today, if you feel uncomfortable working here, please leave as soon as you want. No one should make you feel helpless or ashamed. Please know, you are an amazing person and we have enjoyed having you. I truly apologize for their behavior."

"Thank you, sir," Maggie sighed and relaxed her shoulders. "I would like to clean out my desk and leave right away."

"Of course. If you don't feel right giving me their names, please stop by HR on your way out and file a complaint against the offending individual." Mr. Hopkins stood and came around his desk. "I wish you the very best. If you need a letter of recommendation for your next job, I'll be happy to provide one."

Maggie stood and shook his outstretched hand. "Thank you, sir."

Feeling lighter, Maggie left his office and headed straight for the HR department. Once there, she handed them her letter of resignation and filed a complaint against Ana for throwing the empty food wrapper at her face. She felt childish after she wrote it, but Ana had to be stopped. She knew Mr. Hopkins would find out it was Ana, but by the time he spoke to her, she'd be long gone.

"We'll miss you, Maggie." Sandy from HR stood and hugged her. "Best of luck to you."

"Thank you." Maggie left her office and went in search of Isa.

Isa was in John Cummings office, but the door was open. Maggie knocked to get their attention.

"John—" Isa turned and saw Maggie smiling— "I need to talk to Maggie for a minute. I'll be right back."

"No problem. Hey, Maggie. You stay here, I'll go make these copies for you." John got up and left his office.

"Is it done?" Isa asked as soon as John left.

"Yep. And I feel like a weight has been lifted off my shoulders. I told Mr. Hopkins I wanted to leave today so I'm going to go clean out my desk and head out. I did file a complaint against Ana with Sandy in HR."

"Good." Isa hugged her. "I'm so proud of you."

"I put your name down as a witness." Maggie winced at Isa. "Are you still proud of me? They might call you in."

"Let them." Isa grabbed Maggie's hands and held them. "I'll tell them exactly what I saw. I only have about another thirty minutes here with John, so if you want to go to my house, we'll celebrate. Thunder's at work, but call him because I'm sure he'll want you to start tomorrow. They're technically closed today."

"Thank you." Maggie pulled Isa in for another hug. "I don't know what I would do without you."

"Lucky for you, you never have to find out." Isa turned her around. "Now, go get your shit and get out of here."

"Okay." Maggie giggled and said over her shoulder, "I'll see you at your house!"

Chapter 12

Leaving for Greener Pastures

Maggie

While Maggie was cleaning out her desk, her phone rang with an in-house call. It was Mr. Hopkins.

"Yes, Mr. Hopkins," Maggie answered.

"Maggie, I'm sending Sandy down to man the phones and direct clients. Can you please wait for her?"

"Absolutely." Maggie felt bad about leaving Teramar high and dry, but this was proof that they could manage without her. Sandy or one of the other secretaries worked the receptionist's desk when Maggie took a day off or was sick. They would be fine. "I won't leave until I see her."

"Thank you," Mr. Hopkins sighed. "We'll miss you, Maggie. Thank you again for all your hard work."

Maggie didn't get a chance to answer before Mr. Hopkins hung up. There wasn't much left to say except to thank him again. She didn't have a lot of personal mementos on her desk because she wasn't a big fan of clutter. The only photo by her computer was of her family of four at an amusement park before José joined Los Lobos. Her parents hadn't believed in vacationing without their kids, so they did everything together. Not that they had a lot of vacations because money was always tight, but that day their parents had surprised them with a weekend trip to Disney World. Maggie found out years later that her parents had saved their money for five years to take that trip.

Sometimes they would go to the airport and watch the planes take off. Their mom would bring beef empanadas and they would have a picnic cheering the pilots on when they flew over their heads. The family spent other quality time at the beach, in parks, or at their Aunt Inez and Uncle Thomas' house. Uncle Thomas had more money and would splurge on cookouts with chicken or even steak.

"Hey, Maggie." Sandy was out of breath when she approached her. "Melanie is out today with the flu and Mr. Hopkins didn't want to leave the desk unattended, so I volunteered. Is it on active mode or voicemail mode?"

"I'll switch it to active right now." Maggie picked up the receiver and put in the codes. "Done. Is there anything you need from me?" Maggie liked Sandy. She was still nice to her and didn't take part in any office drama.

"No, just be happy Maggie and know that we will miss you." Sandy sat down and the phone started ringing.

"I'll just grab my purse and be out of your way." Maggie grabbed it from her bottom desk drawer.

Sandy picked up the ringing phone. "Good morning, Teramar Studios. How may I direct your call?"

Maggie purposefully brought a big purse today so she could carry all her belongings. She wasn't sure if Mr. Hopkins would want two weeks or release her, since she could sue the company for harassment. Maggie would not have sued. Sure, it was uncomfortable to work there, but it wasn't Mr. Hopkins' or the company's fault. After gathering all her belongings, she left the building and sat in her car to call Thunder.

"Good morning, American Indian Cultural Center. How can I help you today?" Mark's voice sounded out of breath.

"Hey, Surfer Smurf." Maggie started her car and let the call go through her car speaker.

"Fuck." Mark sighed into the phone. "You're never going to stop calling me that now, are you?"

"Not a chance." Maggie chuckled. "What are you doing there on a Monday?"

"Thunder needed to move some crates into the warehouse, and I came in to help him. What are you up to, Ball Buster? I hear you're starting in two weeks."

"Ball Buster, huh?" Maggie didn't let him say anything else. They could continue their banter another day. Right now, she wanted to talk to Thunder and check on her start date. "Maybe sooner. I needed a job change and Thunder was gracious enough to offer me one." Maggie pulled out of the parking lot, heading to Isa's house.

"Are you okay?" Mark asked. "I heard you were having trouble with some co-workers."

"Yeah. I'll tell you about it some other time. Can I please talk to Thunder?" Maggie wanted to tell Mark, but right now she wanted to see how soon she could start.

"Sure, Mags. He's in his office. I'll transfer your call." Maggie heard a click and Native American music on the line before Thunder picked up.

"Hey, Maggie. Is everything okay?" Thunder sounded worried.

"Yeah." Maggie sighed. "I gave my notice, but since I was experiencing workplace harassment, I asked to leave sooner, and they agreed. I can start whenever you need me." Maggie crossed her fingers while driving, hoping he said she could start tomorrow. She had bills to pay and not getting paid for two weeks would impact her bank account which would then impact her night classes. It was all such a domino effect.

"Can you start tomorrow?"

Maggie would have jumped for joy if she could. "Yes," Maggie was smiling as she got on the highway. "That would be great."

"Okay. Come in at ten. I have some insurance forms for you to fill out, and then Tori and Mark can train you. Will that work?"

"Absolutely. I'll be there at ten." Maggie couldn't wait to meet Isa at her house and tell her the good news. "Thank you so much for helping me, Thunder. I really appreciate it."

"My pleasure, Maggie. Tori and Mark will appreciate your help. I'll see you tomorrow."

"Yup, see you then." Maggie hung up and high fived her steering wheel. *Yes! Life was Good.*

Chapter 13

New Employee has Secrets

Mark

After transferring Maggie's call to Thunder, Mark sat at his computer searching for any new rules or classes that would help him in his new career. He was looking forward to helping Thunder keep the cultural center from having any other issues like they'd had in the past. Mark was vigilant when he walked through the main building and checked the warehouse periodically. After Joseph's theft and Tori's kidnapping, they installed several cameras which he watched on a separate monitor connected to his desktop computer.

With this new security system, both Mark and Thunder received alerts on their phones if one of the center's doors was breached. Keeping their employees and guests safe was their number one priority. It had been quiet now for a while since Winston, Reaper, and Bull were arrested. Mark hoped it stayed that way. All three guys were bad news.

Some nights, if Barrett and Holt were shorthanded at the casino, Mark would work a security shift to help them out. The casino always had something going on and he enjoyed staying busy. Without them, he never would've become the knowledgeable, effective security officer he was – not as quickly, anyway. Thunder and Mark had agreed to not run full background checks on their guests, for legal purposes, but to at least make sure they were not on the sexual offender list. With so many kids coming into their cultural center on field trips, they wanted to keep them safe. Mark signed up to receive free email alerts from the FDLE (Florida Department of Law Enforcement) Sexual Offender and Predator system and kept an updated spreadsheet on his computer.

Not finding any urgent information, Mark headed out to the warehouse to stack crates. The center was always closed on Sundays and Mondays, but Mark and Thunder would come in if they needed to work in the warehouse. He'd run Maggie's background check later. After all, it was Maggie, Isa's best friend. *What could she be hiding?*

Mark had almost finished stacking the crates when Thunder came in.

"Maggie is starting tomorrow." Thunder stated as he walked in the door. "Trouble at work."

"What happened?" Mark wiped his hands on his jeans.

"Her story to tell." Thunder grabbed a crate.

"Fair enough." Mark nodded. "Everything stacked the way you want it?" Mark pointed to the empty stacked crates and the broken-down boxes. "Did you need anything else?"

"Nope. I appreciate your help." Thunder nodded. "Go home and enjoy the rest of your Monday."

"Thanks. I gotta do something on the computer and then I'll head home." Mark walked around Thunder but turned back when he reached the door. "Are you done for today?"

"I'm gonna leave by lunch. Isa was only working a half day today." Thunder placed his hands in his jeans pocket. On Mondays, if they came into work at all, they dressed casually.

"Okay. If I leave before you, I'll lock up." Mark heard Thunder say 'sounds good' as he walked to his computer on the lobby desk.

Mark logged onto his computer and opened his background check software. When he got to the appropriate window he entered 'Maggie Walker', and nothing came up. *Well, duh, her first name was probably Margaret.* When he entered 'Margaret Walker' her record stated that her parents were deceased, and she had a brother. It also said she had an alias, Margarita Gomez. *Who the hell was Margarita Gomez?* Mark had never heard Maggie called Margarita. On her profile based on the date of her name change compared to her birthdate, she was a minor when she changed it. Why would Maggie change her name?

Still curious, he entered her alias 'Margarita Gomez' but her records were sealed. He assumed it was because she was a minor when she used that name. Did she get in trouble with the law? What had happened to her between the time her parents died and the date of her name change? Were her parents abusive? How did they die? Was she adopted? What family secrets was she keeping close to her chest. As far as he knew, no one called her Margarita. So many questions and no answers. He had two choices. He could ask Deputy George about why records were usually sealed—he probably needed to know that information anyway or he could ask Maggie. Mark knew it was best to ask Maggie instead of going behind her back.

Looking further into her 'Margaret Walker' report, she didn't have any misdemeanor or felony convictions, her credit report was good, only one speeding ticket, and a clean drug test report. He also saw all her job history. When he got to the education area, he noticed she'd been taking classes at night at a local community college. Based on the classes, he assumed marketing or business. Interesting, he didn't know Maggie was in night school. Now he was starting to feel like a peeping tom. All he'd needed to find out was if she had any felonies, but he just couldn't stop himself from learning more about Maggie. What was up with that? She would be there tomorrow, and he could ask her. Shutting down his computer, he went to Thunder's office.

"Thunder. Did you know Maggie's real name is Margarita?" Mark asked from the doorway.

"No." Thunder turned away from his monitor. "I didn't. Is she Hispanic? I've never heard her speak Spanish."

"She's Cuban. Well, her parents were Cuban, she was born in the States." Mark leaned on the doorframe and crossed his ankles.

"'Were'?" Thunder quirked an eyebrow.

"They passed away when she was around fourteen." Mark crossed his arms. He was surprised that Thunder didn't know these details about Maggie. He was so protective of Isa.

"Wow, I didn't know that." Thunder leaned back in his chair. "I'm sure Isa did. They've been best friends since they met at Teramar a few years ago. I take it you ran her background check?"

"I did." Mark nodded. "Nothing bad. I was just surprised by her name change, parent's death, and that she has a brother." Mark didn't want to verbalize any of his assumptions before talking to Maggie.

"If it's any consolation, I didn't know any of that either." Thunder chuckled. "I guess as long as she doesn't have a criminal record, we're good."

"Yup. That's exactly what I was thinking." Mark agreed.

He'd get to know Maggie over the next few days and ask about her family. He didn't want to make her feel like it was an inquisition. She'd already left an uncomfortable work environment, no need to make this one just as bad.

Mark moved away from the wall. "I'm gonna head out. I'll see you tomorrow?"

"Give me a second." Thunder shut down his computer and stood. "I'll head out with you."

Mark headed home to make a quick lunch and chill for the rest of the day. His curiosity was getting the better of him. He couldn't wait for tomorrow. Getting to know Maggie had never sounded so interesting and fun. That is, if he could get answers from her without her busting his balls. Calling her a ball buster had been right on the money. Mark knew she did it to get a rise out of him and he usually liked the challenge. Tomorrow couldn't come soon enough. But for now, he looked forward to going home and playing with his favorite girl.

Some time last year, when Mark was leaving work for the day, he heard a loud yelping sound coming from a box by the side of the cultural center. When he opened it, beautiful blue eyes from a German Shepherd puppy stared back at him. Talk about pleading puppy dog eyes. Mark immediately picked up the puppy and saw it was a girl. Her eye color reminded him of the beautiful skies back home. After all, they did call Montana 'Big Sky Country'. He knew he couldn't leave the puppy, so he went to the pet store to buy food, toys, and a bed. He named her Sky and set up a vet appointment to get her checked out. She'd been his best girl ever since.

Mark lived in a small craftsman style house halfway between work and the beach. Thunder had offered him the apartment above the cultural center when his lease was up on his apartment, but he preferred space. This house was perfect for him. It had three bedrooms, two bathrooms, a laundry room, an open concept modern kitchen, a breakfast nook, and a living room. The enclosed back patio led out into a nice size backyard, which was perfect for Sky. A couple months after he moved in, he had a sport pool installed so he could soak his sore muscles after his training and workout sessions. Plus, it was South Florida and hot. He loved to come home and chill in the pool.

The privacy fence was added when he realized his married neighbor sat outside in a skimpy bikini, pretending to tan while just so happening to face him every time he was out soaking in the pool or playing with his puppy. How the hell did she know he was out there? Was he that predictable or did she sit by her window and watch for him? At first, he laughed it off, he was used to girls going out of their way to get his attention. But he'd had enough when she invited her friends over to drink wine and stare at him.

Once while he was training Sky, she ran into the neighbor's yard. Mark followed and said hello to the ladies, introducing himself. When they all said hello, he noticed they were all married. Some women had called him a womanizer, but he drew the line at married women. What the fuck? Did their husbands know they were drooling over another man? He was not some side-show attraction. Some women had no boundaries.

After that encounter, he made sure to train Sky to come to him. He never stepped foot into the neighbor's yard again. When he told his deputy friends George and Sean about his crazy neighbor and asked for help, they introduced him to K-9 Deputy Bryan Wright. Deputy Wright was happy to partner with him and train Sky. Sky was intelligent and eager to learn the commands without distraction. She had done so well in her training that Deputy Wright asked if he could borrow her whenever they had an 'all hands on deck emergency' call. Mark agreed to loan her out, now that her training was complete. Sky was now almost a year old and went to work with Deputy Wright one to two times a week to stay sharp.

Mark wanted to ask Thunder if he could bring Sky to work on the days she wasn't with the K-9 unit and help him monitor the cultural center, but was waiting until her training was complete. Sky had been working with Deputy Wright for the past few weeks and he gave her rave reviews. She was ready to help Mark at the cultural center. Now that he had the 'all clear' from Deputy Wright, he'd talk to Thunder next week.

Chapter 14

First Day of The New Job

Maggie

Today is a good day, Maggie thought as she lowered her visor to check her makeup in the cultural center parking lot. She hadn't had one of those in her previous job for at least a couple of weeks. A tingling sensation came over her. She was happy. Happy she was starting her new job at the American Indian Cultural Center, and she wasn't going to hear anyone mumbling nasty words or names under their breath. Happy no one here hated her. Hell, no one here knew Ryan, which was a godsend. Happy to learn the specifics of her new job and hang out with her friends. Isa had introduced her to Tori during their first Girls' Night Out. They had hit it off even though Maggie was more like Frey (Alex's sister and Tori's best friend) and wilder than Tori.

Tori always had a calm demeanor and was quieter, especially after what happened to her. Maggie was glad Tori had finally agreed to date Alex. Speaking of Alex, he was a certified hunk. Too bad he was off the market and planned on marrying Tori. Alex looked mean with all his tattoos, but he was a softy when you got to know him, and man, could he cook. *Ooh, I get to eat his cooking for lunch every day. I don't have to pack my lunch – winner, winner, chicken dinner!*

Maggie smiled, got out of her car, and pranced inside. Mark sat behind the lobby desk in a security guard uniform. She decided she loved teasing Mark the first time she met him. They had an easy banter because Mark gave as good as he got. She'd never seen him in his uniform—he looked good. No, good was too tame a word. He looked hot. As soon as he saw her, he stood up to greet her with a welcoming smile. *Ay Dios mio*, he looked so sexy in his uniform with the gun holster, zip ties, and taser strapped onto his waist.

He'd slicked his brown hair back and looked ultraprofessional as he waited for her to approach the lobby desk. She had always thought he had a sexy body with his eight-pack abs, but wow, there was a difference between knowing that and seeing him in uniform...he packed a powerful punch. She didn't realize a man in uniform turned her on. Her bad boys were never in uniform.

"Are you just going to stare at me like a piece of meat or are you going to come over and say hello like a good girl?" Mark quirked an eyebrow and crossed his arms.

Maggie realized she had stood frozen to the spot while she drooled over him. *Shit. Get it together, girl.* She walked to the lobby desk and gripped the top. Mark came around the desk and pulled her in for a hug. Maggie's stomach sprung butterflies, her pussy quivered, and she clenched her thighs to stop the throbbing. *What the hell? Say something...speak...hell...give him shit.* Oh wow, his abs were rock solid, and she fit perfectly in his arms. Those strong, sexy arms that held her tight and made her feel safe. Crap...was that his gun, or was he happy to see her? *Shake it off, Maggie, and say hello. You're better than this.*

"Good morning," Maggie mumbled against his chest.

"Good morning." Mark pulled her back, beaming at her. "Ready for your first day?"

You've never reacted to him like this before. Remember, he's a friend and now a co-worker. Don't let those sexy hazel eyes suck you in. Is there some green in his eyes?

"Maggie?" Mark ducked his head down to her eye level, a frown on his face. "Are you okay?"

"Yeah, just nervous I guess." Maggie tried to smile, but it came out more like a wince.

"Hey." Mark pulled her into his chest again and rubbed her back.

Maggie knew he was trying to soothe her nerves, but it wasn't her nerves that needed his attention right now. *Shit, if he kept hugging her, she wouldn't be able to clear her head. Get those thoughts out of your head—now. Getting a hug from Mark was nothing new, so why was she so turned on right now? What had changed? Was it the uniform?* Her group of friends hugged each other for just about anything. They were very touchy-feely. But, somehow, seeing Mark in uniform as he comforted her made this hug more intimate.

"It's going to be okay. This job is a piece of cake, and you get to work with us." Mark chuckled as he stepped away from her. "You know we like you and we won't be saying shitty things about you. Well, I might piss you off with my sarcasm, but you know it comes from a good place." Mark playfully punched her arm, snapping her out of her Sexy Mark trance.

"Yeah, right, Surfer Smurf." Maggie smirked at him. Calling him a Smurf helped her gather her wits—finally. "Where's Tori?"

"There's my Maggie." Mark laughed and turned around to head back to his side of the desk with his arms raised. "And she's back, ladies and gentlemen!"

Maggie smiled and followed him. *Was she his Maggie? Snap out of it, girl. Do your drooling at home, not in front of him.*

"Tori is in the kitchen with Alex. Enter at your own risk." Mark wiggled his eyebrows.

Isa had told Maggie about how Thunder sometimes caught Tori sneaking kisses from Alex in the kitchen. Nothing hot and heavy, but Thunder always pivoted quickly and left. He wasn't opposed to them dating, he just wanted to give them privacy. Maggie knew Isa teased Thunder about it and told him maybe he should text Tori instead of looking for her in the kitchen. With that in mind, she decided to look for Thunder instead of Tori. She had to get away from Mark before she made a fool of herself. Where were these feelings coming from? Hell, she'd seen him in a swimming suit with no shirt and she didn't remember reacting to him like this.

Thunder was on the phone when Maggie peered into his office. She didn't want to interrupt his call by barging in, so she stood just outside the door. Thunder saw her and waved her in. Maggie stood quietly just inside the door.

"That sounds great, Mr. Atkins. We'll see you on Thursday. Have a great day." Thunder hung up and came around his desk to hug Maggie.

This was what a friendly hug normally felt like. Hugging Thunder was like hugging her brother. Not like Mark's hug. Fuck! When she hugged Mark, she wanted to climb his body like a tree. *Stop thinking like this, Maggie,* she told herself. *Now is not the time to daydream about fucking Mark.*

"Are you ready for your first day?" Thunder stepped back.

"Absolutely. I'm so excited!" Maggie beamed at Thunder as she sat down. "Thank you so much for this opportunity. It means so much to me."

"My pleasure. Let me text Tori that you're in my office so she can come and give you the grand tour." Thunder grabbed his cell, and his fingers flew over the keyboard. Maggie smiled because she knew he was taking Isa's advice. "She was with Alex. She's on her way." Thunder put his cell aside and a few seconds later Tori came flying into the room with Alex on her tail.

"Maggie! I'm so glad you're here." Maggie stood and turned just as Tori barreled into her for – yep, she knew it – a hug.

"Hey, Tori." Maggie chuckled. "I'm glad I'm here too. Hi, Alex."

"Hey, Maggie." Alex gave her a quick hug. "Welcome to the AICC family. Will you be eating lunch with us?"

"Duh." Maggie made a silly face. "I tried your cooking when Isa brought it to Teramar. I can't wait to eat your fry bread when it's freshly made."

"Sounds good. I gotta go." Alex kissed Tori on her cheek, waved to everyone, and was ready to leave when Thunder stopped him.

"Alex, can you get Mark and come back for a minute?" Thunder stood, walked around his desk, and leaned on it. "Ladies, have a seat. I just want to have a quick meeting." Maggie and Tori sat, chatting until Alex and Mark came back in a few minutes later. Alex sat next to Tori. Mark stood by the door.

"What's up boss?" Mark leaned against the door frame. Maggie noticed he watched Thunder and kept an eye on the center.

"I just got off the phone with another school. Mr. Atkins from Nob Hill Elementary School is going to be bringing his fourth graders here on Thursday for a field trip. They will arrive around ten and leave at one. Alex, can you please make them some of your fry bread?" Thunder stopped to look at Alex.

"Yes, sir." Alex nodded.

Thunder turned to Tori. "Tori, please explain to Maggie how we do field trips and teach her the Stomp Dance so she can join us when we teach the kids. There will be twenty-five of them and the more of us that can help them the better."

"I can ask Barrett if he can come help?" Alex suggested putting his arm around Tori.

"Great idea." Thunder pointed toward him. "Ask him and let me know what he says."

Alex nodded.

Tori gave Alex a quick kiss on the cheek. "Good idea, honey." Then Tori looked at Maggie. "You will love field trip days. The kids are always so much fun to be around."

Maggie nodded. She wasn't afraid of kids. She loved kids, but she hadn't been around so many of them at one time since she was in school. Maggie wiped her sweaty palms on her pants and found herself smiling back at Tori. Her excitement was contagious.

"Mark, if you want to run a background check on Mr. Atkins for extra practice, go ahead, but the county checks teachers' backgrounds before hiring them, so I'm confident it will be clean." Thunder glanced at Mark.

Mark nodded at Thunder. "I might just do it for practice. I can also help with the Stomp Dance if you need me."

"Sounds good." Thunder pushed off the desk and placed his hands in his pockets as he looked at everyone. "If anyone has any questions, please let me know. Let's get back to work."

Tori grabbed a pad and pencil before they left Thunder's office. "Maggie, let's start in the exhibit room. I brought you this pad and pencil so you could write down whatever you need to remember as we go over the exhibits in here." Tori handed them to Maggie.

"Thank you." *Great thinking.* Maggie was so excited to leave her apartment this morning, she totally forgot to grab a notebook, even though she knew she would need to remember a lot of details.

Maggie followed Tori to the first exhibit and began taking notes. Tori explained every item in the exhibit. Some were Seminole and others in the permanent exhibit were Lakota. Every artifact was beautiful and filled with interesting history. Maggie wanted to learn as much as she could from Tori and continue to research the Seminole and Lakota cultures. The more she knew about the cultures and the people, the more she could teach their guests if they requested a tour. This job was an opportunity to make a change in her life and be an asset to Thunder and Tori. She hoped when she finished her classes next semester, they would consider letting her do some marketing for them.

Between Tori being so animated about every piece on display and Maggie soaking up all the knowledge Tori had to offer, it was no surprise that they had a late lunch. They both lost track of time until Alex came in to let them know lunch had been ready for over an hour. After lunch, Tori went over the items in the gift shop.

"Hey, baby." Alex walked up to Tori. "It's time to go."

"Oh, wow. Is it that time already?" Tori looked at her watch. "Maggie, we'll continue with the rest of the items tomorrow. Alex and I usually leave now since he works a dinner shift at RUSH. Let's see if Thunder is here. He usually visits local schools or businesses promoting the center in the afternoons."

"No problem." Maggie followed Tori to Thunder's office and noticed he wasn't there. Tori grabbed her purse out of a filing cabinet. "I'm not sure where you put your purse today, but you can keep it in here with mine. Let's ask Mark if Thunder left. If he did, then you and Mark will close today. Mark is always the first and last one here." Maggie followed Tori to the lobby desk where Alex was waiting for her.

"Mark," Tori called before wrapping her arms around Alex's waist, "did Thunder leave?"

"He did," Mark confirmed.

"Can you teach Tori how to check in our guests and where to find all the files on that computer?" Tori pointed to the other computer to the left of Mark's setup.

"Yup." Mark nodded. "You lovebirds can take off. I got this."

"Thanks, man." Alex smirked and kissed Tori's temple.

"Thank you, Mark." Tori glanced at Maggie. "We'll finish tomorrow, and I'll teach you the Stomp Dance, so you'll be ready for the field trip."

"Thanks, Tori." Maggie sat down at the computer station. "You guys have a great night."

"Don't bring lunch tomorrow, Maggie. I'm going to cook homemade manicotti for us." Alex grabbed Tori's hand and pulled her toward the front door.

"Oh, wow. I love this job already." Maggie licked her lips. She couldn't wait to eat lunch tomorrow.

Alex chuckled. "Good night," he hollered on his way out with Tori.

"She is so lucky." Maggie sighed and placed her elbow on the desk, resting her chin on her hand as she watched them leave.

Chapter 15

Let the Crazy Names Begin

Maggie

"Hey! Miss Mooney!" Mark snapped his fingers in front of her face. "Snap out of it and wipe the drool off your chin. He's taken."

Maggie jolted back and stared at him. "Listen Surfer Smurf, I know he's taken. But a girl can dream about having a guy who will cook for her and treat her with so much love."

"I can cook," Mark scoffed. "I also give girls all the love they can handle. And believe me it is a lot of love." Mark wiggled his eyebrows and pointed to his cock.

"You are such a slut," Maggie laughed at him. "Jealous much? Besides, I've never seen you with a girl. You've never given me the opportunity to drool over your gooey romantic side. Do you bat for the other team or are you all talk and no action? You're probably not very romantic and I seriously doubt you can cook." Maggie knew he liked girls, she just wanted to mess with him. Isa once told her how he slept around, but never got serious.

"Are you done? Judge Judy? I can show you how much I like girls and how romantic I can be." Mark held out his hand. "Care to place a bet and put your money where your mouth is?"

Maggie spun her chair around, crossed her arms, and raised an eyebrow at him. "What do you have in mind?"

"One date with me. I'll cook for you and provide a romantic environment." Mark crossed his arms, matching her posture.

"What's the catch?" Maggie squinted at him.

"You have to kiss me at the end of our evening and I guaran-fucking-tee you your panties will be drenched." Mark smirked.

"You're that sure of yourself?" Maggie scoffed.

"Yup, Debbie Doubter." Mark wheeled his chair closer to Maggie and put his hand out again. "Deal?"

"Sure. 'Cause I will win. You will not get me panting for you, Surfer Smurf. I won't even bring a change of panties since they'll be as dry as when I put them on." Maggie shook his hand and wondered what she had gotten herself into. That twinkle in his eyes warned her that she would regret this bet.

"Friday. Seven o'clock. My place," Mark said, while still holding her hand in his. It took Maggie a minute to realize he wasn't just holding her hand–he was rubbing his thumb across it, soothing her. Maggie pulled her hand away and rubbed her palm on her leg. "BYOP"

"What the hell is that? Surfer talk?" Maggie squinted at him.

"Bring your own panties. Just warning you, if you don't plan to bring a spare, you'll be stuck going home commando." Mark laughed.

"Yeah, right, Surfer Smurf." Maggie rolled her eyes.

"I'll text you my address." Mark smiled at her before he grabbed his phone. Her phone beeped seconds later.

"How do you know my number?" Maggie swung narrowed eyes from her phone back to him.

"Put the magnifying glass away, Nancy Drew. I'm a security officer and I run background checks on everyone who works here or comes in here. It's my job to keep this place and its employees safe."

Maggie stiffened. *Did he know her real name and about her family?*

"Which reminds me, Nikita. Why didn't you write your real name on your application for employment?" Mark watched Maggie's reaction.

Fuck! How much does he know? Should I come clean? No, I'll just give him some bullshit answer and change the subject. The day was almost over, and he still hadn't told her about her receptionist's job.

"Funny, Surfer Smurf." Maggie pretended to blow off his comment, waving her hand in a shooing motion. "I've gone by Maggie for so long that I didn't think to write Margarita. Now, let's get back to work. Tori wanted you to teach me how to check in a guest and my workday is almost over." Maggie ignored his skepticism and wheeled herself under the desk, facing the computer and clicking a key to wake up the monitor. "So, what do I need to do?"

"Fine, Nikita." Mark wheeled his chair next to her, leaned into his armrest with his shoulder touching hers, and pointed with his other hand at the sign in window on the computer monitor. "Click this icon, then select 'new user'. Let's set up a sign in for you. I keep the computers locked down so no one can access our files. Pick a password you'll remember and don't give it to anyone."

Between the woodsy scent of his cologne and his deep voice near her ear, Maggie was having a hard time focusing on his instructions. *Why is this happening?* She hung out with Mark all the time when their group got together, and she never had this reaction to him. It had to be the uniform and what she knew was under it. *But why now?*

"That hard to pick a password, Smarty Pants?" Mark turned his head to look at her.

Maggie could feel his breath on her cheek. *Fuck!* She could feel her nipples harden and her breath quicken. This had to stop. *Focus Maggie*, she told herself. *Get this shit done and go home! And what is up with all his quirky names for me?* She would normally be mad at him and give him shit, but she found it funny, even though she would have to look up some of the names he called her. *Who the hell was Nikita? Where did he come up with this stuff?*

"Stop breathing down my neck. I just want to pick one that I'll remember. Us mere mortals are obviously not as smart as you." Maggie muttered and typed in her mom and dad's names with the date of their death. Not a great password if anyone knew who she really was, but it was all that came to her at the moment. She could always change it later.

"Right." Mark pointed to her pad. "You might want to take notes on that fancy pad of yours, little miss secretary, since you're not as perfect as me."

"Okay, Surfer Smurf or should I call you Arrogant Smurf?" Maggie grabbed her pad, ready to take notes. "Are you sure you remember everything you need to teach me? That blue hair dye from a few days ago didn't fry your brain?"

"Not a chance, Snarky. I'm as sharp as a tack." Mark tapped his temple. Grinning, he taught her how to sign in guests.

Maggie wrote down everything he said, but the program seemed simple and easy to use. He then showed her the files Tori was talking about and how to put the computer to sleep.

"Don't turn off the computer after you sign out, Madame Reporter. I created a program that backs them up every night." Mark pointed to her notes. "Do you want to write that down, too?"

Instead of writing down what he said, Maggie wrote 'Surfer Smurf is really Asshole Smurf' and underlined it three times before she threw her pen down and smiled at Mark. "Got it, Surfer Smurf." Maggie left her notebook open on her desk purposely. She heard Mark chuckle when she opened her top drawer and grabbed her keys. She stood and walked around the lobby desk, ready to leave.

"Wait for me." Mark bolted from his seat. "Let me close everything up. I'll walk you to your car."

"You don't need to walk me, Surfer Smurf. I'm good." Maggie turned to leave, but Mark grabbed her arm, stopping her. How did he get to her so fast? Damn, he was becoming as stealthy as Thunder.

"Listen, Elektra, after everything that happened to Isa and Tori, I feel better walking you to your car. Consider it part of my job." Mark pointed to the floor. "Stay right there. I'll be back to get you."

Damn, that was sexy. His no-nonsense alpha attitude had her breasts tingling and her nipples poking through her blouse. Maggie crossed her arms, hoping to cover her perky nipples.

"Fine." She watched him walk into every room, leaving the lights on. When he approached her, she turned her body away from him. If he saw her nipples waving hello, he'd know he got to her.

"Okay. Let's go." Mark pulled his keys from his pocket and placed a hand behind her back, leading her out. "Did they give you a key?"

"No." Maggie looked over her shoulder. "Why do you leave the lights on?"

"When a business has the lights on, believe it or not, it deters thieves. Plus, it allows the police to see any suspicious activity happening inside. You know deputies George and Sean?"

"Yes, I met them at Thanksgiving." Maggie stepped out and watched Mark set the alarm.

"They drive by during their shift, along with some of their officer friends, and they asked us to leave the lights on. Our light bill is a little higher, but if someone steals something, it would cost us more." Mark escorted Maggie to her car. "I'll go make you a key tonight and tomorrow I'll teach you how to arm and disable the alarm with your key so we can make sure it works." He kept his hand on her lower back until she got in her car. He watched her and waited until she backed out of the parking spot before raising his hand to say goodbye. She waved before pulling out into traffic.

Checking her rearview, she saw him walk toward his truck. Maggie realized he hadn't moved from his spot until she left the parking lot. He seemed very thorough. She was going to have to watch herself if he ever mentioned the information on her application. Hopefully, he bought her excuse.

Chapter 16

Jail Visit

Reaper

Reaper was called out of his cell for a visitor. He hoped like hell it was his daughter. As a small child, she had been daddy's little girl, following him around wherever he went. Then she turned into a know-it-all teenager and looked at him like the devil on the logo of their motorcycle club. He missed the hero worship days and brought her to the club as soon as she turned eighteen, hoping to share his love of drinking with her. At his club, she could drink, dance, and bring a couple friends. He'd warned all his brothers to treat her and her friends with respect or they would answer to him.

Reaper was over the moon when she fell for one of his brothers, Tools (their mechanic). Tools loved Angel so much, that when he found out she was pregnant, they married, and he tried to get the club to go legit by opening an auto shop next to the clubhouse. He loved his wife and his brothers too much to lose any of them.

Tools was doing well with the auto shop. Word had gotten around that Tools could fix anything from cars to motorcycles and people were lining up for his services even though most knew he was part of Lucifer's Renegades. He kept his business professional with honest prices. Several of the brothers helped him in the shop.

But Tools' luck ran out, along with a couple other brothers, on that fateful night that Los Lobos de Muerte came seeking revenge for the death of one of their prospect's parents. That prospect, José, had been sticking his nose in Reaper's business. Reaper sent several members to shoot up José's house. He knew someone might be home, but he didn't care who got hurt as long as he shut José down. Reaper later found out that his brothers had killed José's parents, but the sister had escaped.

Reaper expected a retaliation, but not that same night. José was now called "El Loco" because he rode his fucking bike in front of their clubhouse and sprayed bullets as he rode past. Tools and several brothers were outside talking. Numbers survived, but Tools and two other brothers met their maker that night. Angel was inconsolable. She was pissed and blamed Reaper for the death of her husband. She'd never forgiven him.

Reaper didn't want Angel's forgiveness, just her obedience and silence. She needed to fall in line with the club and accept his decisions. Reaper hated loose ends. It was now eleven years later, and they still hadn't found El Loco's fucking sister. Plus, José and his fucking club were still sticking their nose in his business. The best way to fuck with El Loco was to find his fucking sister and kill her.

Reaper followed the corrections officer to the waiting room. He had hoped she would come, but never actually expected to see her here. Angel wore a dark blue power suit, white blouse, and conservative heels—her professional lawyer attire. Reaper had seen her wear this outfit often in the courtroom when she represented the club. The officer uncuffed him, shut the door, and stood outside.

"Finally," Reaper grunted. "I'm glad you're my new lawyer."

"I'm not. I just told them I was so I could tell you to your face." Angel stayed in the chair, not even getting up to hug her old man. "I do not want any part of this."

"Well, you wanted a part of this when you fucked and married one of my brothers." Reaper glared at her. Angel's beauty, with her long blonde hair and blue eyes, captivated many of his brothers, yet only Tools dared to pursue her. That good looking young fucker had caught and married Angel guiding her gently closer to Reaper and their club. But with Tools gone, Reaper no longer saw love in her eyes when she looked at him. He only saw hate, anger, and disgust.

"You're an asshole." Angel got up to leave. "Fuck You! He tried to save the club, and you just had to go on a killing spree."

"Yeah, well, I had to stop that fucking prospect." Reaper dropped into his chair and pointed to the other. "Sit, let's talk. I miss you and I haven't seen my grandson in several months."

"And who's fault is that?" Angel placed her hand on her hip. "Whenever he spends time with you, he comes home meaner and angrier. You're filling his head with MC shit. I want a different life for my son. Tools wanted a different life for Steele. I'm gonna make sure he stays away from the club. Over my dead body will you turn him against me. You're lucky I let him visit you at the club. But like hell will I bring him here."

"Fine. I won't convince him to join me and my brothers. But I need a favor from you." Reaper crossed his arms and rested them on the table. *Fuck yeah, he was going to make Steele a member of Lucifer's Renegades, but now wasn't the time to argue about that with his rebellious daughter.*

"What is it?" Angel sat down, glaring at Reaper.

"Call Numbers. When they find the girl, I need you to pay her a visit and verify where she lives and works."

"That's it? All you want me to do is find out where she lives and works?" Angel quirked her eyebrow. "Why? Are you going to hurt her?"

"Why the hell do you care? Her motherfucking brother killed your husband," Reaper growled. For a minute there, he forgot the cops might be listening. Reaper was going to make sure El Loco's sister paid for what he did. Tools had brought him closer to his daughter when he was alive, and El Loco had ruined that. He'd always be grateful to Tools for reuniting them and hate El Loco for pulling them apart.

"I know what her brother did. You don't have to keep reminding me. But this all started with you going after El Loco and killing his parents. YOU" –Angel pointed her finger in his face– "started this. Tools wanted peace and you fucking made war."

"And I'm going to fucking end it!" Reaper backhanded her finger away from his face. She always could piss him off.

"Do. Not. Kill. Her." Angel said through gritted teeth. "Tools would not have wanted that. Steele and I have moved on. Leave her alone."

"Okay, fine. I'll leave her alone." Reaper wondered if she knew he was lying through his teeth so she would help him.

"I don't believe you. You're up to something." Angel crossed her arms.

"Can't you just fucking do this for me since you're not going to be my lawyer?" Reaper stood abruptly. His blood was boiling. He had to get her out of here before he lost his temper and hit her. That wouldn't bode well for him.

"Fine." Angel stood.

"Good." Reaper nodded. "Since you won't be my lawyer, they won't let you in here. But I can still facetime you from that monitor." Reaper pointed toward a monitor in front of a small bench seat. "I expect to hear from my grandson in a few days. If you don't let Steele call me, Numbers will make sure to pay you a visit."

"Are you threatening me?" Angel stiffened and took a step back. She knew how dangerous Reaper could be when his authority was tested. Tools protected her from Reaper's temper while they were together, but he was gone now. Reaper had hit her before to keep her in line, but lately he'd tried to be nicer. He was afraid she would run with Steele while he was in jail, and he'd never see his grandson again. He had to play nice until he got out of this shithole.

"No, just reminding you who your father is." Reaper smirked at her and watched a shiver run down her spine. He knew he got his point across.

Angel took a deep breath. "Fine. I'll let him call you."

"Now hug your daddy before you leave." Reaper grabbed her and hugged her. "I do love you even if you don't think I have a heart. I won't let my boys kill the girl." The girl would go back to her brother in one piece and not in a body bag. Reaper would stand behind his comment, but he never said he wouldn't allow his brothers to play with her before returning her to El Loco.

"Okay." Reaper could feel Angel's body trembling in his embrace.

"I...I gotta go." Angel pulled away and stood by the door.

Reaper banged on the door, letting the guard know he was ready. Once the guard opened the door, Angel scurried out. The guard cuffed Reaper again and led him back to his cell.

Chapter 17

Where the Fuck is Margarita?

José

José drove by Teramar several times a week to check on Maggie. He never went in, but seeing her car in the parking lot gave him peace of mind. He never drove by Nancy's apartment where Maggie lived because it would have been more suspicious. It had now been a few days and Maggie's car wasn't in the lot. Pulling into a parking spot, he started to panic and needed to make sure she was okay. He texted Maggie on her burner phone. The one he'd given her the day Aunt Inez picked her up from the clubhouse.

> José: Why haven't you been at work? You, ok?

> Maggie: Sorry. I left that job and I'm working somewhere else.

> José: Where?

> Maggie: American Indian Cultural Center

> José: Why?

> Maggie: Trouble with co-workers

> José: I'm coming by.

> Maggie: No! I'm good.

José needed to see her and make sure she was okay, even though she didn't want him to visit her at her new job. Since he made a run this morning, he was in his truck instead of on his bike. It was less conspicuous. Besides, he didn't give a fuck if any LR's saw him in their area. He could take care of himself. Seeing his sister was more important than those fuckers.

José googled the address and put it into his GPS. It didn't take long to drive from Teramar to the cultural center. He parked, took off his Kutte (a vest with the MC's logo on the back), and got out of the car, scanning the area for any LR's on their bikes. Seeing that the coast was clear, he walked into the center. The first thing he noticed when he opened the door was the security officer sitting next to his sister, laughing with her. They both looked up when he walked in.

"Hi." Maggie stopped laughing and her eyes widened.

"Good morning, welcome to the American Indian Cultural Center." The security officer said. "How can we help you?"

"I'm here to find out about the center." José walked up to the desk in front of Maggie. He acted like he didn't know her to keep her safe, but his eyes wandered over her body, checking for any bandages or bruises. He was relieved to see she was okay.

"Maggie?" The security officer called her name, watching her.

"Oh, sorry." Maggie jolted out of her seat. "Would you like a tour?"

"Sure." José looked around and saw the exhibit room. "Could you show me that exhibit?" José pointed to the room.

"Of course." Maggie grabbed a brochure and handed it to José. "Please, follow me."

José smiled at the security officer whose eyes kept bouncing between him and Maggie. José followed her into the room with the sign that said "Unconquered Path Exhibit". He had just walked into the room when Maggie spun around and poked him in the chest.

"What are you doing here?" Maggie whispered through gritted teeth.

"I needed to see you and make sure you were okay. You never miss work and I've driven by Teramar every day for the past week and didn't see your car. I was worried about you." José placed his arms on his hips.

"Sshh. Keep your voice down." Maggie grabbed his forearm and pulled him further into the room. "As you can see, I'm fine."

"Who's the guard dog watching your every move?" José pointed his thumb over his shoulder toward the doorway.

"Mark is a security officer who is very observant and takes his job seriously. Which is why I didn't want you coming here." Maggie rubbed her temples.

"Why did you leave the other job?" José crossed his arms over his chest, waiting for her answer.

"I was having issues with some co-workers and couldn't take it anymore." Maggie fidgeted with her hands and looked down.

"What the fuck? Were they hurting you? I'll fucking kill them." José could feel the anger rising from the pit of his stomach. No one fucked with his sister. She was the only immediate family he had left except for his brothers. Sure, he still had his aunt, uncle, and cousin – but he only had one sister.

"No, José." Maggie looked up and placed her hand on his crossed arms. "I handled it. It's fine. I'm here now and I love it. My friends work here. You remember me telling you about Isa?" Maggie waited for José's nod. "Her husband, Thunder, owns this center and he hired me when I needed a job."

"Wasn't this the center Lucifer's Renegades stole from and kidnapped that girl?" José was getting madder by the minute.

"Yes, but now we have more security and Mark is authorized to carry a gun. He's constantly scanning for trouble." Maggie grabbed his hand and tried pulling him out of the room. "Which is why you shouldn't have come here."

"Like I said, I needed to see you. I love you, Margarita." José pulled her into his arms. "I worry about you all the time. You are the only sister I have, and I need to keep you safe. If you have any trouble with the LR's, please call me." José pulled back and stared her down, trying to convey with his eyes how important it was for her to take her safety seriously.

"I will. I promise." Maggie kissed his cheek and went in for another hug.

"Is everything okay in here?" Mark asked from the doorway.

"Shit," Maggie mumbled.

Maggie stepped back and laughed. "Mark, this is my brother, José."

"Oh. Well, why didn't you say so when he came in?" Mark stepped up to José and shook his hand. "It's nice to meet you man." José watched Mark closely and didn't see any animosity toward him. He wondered if Mark would have given him a different reception if he was wearing his Los Lobos Kutte. Most people treated him differently when they knew he was a member of a motorcycle club.

"It's a game we've played since we were kids." José wrapped his arm around her shoulder. "Maggie hates when I check up on her. She likes to pretend she doesn't know me. I can be overprotective." José glared at Mark, making his point about how he should treat his sister. "I'm always watching out for her. It drives her crazy, so she likes to mess with me. Right, Maggie?" José squeezed her shoulders closer to him.

"Right." Maggie glared at José. "Now that you can see I'm okay. You can go back to work." Maggie pushed him away, but José gripped her shoulders tighter and pulled her in for a kiss on her temple. He used his hand over her shoulder to walk her to the entrance of the center.

"Where do you work, José?" Mark asked from behind him.

"I'm in marketing," José answered and glanced down at Maggie with a smirk on his face. Maggie didn't look amused, but he thought it was hilarious.

"Okay, *hermanita. Te quiero mucho, cuidate*," José mumbled in her ear while he hugged her tightly. José noticed Mark behind them, so he kept one arm around his sister and extended the other to shake his hand. Since Maggie couldn't see his face, he glared at Mark, making sure the guy understood how serious he was about protecting Maggie. "It was nice to meet you, Mark. Please take care of my sister while she is here." Mark never broke eye contact and shook his hand again. His firm grip and nod comforted José, who gripped harder this time. *Good, we understand each other.* "You all have a great day."

José left feeling better about his sister's whereabouts. Mark seemed to be aware of everything that went on around him. José was glad Mark came into the room to check on Maggie. He didn't think Maggie had caught on, but he saw how the security officer watched her like a hawk. There was something between them.

He would have his brothers keep an eye on the center. The LR's were never going to mess with the center again. Not while Maggie worked there.

*** Maggie ***

Maggie panicked when she saw José enter the cultural center, but remained calm as he approached the lobby desk so Mark wouldn't get suspicious. It had slipped her mind to let him know she had switched jobs. She wished he would switch jobs and get out of the Los Lobos Club, but like he'd told her before, "once you're in, there is no out"–not that he wanted out. He loved his brothers and would do anything for his club.

Worrying about José had become a constant buzz in the back of her head from the first day he joined the club. She remembered the day she and her parents found out he was a prospect.

Maggie was sitting quietly in her room, studying for a test when she overheard her parent's raised voices. Wondering why they were talking so loudly, she stepped out of her room and headed toward the kitchen. She froze in place when she saw José wearing a black sleeveless leather vest with the biker club logo and the word 'prospect' on the bottom. That was the name of the motorcycle club all the kids at school were talking about. Some boys thought they were cool, but most people stayed away from them. Maggie crouched down, leaning against the living room wall that led to the kitchen. Leaning forward into the entryway, she eavesdropped on their conversation.

"José, money isn't everything. We have a car, a roof over our head, and food which is more than we had in Cuba. We will be fine. You need to quit this new job'. Your mother and I do not want you joining that motorcycle club. Coño, take off that vest," Ramon pointed to his son's chest.

"No, Papi. I love making more money and helping. Maybe now you only gotta work one job instead of three."

"No, mijo." Her father raised his voice again. "I can take care of my family. You need to take off that vest and quit so your mother can sleep at night."

"Mami, you don't sleep?" Maggie peaked into the kitchen and saw José's sorrowful eyes on mami. Maggie knew José would never do anything bad, he was a good guy. Why didn't papi understand that José was just trying to help them?

"No." Mami admitted. "I never know if you are going to make it home in one piece. We left a communist country to keep you safe and now you join a biker club. What were you thinking?"

"I'm fine. They're good guys and I'm part of a brotherhood. It's cool when we ride down the road and everyone watches us." José placed his hand over his heart. "We look out for each other."

"How can you say they are good guys when they do things that aren't legal? Everyone watches you when you ride down the road because they are afraid of you. Do you not see how they hide or scurry away? Those bikers sell drugs and guns. Coño, you probably carry that on you when you go on deliveries."

Maggie gasped and covered her mouth, but too late. Papi turned toward her hiding spot with a frown.

"Margarita, go to your room!" Papi yelled and Maggie scurried away. She had heard enough to know her brother was in trouble and the bikers he hung out with were trouble.

Her father had been right. The next night, José told her the truth about how he was paid a lot of money to deliver things for his brothers along with the fast food they used as a front. Through the years, Maggie had heard that the Los Lobos were not as ruthless as the LR's, but they were a one-percenter biker club involved in illegal activities. Maggie didn't approve of her brother's choices, but he was her brother, and she loved him.

She was glad she had told Mark who he was near the end of his visit instead of pretending he was a guest, but now Mark would have more questions for her. It was important how much she told Mark because keeping her brother out of jail was her number one priority. Thank goodness José hadn't worn his kutte when he came in. That was not a discussion she was ready to have with Mark—not yet.

*** Lucifer's Renegades Prospect ***

"Prospect, where the fuck are you?" Numbers voice came over Red's cell phone so loud he had to pull it away from his ears.

"I was on my way to the clubhouse when I spotted El Loco's truck at that cultural center Reaper tried to rip off a few months ago. So, I parked across the street. I've been sitting here waiting to see if it's him." Red explained and hoped Numbers wouldn't get too mad at him. As a prospect for Lucifer's Renegades, he couldn't afford to fuck up. He'd been prospecting for almost a year and still hadn't proven himself worthy of becoming a full patch member of the club.

"Is he alone?"

"Looks like it. Although the motherfucker has such dark tinted windows, I can't see if there's anyone inside the truck." Red didn't think he saw movement.

"Is the fucking truck running?"

"No," Red answered.

"Then there's no one in the fucking truck, Prospect." Numbers screamed again. "It's fucking ninety-five degrees. Do you think someone would sit in a truck without AC?"

"Guess not." Red hated when one of the brothers yelled at him and made him feel like a fuck up. "Wait, he's leaving and he's hugging a girl inside. Fuck! It's him! Do you want me to follow him?" Adrenaline amped up his body and he was ready to ride after El Loco. Part of him feared being alone, but another part figured if he killed El Loco, maybe they would patch him in sooner.

"No, asshole. He's probably going back to his clubhouse. Besides, with that big ass truck, he could run you off the road and kill your ass. Just get the beer we asked for and get your ass over here ASAP. We'll take care of El Loco."

"Okay. On my way." Red hung up, dejected. He thought he could prove himself worthy of being a brother, but Numbers wanted him to get the fucking beer and head back—so that's what he would do. When a brother gave you an order, you followed it, come hell or high water. He'd wasted so much time making sure it was El Loco that he had to drive like a bat out of hell to the food store closest to the clubhouse and buy cold beer from the refrigerated section. If he wasn't back quick with the beer, it would be his ass.

Chapter 18

Tools, I Miss You

Angel

"Numbers? Why are you calling me?" Angel was panting into the phone, trying to catch her breath. Steele had gone to a friend's house, and she had gone for a run to clear her head. She hated doing anything for her father, but if all she had to do was recon, it was worth it to avoid his wrath. She was walking back from the end of her run when her phone rang. "I went to see my fucking father. What else do you want?"

"Well, hello to you too. You know there was a time when you were much nicer to me—to all of us."

"Yeah, well, that was before you all got my husband killed." Angel opened her door and stepped into the welcoming coolness of her air conditioning.

"Whatever. I'm not going to argue with you. I know you went to see your dad and you haven't called me." Angel could hear clubhouse noises in the background. Walking into her kitchen, she opened her fridge and grabbed a bottle of water. She knew Numbers would just continue talking, so she guzzled half the bottle while she listened for his next words. "You were supposed to call me."

"How do you know I was supposed to call you?" Angel wiped her mouth and carried her bottle to the couch. She needed to sit for the rest of this conversation.

"Because I talked to Reaper, and he told me his plan."

"Terrific." Angel sat on the couch and leaned her head back. Closing her eyes, she used her feet to slip off her shoes. "Now that you know I saw him, you can leave me alone."

"Not gonna happen. Our timeline just moved up."

"What do you mean it 'moved up'?" Angel's eyes popped open, her body stiffened, and she held her breath, waiting for the hammer to drop.

"We think we found the girl. I need you to take Steele to the American Indian Cultural Center and meet this girl. Find out if she's El Loco's sister or girlfriend."

"How the hell am I supposed to find that out?" Angel didn't want to do this, but not helping her father could drive a wedge between her and Steele. Reaper had become close to Steele during the early months when she fell apart after losing her husband. She'd been so busy grieving Tools' death, she didn't realize how much time Reaper was spending with Steele, molding him into his mini-me biker.

Steele was now thirteen and had a mouth on him that Angel tried in vain to clean up. She tried to tell him about the good things his father wanted to accomplish within the club. She desperately wanted him to stay away from the dangerous club, its reputation preceding it with whispers of trouble and violence. Unfortunately, he thought his grandfather was cool since he was president of a motorcycle club, and everyone respected him. The community didn't respect him—they feared him—but Steele didn't see it that way. Or maybe he did and didn't care.

"I don't know." Angel heard the frustration in Numbers' voice as it got louder. "You're a lawyer. You know how to lie, so make this happen. Ask for a tour or some shit, but get to know her or I'll fucking tell your father you didn't do what he asked."

"Fine." Angel rubbed her face. *Would this ever end?* "I'll go by there, but I'm not taking Steele." She didn't want him to be a part of this.

"You will take him. That was your father's command, not a suggestion."

"Why? I can handle this myself." Angel was getting agitated. *Why was her father involving Steele?*

"Steele knows what to do." Numbers answered curtly.

"What do you mean?" Angel's heart started racing. *What did Reaper tell Steele? She needed to talk to him.* Checking her watch, she saw Steele would be home in about an hour for dinner. "Numbers, I don't want Steele involved. He's just a little boy. Please don't make me take him."

"I'm not making you do shit—your father is. Steele has to go, Reapers' orders. Make sure you do this within the next couple days and report back to me. I do not want to go see Reaper as his pretend secondary lawyer and not have news to report. Get your shit together Angel and get the job done."

Angel winced when she heard the click announcing Numbers had hung up on her. *Fuck!* Angel threw her phone on the couch. She knew what her dad wanted her to do was not as easy as he made it seem. Of course, the asshole didn't tell her she had to bring her son in person because she would've been screaming and yelling at him so loud it would have brought multiple officers to that fucking jail room.

Angel got up and walked to the shelving unit which held photos of her life with Tools. Angel grabbed the photo where she and Tools were laughing at Steele trying to bite into a smore while the marshmallow dripped onto Tools' leg. Her father had taken the photo. Tools had wanted to go camping and Reaper offered to go with them to help watch over Steele, who was only two, so they could have some alone time.

Tools begged her to get closer to her father. He knew Reaper had hit her growing up, but Tools promised her Reaper had changed and would never lay a finger on her again. Tools didn't expect her to forget, but he wanted her to forgive him so they could all be one big happy family. She knew Tools felt a tremendous tug of war between his brothers and his wife, always trying to keep everyone happy. Deep down she would never forgive her father, but she loved her husband and was willing to be the family Tools never had.

Tools had been an orphan when he found Lucifer's Renegades. One day when Angel went to talk to her father, she met Tools. It was love at first sight. Her father had been ecstatic. Being married to one of his brothers meant he could still control her fate. They married quickly and Tools became her world. During their brief marriage, Reaper behaved and acted like the doting father. Angel never forgot all the horrible things Reaper had done to her, but seeing her husband happy helped her to deal with her father. That camping trip helped to reunite them—until Tools was killed.

"Tools, what am I going to do? I miss you so much." Angel hugged the photo to her chest as tears slid down her face. "It's so hard to raise Steele without you. I wish you had never brought my father back into our lives. We should've moved away when we found out I was pregnant. I miss your love, your arms around me, the warmth of your body at night, your laughter, and your beautiful smile. You were my everything. I feel so lost and alone without you." After eleven years, she thought the pain would've eased, but she still missed him like it happened yesterday. She didn't know how long she stood there crying, but suddenly she heard the front door. Wiping the tears from her face, she placed the photo back on the shelf and turned around.

"Mom? Are you okay?" Steele stood in front of her.

"Yeah." Angel tried to smile. "Just thinking about your dad and all our good times."

"Oh. Well, I'm gonna shower."

Angel tried so hard to tell Steele about Tools, but he was too young to remember his father. It hurt her whenever he was indifferent about Tools and his memory.

"I need to talk to you before you go shower." Angel grabbed her bottle of water and took a sip. *What she really needed was several shots of tequila for this conversation.*

"About what?" Steele placed his hands on his hips, waiting for her response.

"Your grandfather wants me to take you to the American Indian Cultural Center and meet a lady that works there. Did he talk to you about that?" Angel watched Steele's reaction. He was so volatile sometimes that any little thing would set him off.

"Yep." Steele puffed out his chest. "I know what to do. When are we going?"

"What do you mean, you know what to do? When did you talk to him?" Angel crossed her arms and stared him down.

"I know he was looking for the girl whose brother killed my dad. We talked about it a lot and I know what he wants me to do." Steele shrugged.

"You talked about it. You know what to do. What the fuck is going on around here?" Angel lost her temper.

"It's no big deal, Mom. Stop!" Steele screamed at her. "I'm not a fucking baby!"

"You're not an adult either. Besides, you will always be my baby." Angel watched Steele roll his eyes at her. "What exactly did your grandfather expect you to do?"

"I just need to talk to her and get to know her. That's all." Steele waved his hands out in front of him. "So, when are we going?"

"I want to get this over with." Angel sighed and rubbed her forehead. "I'll call the school and tell them you don't feel well, and we'll go during the day."

"Yes!" Steele pumped his arm in the air and turned to leave.

"Don't get so excited. You're going to have to make up all your work." Angel hollered at his back. "I hate taking you out of school."

"Yeah, yeah, yeah. Goodnight." Steele left the room with more pep in his step than when he came home.

"Aren't you going to come back down for dinner?" Angel followed him for a few steps.

"Nope. I ate at Benny's house."

"I'm still going to make some spaghetti. I'll leave the leftovers in the fridge in case you get hungry later." Angel stopped following him when he shut his bedroom door in her face.

"Fine!" Steele screamed through the door.

Fuck my life! Tools, fuck you for helping create this bond between your son and his asshole grandfather! What the hell had Reaper told him to do? She would watch him carefully and make sure it wasn't anything illegal. Angel went to her room to shower before starting dinner. She wasn't hungry, but Steele was known to come down and eat more before going to bed. He was a growing boy and instead of gaining too much weight, he just kept growing taller and taller. Soon, he would be as tall as Tools—over six feet.

Chapter 19

Strange Visitor

Maggie

Maggie enjoyed working at the center. She wished her brother hadn't shown up at the cultural center, worried about her, but it was her fault she hadn't let him know she'd quit her job at Teramar and gotten another one. She knew how overprotective José was toward her. Mark didn't have time to say anything about her brother because shortly after his visit, the fieldtrip students came in and it was all hands on deck.

Today should be a slower day. It was Friday and the only planned item on the schedule was the shelter kids coming to visit. The shelter kids were a group of boys from the Boys Shelter in town who Thunder mentored. She'd met them at the Panther's Thanksgiving Dinner at the Rock 'n' Roll Resort & Casino. Alex's parents had been gracious enough to invite them all over to eat and swim in the resort pool after dinner. The kids were so excited and very respectful. Something you don't normally see in young kids, especially ones that have had it hard growing up.

"So." Mark wheeled his chair over to her. "We're still on for tonight, right?"

"Yep. What are you cooking for me?" Maggie continued to sort through her work emails. She wasn't sure how tonight was going to go, but if the butterflies in her stomach were any indication, she might just get lucky tonight. *Where the hell did that thought come from? Lucky with Mark?* Shit, she had to get her hormones under control or tonight was going to end with them in bed naked after having marathon sex. *Marathon Sex?* He was turning her into a nymphomaniac. He was even entering her dreams at night in his sexy uniform.

"That, Miss Impatient" –Mark pushed her chair away. He loved to mess with her and vice versa. Several times a day, one of them would push the other's chair away to get their attention. She knew it was immature behavior, but it worked. Maggie rolled herself back to her computer, laughing and pushed him away as he finished his statement– "is a surprise."

"Maggie, Mark." Thunder came up behind them. *Oh, Shit.* She hoped they weren't in trouble since they were acting like five-year-olds. "Holt and Frey are coming in this afternoon when our kids are here. Just wanted to give you a heads up." Thunder had referred to the shelter kids as "our kids" from the first day he began mentoring them and inviting them over for visits.

"Sounds good, Boss." Mark grinned at Thunder and pulled himself back to his station.

"I gotta step out for a quick meeting, but I'll be back before they all arrive." Thunder pointed toward his office. "Tori is in my office if you need her."

"Okay." Maggie smiled at Thunder. She loved that they called the Shelter Kids "our kids" and treated them like family. "Have fun."

After Thunder left, they had several guests come in for tours or lunch. Most of the companies nearby had gotten wind of the center having a talented chef and their employees came in for lunch. Alex always served his Fry Bread with a variety of toppings, but also had specialty sandwiches and wraps on the menu. Once a week, he provided a hot lunch which usually consisted of Lasagna, Stuffed Shells, Ropa Vieja, or Beef Stew. Those were the days when they were the most crowded and Tori would help Alex in the restaurant. But they all loved his home-cooked meals, and it brought more people to visit the center.

After lunch, a beautiful blonde woman with a teenage boy came in.

"Good afternoon. Welcome to the American Indian Cultural Center. How can I help you?" Maggie greeted her when she walked up to the lobby desk.

"Hi. My son and I would like a tour, if possible?" Maggie noticed she was fidgeting with her purse strap and the boy's eyes were bouncing around the center, looking everywhere.

"Of course. Can I have a driver's license to sign you in?" Maggie reached out her hand.

"Why?" The woman clutched her purse tighter, pulling it toward her body. Maggie noticed Mark turn in his chair and face her, his hand by his side–the side where he wore his firearm.

"It's just procedure so we know who is in the building in case of an emergency." Maggie smiled.

"Oh, okay. Sure." The woman dug into her purse, pulled out her wallet, and handed Maggie her license.

Maggie swiped her driver's license to sign her in. It was a new system Mark installed for an easier and faster sign in. Plus, now that her info was on the computer, Mark could verify who she was if the need arose.

"Perfect." Maggie stood and handed the woman back her license. Walking around the desk, she approached the woman and child. "My name is Maggie. That's our security officer, Mark." Mark did a two-finger salute and watched them.

"Hi Maggie, Mark. I'm Angel and this is my son, Steele." Angel placed her hand on her son's shoulder.

"Nice to meet you both. Let's start with the exhibit room." Maggie grabbed a brochure and pointed toward the exhibit room door. "Right this way." Maggie stepped ahead of them and turned to give them the brochure. "Here's a brochure for you. It has our current exhibit, hours, and any special events we have during this exhibit." Maggie continued to talk as she led them into the Unconquered Path Exhibit.

"Let's start with the way the Seminole Tribe of Florida escaped capture from the American soldiers. They were the only tribe to not be conquered and made to live on a reservation. Around 300 of them ran deep into the everglades and lived in chickees. They built these elevated houses from palmetto leaves and cypress-log stilts." Maggie pointed to several photos of different chickees.

"Where do you live?" Steele asked, staring at Maggie.

"I live with my cousin in an apartment." Maggie thought it was a strange question, but chalked it up to kids always saying the darndest things. "Where do you live?" Maggie smiled at Steele.

"I live in a house with my mom." Steele glared at her, making Maggie uncomfortable. "My dad's dead."

"Steele!" Angel reprimanded her son. She grabbed his arm and stepped in front of him. Maggie couldn't see her face, only Steele's and he was still glaring at her. "Steele" –Angel's voice sounded calm and soothing as she spoke to her son– "don't be rude to the lady. Be nice and let's hear what she is going to teach us about this exhibit." Steele's gaze shifted to his mom, and he nodded. Angel turned to Maggie. "I'm sorry. He misses his dad."

"It's okay. Kids always say what's on their minds. No worries." Maggie looked between Steele and Angel. She didn't miss the angry glare he sent his mom. "I'm sorry for your loss."

Maggie noticed Steele opened his mouth, ready to say something, but shut it when his mom placed her hand on his shoulder. He didn't say another word until after she explained the next artifact. And that's how the rest of the tour went. Maggie gave her spiel on an artifact and the kid followed up with uncomfortable questions about her personal life. *Do you have any kids? Do you have a large family? Do you have any siblings? Are you married? Where are you from? What days do you work here?* She tried to answer him since he was just a child, but after a while, the questions got more troubling and the whole thing was getting old. His mom tried to intervene, but he just continued ignoring her.

Maggie kept her calm demeanor and after the tour, she showed them the storytelling room and the gift shop. They purchased a couple items and then she left them in the restaurant so they could try Alex's fry bread. Usually, Alex left after lunch but since 'their kids' were coming, he stayed to make them fresh fry bread with lots of leftovers to take back to the shelter for themselves and others.

Chapter 20

Heebie Jeebies

Maggie

"That was the weirdest tour I've had so far," Maggie mumbled to Mark before sitting down.

"How so?" Mark glanced in her direction.

Maggie turned to face him so the woman and her creepy kid couldn't see her while she talked about them. "The boy kept asking me personal questions. At first, they were related to what I was showing them, and I thought, wow, what a smart kid. But then he continued with random personal questions."

"Like what?" Mark stopped what he was doing, giving her his full attention.

"Did I have a large family? Any siblings? Was I married? Those were just a few. I can't remember all of them." Maggie ran her hand through her hair.

"That is weird. It looks like it creeped you out. Are you okay?" Mark wheeled his chair over to her and rubbed her back. Maggie looked up and saw Mark looking toward the restaurant.

"Don't look over there." Maggie squeezed Mark's thigh to get his attention. "I don't want them to know we're talking about them. I'm sure it's fine. I'm just overreacting."

"Maggie, you are a lot of things, but you don't normally overreact." Mark bent his head to look into her eyes. "Look at me." Maggie looked up. "Go into Thunder's office and I'll let you know when they leave."

Maggie sighed. She should've kept her mouth shut. It was probably nothing. Now Mark was acting like her brother. Getting all alpha male and shit on her.

"I'm fine." Maggie straightened her back and moved away from Mark.

"There's the Ice Princess I know," Mark muttered.

"You know what, Surfer Smurf?" Maggie spun in her chair and crossed her arms, ready to face him and his smart-ass comments. "I can take care of myself. I never should've said anything to you. Just forget I mentioned it."

"Fine," Mark snapped. "I was only trying to help you, Miss Stubborn."

"Well, I don't need your help. And stop fucking calling me stupid ass names." Maggie turned back to her computer.

"Okay, Maggie. I'm trying to help you, and this is the thanks I get." Mark bolted out of his chair, sending it rolling back and stormed off to make his safety rounds around the center. She knew after he finished inside, he would go outside and check all the doors.

She had really pissed him off this time. She knew he was walking away so he didn't yell at her. They were pros at swapping insults, but usually they were joking and not intentionally hurtful. In this case, Maggie knew she was wrong and felt guilty for snapping at him in anger. Seeing her brother in person had made her jumpy and had her questioning everyone's behavior. Shit, it had been eleven years since her parents were murdered. No one had approached her or threatened her in all that time. She needed to stop being so paranoid.

When she thought back to how their conversation had started, she realized Mark had been nice and supportive. He was only trying to help her, and she'd cut him off at the knees. She had to make this right and apologize. Not only were they friends, they worked together. She didn't want to be in another uncomfortable workplace situation. Maggie saw Mark come back to his side of the desk out of the corner of her eye. He plopped down with a heavy sigh.

"Mark." Maggie leaned her elbow on the desk and placed her chin in her hand, looking in his direction.

"Yeah?"

"I'm sorry. I know you're just trying to help." Maggie wished he would look at her, but he didn't. He stayed focused on the computer. "Are we still on for dinner?"

"Yeah. Sure."

Those were all the words she got from Mark. Luckily, she heard the door and looked up to see the shelter kids coming in. Mark's attitude immediately changed, he stood and went around the desk to fist bump each one. Maggie hugged them. They were causing such a commotion, she glanced at the restaurant and caught Angel and Steele staring at them.

"Where's my boys?" Frey yelled as soon as she walked in the door.

"Frey!" Bryce, the smallest of the kids, ran to her for a hug. "Where's Holt?"

"He's parking the car. He'll be here in just a minute." Freya walked to Maggie for a hug. "How's the new job?"

"Great." Maggie was so happy to see Frey. They were the troublemakers of the girls group. "I'm so happy to be here. I'm glad you came today."

"Hey, gentlemen," Holt hollered as he and Barrett walked in the door, "guess who I brought?"

"Holt!" Bryce screeched and ran at him, full throttle. Bryce had gotten close to Frey and Holt after meeting them at the cultural center last month. Holt bent down and swooped him up, swinging him around as Bryce laughed. Holt brought him in for a hug before resting him on his waist as he shook all the other boy's hands.

"Hey, guys." Barrett fist-bumped each of the boys.

"Hi, Barrett." Bryce reached out for his fist bump while still clinging on to Holt's neck with his other hand.

Maggie watched Frey laughing at Bryce while he clung to Holt.

"I see you and Holt both share an attachment to Bryce." Maggie shoulder bumped her. Maggie stepped aside when she saw Tori heading toward Frey. They were besties, like her and Isa.

"Hey," Tori said before hugging Frey. "I'm glad you came. I see you dragged Barrett away from his daytime prowling for girls."

"I heard that." Barrett came up behind Tori and gave her a hug.

"I can't believe you're here two days in a row?" Maggie elbowed him in the side. "No hot girls by the pool?"

Before Barrett could make a smart comeback, Maggie felt something shove into her back. Luckily, Barrett had quick reflexes and caught her before she face planted into the ground. She turned around quickly to see who pushed her.

"Sorry," Steele mumbled with a smirk on his face.

"Steele," Angel reprimanded him and grabbed his arm. "I'm sorry, Maggie. Thanks again for the tour. Have a good day."

"You're welcome. Come back anytime." Maggie forced a smile on her face, hoping they wouldn't come back. She felt like crossing her fingers behind her back. Angel seemed nicer than her son. But what was his beef with her?

"Stay safe," Steele grumbled at her before Angel pulled him away.

A shiver ran down Maggie's spine, her hair standing on end. Was that a warning? Did he just threaten her? Maybe she misheard him.

"Mags." Maggie jumped when Tori laid her hand on her shoulder. "Are you okay?"

"Who the hell was that?" Barrett watched them leave.

"She was hot." Tim, the oldest shelter kid, smiled at Barrett. "I know her from somewhere, I just can't place her."

"They came in for a tour. I'm okay. Just cold." Maggie rubbed her arms, feeling goosebumps and trying to calm her breathing. She looked around and saw Mark watching her. His gaze intent on her reactions. How much had he seen? He couldn't possibly have heard Steele. Maggie took a deep breath and knew what they would be discussing tonight at their supposedly romantic dinner. Shaking herself out of her funk, she saw Thunder come in the front door and tell everyone to go to the storytelling room.

Mark was heading her way. She didn't want to have to face him right now, so she pivoted and grabbed Frey's arm, trying to join in the conversation. Out of the corner of her eye, she saw Mark put his hands on his hips and release a heavy breath. Cowardly Lion is what he would call her next–if he could catch her.

Having the boys there changed the mood, transforming what had become a tense morning into a lively and fun afternoon. They heard stories, danced, and ate fry bread before the boys left with smiles on their faces. Barrett, Holt, and Frey left soon after so they could get ready for their shifts at the casino. Frey was a blackjack dealer while Holt and Barrett worked security. Alex and Tori followed them out and Thunder left a few minutes later.

Soon it was just Mark and Maggie. Maggie logged into her homework for her marketing class and took notes on some slides that she had to study for a test next week. Thunder told her if her work was done, she could do schoolwork at the office.

"Do you want me to pick you up tonight?" Mark blurted, out of the blue.

"Uh, no." Maggie continued to write in her notebook. "I'll drive myself. I'd rather have my car there, so I don't have to inconvenience you to drive me home."

"You're not an inconvenience, Miss Congeniality." Maggie was glad to hear Mark call her quirky names again. After yelling at him, she wasn't sure he would do that. Truth be told, she liked all the crazy stuff he came up with.

"Thanks, Surfer Smurf." Maggie glanced at him and smiled when he winked at her.

They stayed quiet until quitting time rolled around. Mark walked her out to her car.

"See you at seven?" Mark asked before he shut her door for her.

"Yup." Maggie started her car and gave him a quick wave. She needed a shower before she went to Mark's place.

Chapter 21

Romantic Dinner...Gets Hot Quick

Mark

After work, Mark drove to the grocery store to get fresh steaks, broccoli, baked potatoes, and a bouquet of flowers for Maggie to take home. He didn't have enough time to make homemade mashed potatoes–although his mom had taught him how–so he would bake some potatoes in the oven.

He seasoned the steaks and let them marinate. Turning on the oven, he cleaned the potatoes and wrapped them in foil while the oven heated. When the oven beeped, he put them inside and went to take a quick shower. Mark put on a pair of black dress slacks. He was dressing up to show Maggie he knew how to treat a lady on a date. After he shaved, he applied his favorite aftershave lotion and sprayed cologne on his neck. Walking into his closet, he grabbed his tailored hunter green button-down dress shirt. This shirt accentuated the flecks of green in the outer rim of his hazel eyes. A look that attracted the girls like bees to honey. He was pulling out all the stops tonight.

Walking back into the bathroom, he tucked his shirt into his pants, rolled up his sleeves, and finger-combed his hair. Reaching for his watch to put it on, he checked the time and saw he had about half an hour before Maggie knocked on his door. He sat on his bed and put on his dress socks and shoes.

Mark knew he was a good-looking guy–or so he'd been told, many times. He always made sure to look his best for his dates or when he was on the prowl. First impressions helped him decide whether or not he would ask for a second date. He assumed it was the same for the women he dated. Steve, his brother, constantly told him he was too picky and a commitment-phobe. Sure, he dated a lot, but he was trying to find 'the one'. He liked a strong woman so if they got too clingy or he didn't see a future with them, he would end it. Mark figured if he was going to be with this woman for the next fifty years or so, he had to make sure he picked the right one.

Mark turned on some soothing, sexy music to play in the background, smiling to himself. He knew Maggie would give him shit for setting the mood, but he promised her romance and he was going to deliver, tenfold. He found the linen tablecloth and napkins his mom gave him for special occasions. He'd never used them before, so he knew they were clean. Pulling out some candles, he set the table for two with the bouquet of flowers as the centerpiece. The intimate setting of the table would be more romantic than sitting at his island or on tray tables in front of the couch. Turning off some lights and using the dimmer settings on the others, he was able to create the perfect romantic ambiance.

Once the inside was set up, he let Sky out. She loved to run around the backyard. Mark wanted to grill the steaks outside, so he turned on the grill to get it to the right temperature. Walking back to the kitchen, he put the broccoli in a bowl, added butter and some salt, then placed it in the microwave. Poking the potatoes with a fork, he gauged they were almost ready. Now, he just needed his date.

Maggie must have telepathy because the doorbell rang as he finished his last thought. Mark checked his phone. She was right on time.

"Hey." Mark opened the door, and his jaw dropped. Maggie was wearing a spaghetti strap summer dress that fit snug on her breasts while showing some skin. Mark was salivating, he would love to put one of those round globes in his mouth. Continuing his gaze down her body, he noticed the dress flowed down to mid-thigh. She had paired it with high heeled, strappy sandals. *Oh, fuck! She's playing hardball too.* He might drench her panties, but she was getting a rise out of him. If he didn't stop thinking about fucking her, he was going to have a hard time hiding it, let alone walking.

"Hi." Maggie sounded breathless. "I brought wine." *Had she been checking him out at the same time?* Mark's gaze darted to her face before seeing the bottle of wine she had raised in her right hand. If the pink on her cheeks was any indication, she sure as shit was checking him out. At least the feelings were mutual.

"Uh...Come in." Mark opened the door and stepped aside. "You look beautiful."

"Thanks, so do you, Surfer Smurf."

"I look beautiful, huh? Thanks, Jessica Rabbit." Mark grinned until Maggie purposely rubbed up against his hard on with her hips as she sashayed her sexy ass past him. *Motherfucker!* Mark grunted. Taking a deep breath to get himself under control, he inhaled a huge blast of her earthy scent with a hint of jasmine. Mark dropped his head down and prayed he could handle this fiery, sexy, Maggie.

"Ahh!" Mark heard Maggie scream, and he looked up. *Shit, he forgot about Sky.*

"Sky! Sit!"

Maggie raised her arms to cover her face, bracing herself for Sky's assault, but Sky was well trained. When she heard 'sit', she came to a screeching halt, inches away from Maggie and sat, her tail wagging like crazy.

"Sorry," Mark walked around Maggie and placed his hand on Sky's head. "Maggie, this is Sky."

"I didn't know you had a dog?" Maggie lowered her hands away from her face. "Can I pet her?"

"Uh. Yeah. I've had her for just over a year. Believe it or not, she is a trained police dog. Put your hand out slowly and let her sniff you." Mark had never seen Sky run up to a stranger so fast to play.

"Here take this." Maggie gave Mark the bottle of wine while she squatted down in front of Sky. "I didn't know what we were having but I picked red because I didn't have to refrigerate it. Hi, Sky. Aren't you a beautiful girl?" Maggie continued to coo and pet Sky until Sky laid down and rolled onto her back for a belly rub.

Mark's mouth dropped open at the sight. Sky never gave up control like that to anyone but him and Bryan. Maggie must be a witch who put a spell on him and Sky because neither one could stop looking at her. It's a good thing Maggie wasn't a criminal, or he'd be worried that Sky had lost her touch.

"Are you feeding me or are you just going to stand there and stare at us?" Maggie sat with her legs crossed in her dress on his floor and continued to pet Sky. "Sky, I don't think we're going to get to eat tonight unless your daddy stops staring at us and starts cooking."

Sky, the traitor, shifted her head toward Mark and whined.

"Great, now I have two women riding my ass," Mark protested and walked away. Sky had stolen the show. So much for his romantic ambiance. He should have told Bryan to keep Sky overnight. Mark took out the potatoes, set them on a platter to cool, and turned off the oven. Time to start cooking the steaks. He took them out of the fridge and carried the bowl out to the patio, shaking his head when he passed Sky and Maggie playing on the floor. Mark heard the door open behind him as he placed the steaks on the grill.

"How do you like your steak?"

"Medium well, please."

Mark nodded, glad she didn't say well done. He hated to overcook a steak and make it charred. Growing up on a ranch, the most they ever cooked their steaks was medium well. Hell, most of his family ate it rare. That, he couldn't do. As a child he named most of the cattle and hated when he had to load them into a truck headed to the slaughterhouse. Mark shook his head, attempting to get those thoughts out of his head. No dark thoughts allowed on this romantic date.

"Hey, does she have a ball to play catch?" Maggie asked from behind him. "That way I can play with her out here and keep you company while you grill."

"Yeah." Mark pointed toward an outdoor box with doggie toys. "In that box."

"You have a beautiful home." Maggie stood next to him while she tossed the ball. Sky loved to play fetch.

"Thanks. I would've given you a tour, but my dog seemed to steal your attention, Miss Easily Distracted." Mark pouted.

"Aww, are you feeling jealous, Surfer Smurf?" Maggie rubbed Mark's back. Mark wished she'd rub something else to comfort him.

"Considering the fact that I invited you over for a romantic date, not a doggie play date, I'd say yes, I feel left out and in need of some of your attention." Mark winked at her.

"All right." Maggie threw the ball and turned her attention to Mark. "Show me what you got. Sweep me off my feet like you would if I was a real date."

"Now?" Mark flipped their steaks.

"Yep, show me what you got, Loverboy." Maggie braced herself and straightened her back.

"Are you preparing for a firing squad?" Mark laughed at her getting herself ready.

"Are you going to do something or not?" Maggie placed her fist on her hip and tapped her foot, waiting for him. *Damn, she looked like a sexy schoolteacher ready to reprimand him. He wouldn't mind doing detention with her.*

Mark grinned and pulled her into his arms, pressing her tightly against his body. He placed one hand on the back of her neck while the other stroked her back slowly. He bent his head down as he slowly ran his nose along her neck, breathing her in. "You smell so good," Mark moaned, the hand on her neck grabbed her hair and tilted her head to the side to gain better access. He repeated his previous path but with light kisses and slow licks. He could hear Maggie's breath coming faster. She had a death grip on his biceps. Good. She needed to hold on because he was about to assault all her senses.

Mark ran the tip of his tongue over her jaw on his way to her mouth. Maggie opened for him. He could feel her breath on his lips. He shifted his eyes to look at her. He wanted Maggie to accept his kiss – No, needed her to accept it. His heart was pounding in his chest, waiting for her to give him the go ahead. She must have sensed his question because she opened her eyes and let out a soft moan. Her eyes were filled with desire.

Once she gave a slight nod, Mark attacked her mouth. The hand in her hair tightened into a fist holding her head in place while his other hand travelled down her back. Grabbing her ass, he pressed her against his raging hard on. Maggie was undulating against him with wild abandon, her hard nipples poking him every time she pushed against him.

Mark hadn't meant to go that far, but he was lost in the taste of her mouth, the smell of her perfume, the sound of her moans, and the feel of her ass. She had overwhelmed his senses, and he didn't want to stop. He released her ass and slid his hand up her sides and over her breast, slowly pulling her spaghetti strap down. Releasing her mouth, he ran his tongue down her neck toward her breast. He couldn't wait to suck on her beautiful breasts.

"Mark. Stop." Maggie's voice sounded far away. Did she just ask him to stop? Why?

Mark stopped and gazed into her eyes. Why did she stop him? Her eyes were full of lust just like he was sure his were. He took a couple deep breaths to calm his racing heart. When a woman says 'stop' you stop. "Why? What's wrong?"

"Um," Maggie pointed behind Mark. "I think the steaks are burning."

"Oh, Shit!" Mark released her and grabbed the tongs to flip them. "Fuck! I hope you like your steak well done."

"That's fine, Surfer Smurf." Maggie chuckled and adjusted her dress strap. She took a few steps back. "I'm gonna use your restroom."

"Betty Boop, you don't know where it is?" Mark said while he cut into the middle of the steaks. He would give her the one that was medium well. He'd eat the overcooked one.

"Your house isn't that big. I'll find it." Maggie hurried inside.

Mark was smiling to himself. Mission accomplished. From the way she was humping him, he knew her panties were totally drenched. Unfortunately, so were his boxers. He was sure he leaked and almost lost it, like a pre-pubescent boy looking at his first nudie magazine. It's a good thing Maggie went to the bathroom because he needed to cool off too.

Mark looked down and saw Sky laying on the ground with her head on her paws watching him grill. "Sky." Sky lifted her head and tilted it at him. "I think we bit off more than we could chew. That girl" –Mark looked toward the house and pointed with the tongs– "is going to be the death of me."

Chapter 22

Romantic Dinner...Turns Ugly

Maggie

Maggie walked around the house looking for a bathroom. She found the master bedroom, but using his personal bathroom would not help her stop thinking about skipping dinner, stripping, and fucking Mark. He was so fucking sexy and such a good kisser, who knew? And he wasn't even in uniform. What would he say if he found her naked on his bed. Shaking her head, she left that room and found the jack-n-jill bathroom that connected the two other bedrooms.

Maggie locked herself in and stared at herself in the mirror. She was panting, her face was flushed, her hair was all over the place from Mark's hand, and her lips were swollen from his kisses. She was so turned on right now if she touched herself, she would go off like a firework. Closing her eyes, she took several slow deep breaths. If she didn't calm down, she would have to admit to him that he turned her on. She would never live that down. He'd probably tell the guys, and they'd laugh about it for hours. She'd tell the girls, and they would give her a hard time and tease her.

Maggie used the restroom and debated between taking off her drenched panties or keeping them on. Keeping them on was a constant reminder of her mini orgasm and the wetness was uncomfortable. But if she took them off and he got her going again, and it dripped down her leg because her underwear wasn't there to catch it, she would be mortified. *What the hell?* How did she get herself into this predicament? She should have brought a spare pair, but then he would've been right. She should've cancelled. There was no way she was going to let Mark win this bet. Although, technically he'd won, but she didn't have to tell him. She had to do something that stopped him from making romantic moves on her because her body was betraying her.

Deciding to go with option one, she dried herself and her panties as best she could, then left the bathroom. She sat at the table to wait for Mark. Watching him grilling in his Sunday best was sexy as hell and too distracting. Not only did she sit her ass down at the table, but she also opened the bottle of wine, and was on her second healthy serving by the time Mark came inside with the steaks.

"Hungry much, Miss Impatient?" Mark smirked and said when he placed the steaks on the table. "How much have you had?"

Rude. He had no right to comment on her drinking. She was a big girl and could drink her wine however slow or fast as she wanted. So what if she was guzzling it down like water? What was it to him?

"Do you want to drink out of the bottle?" Mark pointed to the almost empty glass of wine.

Maggie looked at the bottle and realized he was right—half the bottle was gone. No wonder her head was feeling fuzzy. Maybe she should slow down. But then Mark would think he was right and that was not happening. Damn her stubborn, competitive self. If she kept this up, she was going to pass out.

"Ha, Ha." Maggie finished the last drops and poured another full glass for spite. Drinking half of it when he came back from the kitchen with the broccoli and potatoes.

"Betty Ford, I think you need to slow down." Mark raised an eyebrow at her.

"I'm fine, Surfer Smurf." Maggie began cutting her steak. Once Mark put down the other plates, she forked a baked potato and slapped it onto her plate. Grabbing the bowl of broccoli, she scooped some onto her plate as well. When a couple pieces fell on the table, she forked them and shoved them into her mouth.

With the half-chewed broccoli still in her mouth, she chewed like a cow and said, "These are really good." Then shoved a piece of steak in her mouth, because why the hell not? Maggie could feel her cheeks so full her mouth almost didn't close. She must look like a crazy chipmunk pocketing her food.

Mark was squinting at her, watching her every move. "Are you okay?" Mark was getting ready to eat a piece of meat on his fork when his hand froze on the way to his mouth.

"Yup, fine," Maggie said and chewed the rest of her meat and broccoli with her mouth open. "This is delicious". If she couldn't keep her hands off him, then she had to do things to turn him off. Maggie could tell her plan was working, because Mark kept looking down while he ate—no eye contact.

Maggie kicked him hard on his shin under the table. Mark winced and looked at her. "Sorry, my foot slipped."

Mark leaned down and rubbed his leg. "No problem. Are you sure you're okay?"

"Never better." Maggie stuffed her mouth with so much food that when she talked while chewing, some of it fell out of her mouth. She scooped it right up and shoved it back in her mouth mid-chew. *Oh, sweet baby Jesus.* She was disgusting herself.

Mark didn't ask her any more questions while they were eating, probably because it was gross to watch her. But that didn't stop Maggie from rambling on and on about work. She was on another glass of wine before she realized that drinking that much was not a good idea. The room was spinning, she was seeing two Marks, and her dinner was swirling around in her stomach. Maggie grabbed her stomach. Mark looked concerned and his lips were moving, but she couldn't hear what he was saying. Oh no, she was going to be sick.

Maggie bolted out of her seat to run to the bathroom. In her hurry, she bumped into the table and spilled her wine all over herself and Sky.

"Maggie?" She heard Mark call her name, but she couldn't stop. She had to make it to the bathroom before she hurled on his floor. Maggie made it just in time to hold the toilet seat and release her dinner and wine into it.

"Shit, Mags. What the hell?" Maggie felt Mark kneel next to her and pull her hair back away from her face. "Sky, sit."

Maggie's head felt like it was about to explode as she dry-heaved into the toilet several times. Mark held her hair in one hand and sat behind her holding her against his chest. Why did he have to follow her and take care of her? How many glasses had she drunk? This was a stupid ass plan. What the hell was she thinking? That was the problem, she wasn't thinking. She was too busy trying to beat Mark and one up him. Fuck, she hated feeling drunk. *I'm never doing this again.*

"Come on. I think your stomach is all empty now." Mark pulled her up and walked her to the sink. "Rinse your mouth. Stay here." Mark placed her hands on either side of the sink. "I'm gonna get you something to change into."

Maggie leaned against the sink and cupped her hands to get water for her mouth. After rinsing twice, the room started spinning, and she gripped the sink. Her body felt so heavy, she could see herself swaying in the mirror. The image made her dizzy and she fell.

"Shit, Mags!" Maggie heard Mark yell. Arms wrapped around her seconds before she smacked her head on the floor. Mark picked her up in his arms and carried her to his bed. He laid her down and began to take off her dress.

"What are you doing? You can't fuck me now. Didn't I disgust you enough to stop flirting with me?" Maggie weakly smacked his hands. Mark ignored her and fully undressed her.

"Was that your endgame when you realized I was right?" Mark held up her panties. "Too bad it didn't work because these bad boys are soaked and it's not from all the wine you drank."

"Fucker! Fine, you win. Take your prize." Maggie spread her legs on the bed.

"Yeah, no thanks. I don't fuck drunk girls." Mark closed her legs and put a pair of his sweatpants on her. Mark pulled her up into a sitting position and put a t-shirt over her head. He tried grabbing her hands to put them through the shirt, but Maggie was flailing, trying to smack him. When that didn't work, she preceded to try to tease him.

Maggie cupped her breasts and massaged them. "You know you want to suck these. You've been staring at them all night."

"Not tonight and not like this." Mark finally got her arms in the shirt and let her go. Maggie dropped back onto the bed.

"Asshole. You may as well fuck me now, it's not like if I was sober, I'd remember it anyway," Maggie snorted. *Why was she being so mean to him? She was usually a happy drunk.*

"Oh, Beautiful. You'd remember it. But it's not happening tonight." Maggie felt Mark pull her up and tuck her into bed before she passed out.

*** Mark ***

Everything was going great until that kiss. Then Maggie went batshit crazy. At least now he knew she was purposely trying to turn him off. *Why?* Hadn't they just been messing around? Unless she was getting as turned on as him and it meant something to her. Was she afraid of falling for him? Was he falling for her?

Mark looked at Sky.

"What the hell was going on in her head to eat like that and drink so much, Sky?" Sky wasn't listening, she was trying to lick the spilled wine on her face. Shit, the last thing he needed was a drunk dog to go with the drunk girl in his bed. Mark got up and grabbed a towel. Wetting it in the sink, he wiped the wine from her head. Luckily, most of it was on Maggie's clothes and not Sky's face.

Mark grabbed Maggie's dress and panties tossing them in his laundry hamper. He might as well do a load of laundry so he could stay awake and keep an eye on her and Sky. He didn't think Sky drank too much of the spilled wine on the floor, but he would have to watch out for vomiting and diarrhea. The last thing he needed was to have to leave Maggie to take Sky to the overnight vet. That was never a quick visit, and Maggie would be alone. What if she needed him? He watched Sky wobble into her crate to sleep. He wished he could wobble into his bed to sleep too. It was going to be a long night.

Mark put the clothes in the wash and went into the kitchen to clean up. When he finished, he grabbed a beer from the fridge and sat down on his bed, leaning against the headboard, staring at Maggie. She was going to feel like shit tomorrow. They had work, but maybe Thunder would let her take the day off if he knew she was sick. Saturdays weren't always busy. It was hit or miss.

Mark picked up his phone and dialed Thunder's number.

"Hey, Mark. What's Up?"

"Hi, Thunder. Sorry to interrupt your evening." How was he going to tell Thunder what happened? He hadn't thought this through.

"It's fine. Isa and I are just watching a movie at home. Did you need something?"

"I just wanted to let you know Maggie might not come in tomorrow." Before Mark could finish, Isa jumped on the call.

"Why? Is she okay?"

"Sorry," Thunder interrupted. "You're on speakerphone."

"No problem. I..uh..we went to dinner and something made her sick. When I left her, she wasn't feeling so good." Mark winced and pinched the bridge of his nose. Could Thunder hear in his voice that he was lying? He hated lying to his boss, let alone his friend.

"I gotta go see her, Thunder. I'll be back." He heard Isa say.

"No!" Mark screamed into the phone and looked at Maggie, but she was totally out. He had to stop Isa from going to Maggie's apartment and he sure as shit wasn't ready to tell her Maggie passed out on his bed. "She said she wanted to be alone. I'm sure she'll be better by tomorrow. Hell, she'll probably still come in just not at nine." He was fucking this all up. Mark got up and began pacing. This conversation was getting out of control. Why the fuck did he call anyway? Maggie would probably wake up tomorrow and hate him for telling Thunder she was sick. She'd rip him a new one.

"Okay." Isa sighed. "I'll check on her tomorrow. I'm sure Nancy will help her if she needs anything."

"Thanks for letting me know. It's okay if she comes in late." Thunder said. "I just hope she feels better soon."

"Thanks. I'll check on her in the morning and call you Isa."

"Okay. Thanks, Mark," Isa said before they hung up.

Fuck me! This night needs to end. Mark waited until the laundry was dry. He folded everything, placing Maggie's dress and panties on the back of the couch separate from his. Mark finished his beer and brushed his teeth. He normally slept naked, but if Maggie woke up, he didn't want to freak her out. He dug out a pair of pajama bottoms and slipped into bed. Maggie rolled into him and used him as a body pillow, her leg draped between his legs and her arm around his waist. *Fuck!* Mark lifted his arm, and she snuggled into him. It was going to be a long night. Why the hell did he put her in his bed? *To make sure she was okay, asshole. His* subconscious answered him.

Chapter 23

I'll Never Drink Again

Maggie

Maggie felt a light touch stroking the side of her right breast as her hand ran down a sculpted chest. Her fingers memorizing and counting abs. Eight, he had an eight pack. This was an awesome dream. Who was this sexy man lying in bed next to her? Maggie trailed her hand further down and met an elastic waistband. Hmm, why was he wearing pants? She would've preferred her dream man to be naked and hard. The stroking on her breast stopped. He felt so good, it was time to go big or go home.

Maggie's hand dove into his pants and she grasped a long, wide, hard cock. Her hand could barely close from his girth. *Oh, hell yes.* Just the way she liked them. The hand was back at her breast, but this time it was massaging her whole breast and tweaking her nipple. She wished she dreamed this sensually every morning. She continued to stroke his perfect cock slowly from the bottom, where it met his balls all the way to the top. He was leaking and her hand spread the liquid all over the bulb of his head. He moaned and she felt a hand on the back of her head, attempting to push her down his body.

"Fuck, Maggie. I could wake up like this every morning," the man's deep, raspy voice murmured.

Wait, that hand felt real, and the voice sounded like Mark. Maggie snapped out of her dream state and opened her eyes. She was staring at the sexiest abs that led to the biggest cock she had ever seen. *Oh Shit!* She'd know that chest anywhere. It was Mark and this wasn't a dream. Flashbacks came back to her from last night. Drinking too much, spilling wine, and throwing up. Why the fuck was her hand still pumping his cock? Now what was she supposed to do? Finish him off with throw up breath or get the hell out?

"Babe, suck my cock and put me out of my misery. I want to feel your lips wrapped around me." Mark's bedroom voice was so damn sexy, and his hips were pushing up into her hand while his hand pushed her down until his cock touched her lips.

She couldn't help herself. She loved having a man at her mercy. That was the last rational thought she had before her mouth licked his weeping head and she swallowed as much as she could.

"Oh fuck!" Maggie heard Mark moan as she sunk her mouth down until his cock reached her throat and she swallowed, causing him to moan even louder. She pulled back and repeated her movements until she could hear him panting. Then she began to stroke him while sucking the head.

"Babe, please let me cum down your throat?" Mark sounded desperate between his words and all his grunting, so Maggie put him out of his misery. Sinking her mouth all the way down, she felt his hands holding her still while he fucked her mouth. She swallowed and sucked several times before he stiffened and released his orgasm down her throat. His hands trembled as he stroked her hair and cheeks. Maggie was good at giving head. She'd had several boyfriends who taught her what to do and how to breathe through her nose while taking their cocks down her throat. It also helped she didn't have a gag reflex.

Mark's body relaxed and he dropped his hands off her head, his breathing slowing down. She was surprised to see his penis growing again as he pulled it from her mouth. *What the hell? He was one of those guys that didn't need much time between fucking. Down boy.* She stared at it and watched it harden. Shit, she had to get out of there fast. Before she could move, Mark grabbed her and rolled them over, so he was on top.

"Babe, where are you going? It's your turn and I'm hungry for my breakfast." Mark mumbled into her neck. *Was he still asleep? There's no way, not after he exploded in my mouth.*

"Mark." Maggie tried pushing him off her, but he was stronger than her. "Mark! Get Off!

Maggie felt him stiffen and he raised his head, staring into her eyes with a smirk on his face. "Why? Are you embarrassed for me to see your pussy and eat you out?"

SLAP!

"What the fuck, Maggie!" Mark scrambled off her and jumped out of bed. Throwing his arms up and placing them on his hips he glared at her. "Why'd you fucking slap me?"

Maggie's eyes widened. She couldn't believe she just slapped his face. All she wanted to do was get him to snap out of his sex induced mood so she could get out of there. She had taken it too far. If looks could kill, she'd be dead right now.

"Sorry." Maggie looked down and scooted off the bed. "I gotta go."

"Sorry, doesn't cut it, Looney Tunes."

Maggie looked around for her clothes. *Where were they?*

Mark grabbed her arm and pulled her around to face him. "What the hell is going on with you? You were acting crazy last night, but then this morning you gave me the best blow job of my fucking life and then you slap me so hard your fingers might be permanently imprinted on my cheek."

"Don't be so fucking dramatic. I didn't hit you that hard." Seeing Mark angry made Maggie angry enough to forget about her embarrassment over what she did. Placing her hands on her hips, she faced him down, watching his cheek get redder by the moment. "Where are my clothes?"

"In the fucking living room. You spilled wine all over your dress along with a touch of throw up and I washed it for you." Mark pointed toward his living room.

"Great. Thanks. See you at work." Maggie spun around and ran into the living room. She should not have turned so fast. Leaning on the couch for a second, she took a breath before grabbing her dress and dropping it over her head. Shit, how was she going to drive home if she was dizzy? She grabbed her purse and heard Mark come out of the bedroom.

"Forget something?" Her strappy shoes were dangling from his fingers.

Maggie reached out for them, but he held them up above his head. There was no way she was reaching them. He was at least a foot taller than her.

"Give me my shoes." Maggie jumped up to grab them.

"No. Tell me what the hell is going on with you."

After a couple more attempts at grabbing her shoes and Mark raising them out of her reach, Maggie was pissed. She kneed him in the balls, causing him to drop her shoes to the ground and grab his goods before he fell to the ground in the fetal position.

"Ow!" Mark howled. "Fuck! Shit! What the hell, Kill Bill?" Mark groaned from the floor as Maggie picked up her shoes. Sky immediately came running out of the bedroom and sat in front of Mark, growling at Maggie.

"I told you to give me my fucking shoes!" Maggie shrugged. "Why is she growling at me? Is she going to bite me?" Maggie became nervous, she had forgotten about Sky. The sweet German Shepherd was now growling like she was about to attack.

"Sky, no, sit." Mark grumbled.

"See you at work." Maggie took a few small steps back before turning to leave.

"You don't have to go in." Mark growled between breaths. "Please, talk to me."

"What? Why?" Maggie stopped in her tracks and faced him. Her sudden move had Sky growling again.

"Sky, no, it's okay." Maggie watched Mark struggling to get to his knees. "I called Thunder and told him you were sick. Upset stomach from something you ate." He braced one hand on the cocktail table while still holding his goods. "Fuck Maggie, that fucking hurt." Mark looked up at Maggie in horrified astonishment, his teeth clenched from the pain.

Maggie didn't know what to do other than get out of there. Maggie bolted to the door. She could hear Sky barking and Mark calling out her name, but she didn't stop. Getting in her car, she started it and looked up before she backed up out of his driveway. Mark was hunched over in the doorway holding Sky's collar in one hand and...were those her panties in the other? She felt tears stream down her face as she backed out of his driveway and drove off. Looking back on the entire evening and night, she realized Mark hadn't done anything wrong.

He'd prepared the romantic date he promised, and she had freaked out and ruined it. He had game. She'd give him that. Mark had told her he could be romantic, and he had proven it. How was she supposed to face him now? Her actions were worse than a walk of shame. What had gotten into her to kick him in the crotch? She'd never kicked anyone in their privates. He'd done nice things for her, and she thanked him with pain. She was a bitch. *Fuck!* She should take the day off. Her head was pounding, and her stomach felt queasy. Medicine and bed would be her best friends today.

*** Mark ***

What the fuck just happened? Talk about a date going down in flames. Mark limped into the kitchen for some ibuprofen and laid down on the couch until the pain in his balls went away. Sky climbed up on the couch and laid at his feet. At least one girl still loved him. Hell, he wasn't even sure if, after last night, Maggie still liked him as a friend. Why had she given him the best blow job of his entire fucking life only to give him a shitload of pain later? He would give anything to know what was going on in her pretty little head.

Last night he was just trying to show her his moves, friend to friend, and she freaked out. Was he that bad of a kisser? He'd never had complaints before. The steaks were overcooked, and the dinner conversation went south quick after she drank all those glasses of wine. He'd held her hair back when she was hurling in the toilet. How many friends would do that? You'd think she'd be grateful, but not Maggie. She was such a ball buster–literally.

Placing her in his bed had been a big mistake, but he wanted to keep an eye on her. Mark was afraid she would throw up and choke on it. He'd read about how people dying from their own regurgitation. Most of the night, he stayed up watching her or reading. Sleep had finally caught up with him in the early morning hours.

When he felt her hand feeling up his chest, he thought he was dreaming until she grabbed his cock. That had jolted him awake, but he was afraid to move. Unfortunately, once she got going, he lost all sense of control. His body reacted to her touch and mouth. After he exploded in her mouth, he remembered thinking he wanted to make her his girlfriend. That thought had him hardening again. He'd never gotten that hard that fast after a blow job in his life. Sure, Maggie had acted crazy during dinner, but once they talked it out, he knew everything would be okay. He liked strong women, maybe Maggie was 'the one' and she'd been right in front of him this whole time. His plan to just tease her had backfired, because now he wanted her in his bed every night.

Wanting to return the favor and get her off, he'd laid on top of her. He couldn't wait to taste her. Then she'd slapped him so hard his head spun to the side. He hadn't been expecting that, so he let her go.

She had turned on him so fast and become the sassy little spitfire he knew her to be. Though never in his wildest dreams did he think she would knee him in the balls. That fucking hurt. He still felt a dull throbbing pain which he would have to ignore in a few minutes because he had to get up, shower, and get to work.

Mark slowly sat up and petted Sky. *Shit, even that hurt.* He hoped the ibuprofen kicked in soon.

"Come on, Sky. Potty time." Mark let Sky out to do her business. He would talk to Thunder today about bringing Sky to work on the days she was off duty from the police department. He hated leaving her at home when she could help him out with security at AICC.

As he showered, he prayed that Maggie took the day off. He wasn't ready to see her. She was giving him whiplash with her behavior. Maybe she didn't like him? But why would she give him a blow job if she didn't like him? To him that was a very personal act. He had to talk to her, but not today. He needed to cool down. He was so pissed, hurt, and confused; he was afraid of what he might say to her.

Chapter 24

Shitty Day at the Office

Maggie

Maggie called in sick on Saturday and ignored all calls that weekend except for Isa's because she knew Isa would keep calling until she answered. She used that weekend to do laundry, help her cousin clean the apartment, and cook a couple of meals.

By Tuesday, she was ready to go to work and face Mark. He'd tried to call and text her on Monday, but she didn't respond. Taking a few deep breaths, she left her car and walked into work with a smile on her face for Mark. She preferred to forget everything that happened Friday night, but she wasn't so sure Mark would let her. It was worth a try.

"Good morning," Maggie smiled at Mark and sat at her desk.

"Mornin'," Mark mumbled and barely looked at her.

Well, so much for forgetting. Maggie felt something nudge her thigh. She looked down and saw Sky.

"Oh, my goodness, Sky." Maggie rolled her chair out from under the desk and bent down to pet her. "How is she here?"

"I asked Thunder if she could help me with security. He said yes." Mark was being curt with her.

"You are such a good girl. I'm so sorry I made you mad on Friday." Maggie heard Mark grunt while she placed kisses on Sky's muzzle. Apparently, he wasn't going to talk about it. Then why the hell had he called and texted her yesterday?

"Mark, about Friday?" Maggie never liked the silent treatment. It was time to eat crow.

"It's fine, Kill Bill. Forget about it." Mark continued to work without looking at her.

"Mark!" Maggie raised her voice, not quite yelling. Although, from the look on Sky's face, she better be careful.

"What?" Mark turned and growled at her.

"I'm sorry." Maggie was rubbing Sky's back to keep her calm.

"For what? Spilling wine on my dog? Throwing up in my bathroom? Ruining our night? Giving me one hell of a blow job or slapping and kicking me in the balls?" Mark quirked his eyebrow as he glared at her.

"All of it, asshole," Maggie said through gritted teeth.

"Children, play nice," Thunder said from behind Maggie.

"Sorry, boss," Mark mumbled.

"I'm sorry, Thunder." Maggie spun her chair to face Thunder, embarrassed that he heard her comment to Mark at work. She hoped Thunder only heard her calling him an asshole and not what Mark said. Isa always told her how Thunder could sneak up on her and she had just experienced it firsthand. Maggie hadn't heard his footsteps behind her. *She really needed to act more professional at work. Hadn't she learned from her last job?* She would find out soon enough because if Thunder had heard Mark's side of the conversation, Isa would be calling to chat. "It won't happen again."

"Yeah, right," Thunder scoffed. "You two can't stop messing with each other no matter how hard you try. Hold down the fort. I have a meeting with Osceola about his new expansion. I'll be back later this afternoon." Thunder turned when he reached the door and gave his parting words like a dad reprimanding his children. "Oh, and no name calling. It's not nice."

Maggie nodded to Thunder and mumbled, "Yes, sir."

After Thunder left, Mark blurted, "Fine. I accept your apology, but what the hell happened?"

Maggie stiffened and turned to her computer. She didn't want to tell Mark that he had swept her off her feet with his romantic gestures and she had panicked. She hadn't expected him to pull out all the stops for their date.

"Let's just say you won. You were right, you are a very romantic guy." Maggie signed in to her computer. She could feel Mark still staring at her. She would not turn her head and look at him until she had her inner armor in place. They were just friends who liked to joke around. Mark was not interested in her as a girlfriend.

"Okay, Teller, don't tell me what spooked you." Mark turned back to his computer. "I'll get it out of you eventually. I knew I won when I took off your panties. They were soaked."

Maggie spun her head around to look at him. *Oh, he did not just say that. Arrogant Ass.*

"Yeah, 'hell of a blow job', huh?" Maggie smirked.

"It was, Miss Deep Throat." Mark glanced at Maggie and chuckled. "Let it be known that I would have returned the favor if you had let me."

"Noted." Maggie's face was on fire. And just like that, they were back to their bantering and teasing.

*** Mark ***

Mark was glad they cleared the air somewhat, but he was still going to find out what was going on in that head of hers. He'd leave it alone for now, they had work to do and he needed to walk around with Sky. Thunder had given him the go-ahead on Saturday. At first, Thunder had been shocked to find out that Mark had a police dog he shared with an officer. But after their talk, Thunder agreed that a security officer and a K-9 officer were a good idea. He'd tried to tell Maggie yesterday that Sky was going to be at work, but she never called or texted him back. Just as well, he figured she would find out soon enough when she saw Sky.

Sky was friendly unless Mark gave her commands in German to attack or apprehend. Most guests that came in wanted to pet her, but Mark always told them no because when she wore her vest, she was on duty. Sky knew the vest meant it was work hours. However, Mark told Thunder if a fieldtrip came in, he would take off the vest so the kids could pet her. Thunder agreed to fieldtrips and the shelter kids. Dogs could be great therapy for kids and adults.

Several times that day, Mark heard motorcycles revving by the office. Sky would sit up and stare out the window every time she heard them. Mark noticed Maggie would stiffen and jerk her head to the window as well. One time, instead of looking at Maggie, he looked at the road. Several bikers stopped in front of the center and one guy pointed to his eyes and then inside the center before he drove off. Mark turned to Maggie and saw her jaw clench.

"Maggie? Are you okay? Do you know that guy?" Mark pointed out the window. Sky growled.

"Uh, no." Maggie jerked her gaze back to her monitor. But Mark noticed her leg bouncing under her desk. Behind them he heard a gasp and turned around to see Tori hugging her trembling body.

"Tori?" Mark got up and called into the kitchen on their office phones.

"Hello," Alex answered.

"I need you to come out here right now." Mark slammed the phone and walked to Tori, gently placing his hand around her shoulder. "Alex is on his way." Tori shook her head before she turned into Mark's arms.

"What's going on?" Alex hurried over to them. "What happened?"

Tori pulled out of Mark's arms and ran to Alex, holding him tightly. Alex looked at Mark for answers.

"A biker guy from Lucifer's Renegades MC just stopped in front of the center and pointed inside at Tori." Mark recognized the kutte. Anyone would recognize them. They were the local one percenters motorcycle club in town that you stayed away from. Mark figured they were threatening Tori because their previous kidnapping attempt put their president in jail. But it had been quiet for a while. Mark thought it was over.

"Come on, Baby." Alex was pulling Tori toward the kitchen. "Where's Thunder?"

"He went to the resort to meet with your dad. I'll tell him when he comes back." Mark rubbed the back of his neck.

"Okay, thanks for taking care of Tori. I'm gonna take her back into the kitchen with me." Mark nodded at Alex and watched him rubbing her back trying to calm her down.

Mark looked at Maggie, she was pacing behind the desk and biting her fingernail. "Maggie? What's wrong?"

"Nothing," Maggie snapped, pacing like a caged tiger.

"Then why are you pacing?" Mark stopped in front of her to stop her movement. "What are you not telling me?"

"I. Said. Nothing." Maggie enunciated every word as she glared at Mark.

"It doesn't look like nothing, Miss Stubborn." Mark crossed his arms, blocking her path every time she tried to walk around him. "Talk to me. Tori is going to be okay now that she's with Alex. Sky and I will keep an eye out for the bikers."

"I need a Girls' Night Out," Maggie huffed and waved her hands in the air in frustration.

"Where the fuck did that come from?" He didn't understand women. What did a night out have to do with bikers pointing at Tori?

"Men suck!" Maggie screamed in his face.

"What did I do?" Mark's eyes widened. He pointed to his chest, refusing to budge from his spot. He needed answers from Maggie, and he wasn't moving until she told him what was going on in her head. "Explain yourself, Looney Tunes. I'm getting whiplash from this crazy ass conversation."

"Just leave me alone, Mark." Maggie pushed him out of the way and headed to the kitchen. "I'm gonna check on Tori and then text the girls. I'll be right back."

What the hell was going on? Was he being punked? Mark looked around for any hidden cameras. He'd talk to her later when she calmed down and came back to the desk. Wanting to do an outdoor perimeter check, but with no one at the front desk, he settled for stepping outside the front door and looking both ways while Sky stood by his side.

"See anything, Sky?" Mark mumbled as he and Sky scanned the road. "Yeah, I don't either."

*** Maggie ***

Oh Shit! At first, Maggie thought they found her and were pointing at her. But then Tori gasped behind her, and she figured they were pointing at Tori. She knew MC's held grudges and Reaper was still in jail because of Tori's kidnapping attempt. Her brother was a perfect example of the kind of revenge they dealt. He had gone after the LR's after her parents' death–the same fucking day. Were they now after her or Tori? José had always kept her hidden so they wouldn't find her, but had they found her? Would they hold a grudge for eleven years? She needed to text her brother and let him know what happened. He could help her figure it out.

Maggie reached for her phone in her pocket, but it wasn't there. *Fuck!* She had left it by her computer. *Wait, she had to text him from her burner phone.* José was anal about her not using her regular cell phone when calling him. She'd have to text him later. She had to keep this away from Mark. Mark met José, but he didn't know her brother was the Sergeant at Arms of the Miami based Los Lobos de Muerte Motorcycle Club, and the LR's rival. She didn't think that conversation would go well.

For the millionth time in her life, she wished her brother had never gotten involved with the MC, then none of this would have happened and her parents would still be alive. José had once told Maggie he didn't regret joining the MC, he'd made a family with them. His only regret was getting to the house late on that fateful day when his parents were gunned down. He wished he could have been there to defend his family from the LR's that were there that day. Which was why he was so overprotective of her now.

"Tori." Maggie ran into the kitchen. Tori clung to Alex while he rubbed her back. "Are you okay?"

"Hey, Maggie." Alex gave her a fake smile. "She's gonna be okay. I'm gonna keep her in here with me until we leave. I called Thunder and told him what happened. We'll leave when he gets back."

"Okay." Maggie nodded. "If you need anything, let me know."

"Sounds good. Thanks," Alex sighed.

Maggie felt helpless. She didn't know whether to comfort Tori and tell her they were probably there for her, not Tori. But what if she was wrong and they were there for Tori? This was so messed up. She needed some fun to clear her head and the best way to do that was to hang out with her girlfriends and go dancing. Going clubbing always helped her relax. Between the music and dancing, she felt free. Dancing had always been her escape from reality. But first she had to walk out there and face Mark.

"Before you ask" –Maggie held up her hand to Mark– "I'm fine. Tori's good with Alex. Alex called Thunder and told him what happened, and he'll be back as soon as he can. I'm texting the girls so we can go dancing tonight and leave all our worries behind." Maggie couldn't look at Mark because she didn't want him asking any more questions.

"I know. I texted Thunder and he told me he already talked to Alex. Are you sure going out tonight is a good idea after that threat from Lucifer's Renegades?" Mark pointed toward the door. "Are you crazy?"

"Don't call me crazy." Maggie stomped her foot. "The LR's are assholes, but they aren't going to do something at a crowded nightclub." Maggie wasn't sure about her statement, but she wasn't going to let the them rule her life. She was tired of running and hiding.

"How are you so sure about that?" Mark didn't sound convinced. "They kidnapped Tori from under our noses in a crowded museum opening."

"Well, that was one time. I've heard they usually like to get people when they're alone, not in crowds." Maggie's words sounded stupid even to her ears.

"Where are you coming up with that shit? You are not going to a club tonight, Mrs. Magoo." Mark growled.

"The fuck I'm not. Who do you think you are?" Maggie grabbed her phone and sent a text to her Girls' Night Out group chat. "You can't tell me what to do."

"I'm your friend and you're not going. I bet you none of the other guys will let their girls go when they find out about the threat today."

Maggie looked at Mark's smug face. "Then I'll go alone. It wouldn't be the first or last time I go clubbing by myself." Maggie smirked at him. "Maybe I'll even meet a fun guy to take home and fuck." Maggie should have stopped before she threw those last words out at Mark. She could see his face become angrier and redder by the minute. If he was a cartoon character, steam would be pouring out of his ears.

"The fuck you will," Mark grumbled and pointed at her. "You will stay home and behave, Wile E. Coyote."

"Watch me." Maggie finally looked at him and smiled an evil grin. Plopping into her seat, she chose to ignore the rest of his ranting and raving. Eventually, when she didn't react to any of his words, he ran out of breath and stopped berating her.

"I'm gonna walk the perimeter. I texted Alex and let him know." Mark got up from his chair so abruptly it rolled back until it hit the tree. "Sky. Come."

With those final words, he stormed out of the center with Sky. *Good riddance.* Maybe when he came back, he would be in a better mood. He was not the boss of her. Her phone buzzed and the girls were telling her their men said they were not allowed to go out. They could go out another night, but not tonight after that threat. *How did they find out so soon?* Alex must have sent out an alert. *Fuck it.* She didn't have a man in her life telling her what to do, so in her last text, she told them where she would be and at what time. She was going out anyway. Screw all those damn alpha men in her friends' lives.

After that, she texted her brother from her other phone before Mark got back. She let him know what happened. He told her to be careful. She didn't tell him she was going to the club tonight because he would've told her to stay home. And tonight, she wanted to dance her cares away.

Chapter 25

Girls Gone Wild

Mark

After his perimeter check, Mark returned calmer than when he left. He tried to talk some sense into Maggie, but she had made up her mind. She refused to tell him when or where she was going, but Mark knew he could ask Alex or Thunder, and they would tell him. He was right. Placing a text to his boy's group chat, he found out Maggie told everyone she was still going to The Dragon at 9:00pm, whether or not they joined her.

Mark wasn't in the mood to go out, but the thought of Maggie alone at the club made him sick to his stomach. He knew the guys were telling their girls not to go, but would they listen? The girls were a stubborn lot that didn't like to be told what to do. When a girl from their tribe felt lost, they all gathered around her. He was glad Maggie had them, but he wished she would go dancing in one of their living rooms and not at a club by herself.

At least he knew Tori wouldn't show up. She was more fearful with reason. Tori would stay home and away from the club scene tonight. She'd still looked shaken when she left with Alex. *Fuck!* He had to go to the club just in case the men won, and Maggie was by herself.

After a shower and dinner, Mark left for The Dragon. He should've known Maggie would want to go there. She loved dancing and The Dragon not only played good 80s dance music, but if you went downstairs to "The Dungeon" they played 80s new wave/punk music, her favorite. Then at midnight, the bouncers would move people away from an area of the dance floor as smoke surfaced from the floor and a huge animatronic dragon face emerged. The dragon's mouth would open and roar with more smoke. No one left before midnight. Everyone loved watching the dragon reveal himself. Then the place would go nuts until 3:00am. It was a fun club and great hook up joint, but the last place he wanted to be tonight.

Mark got to The Dragon before nine and went to the back corner of one of the bars where he could see the dance floor and remain inconspicuous. Maggie was still mad at him when they left work. He didn't want to ruin her night, just make sure she was safe. If she got too drunk or a guy got too handsy, he'd step in even if she yelled at him. He was going to take care of her, whether she liked it or not.

After sitting at the bar and ordering a beer, several women approached him. One thing about Broward, Dade, and Palm Beach County, they all had beautiful girls with hot as fuck bodies. Must be because they stayed in shape for the beaches. Whatever it was, he loved looking at them and taking one home. But tonight wasn't about him. It was about watching over Maggie and any of the other girls from their group that showed up. Because he knew someone would. There was no way all of them were going to listen to their men and stay home. He'd bet money on that.

Mark gently turned down the ladies who approached. He didn't want them to distract him from watching out for Maggie. A couple minutes later, while a blonde bombshell was flirting with him, he saw Maggie walk in through the front door and order a shot at the other bar. Maggie downed the shot as soon as the bartender placed it in front of her and headed straight to the dance floor. Several guys swarmed around her, attempting to get her attention, but they were harmless. No one was touching her...yet.

For the next hour, Mark watched her take a shot then dance for a couple songs and repeat. The guys must have gotten through to their girls because none of them had shown up yet and it was almost ten. No sooner had that thought entered his mind than in came Frey, Isa, Gaby, and Sarah. He was right–Tori stayed home. Frey, Gaby, and Sarah continued to have their fun and followed Maggie's drinking and dancing pattern except for Isa. She was pregnant and smart enough not to endanger the baby's health.

After another hour, four men came up behind them, running their hands down their sides and attempting to pull them back into their chests for more of a sexual exploration dance. *Oh, Hell No!* Mark whipped out his phone and texted the guys.

> Mark: Ah, where the fuck are you guys?

> Alex: Who?

> Mark: Holt, Thunder, and Grayhorse.

> Alex: Why?

> Mark: Because each of their women have a man attached to their ass on the dance floor with roaming hands.

> Thunder: What the fuck are you talking about? Isa is at Sarah's.

Mark: Ah, no. She's here with Maggie.

Grayhorse: Isa is not here, I thought Sarah was with Isa at your house.

Matteo: I thought Gaby was with Isa at your house, Thunder.

Mark: They are all here!

Thunder: What the fuck are you doing about it, Mark?

Mark: Texting you.

Thunder: Get the fuck out there and stop those assholes.

Holt: Didn't Barrett and I teach you anything. Fuck I'm on my way. Damn independent women.

Mark: Fine. I'm heading over there, but hurry. The odds are against me.

Thunder: Fucking Pussy. Go kick some ass. Leaving now.

Grayhorse: Bring Sarah home. I have the kids. I can't leave.

Matteo: Drop them off at my house on the way. My mom is here. She said she'd watch them.

Thunder: Coming to get you Grayhorse. We'll drop off your kids on the way.

Grayhorse: Got it.

Mark: Fucking hurry.

Mark sighed and put his phone away. He didn't like his odds. Holt, Barrett, and Alex had spent a lot of time training him in self-defense, but four against one was not good. It didn't matter that he was going to get his ass kicked, he had to get those guys away from the girls. Making his way over, he noticed the guy behind Isa pull his hands away when he realized she had a baby bump. Panicking, he turned and ran while Isa laughed. One down, three to go.

He started with the guy trying to press his pelvis into Sarah's ass. He was the most daring at the moment.

"Hey, get your hands off her." Mark yelled over the music and grabbed Sarah's bicep, pulling her toward him. Sarah looked confused. *How many shots had she had? How could she not notice some dickhead grabbing her.*

"What the fuck man? Are you her boyfriend?" The guy tried to take her back.

"I'm her fucking husband." Mark didn't know what to say. He pulled Sarah's hand up and showed him her wedding ring. Smirking at the guy, he grabbed Sarah's hand and pulled her toward Gaby. The guy raised his hands and walked away. Now it was only two to go. His plan had worked, so he thought he'd try it again.

"Get your hands off my wife!" Mark yelled at the man behind Gaby while pulling a dancing Sarah with him.

"If this is your wife, who the fuck is that?" The man pointed at Sarah. Mark sighed. The man had a good point. How the hell was he going to say they were all his wives? He looked up at Maggie and saw her smiling while she watched the show and the guy behind her had his hands a little too close to her breasts. This was getting ugly fast.

"Sister wives." Mark hollered over the music and grabbed Gaby with his other hand. Now he was pulling both dancing queens behind him as he walked to Frey.

"Get your hands off my wife!" Mark screamed at the man who was facing Frey and grabbed her ass.

"Hey, asshole. I thought you said this one was your wife?" The guy that had been with Sarah got bold and came back to try to grab Sarah.

"The Dick said both of them are Sister Wives." Gaby's guy piped up.

"That's fucking bullshit." Sarah's wannabe date got in Mark's face and grabbed Sarah. None of these guys were small. They were about the same size as Mark and around the same height. One on one, he could take them, but three on one...he was going to be in a world of pain. Still, Mark was glad it was just three. Obviously, the guy that had gone after Isa wasn't fighting to keep a pregnant woman.

"We are sister wives" –Sarah poked the man on the chest– "and that is our hot man. So, get your fucking hands off me." Sarah pulled her arm out of the man's grip and draped her arms around Mark's neck, kissing his cheek. The girls started giggling.

Great, now we are all going to get our asses kicked. How the hell was he supposed to defend them with only one hand and Sarah plastered to his chest?

"Uh, mine isn't wearing a wedding band, dude." The guy feeling up Frey's ass said while he ignored Mark and smiled at her. "Lay off. You already got two women. Give a guy a break."

"Get your fucking hands off my fiancée or I'll give you a fucking break." Mark screamed in the guy's face. If he was getting his ass kicked, he wasn't going down like a pussy.

"What he said." Holt used the palm of his hand to push the guy back and grab Frey.

Relief washed over Mark at the sound of Holt's voice. *The cavalry had arrived–Thank fuck!*

"Hi, Holtie." Frey wrapped her arms around his waist and sucked on his neck.

"Get the fuck away from us." Holt pointed at him. "Before I put you in the fucking hospital where you'll have to drink from a fucking straw for the rest of your fucking life."

"Alright. Alright." The guy held up his hands. "Sorry, man."

Mark watched the man turn and run. Grayhorse came up behind him and slapped his back. "Good man. We'll take it from here." Mark spun around and sighed, releasing Gaby and Sarah into their husbands' waiting arms.

"You guys came just in time." Mark ran his hand over his face.

"I think you have one more to save." Thunder pointed toward Maggie. Mark followed his direction and saw Maggie facing a guy with her leg between his, arms raised in the air, kissing him while he gripped her ass. *Fuck Me.* Adrenaline shot through his body as he walked over to her, grabbed a chunk of her hair, and dragged her away from her dance partner's lips. Turning her head so she could look at him, he released her hair.

"What the fuck are you doing?" Mark growled, glaring at Maggie. He was so mad—he could feel his eye twitching.

"Having fun. You should try it sometime." Maggie fucking laughed at him.

"Hey, dude. Get your own girl." The guy pulled Maggie further back on the dance floor. "Babe, that guy's intense."

"Yeah, just forget about him." Maggie shifted her eyes from the guy to Mark. "I already have."

Mark felt gutted. He came to watch over her and make sure she was okay, but she plunged a dagger into his heart when she told him to fuck off. Fine. He was done playing knight in shining armor. Mark walked up to Thunder and Isa, who were slow dancing to a fast song. Didn't they hear the beat?

"I'm leaving now that you guys are all here. Maggie doesn't want me here so I'm heading home." Mark pointed to where she was bumping and grinding with some guy on the dance floor. "Keep an eye out for her."

"I can go get her." Isa pulled out of Thunder's arms.

"No." Mark stopped her. "It's fine. This is what she wanted to do tonight, let her have her fun. But this is a trainwreck waiting to happen and I no longer want to watch. Goodnight."

Mark heard them say goodnight as he walked off the dance floor. He'd done what he came to do—protect the girls from horny guys. If Maggie wanted to fuck one of them, then let her. She was an adult and didn't owe him anything. But he didn't have to stay for the show.

Chapter 26

I Fucked Up

Maggie

The guy dancing with her was the perfect guy to make Mark jealous. Mark had to know he couldn't tell her what to do. She was no one's property. She had spotted Mark with a blonde by the bar when she came in. Of course, the asshole would choose to come to the same bar where she wanted to let loose after a shitty day. After Mark saved her friends and walked away, she realized she didn't need this guy anymore. She wasn't interested in him; she had just wanted to piss off Mark. Now she had to get away from the guy she was dancing with.

"Mags." Maggie heard Isa's voice and felt her hand on her shoulder. "It's time to go." *Perfect timing, Isa.*

"I gotta go." Maggie pushed the guy away from her.

"Come on, babe. I'll take you home." The guy tried to pull her back, then froze with a crazed look on his face. Maggie turned around and saw Thunder, Holt, Matteo, and Grayhorse standing with their arms crossed and angry looks on their faces.

"The lady said she had to go." Thunder's voice boomed over the music. "Let. Her. Go."

"Yeah, yeah, sorry." The guy backed up and scurried away.

"Thanks. Where's Mark?" Maggie asked, wondering if he left or was at the bar.

"He left." Thunder quirked his eyebrow at her. "You know he came here to watch over you. He didn't deserve how you treated him. I hope you guys work it out quick or you're going to have another uncomfortable work environment."

Maggie winced. Thunder wasn't wrong. She needed to apologize to Mark. "You're right. Let's go." They all walked off the dance floor toward the exit.

"Can you drive?" Isa asked Maggie.

"Yeah, I stopped the shots when Mark came over with his Sister Wives story." Maggie knew she wasn't a hundred percent, and she shouldn't be driving, but she didn't live far.

"Sister Wives, what?" Holt had his arm around Frey's shoulder as they walked out.

"He told the guy that was with me, that I was his wife. Unfortunately, then he told Gaby's guy the same thing. Gaby's guy was paying attention and told him he already said he had a wife, so he came up with the Sister Wives story." Sarah and Gaby were laughing.

"Quick thinking on his part." Thunder and the rest laughed all the way to the car. Maggie found it funny but wasn't laughing because she had some groveling to do and wasn't sure how to do it. Mark had been there for them tonight. She had seen him earlier in the night and knew she would be okay. She'd been right. Did she really have to throw that guy in his face? That had been a shitty move.

They all said goodnight and went their separate ways. Some had carpooled and others left their cars behind. They would get them tomorrow. But the guys didn't want the girls driving home after drinking. Maggie was the exception because she told them she was sober. She lied. Not that Isa believed her because Thunder was in the car behind hers.

Driving home, she took her time and made sure she didn't go over the speed limit. At least she thought she didn't. Once she parked in her apartment complex, she heard Thunder honk his horn as he continued out of her parking lot. Maggie honked back and watched their taillights drive off. She took a couple of deep breaths–glad she made it home in one piece. Getting out of her car, she stepped back to close the door when she felt something hit the back of her head, disorienting her. As she felt her body falling, her fingers scrambling desperately for the car door, a cold, metallic chill spread through her body.

***

Waking with a gasp, Maggie realized she'd been asleep for far too long. Her head pounded like a drum, and her body was stiff and sore. Tequila could do that to her. She'd had at least four shots that she remembered. Her mouth was dry from the rag they shoved in her mouth. Slowly coming back to reality, she raised her head and tried to open her eyes. She was in a small empty room by herself. When she tried to move her arms and legs, she realized someone had tied her to a chair.

Where the hell was she? Who had taken her? She had been tipsy and not aware of her surroundings. If only she had let Mark take her home, she would not be in this predicament right now. Did anyone know where she was? Thunder and Isa had already driven off. Did anyone see anything? She hoped a neighbor saw something and called the police. The door opened and three bikers walked in with the blonde that toured the center with her child. What the hell was going on?

"Sleeping Beauty is awake." One biker said as he approached her and pulled the rag out of her mouth.

The lead biker turned around, and she saw the back of his kutte. Lucifer's Renegades had found her. Maggie's body trembled in fear. She was in deep trouble.

"I think she knows who we are now, Numbers." Another biker in the back with the blonde laughed. What was the blonde's name? Maggie was wracking her brain to remember. Annie, Amber, Angie, Angel...that was it. Her name was Angel, and her son was Steele.

"You recognize my kutte, bitch." Numbers sneered and shoved his face in hers. Maggie could smell his foul breath and pulled her head back. "We're gonna fuck your skanky ass up and then return you to your fucking brother's doorstep with a nice note from us."

Maggie sucked in her breath, her eyes seeking Angel's. But Angel was staring at the floor, not making eye contact. She didn't look like she wanted to be there. Then why the hell was she not helping her? Maggie tried to scream, but the rag muffled it.

"You want to say something, bitch?" The bearded biker pulled the rag out and Maggie let out a blood-curdling scream right before the one named Numbers punched her in the face. "Don't fucking scream in my face, bitch."

Maggie's face snapped to the side, pain shooting from her eye to her head. *What were they going to do to her?*

"I bet you're wondering why we have you?" Numbers licked the side of her face from her jaw to her forehead. Maggie was disgusted but tried not to move. Her head lulled to the side.

"We're gonna beat the shit out of you and then fuck you." Numbers grabbed his knife from his side holster and ripped her top from her neck to her stomach. "But don't worry. We'll leave you alive so you can give your asshole brother a message."

"No!" Maggie heard Angel yell. When she looked up, the other two bikers were holding Angel back as she struggled to get away from them. "My father promised none of you would rape her. You can't touch her. Just give her the message and let her go."

"Prospect, take her ass out of here. Now!" Numbers yelled over his shoulder before he used his knife again to cut Maggie's skirt down the front.

Maggie was trying to keep her body still. He had already nicked her with the tip of the knife. Maggie stared into Angel's eyes, pleading for help, but the two men opened the door and pulled her out of the room.

"Well, lookie here." Numbers put his knife away and grabbed her breasts. "Nice lingerie. Were you hoping to get lucky at the bar?"

"You...You were following me?" Maggie snapped her head to look at the long-bearded biker.

"Yup. Been following you for a while. Just couldn't get to you at the center because of that fucking security officer and his damn dog." Numbers continued to play with her breasts. Maggie turned her head, trying to ignore the pain every time he pinched or pulled her nipples. Tears were forming in her eyes, but she didn't want to give him the satisfaction of watching her cry.

"What do you want?" Maggie whimpered.

"I want to make your brother suffer like he made us suffer when he killed three of our brothers and wounded me." Numbers bent down and bit her breast. Maggie couldn't stop the scream from escaping her mouth.

"We already suffered when you killed our parents." Maggie wanted to keep him talking. If she could gain his sympathy, he might let her go.

"Not enough!" Numbers stood up and slapped her face on the same side where he had punched her. *Fuck, that hurts.*

"Please, let me go. I'll give José any message you want me to give him." Maggie watched him out of the corner of her eye as he stepped back. She would take a message as long as she got out of there alive.

"Oh, you will have a message for him. I'm gonna carve it into your fucking skin so you don't forget." *Did he just say carve into my skin?* Maggie's eyes darted to the knife in his hand. *He didn't actually mean to carve words on her, did he?* She never got a tattoo because she didn't think she could handle the pain, and this lunatic was going to cut her skin. *Oh shit!*

"Please, don't hurt me." Maggie's body jolted and shook harder than before. Tears streamed down her face as she pleaded with him. "I...I've never done anything to you. I don't even know you."

The door opened and the other two men walked in without the blonde this time.

"I'm gonna cut you out of this chair. Don't. Fucking. Move." Maggie felt the knife pressing against her neck as he said each word with menace. She swallowed and did a slow nod.

Was he letting her go? Maybe he had changed his mind. But then why were the other two guys licking their lips and staring at her body? Once she was free, she thought about running, but where would she go? She couldn't fight three men that were double her size. Remaining passive, she waited for further instructions and her chance of escape.

"Come here, boys." Numbers waved them over. "Hold her down. One of you grab her arms and the other her legs."

"No! Please!" Maggie begged, pleaded, and cried while they punched her a few more times in the face and kicked her in the stomach. When she fell, they laid her flat on the ground holding her arms and legs so she couldn't move.

"I promised Reaper, we wouldn't fuck you and share you with the club. But if your brother doesn't answer our call in the next couple days, I will find you and fuck you in every hole you have, then hold you down while every brother, prospect, and hang around fucks you too. Do you hear me?" Maggie was in so much pain from the beating she could only nod. Words wouldn't form. All she could do was pray that this would all be over soon, and she would be in a place with no pain.

Suddenly, she felt the knife cutting her abdomen area and she howled in pain. He was leaving his message, but she couldn't make out what he was writing. Her entire body felt like it was going up in flames. She couldn't breathe, but she could smell the brassiness of blood and hear them laughing. Their voices filled with excitement over how José would react when he found her.

She knew how José would react when he found her, but she wasn't about to tell them. It would break him and then he'd go after them. Hopefully with his brothers this time or he might not survive. Would she be dead or alive when they dropped her off?

Maggie was in so much pain, she let her mind wander to another place and time. She wished she had told Mark that she cared about him and was just scared to admit she had feelings for him. She would've loved to thank Thunder for helping her. Isa would be devastated when she found out what happened to her. Tori would feel like it was her fault because of Reaper.

If she survived this hell, she swore to be nicer to Mark and be a better friend. The sharp pain became too overwhelming, and she finally succumbed to the darkness.

Chapter 27

Where's Maggie?

Mark

Mark woke up frustrated with himself for letting his anger override his protection of Maggie. She had pissed him off with her sassy ass, snarky attitude last night at the bar. He'd gotten so mad he stormed off, knowing her friends were still there and they would take care of her. But he felt like a piece of shit because all her friends were coupled off and at the end of the night, she would still be alone. Maggie wouldn't tell him what she had been worried about and when she pushed him away, like a coward, he'd left.

Today, he vowed to get it out of her and make sure she was okay. He'd never gone partying with her, but last night she seemed like a different person. One who didn't give a shit about her safety or her life. He watched her grind on any guy who danced with her with no shame.

Mark showered and dressed. "Come on Sky, let's go talk to Maggie before work." Mark hoped seeing Sky would make Maggie smile, she loved Sky. The best part of working with Maggie and being a security officer was that he knew her address. He also knew she lived with her cousin and her husband, so he had to tread lightly or he would get kicked out by her family before he got a chance to talk to Maggie. He saw her car in the parking lot and pulled in next to her. But why the fuck was her car door open? Had she forgotten something in the apartment and ran back in to get it? He'd have to talk to her about leaving her car door open. Any asshole could get into her car and steal it or worse yet, wait for her to hurt her.

Getting out of his car, he walked to her open door. *Shit!* Was that her phone on the ground? Was that blood by her phone? *What the hell?* Mark spun around, looking for anyone who might know what had happened. He knew better than to touch anything if this was a crime scene. But what if she was in the apartment and ran up to get something at the last minute? No, Maggie would not leave her phone on the ground.

Sky was going crazy, walking around in circles, smelling the ground and crying. Mark looked inside her car, careful not to touch anything. He spotted her purse on the passenger seat and her keys in the cupholder. All he could think was that Maggie was kidnapped. He pulled out his phone and called Thunder.

"Hey, Mark. What's up?" Thunder answered on the first ring.

"Sorry to call so early." Mark checked his watch. It was seven and they didn't have to be at work until nine.

"No problem." Mark heard Isa ask who was on the phone. "I went for a run and just got out of the shower. What's going on?"

"Did you follow Maggie home last night?" Mark held his breath, praying for the right answer.

"I did. As soon as she pulled into her parking spot, I honked, she honked back, and we drove off. Why?"

"I just came to her apartment to talk to her about last night and her car door was open, phone on the ground, keys and purse inside, but no Maggie. I was getting ready to go knock on her door, but I thought I would call you first in case I'm overreacting, and she wasn't taken but is safe inside her apartment."

"You are not overreacting!" Isa shouted.

"Sorry, I had you on speaker phone while I got dressed. Don't touch anything. I'll be right over." Mark heard Thunder say to Isa. "What are you doing?"

"I'm coming with you," Isa answered back. "You don't know Nancy, Maggie's sister. I do. She might not let you guys in to talk to her, but she knows me."

"Okay." Thunder sighed. "Mark, we'll be there in twenty or less. Call George and tell him what's going on."

"On it." Mark hung up and called Deputy George Smith. George had been one of Thunder's shelter kids who Thunder and Mark mentored. After George turned eighteen and wanted to stop bartending, he became a police officer.

"Mornin' Mark. What's up?" George grumbled when he answered the phone. Mark realized he must have woken him up.

"I think Maggie was kidnapped." Mark blurted into the phone to get George over there quickly.

"On my way. Text me the address." George's voice sounded clearer before he hung up. Being a police officer must teach you how to wake up fast. Mark texted George the address. Then he shot off a quick text to K-9 Deputy Bryan Wright, letting him know to come get Sky.

Mark was pacing back and forth behind their cars when Thunder, Isa, George, Sean (George's partner), K-9 Deputy Bryan Wright, a detective, and the CSI Police Unit pulled up next to him. They all looked at the evidence and photographed it while they dusted for prints. Bryan let Sky sniff everything and followed her a few steps before she froze and looked around. George put on gloves, picked up the phone, placing it in a Ziploc bag, and handed it to one forensic officer. Isa, Thunder, and Mark walked to Maggie's apartment to see if Maggie was home.

Mark was praying that he was wrong, and the police and CSI team had been called out for a false alarm, but the hair on the back of his neck was tingling. He had a bad feeling about this. Isa knocked on the door. The way his heart was racing with adrenaline, Mark was afraid if he knocked, he would end up pounding on the door instead.

"Hi, Kevin." Isa smiled when a man answered the door. "Is Maggie here?"

"I don't know." Kevin looked from Isa to Thunder to Mark. "What's going on?"

"We're not sure yet. We need to talk to Maggie," Isa answered. They had decided on the walk to the door that it would be best for Isa to talk to Maggie's family. Mark was in no condition and Thunder had only met them twice.

"Kev, who's at the door?" A woman, yawning and hugging her robe closed, asked. She looked a little like Maggie, but with dark brown hair.

"Hi, Nancy. Can we come in and talk to Maggie?" Mark could tell Isa was getting worried. He watched her wring her hands.

"Sure. Come in. I'll get her." Nancy smiled and walked away. Mark sighed in relief. Maggie was home. Thank fuck.

"Follow me." Kevin led them into their living room, and they sat down, waiting for Maggie. She was going to be so pissed that he called Isa and Thunder. Then she would explode when she realized CSI was all over her car.

Nancy ran into the living room and stared at all of them, her gaze bouncing from person to person. "She's not in her room, and her bed's still made. It looks like she didn't come home last night. She wasn't with you?" Nancy focused on Isa.

"Fuck!" Mark bolted up and began pacing.

"What's going on?" Nancy watched Mark and walked to Kevin.

"She was with us, and we followed her home. When she parked, we drove off." Isa began crying and Thunder tucked her into his arms and rubbed her back.

"Why the fuck didn't you walk her to the door?" Mark screamed, raising his arms in exasperation.

"Why the fuck did you leave her at the club?" Thunder growled at him while he stood with Isa in his arms. "Don't be fucking pointing fingers right now. Calm the fuck down."

"You left my cousin in the bar?" Nancy was livid and trying to get at Mark to hit him. The only thing that saved him from getting a slap or punch to the face was Kevin holding Nancy back.

"She pissed me off," Mark said through gritted teeth with his hands on his waist.

"She pisses off a lot of people, but we don't leave her. How old are you? Five?" Nancy kept trying to get out of Kevin's arms to get at Mark. Yep, she was a little spitfire, just like her cousin. Now he could see the resemblance.

"He sure is acting like it." Isa stepped away from Thunder toward Mark.

Shit, now he had two angry women who were going to kick his ass—which he deserved.

"Okay." Thunder stood in front of Mark, one hand out to stop Isa and the other to stop Nancy, who had broken free from Kevin. Obviously, Kevin agreed with Nancy because he stopped trying to hold her back. He just stood with a smirk on his face and crossed arms, watching his girl take a fighting stance. "Let's all calm down and think this through. Who would want to get Maggie? Where could she be?"

Knock, knock, knock.

"Now what?" Kevin said before opening the door.

"Hi. I'm Deputy George Smith and this is my partner, Deputy Sean O'Reilly. We've been in the parking lot dusting for prints and trying to find any witnesses to figure out what happened to Maggie. Can we come in?"

"Absolutely." Kevin opened the door wider for George and Sean to step in. "Did anyone see anything?"

"No," George sighed. "No one saw anything, and no one heard anything. But we still need to ask several other apartments that don't face the parking lot. We saw a couple of cameras outside. Can you tell me the name of the owners of this complex so we can get the footage?"

"Of course. I'll go get the info for you." Kevin turned and walked away.

"Any leads?" Sean asked the group assembled in the living room before turning to face Nancy. "When was the last time you saw her?"

"We were just talking about that." Thunder also faced Nancy.

"Last time I saw her was when she left yesterday to go clubbing with the girls." Nancy smirked at Mark. "I can call her brother. Maybe he knows something."

Just then, Isa's phone started ringing. Mark saw Isa look at her phone and grimace before hanging up. Then it rang again.

"Who's calling you?" Thunder didn't miss much, and he noticed Isa turning off her phone every time.

"I don't know. I don't recognize the number." Isa crossed her arms and glared at him.

"Answer it. What if it's Maggie?" Thunder laid his hand on her shoulder.

"Shit! I didn't think of that." Isa's eyes widened as she looked at everyone. Then her phone buzzed with a text.

> Unknown: Answer the fucking phone. It's about Maggie.

Isa lost all color in her face as she turned her phone around to show Thunder and Mark. This time, when the phone rang, she answered immediately.

"Who is this? Where's Maggie?" Isa rattled off, desperate to find Maggie. Thunder pulled Isa's hand down and pressed the speaker button so they could all listen in.

"I'm her fucking brother and I need you to get your ass to my clubhouse, NOW!" He screamed into the phone.

"Don't you fucking talk to my woman like that, asshole. Have some respect. She's worried about her friend." Thunder took the phone away from Isa and roared into it.

"Sorry. It's a shitshow over here." Mark heard other male voices in the background. "Maggie's here. She wanted me to call some guy named Mark, but she couldn't remember his number. She lost her cell phone."

"What clubhouse?" Thunder asked while Isa bit her nail, a deep frown on her face.

"The Los Lobos de Muerte Clubhouse in Miami. I'll text you the address. Hurry."

"Oh my God!" Isa covered her mouth and stared at her phone.

"Fuck!" Mark exclaimed. Maggie's brother hung up. Seconds later, Isa's phone was buzzing with an incoming text message. Thunder clicked on it and googled the address while Mark looked over his shoulder.

"It's a fucking hour away!" Mark ran his hand over his hair. "Shit! I gotta go." Mark turned to leave, but Thunder grabbed his bicep.

"Not without me you're not. Give Isa me your car keys. I'm driving." Thunder kissed Isa's temple. "Go home or go to Sarah's. I'll call you as soon as we have any news."

"I'm going with you." Isa crossed her arms and glared at Thunder.

"No, you are not. I am not putting my woman and child in danger. And you are most definitely not going to a motorcycle club clubhouse. You will do as you're told and go home." Thunder roared at her. "This is not the time to argue with me."

Mark stood back, watching the icy stare down. No one said a word. It was like they were talking to each other through their eyes. Finally, Isa stood down.

"Fine. But we need to talk when you get home."

"Fine." Thunder squinted at her before bending down close to her ear. Mark stood so close to them he heard Thunder whisper, "I love makeup sex with you. Make sure you eat something. You're gonna need your strength." He kissed her cheek, and turned to Mark and said, "Let's go." Thunder placed his hand on Isa's back and led her out of the apartment.

"Someone call me as soon as you know anything?" Nancy cried out.

"Absolutely," Mark said over his shoulder.

"We'll follow you, but stay parked on the street," George stated. "The MCs don't let us into their clubhouse, and we don't want to start a shoot-out."

"I'll take Sky with me back to the station." Bryan held her leash. "Update me when you know anything."

"Will do." Mark got in Thunder's truck, waiting for him.

Thunder made sure Isa got in Mark's car and drove home before he started his truck. Mark was already waiting inside.

Chapter 28

I Will Kill Them!

José

José heard banging on his door. He lived in one of the many rooms in the Los Lobos Clubhouse. He'd slept with Lola, his favorite sweet butt. Sweet butts were the girls that hung around the clubhouse and slept with the brothers. The brothers passed them around until one claimed a girl as his girlfriend. José hadn't claimed Lola yet because he didn't want to put a target on her back, but everyone knew she was his and off limits to anyone else.

Sitting up, he grabbed his phone and looked at the time. Fuck, who was banging on his door this early in the morning?

"*¡Loco, levantate. Rapido. Apurate!*" José heard one of his brothers yelling while he pounded on the door. *What was happening at fucking six o'clock in the morning that couldn't wait another hour or two?*

"Lola. I gotta go. *Quédate aquí.*" José got up and grabbed his jeans. Lola rolled over and pulled the covers up to her shoulders. José heard more pounding on his door.

"*¡Ya, voy, pendejo!* What the fuck is going on? It's six o'clock in the fucking morning." José swung the door open and saw Machete, their president, with an angry look on his face. "*Perdon, jefe.*"

"You need to come with me now." José hadn't done anything wrong. He didn't know why the club president was knocking on his door so early in the morning. Machete did not look happy.

Once they got downstairs, Machete led him to the couch where he saw Deb (Machete's ole lady) leaning over his sister's beaten, bloody body. José was glad she was at least in her bra and panties, or he'd punch the shit out of any brother that saw her naked and didn't cover her up. As it was, she still needed a fucking blanket.

There was a sticky note on each breast. One note said, "Stay out of our fucking business" and the other said "or else. Courtesy of Lucifer's Renegades" Then carved into her skin on her belly were the words "Next Time" with an arrow pointing toward her pussy.

"Fuck! No! Not her!" José screamed out and grabbed the hair on his head pulling it until tears came to his eyes. "Not Margarita. I'm gonna fucking kill them." José dropped to his knees in front of her and felt her pulse before grabbing her hand. "Someone get me a fucking blanket and call Doc."

"Already called Doc. He'll be here in ten." Machete placed his hand on José's shoulder. "We got your back. Whatever you need."

"Here." Chulo, their vice president, placed a blanket over Margarita. "This time we ride together. You do not go alone to meet their demands. We are brothers and we ride as one. We will all avenge your sister."

"*Gracias*," José mumbled against Maggie's hand.

"José?" Maggie's voice was raspy.

"*Si. Soy yo.*" José watched Maggie attempt to open her eyes. One eye remained completely swollen shut, while Maggie could barely open the other.

"I'm sorry they found me."

"Deb." Machete called out to his old lady. "Get her some water and a straw."

"*Mi hermanita*, this is not your fault." José brushed the hair off her forehead. "What can I do for you? Doc is on his way."

"Can you call Mark?"

José was confused, as far as he knew, she wasn't dating anyone. "Who is Mark?"

José took the water for Maggie from Deb. "Thanks, Deb." José helped Maggie sit up, but stopped moving when she cried out in pain. "*Perdon*. Take a little sip of water. Don't drink too much."

"Mark is the security officer that works with me." Maggie said between a couple sips. "Remember, you met him when you came to the center."

"Yes. Do you know his number because you don't have your cell phone?" José remembered meeting the guy. He seemed overprotective of Maggie. So, where the fuck was he last night? Yeah, José was looking forward to talking to this Mark guy.

"No. Can you call Isa?" José looked up when he heard a commotion at the door.

"Yes. Here's Doc. Let him check you out." José moved out of the way.

"Can we move her to a room?" Doc took out his stethoscope.

"She's in a lot of pain when I move her." José didn't know what to do. He would carry her to his room if he could, but he didn't want to cause her more pain.

"Let's move her to that spare room behind the kitchen. It will give her some privacy." Deb touched Machete's arm as if to ask for permission. He nodded. "I'll go change the sheets. Give me a few minutes."

"*Gracias, Machete.*" José ran his hand over his hair. That room was only used when a member of another charter came and needed to crash. But it was good that Deb was changing the sheets, who knew what was on there from the previous night of fun and debauchery.

"It's ready." Deb came out and told José. "You can bring her." He put his arms under Maggie as gently as he could and picked her up—Maggie whimpered. Deb made sure the blanket covered her as he carried her to the spare room.

José softly laid her down on the bed and stepped out of the way.

"Let me talk to her privately." Doc moved around José and sat on the edge of the bed. "I'll come get you as soon as I finish."

"Can Deb stay?" Maggie whispered. José knew Maggie had always liked Deb. When she spent those few days at the clubhouse after their parents' death, Deb looked after her. Deb looked at José and he nodded.

"I'll stay with you, Magpie." Deb went over to the other side of the bed and held Maggie's hand. José saw Maggie crack a small smile at Deb and squeeze her hand. Deb was the only one that got through to Maggie during those dark days before Aunt Inez and Uncle Thomas came to get her. Maggie asked Deb so many questions and talked to her so much, Deb nicknamed her Magpie.

"Thanks, Deb." José nodded. "Thank you, Doc. I'll wait outside." Maggie was in good hands. When Maggie and Isa became friends, José had asked for her number in case of emergency since Isa was Maggie's best friend. He was now grateful he had it.

Chapter 29

Why was Maggie at the Los Lobos Clubhouse?

Mark

T hunder drove like a bat out of hell. Thankfully, since George didn't want Thunder to get pulled over, he called Thunder and told him to get behind him. George put on his siren and took off ahead of Thunder. Mark was grateful because their hour drive only took thirty-five minutes and no tickets. As they got closer, George turned off his siren and stayed parked on the street like he'd promised.

Thunder pulled into a garage that was connected to a clubhouse. Screeching to a halt, he stopped right by the front door of the clubhouse. They made such a raucous that a couple brothers came out the front door with guns. Thunder and Mark stepped out with their hands up.

"We're not armed." Thunder said since he was closest to the door. "We're here for Maggie. Her brother called us."

"Are you Mark?" One of them asked Thunder.

"I'm Mark." Mark walked slowly around the front of the truck toward the clubhouse door. "This is Maggie's friend, Thunder. He's Isa's husband and was with us when we got the call."

"*Si*. El Loco said someone named Mark was coming." The guy lowered his gun. "Are you packing?"

"No." In his hurry to get to Maggie, Mark had left his gun in his car.

"Check them." The guy told the other man.

"All clean." The man said after quick body checks.

"Come in." The man moved aside and let them enter the clubhouse.

Mark looked around for Maggie. The place was trashed, and he saw several guys with prospect vests cleaning up the mess. Then he recognized Maggie's brother walking toward him.

"Where's Maggie?" Mark said before José reached him.

"She's back there." José pointed behind him. "In a room with Doc."

Mark began to move in that direction when José placed his palm on Mark's chest.

"If you are dating my sister, where the fuck were you last night?" José growled at Mark.

"I am not dating your sister. We're uh...friends, co-workers." Mark rubbed the back of his neck. "Can I please see her?"

"Yeah, right." José snorted and crossed his arms. "I saw the way you look at her."

"Can we table this for now?" Thunder stepped in. "I'm Isa's husband and Maggie's new employer. I'd like to be able to tell my wife that her best friend is okay."

"I've heard of you. Thank you for giving Maggie a job after those assholes were bothering her at her old job." José put his hand out to shake Thunder's.

"Maggie's a good friend to my wife." Thunder shook it. "She's family."

"Can we cut the small talk so I can see Maggie?" Mark was losing patience. He needed to see her. His arms were longing to hold her and make sure she was alright.

"We need to talk before you go see her. Let's have a seat so I can tell you what I know. Then, when Doc is done, you can see Maggie." José led Mark and Thunder to the empty stools in front of the clubhouse bar.

Mark was grateful they weren't going to sit on the couch because it didn't look very sanitary. Before Mark could ask any questions, José jumped right in.

"Maggie was beaten and dropped on our doorstep this morning." José tapped the bar, which obviously meant he wanted a beer since one was opened and placed in front of him. "Do you want one?" He asked them.

"No, thank you." Both Thunder and Mark answered.

"I don't think she was raped, but she is in bad shape." José took a drink. "This is all my fault. I thought I was keeping her safe and hidden, but they must have followed me the day I came to check on her at the cultural center. I fucked up."

"Yeah, you sure did." Mark stood facing José, spoiling for a fight.

Unfortunately, so was every other brother in the clubhouse, outnumbering him and Thunder ten to two.

"Mark." Thunder placed his hand on his shoulder. "Take it easy. We're all on the same side. All of us just want Maggie to be okay."

"You're right." Mark's body deflated and he dropped onto the stool, placing his head in his hands. "Who did this to her? Why?"

"I can't tell you why, that's club business. But I can tell you who." José took another swig of his beer and nodded at his brothers to stand down. "Lucifer's Renegades. They have a grudge against us, specifically me."

"Are you saying they were after Maggie?" Mark looked stunned.

"Yes."

"Shit. So, when they came by yesterday, they were pointing at Maggie, not Tori?" Mark was so confused.

"Yes," José replied bluntly.

"Why?" Mark looked from Thunder to José.

"Can't tell you. Like I said, club business." José shook his head. "But I can tell you we'll take care of it." José bolted out of his stool as an older man with a stethoscope came down the hallway. "Doc, how is she?"

"She took quite a beating." Doc placed his stethoscope in his black bag before looking up. "But with lots of rest, she's gonna be fine. Her injuries include a mild concussion and some bruised ribs. I gave Deb some pain pills to give her, but she refused to take them because they'll make her sleepy. She refuses to fall asleep until she sees Mark. Which one of you is Mark?." Doc glanced between Thunder and Mark.

"I'm Mark." Mark raised his hand like he was in school waiting to get picked to answer a question. "Are you a real doctor?"

"I am." Doc nodded and smiled. "I served as a medic in the Army before I opened my practice."

"Thank you." Mark released his breath. "Do I need to take her to a hospital?"

"No need. I could feel her bruised ribs and saw signs of a concussion. She wasn't raped. But if it will make you feel better to take her to the hospital, go ahead." Doc smiled again.

"You can trust Doc." José said. "He's taken care of us for years."

"What if she has internal bleeding?" Mark rubbed the back of his neck.

"I can see you will feel better if you take her to a hospital." Doc looked at José. "Get your story straight. Let me know what happens." Doc patted José on the back and left.

What did Doc mean by get your story straight?

"Come with me." José spun on his heels and headed down the hallway. "Sounds like she wants to see you. We'll talk when you're done. Do you know why the cops are sitting outside our gate?"

Mark had forgotten all about George and Sean. *What was he going to tell them?*

"They're friends ready to escort us if we need to take her to the hospital." Thunder answered. "I'll stay out here while you talk to Maggie. I'll call Isa with an update."

José opened the door and whispered to Mark before he walked in. "She doesn't look good. Control your temper and facial reaction. Don't scare her."

Mark nodded and walked in. Maggie looked so tiny in that big bed. The lady named Deb was running a washcloth over her face.

"Mags." Mark spoke softly as soon as he entered the room.

Maggie turned her head and looked at Mark with tears rolling down her face, her lips trembling. Mark placed his hands in his pockets so Maggie couldn't see his balled-up fists. He wanted to beat the shit out of every person who hit Maggie. Taking a couple of deep breaths, he forced a smile. Maggie didn't need his anger right now; she needed his support.

"I'll be back," Deb said before she stood up and left the room.

Mark walked to the bed, took his hands out of his pockets, and sat down.

"I was so worried about you." Mark grabbed her hand and brought it to his lips. "I'm sorry. I was such an asshole last night. I shouldn't have left you there."

"What happened to me wasn't your fault. They would have found me sooner or later." Maggie whispered, with a slight smile. "I should've left with you, Surfer Smurf."

My sassy Maggie is trying to find her way back.

Mark kissed her hand. "Why did they want you?"

"I don't want to talk about it right now. Can you take me home?" Maggie's swollen eyes were pleading with him.

"I'm not taking you home." Mark saw Maggie's eyes turn angry–her mouth open, ready to yell at him if he didn't diffuse the situation. "It's not safe there. I'll take you to my house where I can take care of you. I live in a gated community and my house has security cameras all over the property."

Maggie raised an eyebrow.

"What can I say?" Mark shrugged his shoulders. "When I started this security job, I practiced on my house. It's safer than Fort Knox, Princess."

Mark finally got a smile out of her.

"Take your medicine and I'll carry you to Thunder's truck so he can take us home." Mark realized he said home like she lived with him. Usually, he would panic, but after he said the words, a calm settled over him. Was Maggie his home?

"Thunder's here?" Maggie tried to sit up.

"He is." Mark helped her. "He came with me so I wouldn't kill myself driving over here to come get you. Although several times, I thought he was going to kill us with his driving. Luckily, George and Sean gave us a police escort and are waiting outside the clubhouse to give us another one."

Mark handed her the pills and water. "I think we need to take you to the hospital. Get you checked out."

"Then I probably shouldn't take these. They'll have questions for me I'll need to answer. Talk to José and find out what he wants you to tell them. I don't want the police to come after Los Lobos." Maggie gave him back the glass of water.

Maggie's comments confused Mark. What was she hiding from him? She should tell Deputy George everything so they could find the fuckers that did this to her and put their asses in jail. Deputy George was their friend and could help them. Mark didn't know enough about the Los Lobos de Muerte MC. Were they just as bad as Lucifer's Renegades? Did they sell drugs and guns? Mark had so many unanswered questions that needed to be addressed.

The fact that José and his brothers called a doctor to check her injuries showed Mark they cared about Maggie. To keep the peace and since they were outnumbered, Mark decided to follow Maggie's requests. He wanted her to stay calm. But tomorrow, they were going to have a long talk.

"Okay." Mark placed the glass on the nightstand and stood. "I'll be right back."

"Can you ask Deb to come back in? She can help me get dressed and get me some ibuprofen." Maggie pulled the blanket up to her chin.

"Sure." Mark smiled and walked out. He saw Deb standing in the hallway next to a scary badass biker. "Uh, Deb?" She nodded. "Maggie would like you to help her get dressed. She doesn't want to take the prescription pills, but she's in pain. Maybe get her some ibuprofen? I'm gonna take her to the hospital after I talk to José."

"Got it." She turned and waited for the scary badass biker to nod his approval.

Mark stepped out of the way and went in search of José with the scary badass biker behind him. *Who was this guy?* They had a story to concoct.

Mark found José exactly where he'd left him, with Thunder on a stool. "José, I'm gonna take Maggie to the hospital. I believe your doctor, but I want to make sure she doesn't have any internal bleeding." Mark noticed José looked behind him at the badass biker. Mark turned and saw the biker nod. *Was he asking permission?*

"Okay." José sighed. "If my prez says it's okay, then you can take her to the hospital."

"Prez?" Mark frowned, looking between José and the biker.

"That's Machete" –José pointed to the badass biker– "our president."

Mark saw Maggie coming out of the room with Deb in a pair of loose sweatpants and large t-shirt. She limped to him, and he wrapped his arm around her waist.

"Margarita, Mark is going to take you to the hospital." José faced them. "You can tell them and the police everything that happened to you last night. You can even tell them that we found you this morning on our doorstep and you wanted us to call Mark. But as far as why this happened to you, you must play stupid and tell them you don't know why you were a target for them." José reached out and touched her cheek. "Do you understand what I am asking of you?"

"Yes, I do." Maggie nodded.

"Do you agree with this Machete?" José turned to his prez.

"I do." Machete walked up to Maggie. "Your brother can't go to the hospital with you, but Mark" –Machete pointed at Mark– "will keep us updated. Won't you Mark?"

"Yes, sir." Mark was caught off guard when Machete glared at him. Hell, he wasn't about to piss off the president of a motorcycle club.

"We will take care of this, I promise you." Machete turned back to Maggie. "We love you, Margarita. I'm sorry this happened to you."

"Thank you," Maggie whispered.

José gave her a hug and nodded to Mark. "Please take care of my sister and keep me updated."

"Of course. Can I talk to you for a minute?" Mark needed to talk to José, but not in front of Maggie. "Thunder, can you help Maggie into the car? I'll be right there."

"Sure thing." Thunder walked over to Maggie and helped her walk out.

"What is it?" José squinted at Mark.

"The police are going to ask if I have any photos of how she was found. For evidence. I didn't want to ask you this in front of Maggie." Mark rubbed his neck. "Do you have anything?"

"I have the one my brothers sent me when they were trying to identify her." Machete took out his phone. "What's your number?"

Mark gave him his number. Machete texted it quickly. Mark saw the text come up and clicked on it. His stomach dropped when he saw how they treated Maggie. They had dumped her on the ground like a piece of trash by the front door. She was only wearing her bra and panties. He quickly zoomed in and read the notes over her breasts and the words carved into her abdomen. Mark closed his eyes and took a couple deep breaths before looking at José and Machete.

"We will say what we rehearsed. I don't need to know anything else." Mark shook hands with José and Machete. "Thank you for calling me. I will look after Maggie. You have my word." Mark turned to leave but stopped and looked José in the eyes. "I hope you get those motherfuckers."

Chapter 30

Sticking to the Story

Maggie

Maggie felt like shit. She was grateful Deb had let her borrow some clothes. The LR's had used her as their personal punching bag. Her entire body was throbbing, and she was dying to take the prescription pain pills, but then she would have to explain where she got them from. She didn't want Doc to get in trouble. He was a doctor, but they didn't know he worked on the side for the Los Lobos MC. The MC members rarely went to the hospital, because police reports had to be filed. Maggie knew nothing happened in the brotherhood without the President's approval, so she was grateful when Mark mentioned internal bleeding and José asked Machete to allow her to go. Machete knew how important Maggie was to José and gave his approval.

Maggie would play stupid and not tell anyone why they had targeted her. She knew it was because José shot some of their members when they killed her parents eleven years ago, but she didn't want her brother going to jail. At some point, she would tell Mark the whole story, but not today. Today, she had to focus on parts of the story. The more she rehearsed the story in her head, the better she would be at telling it just like José wanted.

Thunder called Deputy George and asked for a police escort to the hospital. As soon as Mark got in the car, Thunder drove them to Broward General Hospital. Deputy George asked a nurse if they could put her in a temporary room because they needed to question her. The nurse helped her sit in a wheelchair and found a room.

"Maggie. I'm so sorry this happened to you, but we need to ask you some questions." Deputy George squatted down to talk to her.

"I know. It's okay," Maggie sighed. "Let's get this over with."

"Can you tell me what happened?"

"After I parked my car in my parking lot, I waved to Thunder and Isa and opened the door. Then I realized my phone was still in the car, so I reached in to grab it. As I was bent over, I felt someone yank me back and then something hit my head." Maggie touched the back of her head.

"When I woke up, I was strapped to a chair in a room. I tried to get my hands out, but the zip ties cut into my skin. Then three men walked into the room with the blonde lady who came into the cultural center for a tour. I think her name was Angel. Two stood at the back with Angel and one approached me with a knife." Maggie closed her eyes. Her hands covering her mouth were trembling.

"It's okay. I got you." Mark placed a hand on her shoulder from behind.

"Take your time," Deputy George murmured.

Maggie shook her head. She had to continue so she could forget about that horrible night. "The man with the knife turned around and I saw he was wearing a Lucifer's Renegade kutte. I know what a kutte is because my brother is a member of Los Lobos de Muerte Motorcycle Club." Maggie dreaded saying those words, but she had to give them something.

"Do you think they kidnapped you because of your brother?" Deputy Sean looked up from his notepad.

"Maybe. I know the two clubs are rivals." Maggie nodded. "They knew I recognized them. I was scared and asked them not to hurt me. I must have raised my voice because he punched me and told me not to scream." Maggie looked down. Here came the hard part. "He cut off my blouse and skirt. Grabbed, squeezed, and bit my breast. I screamed and he slapped me. He sai...said he was going to fuck me and pass me around but Angel said her father promised they wouldn't rape me. Two men led her out and when they came back, they cut me out of the chair, held me down on the floor, and carved into my stomach." Even though Maggie was shaking and crying, she felt Mark's hand massaging her shoulder. "I must have passed out from the pain because the next thing I remember is Machete picking me up off the ground and bringing me inside the Los Lobos clubhouse. My brother and Deb, Machete's old lady, took care of me until Mark came to get me."

"I hate to ask this, but...do any of you have a photo of how she looked when they dropped her off?" Deputy George looked around.

"I do." Mark pulled out his phone. "Machete texted it to me so I could show you."

Maggie saw Mark's hand next to her face, but she turned away. She didn't want to see that photo. It would show a broken down, beaten girl, and dammit she was a survivor.

"Shit. Can you please text me that photo?" Deputy George asked Mark.

"Yeah."

"Maggie, do you know what the message on the sticky notes mean?" Deputy George zoomed into the photo.

"No. I never saw the notes."

"Maggie, can you come into the station and look at mugshots of the LR members? It would give me great pleasure to arrest the ones who did this to you." Maggie looked at Deputy George and he looked ready to murder someone.

"Yes, I'll come as soon as I can." Maggie would love to put those assholes behind bars. A part of her feared identifying them, but the larger part of her wanted them to pay for what they had done. She would have to let José know if she identified them. He would want to know who they were. Maybe she could also convince him to let the police handle the situation. She didn't want to lose her brother in a turf war.

"Okay, ladies and gentlemen." A nurse came in and interrupted their conversation. "It's time for her X-Ray, ultrasound, rape kit, and CT scan. I promise to take care of her and bring her to a room as soon as we're done. You can all wait in the waiting room."

Maggie was grateful for the interruption. She wanted to get all these tests over with so she could go home. Doc had already told her she wasn't raped, but she couldn't tell them that.

Mark grabbed Maggie's hand before the nurse wheeled her away.

"We'll be in the waiting room until they're done running tests, Merida." Mark kissed Maggie's hand.

"Okay." Maggie smiled at Mark.

The nurse wheeled her out and must have seen Maggie wince when she adjusted herself in the wheelchair. Her ribs were hurting. She hoped she could lay down for the tests they were going to run.

"Are you in pain, honey?" The nurse wheeled her into the elevator and pushed the button.

"Yes."

"As soon as they give me the okay, I'll get you something for your pain." The nurse wheeled her out and down the hallway to an X-Ray machine. "I'll stay with you the whole time."

"Thank you." Maggie was glad the nurse was staying with her. She seemed nice and motherly, which helped to comfort her. She prayed she didn't have internal bleeding. Who knew bruised ribs could hurt so much?

Chapter 31

Woman Down

Mark

"I'm gonna take Maggie to my house when they release her," Mark told Thunder.

"Okay." Thunder rubbed the back of his neck. "I'll tell Isa. I know she wanted Maggie to come to our place."

"I promise I'll take care of her." Mark sat and braced his forearms on his knees. "I fucked up, but I won't let anything happen to her. I have a shit ton of security installed in and around my house."

"Are you sure she will go with you?" Thunder sat next to him. He scooted down in the chair and crossed his arms and ankles.

"I already told her I was taking her to my house, and she didn't argue with me. I'm not taking no for an answer," Mark mumbled. "I don't want to bring any trouble to Isa. She's pregnant and she doesn't need any of this stress." Mark turned his head and stared at Thunder.

Thunder nodded. "I appreciate that. Just make sure it's Maggie's choice. She was pretty pissed at you last night. You can't force her to stay with you."

"I know." Mark rubbed his hands down his face. That was going to be the hardest part of all this. Maggie could be so fucking stubborn when she sunk her heels on something. Thinking back to their conversation, she'd never actually agreed to go home with him.

"I'd feel better if she was with you, but I also need her to be okay with this arrangement or Isa will have my ass." Thunder sighed.

"As if," Mark scoffed. "That woman doesn't stay mad at you."

"True, but even one day in the doghouse sucks." Thunder smirked.

"I gotcha, man," Mark chuckled. "I'll talk to Maggie about her options and make sure she sees mine is the best thing for her."

"Thanks, I appreciate that." Thunder shrugged. "Although, I do love our makeup sex. So, if Isa's mad at me for a few hours, I can take it." Thunder shoulder bumped him.

Mark knew Thunder was trying to cheer him up. He appreciated the effort, but all he could see when he closed his eyes was that damn photo of Maggie lying like a rag doll on the floor in front of the clubhouse door.

"Hey, I heard what happened." Barrett busted into the waiting room. "Tori and Frey wanted to come, but Alex and Holt made them stay at the resort. I promised them I'd see how Maggie was doing."

Mark stood and shook Barrett's hand. "Thanks for coming. I appreciate it. They took her in the back to run some tests and check her for any internal bleeding." Mark sat back down and rested his head against the wall, closing his eyes.

Barrett faced Thunder. "Thunder, Isa is at Sarah's. Grayhorse went to get her. He didn't want her to be home alone."

"Thank you for letting me know." Thunder stood and slapped Barrett's shoulder. "I texted her an update when Maggie was taken for her scans. I'm glad she did what I asked her to do for once. I knew Grayhorse would go get her if she called him. I don't want her driving when she's so upset."

"Hey." Thunder sat next to Mark and gripped his shoulder. "She's gonna be okay. She's a tough little cookie."

"Yeah, but you didn't see her unconscious laying on the floor like a rag doll. Those assholes treated her like trash, man," Mark mumbled.

"I know seeing her like that is killing you, but you've got to get that image out of your head," Thunder mumbled. "She needs you right now and Maggie isn't the type of girl that likes to be pitied."

"I don't pity her." Mark opened his eyes and clenched his teeth. "I want to fucking kill them."

"What image?" Barrett looked between them. "What are you guys talking about?"

"I saw an image of how Lucifer's Renegades left Maggie at the Los Lobos clubhouse, and I can't get the fucking picture out of my head." Mark closed his eyes and dropped his head. "I hate they got to her and terrorized her. What kind of man does that to a woman?"

"One-percenter motorcycle clubs are a different breed," Barrett sighed. "They're all about an eye for an eye. Lucifer's Renegades are the worst of the worst. Los Lobos may not be perfect, but I don't think they're involved in human trafficking. But the LR's don't believe in anything. They have no rules and no morals. Shit, look at what they did to Tori."

"You're right. I just want Maggie to come through this okay–mentally and physically." Mark took a deep breath. The thought of this breaking his sassy Maggie broke his heart. "Hell, I hate to say it, but I hope José and his brothers teach the LR's a lesson," Mark mumbled.

"Don't let George and Sean hear you say that, or they'll be hauling your ass in for questioning." Barrett sat down next to Mark.

"Rival club business should stay between them. Their pissing match shouldn't involve innocent lives." Mark squeezed his fists. "The LR's should've picked on someone their own size, not some defenseless little girl."

"Don't let Maggie hear you call her a defenseless little girl or there will be hell to pay," Thunder chuckled and glanced at Mark.

"Yeah, you're right." Mark nodded. "This time, instead of kicking my balls, she might just cut them off."

"Wait," –Thunder turned in his seat to face Mark– "what the hell did you do for her to kick you there?"

"A misunderstanding," Mark grumbled. *Shit!* He never meant to tell anyone about that because it was after Maggie had spent the night at his house and woken him up with the best blow job ever. He did not kiss and tell.

"A big one, if she kicked you in the balls." Barrett also turned to face Mark with a smirk on his face.

Mark looked between the two of them, knowing they weren't letting up. Even though Barrett's look was amused, Thunder's looked like a storm cloud, which made sense since Maggie was close to his wife and his employee. He would tell them some of what happened but not the whole story.

"Remember that night when I told you and Isa that Maggie was sick?"

"You didn't tell me shit." Barrett quirked an eyebrow at Mark, but Thunder nodded.

"Well, she spent the night at my house." Mark shrugged his shoulders. He tried to pretend like it was no big deal. "She was sick from drinking too much and I wanted to make sure she didn't choke on her own vomit."

"Okaayy, and..." Thunder crossed his arms. "Did you force yourself on her? Because if you did..."

Mark could feel the sweat beading on his forehead. He'd never been given the third degree from Thunder. Damn, the man could look intimidating when he was angry.

Mark held up his hands. "Whoa, whoa, I didn't do anything to hurt her. We had a misunderstanding. She got mad and kicked me—hard." Mark rubbed his sweaty palms on his pants. "Brought me down to my fucking knees and almost damaged my future lineage."

"Then I'm with Thunder." Barrett uncrossed his arms and sat back in his chair. "I don't think you can call her a defenseless little girl."

"Fine." Mark threw up his hands. "But according to her it was three against one, so she was defenseless and shit, she's not very tall and can't weigh more than a hundred pounds soaking wet. Right?"

Thunder waved his hand, dismissing Mark's comment. "I still wouldn't call her that to her face unless you want another kick where the sun don't shine."

"I agree with Thunder." Barrett nodded.

Mark shut up before they asked any more questions he didn't want to answer. He still remembered the pain and having to put a bag of ice on his balls. Damn, her bony knees were sharp as hell. Mark knew she must've fought those assholes, but there were too many of them for her to get away. He sure as hell wished Maggie or José had told him why they targeted Maggie. They already snuck up on her from behind once. *What if they went after her again?* He needed to protect her.

A nurse came into the waiting room and approached them. "Gentlemen, Maggie is in a room waiting for test results. You all can come back and sit with her."

"Thank you." They all stood up and followed her to Maggie's room.

Mark was the first to enter and kiss her forehead. "Hey. How are you feeling?"

"They gave me some meds, but my head is throbbing and my chest hurts." Maggie gave a slight smile.

"We'll wait with you until you get the results." Thunder grabbed Maggie's hand and squeezed. "I'm gonna call Isa and let her know you are okay."

"Thanks." Maggie placed a hand on her stomach. "Barrett, what are you doing here?"

"Tori and Frey wanted to come, but I told them to stay at the resort with Alex and Holt. If the LR's are up to no good, we need them both to stay safe. I volunteered to come and check on you." Barrett stood at the end of the bed.

Mark was glad Barrett came, even though he didn't know Maggie all that well. It would save him several phone calls.

"Hello, everyone. I'm Doctor White." An older gentleman in a white lab coat walked in looking at the clipboard in his hand.

Mark noticed Thunder turn his phone toward the doctor. He figured Thunder had it on speakerphone so Isa could listen to the diagnosis.

"I've looked at all of Maggie's tests and she doesn't have any internal bleeding." The doctor turned to face Maggie and held her hand. "Your body took quite a beating, young lady. I don't know how you managed to protect your ribs so well, but they are only bruised and will heal in about two to three weeks. Don't bind them because it can restrict your breathing. You will need to walk around, breathe normally, and cough when needed to clear any mucus from your lungs. This will help prevent any chest infections. Apply an ice pack to your ribs for ten to twenty minutes, two to three times a day for the first two days. This will reduce the swelling, numb the area and reduce the pain. Try to sleep upright for the first few nights. No exercise and take off work for at least a few days, but you can return when you feel better—no heavy lifting for at least a week. You do have a mild concussion, so I need someone to watch over you for the next forty-eight hours. Limit any activities that require concentration like reading, watching TV, using a computer, or playing video games. Take as many naps as your body needs and try to avoid loud noises and crowds. I don't recommend you stay in a dark room, but don't use bright lights. All these instructions will be in your paperwork, but call me if you feel dizzy, nauseous, or have extreme pain. I'm prescribing pain medication, but if you only want to take over-the-counter meds, that's fine—take ibuprofen. Do you have any questions for me?"

"When can I go home?" Maggie fidgeted with the edge of the blanket.

"As soon as I sign the release papers, I'll have a nurse bring you a wheelchair." The doctor turned, his gaze bouncing between Mark, Thunder, and Barrett. "Who is taking Maggie home?"

"I am." Mark, Thunder, and Barrett replied.

"I got this." Mark stood, held Maggie's hand, and stared at Thunder. *Had they not just had this conversation with Thunder?*

Thunder raised an eyebrow at Mark. "Isa wants her to come home with me."

"Tori said she would take care of Maggie," Barrett commented.

"Well, Maggie." The doctor turned to face her. "It seems everybody wants to take care of you. You are a very lucky girl." The doctor smiled and faced the boys. "Gentlemen, whoever wins this battle, please make sure she has someone staying with her around the clock for the next forty-eight hours." The doctor wrote something on her chart and walked to the door. "It was nice meeting all of you. May the odds be ever in your favor." Doctor White raised two fingers in the air and winked at Maggie before leaving her room.

"Funny guy," Mark muttered before sitting down and squeezing Maggie's hand. "Maggie, I can take you to my house. I have a great security system. I'll keep you safe."

"We all have great security systems, Romeo." Barrett crossed his arms and stared at him.

"Maggie." Thunder handed her his phone. "Isa wants to talk to you."

*** Maggie ***

"Hey, Isa." Maggie took Thunder's phone and clicked it off speakerphone. This was not a conversation she wanted the boys to hear.

"Mags, I heard what the doctor said. You can come home with Thunder. I'll take care of you."

"I don't want to put you in any danger. I could never live with myself if anything happened to you or the baby." Maggie rubbed her forehead. Just thinking about this was increasing the pain in her brain.

"You can't go home with Mark," Isa stated. Maggie looked up and stared at Mark, who crossed his arms and braced his legs for a fight.

"Why not?" Maggie didn't know why Isa sounded so adamant.

"Because if Tori is freaking out and Alex tells her to stay home for a couple of days, then Thunder needs Mark to help him. Please come to my house."

"I can't do that. I will not endanger you or the baby," Maggie said through gritted teeth.

"You won't be endangering Isa or the baby if you come home with me," Mark barked.

"Put me back on speakerphone," Isa insisted.

"Okay, everyone can hear you. I'm giving Thunder his phone back." Maggie sat back and glared at Thunder.

"Boys, I don't want Maggie to stay with Mark. Thunder, make it happen." Maggie, Mark, and Barrett all frowned at Thunder. Thunder's eyes widened and he shrugged. "Thunder will need Mark because he'll be short-staffed since Tori might not work for a couple of days. Maggie doesn't want to come here, so Barrett, can she go hang with Tori at the resort? You guys have good security."

"Yes, we can keep her with us. Tori would love to hang with Maggie," Barrett answered Isa. "She can't stay in Holt's old room because we're getting it ready for Bryce since Holt and Frey are adopting him. He needs to live with them before they'll let the adoption be final. But my mom redid Tori's old room if she wants to stay in her own space.

Maggie stared at Mark as he paced the room. She could tell he was angry, but didn't know what to say.

"Maggie," Isa spoke. "Are you okay in Tori's old room, or will that freak you out?"

Mark stopped pacing, placed his hands on his hips, took a deep breath, and stared at Maggie.

"That's fine. I've never been in that room before, so I don't have any bad memories." Maggie crossed her arms and glared at Mark. He was not going to tell her what to do.

"Fine. If I can't take time off, then she is better off at the resort where a lot of people can watch over her for the next forty-eight hours because of the concussion." Mark looked up and pointed at Maggie. "But on Saturday, I'll pick you up after work and take you to my place."

Who did he think he was, ordering her around? Maggie clenched her fists. "I can take care of myself."

"Like you did when they took you?" Mark snarled at her.

"Listen, Asshole Smurf, you need to back off!" Maggie yelled and leaned forward, holding her stomach and wincing when pain shot up her body.

"Isa, I'll call you back, Honey." Thunder disconnected the call.

"Okay, okay." Barrett stepped in front of Mark. Placing one hand on his chest and the other in a stop motion toward Maggie. "Back to your corners. Maggie, relax, I'm taking you to the resort. Mark, chill dude and go home."

"Barrett's right. Come on Mark, I'll drive you back to Maggie's apartment so you can get your car. Maggie, text your cousin a list of items you need so she can pack a bag for you. I'll drop it off at the resort after I go to Sarah's house and pick up my wife. She wants to see you." Thunder looked at everyone. "Are we all good?"

Everybody nodded.

"Okay, Maggie." The nurse came in with a wheelchair. "Time to go home. Whoever is taking her, pull into the circular drive of the hospital's front entrance. We'll meet you there. Now shoo, so Maggie can get dressed."

Maggie watched Mark storm out after Thunder.

"I'll meet you down there," Barrett mumbled before he left.

"Girl, that's a lot of good-looking testosterone." The nurse waved her hand in front of her as if she was hot. "Whew. Is one of them yours?"

"No, but one of them thinks he owns me and can tell me what to do." Maggie got up with the nurse's help and carried the scrubs into the bathroom to change.

"Don't lock the door in case you get dizzy," The nurse called out when Maggie shut the door. "Which one?"

"The brown-haired, hazel eyed one in jeans and a black t-shirt." Maggie wanted to say the asshole one, but the nurse hadn't been in the room when they were all arguing about who was taking her home. It had been a tricky conversation because wherever she stayed could put those people in danger. She loved her friends and wished she had enough money to stay at a hotel—away from everyone.

"Oh, he's a cutie. I saw the way he was looking at you."

Maggie stepped out and glanced at the nurse. "You mean the angry look on his face because I didn't agree to his plan?"

"Oh honey, that wasn't an angry look. That was foreplay. You kids today don't get that. You're too stubborn to see what's right in front of you. That man wants you." The nurse helped her into the wheelchair.

"You think so, huh?" Did Mark really want her? That night of the romantic date he'd just been showing her he could be romantic with any girl. She did give him a blow job and he had wanted to reciprocate before she incapacitated him. Ugh, that had not been nice. At the Dragon, he'd been looking out for her, but that's what friends do, right? Heck, he'd looked out for all the other girls until their boyfriends and husbands showed up. Her feelings were all jumbled up. She needed to stop thinking about this because her head was starting to throb. Time for more medicine and a nice nap.

"Oh, yeah." The nurse nodded. "And if I were you. I'd let him catch you and you guys could have angry make up sex." The nurse giggled.

Interesting conversation coming from an older nurse, especially when she giggled. The nurse wheeled her out to Barrett's truck. Barrett got out when he saw her and opened the passenger door. Maggie wasn't sure how she was going to get into his jacked-up truck. She didn't need to worry for long. Barrett picked her up and placed her in the seat. Reaching over, he grabbed the seat belt, buckled her in, and shut the door. Some girl would be lucky to date Barrett if this was how he treated women. It's a shame she wasn't attracted to him. Images of Mark flashed in her mind. Mark shirtless in the pool. Mark massaging her head and moaning while she went down on him. Mark's cologne. Mark's kiss. Maggie's face heated and she crossed her legs.

"Are you okay over there?" Barrett glanced at her and put the car in drive.

"Yeah, why?"

"Your face is all red. Are you hot?" Barrett moved the vents around and made it cooler in the truck.

"It must have been from the few minutes when we were outside." Maggie turned her head to look out the window. "I'm fine now." Was she, really? Taking a few deep breaths, she stopped thinking about Mark and started wondering how long this drive would take. She just wanted to lie down and sleep. The pain pills were kicking in.

"Okay. Don't forget to text your cousin so Thunder can get your stuff." Barrett focused on the road. "They are already on their way there."

"Right. I'll do that now." Maggie was glad George had brought her cell phone. He said they had photographed where it laid on the ground. Since no one touched it, it wasn't evidence. Pulling it out of the clear hospital bag, Maggie texted Nancy.

*** Mark ***

Dammit, Mark wanted to be the one to take care of Maggie but with Tori and Maggie out of work, he couldn't leave Thunder high and dry.

"I'm sorry I couldn't give you days off," Thunder said as they drove to Maggie's apartment for Mark to get his car.

It's like Thunder could read his mind or maybe it's because if it had been Isa, Thunder would've wanted to take care of her.

"I understand," Mark sighed.

"I have several important meetings these next two days that I can't miss, and I can't afford to close the cultural center again. Besides, the shelter kids are coming on Friday, and I don't want to let them down."

"It's okay." Mark rubbed the back of his neck. "I get it. Thank you for closing it today so we could take care of Maggie. Do you need me to go in after I get my car?" He didn't have Maggie so what the hell was he supposed to do to keep his mind occupied?

"Not necessary." Thunder rubbed his face. "We'll open up tomorrow at our usual time."

Mark nodded and leaned back in the seat until they got to Maggie's apartment.

"Thanks for the ride." Mark unbuckled.

"Sure. Mark?" Thunder turned to face him. "Are you going to be okay? You're taking this pretty hard. Was there something going on with you and Maggie I should know about?"

"No. Not really." Mark opened the door.

"You can talk to me. I won't say anything to anybody." Thunder rested his wrist on his steering wheel.

"I don't know what to do." Mark slammed the door. "I've never felt like this about any woman. One minute I want to make her my girlfriend and the next I want to strangle her. She's driving me crazy." Mark leaned his forehead on his palms.

"I understand that," Thunder chuckled. "I remember when trying to talk to Isa was near impossible. Shit, when she threw that damn rock threw my window, I just about lost it. But then we talked and got it all out in the open. Maybe you need to sit down with Maggie, have a nice long talk, and tell her how you feel about her."

Mark stared at Thunder and shrugged. "That's just it. I don't know how I feel."

"I think deep down, you do. You're just afraid to see what's right in front of you."

"Maybe." Mark sighed. "Do you think she likes me?" *What the hell am I asking Thunder? It's like I've reverted back to being a teen in high school.*

"I do. But the only way you will find out for sure is if you talk to her." Thunder squeezed his shoulder. "Give her these next couple of days with the girls and then go talk to her."

"Yeah." Mark opened the door again. "Thanks for the talk."

"Anytime. Us boys gotta stick together, or those girls will run circles around us." Thunder smirked and put up his fist for a fist bump.

Mark fist bumped Thunder. "True that, man." Mark got out and leaned down before shutting the door. "See ya tomorrow."

"Yup." Mark watched Thunder park and go to Maggie's apartment to get her stuff before he went to his car and texted Bryan. He needed to get Sky and get her home. Once again, he wished Maggie was with him and not at the resort. They could've watched a movie and talked. The resort was safe, though, and had a lot more people to watch her for the next few days. Mark was still beating himself up about leaving Maggie last night. Once he got home, he took Sky out to the backyard and played catch. Anything to distract himself from Maggie. When Sky started panting, they went back in, and he laid on the couch with his other favorite girl. He couldn't wait until Saturday to talk to Maggie and see how she felt about him.

Chapter 32

Great News!

Maggie

The next day, Maggie woke up to Thunder whispering to Isa. After she got back to the resort from the hospital, Isa and Thunder came over. Isa was worried about her and wouldn't leave. She wanted to take the first watch making sure Maggie was okay. Maggie wasn't going to turn down the offer, so Isa slept in bed with Maggie and Thunder slept on the couch. Thunder didn't want to leave the girls alone.

"Honey, I'm gonna go home, shower, change, and go to work. I'll come pick you up after work." Maggie squinted her eyes and looked over to see Thunder running his hand over Isa's hair as he woke her up. Ugh, she needed a Thunder. What a nice way to wake up.

"Okay. I think Tori and Alex are going to stay with her tonight. I love you." Isa ran her hand over his cheek.

"Love you too." Thunder kissed Isa so thoroughly Maggie closed her eyes and turned her head. She didn't need to see that. She already yearned for a love like theirs. Maggie felt Isa roll onto her back and heard Thunder say. "See you later, little one." Maggie kept her eyes closed until she heard her front door close.

"Wake up." Isa elbowed her. "I know you're awake."

Maggie rolled over and looked at Isa. "You are so lucky. It is so obvious how much he loves you. I am so happy for you."

"Yeah, he is pretty awesome." Isa beamed while she ran her hand over her belly.

"I'm gonna go shower." Maggie's ribs reminded her to go slow.

"Need a helper?"

"Not a pregnant one. The last thing I need is to drag you down if I slip in the shower." Maggie stood with the help of the nightstand. "I'll be fine as long as I don't make any sudden movements."

"Okay."

Maggie stepped into the shower and did a quick job of washing all the important parts. She'd wash her hair another day. By the time she was done, she was exhausted and sat with the towel wrapped around her on the bed.

"That was harder than I thought," Maggie sighed and dropped back onto the bed. "Ouch."

"What do you want to wear? I'll get it for you and help you put it on." Isa sat up and headed to her closet.

"Are there any men's t-shirts in that closet? Alex let me wear one of his last night and it was so comfortable."

"There's nothing in this closet except for your stuff. Wait here." Isa pointed at her. "I'll go knock on their door and get a shirt from him before he leaves for work."

Maggie wasn't going anywhere until she got some energy to move. Closing her eyes, she waited for Isa. It didn't take long.

"Okay. Alex was gone, and Tori wasn't answering. But lucky me, as I was standing out in the hallway pondering my next move, Barrett walked out. I told him our dilemma and he gave me one of his t-shirts." Isa held her hands out, opening the shirt. "Now you too can be a security officer."

Maggie raised her head off the pillow, wondering what the heck Isa was talking about. Isa held a medium gray t-shirt with the word 'security' in bold uppercase black letters. She smiled. "Help me up."

Isa helped Maggie sit up and draped the shirt over her head.

"Why are men's shirts so damn soft?" Maggie murmured as she undid the knot on her towel and stood up.

"I know, right?" Isa grabbed the towel, taking it into the bathroom. Maggie walked to the dresser and pulled out some panties, but every time she bent over, her ribs screamed at her. Reversing course, she tried dropping it on the floor and using her toes to put her legs through the holes.

"Need help?" Isa giggled behind her.

"This is so embarrassing." Maggie ducked her head.

"I'm your best friend. Don't worry about it." Isa grabbed her panties from the floor and pulled them up. "You can return the favor when I'm so big, I can't bend over to see my toes."

"Deal," Maggie chuckled. Isa also helped Maggie pull on some sweatpants. "There, better?"

"Much, thank you." Maggie straightened.

"Okay, go sit on the couch and I'll make you something to eat." Isa led Maggie to the couch, turned on the TV and gave her the remote. "I know you can't have too much screen time, so I found a movie we've already seen. Close your eyes and just listen."

Knock, knock.

Isa spun around. "Where's that coming from?"

"The adjoining door, you goof." Maggie laughed at her.

"Right. I forgot about that door." Isa walked over and opened her side. "Hey Frey, what's up?"

"I thought I'd come over with some nail polish so we could have a spa day." Frey held up a bag that looked to be overstuffed with products.

"Great idea. I'd love a spa day." Maggie perked up.

"I texted Tori. She'll be in after she showers." Frey headed to the table to lay out all her items. Announcing each one as she took them out of the bag. "I brought nail polish, moisturizers, face mask, and an eye mask."

"Wow, thanks Frey." Maggie smiled before she realized she couldn't bend over to do her toes, her smile dropped.

"What's wrong?" Frey looked worried.

"I can't reach my toes." Maggie whined.

"Neither can I for the time it takes to do my toes," Isa sighed.

"Not to worry. Tori and I will do your feet before we do ours." Frey shrugged.

"Is Tori going to be okay being in this room?" Maggie asked Frey. This was the room where Winston had raped her. She didn't remember the rape because he drugged her, but Maggie knew Tori had left this room and stayed with Alex right after it happened.

"I think so." Frey looked around. "My mom did a great job of getting a new bed and changing the paint colors and décor. Plus, Tori gets stronger every day. Being with Alex has helped her."

"Okay. I just don't want to upset her." Maggie was worried about Tori. She had seemed to be doing better, but that was before she saw the LR's at the cultural center.

"Frey, can you help me finish breakfast so we can all eat?" Isa asked from the kitchen.

Knock, knock.

"That must be Tori. I'll let her in and then come help you, Isa," Frey said on her way to the front door."

"Hey, who's ready for a spa day?" Tori shouted from the door.

"Go sit with Maggie while Isa and I finish breakfast. Did you remember the snacks?" Frey followed Tori, but detoured into the kitchen.

"I sure did. We can't have a spa day without snacks, right?" Tori put a bag on the table. "I went downstairs and raided RUSH. So, we have popcorn, chips, cookies, soda, and water. I didn't get wine because it's too early and half of us can't drink anyway."

"Good call." Isa and Frey came out of the kitchen with a plate of eggs, toast, and bacon. "Okay, let's make a plate and eat. Maggie, do you want to sit up here or do you want me to bring you a plate?"

"I'm coming," Maggie called, trying to stand without using her stomach muscles. Tori came over to help Maggie get off the couch. "Thanks."

"Of course."

"How are you feeling?" Tori helped her to a chair at the table.

"I'm better than yesterday, but still in pain. Can you all do me a favor for today?" Maggie looked at all of them. "Can we not talk about what happened? I want to forget and think about something happy. I hate giving those assholes the satisfaction of living in my mind for another minute."

"I totally understand." Tori nodded.

"I have great news." Frey prepared her plate and sat. All the girls glanced at each other with puzzled looks on their faces. Maggie thought for sure Tori would know Frey's news, but she looked just as confused as the rest of them.

"I have good news too." Tori smiled at everyone. "Frey, you go first."

"Holt and I are getting married on New Year's Eve and we're adopting Bryce," Frey blurted out.

"Oh my God!" Isa jumped up from her chair going around to hug Frey. "That is so awesome! I am so happy for you guys."

Maggie got up slower and made her way to Frey. After hugging her, she noticed Tori was still seated with her head down. Maggie nudged Frey and pointed to Tori. Frey stepped away from Isa and Maggie and squatted in front of Tori.

"What's wrong?" Frey grabbed her hands. "I thought you'd be happy for me and Holt."

"I am." Tori smiled but Maggie noticed her eyes were glassy. *Was she going to cry?*

"But?" Frey squeezed Tori's hand.

"Alex and I were going to get married on New Year's Eve, too. We were going to tell the family on Sunday. If I'm marrying Alex, how can you be my maid of honor?" A tear slid down Tori's face.

"Double Wedding." Frey stood up and pulled Tori up with her. "We'll have a double wedding. Right here at the new conference area my dad is building."

"Will it be ready?" Isa asked. "Thunder said it would be ready in January."

"I bet once we tell him, he'll have everyone working day and night to make it ready." Frey hugged Tori.

"Do you really think so? I don't want to take away from your day, but I would love for us to have a double wedding." Tori stepped back and looked at Frey.

"I'm positive. We'd be inviting the same people, and we could split all the costs."

"Sounds like a win-win to me." Maggie stood and leaned on the table.

"Let's do it." Tori jumped up and down clapping with excitement.

"Yay. We'll talk to the boys tonight and let them know what we decided." Frey hugged Tori again.

"Oh, a double wedding sounds so exciting!" Isa joined in the hug.

"Yes!" Maggie hugged them as well but when they started jumping as a group– "ouchie, ouchie!" –Maggie shouted and stepped back.

"Oh my God, sorry." They all said in unison and helped Maggie to her chair.

"This is gonna be great." Frey sat in front of her plate. "We can go shopping for dresses together, pick our food, flowers and cake. I can't wait."

"Do you think we can get it all done in three weeks?" Tori's eyes widened.

"Yep, the hardest part is the venue, and we have that." Frey smiled at Tori. "We'll sort everything out when we talk to the boys tonight. Let's do it together."

"Okay." Tori nodded.

"We will help you with anything you need." Isa pointed to Maggie and herself. "I can make your invitations, and we can have a bridal shower on Christmas Day."

"Can we do the shower the day after Christmas? Only because this will be Bryce's first Christmas with us, and I want to make it as special as I can for him and the boys." Frey spoke around a bite of food.

"True." Isa nodded. "Thunder's been working so hard on the getting the right gifts for his kids, that I would hate to take away their moment. This might be the best first Christmas for all of them."

"Let us know what he's getting. We can all chip in or buy them gifts from us." Tori took a sip of juice.

"I'll talk to Thunder and get back to you guys." Isa smiled. "I'm sure the kids would love to get several gifts."

"Oooh." Frey covered her mouth since she had just taken a bit of her food. "We can do it here. The Bridal Shower and the Christmas Celebration. Mom would love to host them both here. We can decorate the family living area out there." Frey pointed behind her. Maggie knew she meant the living space on this floor. "And the best part about having it here, we wouldn't have uninvited guests. We can have one of our security guards' stand at the elevator downstairs until all our guests arrive."

"I like that idea." Tori smiled at Frey.

"Ladies, a toast." Isa raised her bottle of water. "To Frey, Holt, Tori, and Alex. This will be the best double wedding the Rock 'n Roll Resort & Casino has ever seen. Many blessings to you all!"

"And, to the best Christmas Day the shelter boys will ever have!" Maggie knew those boys were going to be so excited when they came up and saw they each had several presents under the tree.

They all hooted and hollered as they tapped each other's water bottles. Maggie was so excited for them. A double wedding in three weeks. She didn't know how they were going to pull it off, but she would do anything she could to help them.

Their excitement flowed as they launched into wedding planning, totally ignoring the romance movie on the screen while they did their manicures and pedicures. None of the ladies let her do her own nails, Frey did her toenails and Isa did her hands. They applied the face mask but found it hard to talk about the weddings when it hardened, so they washed it off. The topic for the rest of the day was how to merge their dream wedding, guest lists, maids of honor, groomsmen, colors, décor, flowers, etc.

Maggie got wrapped up in their excitement. They had so many decisions to make. Someday, Maggie hoped to be marrying the man of her dreams like Tori and Frey.

Chapter 33

Tell the Boys

Maggie

*K*nock, knock.

"I'll get it. It's probably Thunder coming to get me." Isa came back with not only Thunder, but Holt and Alex.

"Hey, ladies. Maggie, I brought you dinner." Thunder held up a brown bag, then pointed behind him. "I found these two loitering in the hall." Thunder hugged Isa and planted a kiss on her.

"Hi, baby." Alex walked to Tori, gave her a kiss, and sat next to her on the couch.

"Hey, sweetheart." Holt sat next to Frey, gave her a kiss, and draped his arm around her.

"You guys are all so damn sweet." Maggie glanced at all of them, smiling. "You're giving me a cavity."

"So." Frey stood, grabbed Tori's hand, pulled her up, and walked to the side of the room facing everyone. "Tori and I have something to say."

"Oh, Shit." Holt elbowed Alex. "I'm sorry, man."

"It's not bad." Frey glared at Holt.

"Okay." Holt stood and slapped Alex on the shoulder to stand up with him. "Lay it on us."

Maggie was watching in amusement. The boys looked like they were going to be taken to the guillotine and the girls were smiling from ear to ear. Maggie grabbed the snack bowl sitting back to watch the show.

"Tori and I" –Frey pointed to them– "have decided we want to have a double wedding on New Year's Eve."

"Okaayy." Holt looked at Alex and pointed at the girls. "Did you know about this?"

"How would I know about it, if they just decided it, dumbass?" Alex slapped Holt on the back of the head.

"Oww." Holt rubbed the back of his head. "I'm not a kid anymore. I hate when you do that."

"Well, don't say stupid shit and I won't have to do it." Alex shrugged.

"Boys!" Frey yelled at them. "Did you hear what we said?"

"Yup." Holt nodded and stepped over to Frey, taking her hand and pulling her a couple steps away from Tori. "It's your day sweetheart. If you want to share it with your bestie, I'm okay with that."

"It's your day too." Frey held his forearms.

"Yeah, but we all know it's really about the bride." Holt hugged her and kissed her cheek. "I'll do whatever you want. I love you and I want to marry you. I don't really care who's there as long as it's you and me promising to love each other forever."

Maggie wiped a tear from her eye. Damn, Holt could be so fucking sweet. Then she watched Alex make his way to Tori with a huge smile on his face. He picked her up and spun them around, placing a big kiss on her lips when he set her down.

"Baby, I'll marry you any day, any time, and with or without anybody there. I think it's awesome you want to share your day with my sister. I mean, she can be a real pain in the ass. Are you sure you want to plan this with her?"

"Hey!" Frey shoved Alex.

Alex laughed. "I know you will both make beautiful brides. If that's what you guys want, I'm in."

"Congratulations!" Everyone shouted and they all joined in a group hug.

"What the hell's going on and why wasn't I invited?" Barrett said from the adjoining door.

"How did you get in here?" Frey asked him.

"Master key." Barrett held it up with a smile. "I was knocking, and no one answered, so I went through your room. Thank fuck you guys weren't getting it on."

"It would serve you right, asshole." Holt pointed at him.

Barrett shivered. "Not what I want to see, that's for sure. Anyway, what are we celebrating? I heard everyone yelling congratulations."

Frey draped her arm around Tori. "We're getting married."

Barrett pointed at them and squinted. "You and Tori. What am I missing?"

"A lot of brain cells," Alex murmured right before he smacked him in the back of the head.

"Hey! What was that for?" Barrett rubbed his head.

"No wonder you both understand each other" –Alex pointed at Barrett and Holt– "you're both dumbasses."

"Don't put me in that category." Holt pointed to himself. "I know what's going on and I also know that Tori and Frey are not marrying each other. That's just stupid."

"Really, man?" Barrett shoved Holt.

Maggie couldn't stop herself from laughing. They were like a comedy show when all of them were together.

"Boys! Knock it off," Frey yelled at them. "Barrett, Tori is marrying Alex and I'm marrying Holt in a double wedding on New Year's Eve. Isn't that exciting?"

"Will you be my best man?" Holt walked up to Barrett.

"He can't, he's mine." Alex shoved Holt out of the way.

"Oh shit! You guys are serious." Barrett's eyes bounced between Holt and Alex. "Fuck! I'm the Best Man for both of you at a double wedding. Damn, I'm good!"

"Maybe we shouldn't have asked him," Alex said to Holt.

"No take backs! I'm in." Barrett, Alex, and Holt bro slapped each other until Frey pushed them towards her adjoining door.

"Why don't we all talk about the details in our room." Frey turned around. "Tori, come with us. Maggie, Holt and I will watch over you tonight. We'll be back."

"Frey, I'll be okay." Maggie gave her a hug. "I'm tired. I'm gonna eat whatever Thunder brought me and go to sleep. I'll leave my door open just in case."

"Okay." Frey rubbed her back. "But holler if you need anything."

"I will." Maggie nodded. "Thank you for today."

"Anytime." Frey stepped through her door and turned to Maggie. "I'll come by in the morning."

Maggie nodded and turned to Thunder and Isa.

"So, what did you bring me to eat?"

"Isa said you like Chinese, so I brought enough for the three of us." Thunder unpacked the containers. "We'll stay until you fall asleep."

"I'll get the plates," Isa said on her way to the kitchen.

"Thank you both." Maggie hugged Thunder first and then Isa.

They sat down to eat. Isa made sure Maggie took her pain meds. A wave of bone-deep weariness washed over her, leaving her emotionally drained and aching. She barely listened to the conversation, picking at half her food. With her elbow on the table, she tried to cover her yawn with her hand.

"Come on." Isa stood and helped her up. "Let me take you to your bed. You look exhausted."

"I'll clean up." Thunder got up and packed up the food.

"Thanks." Isa helped Maggie into the bathroom.

Maggie half-assed brushing her teeth because standing on her own was zapping her energy. She was so fucking tired. When she walked into the bedroom, Isa had pulled back the sheets, and several pillows lay against the headboard. She couldn't wait to get into bed. Isa helped Maggie get comfy in bed, earning the title of 'best friend ever'.

"I was talking to Frey earlier and she and Tori are going to the cultural center tomorrow to hang out with the shelter kids." Isa sat on the side of the bed. "I'll have Thunder drop me off before he goes to work, and I'll work from here tomorrow."

"Are you sure?" Maggie stayed on her back. Lying flat on her back felt good on her ribs after sitting on the couch all day.

"Yep." Isa rubbed her arm. "Not a problem. I'll see you tomorrow."

Maggie grasped her hand. "Thank you. For everything."

"What are friends for?" Isa stood. "Good night."

"Night."

She lucked out in the friend category when she met Isa. What a crazy day. A double wedding sounded like so much fun. Her friends had done a fantastic job of distracting her from her worries. Tomorrow, she would contact her brother and check on him. She wondered if José and his brothers had already fought the LR's or if they were still planning their attack. Tonight, she would dream of her friends getting married to the loves of their lives and wonder if Mark would ever call her. She hadn't spoken to him since he stormed out of her hospital room.

Chapter 34

Family Visit

Maggie

By Saturday morning, Maggie was anxious for a change of scenery. The Panthers had a nice rotation schedule set up for sitting with her, but if she was being honest, she missed Mark. Who would've thought she would miss his snarky comments and flirtatious ways? She didn't know why he'd stayed away. He was probably still mad at her for not leaving the hospital with him. But if she remembered correctly, he said he was coming to get her today. She wondered if he really would come and get her, secretly hoping he would.

Maggie needed to get up and get ready. Her aunt Inez and cousin Nancy were coming to visit today. She was hoping they had news from José. Maggie tried to call and text him, but he hadn't answered. She was worried about him. Dragging herself out of bed, she strolled into the bathroom. Her ribs were still sore, but they didn't hurt as bad as when she left the hospital. Maggie looked in the mirror, turning her face to look at all the angles of her bruised face. The swelling was down around her eye, but it was still mostly purple and blue with a hint of green and yellow coming through. The doctor had told her it would take about two to three weeks to heal. She couldn't wait because there was no makeup in the world that could cover it up.

Taking a deep breath, she lifted her nightshirt and looked at her belly. Those were going to be the hardest ones to deal with. She could still see the words 'Next Time' with the arrow pointing down. The doctor told her the cuts were shallow and she might want to wait until they healed before she considered plastic surgery. He didn't think the faint, pale lines of the healed scar would be noticeable, but if they bothered her, he urged her to call him so he could recommend a skilled plastic surgeon.

Maggie shivered as she ran her fingers over the lettering. Feeling the slight bump of the letters like a paper cut from a cardboard box, she prayed Dr. White was right and she wouldn't have to live with a reminder of that horrible night. She wasn't against plastic surgery, but it wasn't something she wanted to have on her abdomen before she had children. Skin was supposed to stretch when you were pregnant. What if it didn't stretch because of her surgery and she hurt her child? Maggie wanted to have a family someday. Thank goodness it didn't get infected from the knife they used. She would take Dr. White's advice and wait until the cut healed before she did anything.

She enjoyed a long shower and washed her hair now that she could raise her arms without too much pain from her ribs. Finishing up, she got dressed and left her bedroom.

"Good morning." Barrett was sitting on her couch, legs crossed on the cocktail table, eating a bowl of cereal and watching TV. Maggie smiled to herself when she noticed his toenails were still painted.

"Hey. Nice toenails," Maggie chuckled. "Why haven't you taken it off?"

Barrett wiggled his toes. "Because I don't own the shit you girls use to take it off. Frey was supposed to help me out, but with everyone taking shifts watching your ass, she hasn't had the time."

"Yeah, it has been like Grand Central Station around here. Thank you. I do appreciate you all taking care of me." Maggie sat on the couch. "I thought Holt was staying on the couch today?"

"He was...I told him to go to his room with Frey. I'd watch over you," Barrett said between spoonsful of food.

"No daytime date, huh?" Barrett didn't date. He fucked around with a different girl every night or so Frey told her. He was a strikingly good-looking guy—romance novel cover material. Too bad she was so hooked on Mark. Then again, if Barrett was the love 'em and leave 'em type, she was probably better off. Eventually, she wanted to get married, have kids, and live happily ever after in a nice house with a white picket fence.

"Nope. I coulda, but I turned it down just for you." Barrett smiled, charming her with his dimples.

"You're such a charmer. No wonder the girls drop their panties for you the instant they see you." Maggie rolled her eyes.

"You didn't." Barrett quirked an eyebrow. "I guess my dimples don't work on you?"

"Nope. I know your one-night game and I ain't playin'." Maggie walked into the kitchen, grabbed a bowl, and poured some cereal.

"I bet I know why." Barrett winked at her when she came back and sat beside him, lifting her legs on the cocktail table next to him.

"Why?"

"Because you have the hots for a certain tall, dark, hazel eyed man with a cute-as-fuck dog." Barrett smirked, clearly proud of himself.

"Oh, yeah?" Maggie finished chewing. "Why do you think that?"

"Uh, your foreplay." Barrett glanced at her with a "duh" expression on his face. "Everybody's noticed."

Maggie stopped mid-chew. "What foreplay? What do you mean everybody's noticed?" Maggie set her spoon in her bowl and held it in her lap.

"The snarky names you guys call each other. Ya'll's body language. It's pretty damn obvious you like each other but haven't fucked yet."

Maggie pushed Barrett's shoulder so hard, he almost dropped his cereal bowl. "Shit! Are you serious right now?" Maggie gasped.

"Fuck, Mags, you almost made me spill my cereal. You know breakfast is the most important meal of the day."

"Cereal, really?" Maggie set her bowl down on the table and stood. Putting on her stern face, she braced her hands on her hips and glared down at him.

"That's all I had in my room. Give a guy some credit. I didn't want to leave you alone and go down for breakfast." Barrett shrugged.

"Thank you for that, but you're avoiding my question. Were you serious? Is that what everyone thinks? That Mark and I are flirting with each other?" Maggie watched Barrett unfold himself from the couch, so he could stare down at her.

"Uh, yeah." Barrett snorted before heading into the kitchen. "When is your family coming?"

Why had Maggie never noticed? Now that she thought about it, they were always messing with each other. Maybe that kiss at his house was real. She knew putting him in her mouth was real, she'd loved it.

"Mags?" Barrett hollered from the kitchen.

Barrett's voice jolted Maggie from her thoughts. "What?"

"When is your family coming?" Barrett was washing his dishes.

Maggie looked at the clock. "In about an hour."

"Okay." Barrett nodded. "I'll stay with you until then. Do you know if they're staying until Mark comes to get you?" Barrett looked up and smirked at her. "You know he's coming right?"

"What makes you think he's coming? I haven't heard from him since he stormed out of the hospital. And to answer your other question, I think they are staying until dinnertime."

"Oh, he's coming." Barrett winked at her, his dimple flashing into place. "In more ways than one." Barrett left the kitchen and dropped onto the couch, going back to his relaxed position.

"You're such a jerk." Maggie tapped his legs with her foot. Barrett moved his legs so she could walk past him to the kitchen.

"You know I'm right. That boy's hand must be tired by now," Barrett chuckled.

"Men," Maggie mumbled to herself. "They're like little boys. Everything is about sex. Like Mark is thinking about me all the time. Yeah, right. He hasn't so much as texted, called, or stopped by in three days. Probably forgot all about me and I'll see him next week when I go back to work."

"Don't be so sure," Barrett whispered in her ear, startling Maggie so bad, she jumped and grabbed her stomach. Her ribs were not happy with the sudden movement. Had she said all that out loud?

"Dammit, Barrett. You're as quiet as Thunder, put a fucking bell on," Maggie grunted.

"Sorry, Mags." Barrett slowly turned her around and stared at her. "I didn't mean to scare you. I thought you heard me. Are you okay? Need some pain meds?"

"It's okay. I'm just jumpy, I guess." Maggie ran her hand over her face. "Getting ready to take my pain meds now."

Knock, knock

"I'll get that. You get your meds." Barrett gave her a quick hug.

"Hi. We're here to see Maggie. Is this her room?" Maggie heard confusion in her aunt's voice. Aunt Inez had never met Barrett. Quickly swallowing her pills, Maggie walked into the hallway to greet her family and introduce Barrett.

"Aunt Inez, Nancy. This is Barrett. He's my friend Freya's brother. He works security downstairs in the casino but was gracious enough to stay with me until you guys got here." Maggie wanted them to know Barrett was a friend and not a threat.

"Hello, Barrett." Nancy shook his hand and walked in. "Where's the man that came to my apartment who was so worried about you?"

"He's at work." Maggie didn't want to throw Mark under the bus. Not sure why she was protecting him since the jerk hadn't even bothered to call her, but she didn't want to have to explain the entire story to her aunt and cousin.

"Come in, have a seat." Maggie hugged her aunt and led them into the living room.

"I'll check on you later, Maggie." Barrett opened the front door. "Let me know if you need anything."

"Thanks, Barrett."

"He seems like a nice young man." Her aunt quirked her eyebrow at her.

"If I wasn't married, I'd want to date him." Nancy threw in her two cents.

"Ladies, Barrett is just a friend." Maggie sat down. "Besides, he's a confirmed bachelor."

"Maybe not if he finds the right girl." Aunt Inez sat beside Maggie. "You know your uncle was like that until he met me."

"*¡Ay, mami!* No, not that story again," Nancy groaned.

"Have either of you heard from José?" Maggie changed the subject. No time like the present.

"No, *mi niña*." Aunt Inez shook her head. "You know he never calls me. I couldn't forgive him after what happened to your parents. Nancy, have you talked to him?"

"No." Nancy sighed. "Part of me wishes he would call so I know he's okay, but another part of me wants him to stay far away from us. It's bad enough the LR's know where we live."

"I'm sorry." Maggie leaned back on the couch and held her stomach. "From what I can remember, I think that was the first time they followed me. They know which apartment complex I drove to, but I don't think they know which apartment I live in."

"None of this is your fault, *mi niña*." Aunt Inez held her hand. "José should've never gotten involved with that club."

"This wasn't José's fault. It wasn't his club that hurt me." Maggie would always defend her brother even though, deep down, she knew what her aunt was saying was right. If José had never joined Los Lobos, her parents would be alive, and she would not have been taken and beaten.

"It wasn't his club, but it is his fault because he joined a motorcycle club. All this time, I thought you were safe with our last name and changing your name from Margarita to Maggie." Aunt Inez squeezed her hand. "We let you down. We should've moved to another state or put you in witness protection like the police suggested."

"No, *tía*." Maggie pulled her hand away. "I never would have wanted to move to another state or gone into the protection program. I wouldn't have been able to see you, *tío*, Nancy, or José ever again. That would've broken me. I'm glad I'm still here. They will be arrested, and I will be okay. I just hope José doesn't get arrested or shot by doing something stupid."

"I hope so too." Aunt Inez patted her thigh. "I brought you something special that I know you'll like."

Aunt Inez started digging around in her big purse. As long as Maggie could remember, Aunt Inez carried a purse as big as a medium sized suitcase. Maggie didn't know how the strap didn't hurt her shoulder. The thing must weigh a ton.

"I brought you your favorite," Aunt Inez said before taking out a box of pastries from her favorite pastry shop in Miami.

"Oh wow, a *pastelito de guayaba*." Maggie beamed as Aunt Inez gave her the pastry. "I love you, *tía*. You just made my day."

"I know what you like." Aunt Inez gave her the pastry and went into the kitchen to get a plate. Maggie made sure to suck up every crumb as the pastry fell apart in her hands. By the time Aunt Inez came back with a plate, the pastry was almost gone.

Aunt Inez laughed. "I'll bring you another one. What do you want?"

"What did you bring," Maggie stuffed the last bite into her mouth.

"I also brought a *pastelito de guayaba y queso*, *empanada de pollo*, *croqueta*, and a *capuchino* (the Cuban pastry not the Italian coffee)."

Maggie was in heaven. "Can you bring me the *capuchino* and put the rest in the fridge?"

"Si." Aunt Inez walked the box over and placed the yummy treat on her plate.

Maggie loved *capuchinos*. The sweet treat melted in her mouth and reminded her of her childhood with her parents. She missed her parents but was glad they were spared from seeing what happened to her.

Everyone sat down to eat. Aunt Inez wanted to know exactly what happened to her although Maggie spared her some parts–the carving into her skin. They left after lunch. It was great to see them and be able to talk to them. They had always treated her like their daughter.

Knock, knock.

Maggie didn't know who would be coming at this time. She checked the peephole and saw a very sweaty Barrett.

"Hey. What are you doing here?" Maggie opened the door to let him in.

"Mom called and said your family left. I just finished working out and wanted to tell you that I'll go shower and come back." Barrett wiped sweat off his face with his towel.

"You don't have to." Maggie knew she was staring at Barrett's tight abs and forced herself to look up.

"I am not leaving you alone on my watch." Barrett smirked. "I'll be back in ten. Keep your door locked."

"Hey, since you're going to your room, can I borrow another one of your security t-shirts? They're more comfortable than mine." Maggie would love to get out of the outfit she had on for a big t-shirt, no bra, and her pajama pants.

"Sure. I'll bring you one. See ya in a few." Barrett left and headed to his room.

"Hey, Barrett." Maggie called out, stopping Barrett in his tracks. Barrett turned around. "When you come back, use your key and come in. I'm gonna relax on the couch. My stomach is a little sore from sitting up."

"You got it." Barrett waved and continued to his room.

Maggie shut her door and took a deep breath. Damn, he was a fine specimen of a man. *Why couldn't she like him instead of Mark? Barrett wasn't always scowling at her and calling her snarky names.* Unfortunately, her body didn't have the same effect it had when she looked at Barrett as when she looked at Mark. One look from Mark and she was instantly wet and craving his touch. Barrett was just a friend. Maggie went back to the couch and laid down.

"It's me," Barrett called out when he walked in.

"That was fast." Maggie got up and froze when she saw Barrett with only a towel around his waist and a t-shirt in his hand. "What are you doing?"

"I thought you might want to change since you were uncomfortable, so I brought you one of my shirts before I jumped in the shower." Barrett held it out for her to take it. "Go change and when you're done, I'll go."

"Oh, thanks." Maggie took the shirt and hightailed it to the bedroom to change.

"I'm good now." Maggie found Barrett still standing in the hallway. "Thanks."
Knock, knock.

Maggie kept walking toward the door.

"Whoa." Barrett turned and wrapped his arms around Maggie's waist from behind as she opened the door. "Maggie, you didn't even look through the damn peephole." Barrett growled, pulling her back toward his chest and trying to slam the door shut.

Unfortunately, the door was pushed open by her guest–Mark. If looks could kill, Barrett and Maggie would both be dead.

Chapter 35

Get My Girl Back

Mark

After putting in a full day at work, Mark was ready to take Sky, get Maggie, and go home. Maggie had only been working with him for about a week before the incident, but these last few days without her had been boring. He missed her snarky comments and fun banter. Who would've thought Maggie would be the head strong woman that would twist him all up inside? Hell, she hadn't even called him these past few days after he stormed out of her room. *Didn't she want to know why he was mad? That her decision had hurt him.*

He was giving her space, and fuck if she wasn't taking it. Part of him had hoped she would miss him enough to contact him. Nope, not his Maggie, she would stand alone and take on the world if she had to. Well, enough was enough, he was getting her back today—no one was stopping him. The cultural center closed in ten minutes and then he was off until Tuesday. Once Maggie was with him, he had two whole days to relax and help her get better.

"Hey." Mark heard Thunder coming up behind him. "Are you going to get Maggie?"

"Yup. I told her I was coming today." Mark spun around in his chair. "I promise my house is secure and I'll be with her every minute of the day. Knowing Maggie, she'll want to come to work on Tuesday and I'll bring her if she feels up to it."

"I'm sure she'll come on Tuesday." Thunder bent down to pet Sky. "Isa told me she's going stir crazy and her ribs are feeling better."

"I figured as much."

"I haven't seen any bikers in the past couple of days, have you?" Thunder was usually in his back office, but these last couple days without Tori, he'd spent more time at the lobby desk.

"No, I haven't, and I hope they don't ever come back." Mark sighed. "Not sure if Los Lobos has made their move yet either. I know I have their numbers, but I really don't want to contact them if I don't need to."

"Yeah, I get that. Take it easy when you talk to Maggie. I know you guys tend to set each other off. Don't go all caveman on her when you go pick her up." Thunder looked at Mark while he was petting Sky.

"I know," Mark sighed. "I'm gonna be on my best behavior. I'm even bringing Sky with me."

"Good Luck." Thunder stood. "Ready to go?"

"Yup." Mark grabbed his keys and stood, following Thunder out the door.

Thunder set the alarm and they walked to their trucks. "Have a good weekend. Call me if you need anything."

Mark opened his door to let Sky jump in and turned to Thunder. "I will. Thank you." Thunder waved. Mark got in and headed toward the resort.

"Sky, I hope this works because these last few days have made me realize I miss her."

Sky barked from the passenger front seat.

"You miss her too, right?"

Sky barked again.

"Yeah, we're gonna go get her and I'll need your help."

Sky laid down and covered her snout with her paw.

"I know it's not gonna be easy, I should have at least texted her over the last couple days. We might have to do some groveling, but I think we can do it."

Sky sat up straight, tail wagging.

"We got this, girl." Mark petted Sky's head before she jumped into the backseat to lay down.

"I'm gonna walk in, apologize, and ask her to come with me. She will agree. I'll even help her pack her bags so we can be home within the hour. Once I get her settled, we'll watch some TV or whatever she wants to do. I'll grill some steaks for dinner, and we'll go to bed early—my bed. I'll hold her close, so she feels safe and get a good night's sleep. Right girl?" Mark heard a snore and glanced at the backseat. Sky was dead asleep. Guess talking time was over. He'd let Sky sleep until they arrived at the resort, then she was coming with him as his wing-dog. Who could say no to her sweet face?

Sky woke up as soon as Mark parked the car and opened her door.

"Come on, girl. Time to eat crow," Mark mumbled.

Sky jumped out and followed Mark into the lobby. He knew without a key he couldn't get up to Maggie's room, so he walked to the lobby desk and was grateful when he saw Sehoy.

"Mark, how are you?" Sehoy immediately came around for a hug. "Oh, Sky. I've heard so much about you." Sehoy bent down to pet her. Sky's tail wagged like windshield wipers at their highest speed.

"I'm good. How are you?"

"She's beautiful Mark." Sehoy finally stood and sighed. "I'd be better if those motorcycle clubs would stop picking on my family."

"Yeah. Me too." Mark nodded. "Can I go up to see Maggie?" Mark held his breath. What if Maggie had told everyone she didn't want to see him?

"Absolutely. Let me get you a key to her room so you can use the elevator." Sehoy pointed a finger in his face. "But you must promise me you won't use the key to get into her room. You will knock, young man."

"I promise." Mark placed his hand over his heart. Sehoy didn't know, but he had already decided to knock. If he pissed off Maggie, she'd never go with him. Plus, if he just entered her room with a key, there would be hell to pay. The last thing he wanted was another one of her kicks to the groin.

Sehoy handed him the key and he rode the elevator to the family floor, praying the whole time that Maggie wouldn't kick him out. Once he reached her door, he pocketed the key and knocked. The door swung open then back closed. Mark put his hand out and pushed it open again.

"What the fuck is going on?" Mark stared at Maggie's shirt which looked to be one of Barrett or Holt's security shirts. Not only was she wearing one of their shirts, her tits were swinging free under it. The next thing he noticed was Barrett in a towel behind her with his arms around her waist.

"This is not what it looks like." Maggie shook her head and elbowed Barrett. Unfortunately, that little move dislodged his towel and now Barrett was standing naked behind her.

"Oh shit," Barrett grumbled and bent down to grab the towel to cover his family jewels.

"What are you doing here?" Maggie tilted her head. "You're supposed to be at work for another two hours."

"I bet you would like that, Slutty Smurfette." Mark growled. "Did you fuck Barrett and take his shirt?"

"Asshole!" Maggie's hand flew out and slapped Mark across his face hard enough to leave a red mark.

"Hey, hey." Barrett grabbed the knot on the towel at his waist with one hand and pulled Maggie behind him with the other. "Nothing is going on. Mark, come on man, I would never take your girl."

"I. Am. Not. His. Girl." Maggie enunciated.

"Clearly." Mark braced his hands on his hips and leaned into Barrett while looking at Maggie behind him and screamed. "My girl would not be fucking another guy!"

"Ugh!" Maggie threw up her arms. "You are such a dick!" Maggie tried to step around Barrett to hit Mark again.

"Both of you, stop." Barrett grabbed Maggie's bicep and pulled her into the living room.

"Ouch!" Maggie shouted and Barrett released her arm.

"Let her go, fucker!" Mark followed them and pushed Barrett.

"You know what?" Barrett turned and faced them both. "Mark, nothing fucking happened. Maggie, calm the fuck down. You two need to figure your shit out. I'm outta here." Barrett bent at the waist to pet Sky. "Hey girl. If I were you, I'd stay away from them. They're both batshit crazy right now."

Mark watched Barrett storm out and slam the door.

"What is wrong with you?" Maggie crossed her arms and stared at him.

"What the fuck are you wearing?" Mark mimicked her stance and tried not to stare at her tits which were now resting on her arms with her nipples standing at attention.

"Barrett's shirt." Maggie narrowed her eyes at him. "Why do you care?"

"Pack your shit and let's go." Mark wasn't in the mood for this shit. "Leave that damn shirt. If you want a man's shirt, I'll give you one of mine when we get home."

Maggie smirked with an evil look in her eye. Oh shit, that did not look like a compliant expression. *What is she up to?* Mark didn't have to wait long. Before his next thought, Maggie whipped off the shirt and threw it over her shoulder onto the couch. Standing with her arms on her hips, she pushed her chest out.

"Is this better?" Maggie quirked her eyebrow. "Are you happy now?"

Oh, fuck! Mark had not expected her to take off the shirt in front of him like that. He thought she would go into her bedroom and change. But the view...was fucking fantastic. Maggie had the most perfect set of tits he'd ever seen. Mark's mouth watered and he cleared his throat.

"Please, go put on a shirt." Mark's voice croaked.

"Cat got your tongue?" Maggie smirked.

"You're gonna have my tongue in a minute if you don't go put on a fucking shirt, Miss Sassy Pants." Mark looked up from her tits. Maggie turned to get the shirt back from the couch.

"Not that fucking shirt." Mark came up behind her, placed his hands on her hips, guiding her to the bedroom before he gave her a slight push and closed the door. *Fuck me!* It had taken all his willpower to not ravage her. Mark looked down and squeezed the bridge of his nose. "We're leaving in twenty," Mark hollered before he sat on the couch next to Sky.

"Fuck, Sky." Mark leaned back and closed his eyes. "How did my plan go so wrong so fast?"

Sky whined and placed her head in his lap.

"I had it all worked out, but she just had to open the damn door in another man's shirt...with the man, naked, behind her." Mark wiped his face before laying his hand on Sky's head. "I know nothing happened, but at that moment, all I saw was red. Shit, Sky, now I need to apologize to her and Barrett. Why am I always having to apologize? Maybe Maggie should stay with someone else."

Sky groaned and nudged his thigh when he heard the bedroom door open.

Mark stood and turned to face Maggie. "Where's your suitcase?"

*** Maggie ***

"I'm not going anywhere with you, Surfer Smurf." Maggie walked past him into the kitchen.

"What?" Mark followed her.

"I said–" Maggie grabbed a bottle of water from the fridge.

"I heard what you said." Mark interrupted her. "This isn't a pet friendly hotel. I can't stay here with Sky, so let's go."

"I'm sure the Panther's would make an exception for you, but it doesn't matter because you don't need to stay here at all." Maggie took a big gulp of water.

"Mags, I don't have time for your shit right now." Mark leaned against the counter, staring at her. "I'm tired and I want to go to bed."

"Who's stopping you? Get the fuck out and go to bed." Maggie pointed toward the door. "I don't have time for your shit either."

Maggie watched Mark turn around and walk out of the kitchen. *Why were they so volatile when they came together?* She did want to leave with Mark, but when he came in all judgy, she snapped. Maggie didn't want Mark leaving angry, so she set her water on the counter and resolved to talk to him.

"Mark, wait." Maggie left the kitchen, but he wasn't by the door. Had he left already? Maggie turned and saw Sky still sitting on the couch. Where was Mark? Maggie walked toward Sky when she saw him out of the corner of her eye coming out of the closet with her clothes.

Maggie stormed to her bedroom and held the doorframe. "What are you doing?" Mark was shoving all her clothes into her bag. She knew what he was doing, she didn't know why he was acting so alpha male. He was usually so laid back.

"I'm packing up your shit, Miss Stubborn." Mark looked up and pointed at her. "You're coming with me. You can either walk beside me or I'll pick your ass up and carry you out. But I warn you, if I drop you over my shoulder fireman style, your ribs are going to hurt."

"Mark." Maggie was tired of fighting and her head was throbbing. She walked up and blocked him from entering her closet again. "Please stop. My head hurts and I don't have the energy to fight with you." Maggie rubbed her forehead.

"Is this a trick?" Mark took a step back. "Are you going to kick me in the groin again?" Mark cupped his manhood.

"No. I'm not," Maggie sighed. "If I'm being honest, I want a change of scenery and I want to go to work on Tuesday. You're my best shot and my ride."

"Okaayy." Mark didn't look convinced.

"I promise I'm not going to kick you." Maggie spun around and walked into her closet.

"Stop, Mags." Mark came up behind her and placed his hands on her shoulder. "Go sit on the couch. I'll finish your packing. Do you need some pain meds?"

"Yes, please." Maggie left the closet for the couch. Sky shifted on the couch when Maggie laid down. "It's okay, Sky. You can lay with me." Maggie patted her thigh and Sky laid her head on Maggie's legs.

"Here, take these." Mark brought Maggie her water bottle and the pain pills. "Sky, down."

Maggie sat up and placed her hand on Sky's head. "No, Sky can stay with me. It's okay," Maggie said before she took her pills. "Thank you."

"Do you want to take a nap?" Mark took the water back. "We can leave after that."

"No. I'd rather get going. Just let me know when you're ready." Maggie closed her eyes. "Can you also get the pastry box in the fridge?"

"Of course," Mark murmured.

*** Mark ***

Mark packed everything up and helped Maggie downstairs to his truck because the pills had made her sleepy. Once they got home, Mark carried her to his room and tucked her into his bed.

"Sky, stay with Maggie." Mark patted the bed. Sky jumped on the end of the bed and curled up facing the bedroom door, ready to protect Maggie. "Good girl."

Mark went into the kitchen to find something to make them for dinner. He was going to cook a steak, but then changed his mind. The last time they had steaks had been a weird night and he didn't want a repeat. He had plenty of chicken in the freezer that he could defrost and cook with a side of broccoli. It would be healthy and not too heavy. He would ask her during dinner what she liked to eat and go to the grocery store if she chose something he didn't have at home.

Setting the package of chicken in a bowl of water to defrost, he went into his living room to watch TV until Maggie woke up.

Chapter 36

Getting to Know Mark

Maggie

Maggie rolled over and took a deep breath. Her bed felt so much more comfortable than she remembered. Sniffing her pillow, she inhaled a woodsy scent that smelled like Mark. Maggie's eyes popped open, and she sat up, looking around. *Was she in Mark's room?* The last thing she remembered was sleeping on the couch in her room at the resort. Sky turned her face and whined.

"Hey, girl." Sky came over and licked her face. Maggie laughed. She loved dogs, but her parents couldn't afford one. When she lived with her aunt, they couldn't get one because her uncle was allergic. Maggie rubbed Sky's neck and kissed her muzzle. "Thank you for taking care of me." Sky barked.

"Shit," Mark said when he entered the room. "Did she wake you up?"

Sky laid down next to Maggie with her tongue hanging out of the side of her mouth.

"No." Maggie chuckled and rubbed her belly. "It's hard to believe she can be so vicious when she is laying like this."

"Yep." Mark tapped his thigh. "Sky, come."

Sky immediately rolled over and jumped off the bed, sitting at attention and staring at Mark.

"Are you hungry?" Mark patted Sky on the head and looked at Maggie.

"I could eat." Maggie scooted to the edge of the bed.

"I'll start cooking. Take your time." Mark turned to leave and stopped in the doorway. "Why were you wearing Barrett's shirt?"

Maggie saw the hurt in his eyes and decided not to be glib with her answer. "Because it was loose and soft." Maggie pushed her hair back behind her ears and noticed Mark go into a dresser.

"I'm not sure if you want to wear one of mine, but this one's soft and it will be big on you." Mark laid a t-shirt on the end of the bed. "I'll see you out there."

Maggie watched Mark leave with Sky. He closed the door on his way out. Maggie got up and used the bathroom. When she came out, she grabbed his shirt. He was right, it was very soft. She opened it up and read the words Big H Ranch with mountains above the words. Taking off her current shirt, she put

Mark's shirt on and immediately wanted to get back in bed. Then her stomach grumbled, and her hunger outweighed the comfortable bed.

She had to let Mark know she couldn't sleep in his bed—not with this nice Mark. It would be too tempting to curl up with him and use him as her pillow. It didn't matter how crazy they drove each other, she still wanted him. He made her feel safe. Unless, he liked her?

"What are you making?" Maggie found Mark in the kitchen with Sky laying on the floor next to his feet.

"Cooking some chicken. I didn't want to make anything too heavy." Mark flipped the chicken and turned to face her. The minute he saw the shirt, he looked at her face and smiled.

"What's the Big H Ranch?" Maggie pointed to the shirt.

"My family's ranch." With the tongs, Mark pointed to the island. "Have a seat. Can I get you something to drink?"

"Just some water." Maggie sat on a high stool. "Your family has a ranch? Where?"

"Montana." Mark poured her a glass of water and set it in front of her.

"What type of ranch?" Maggie took a sip.

"We're cattle ranchers, but also have chickens, goats, and pigs." Mark flipped the chicken.

"Wow. That's really cool. I've never been on a ranch."

"You've been to Grayhorse and Sarah's house." Mark grabbed some plates.

"Oh, you're right." Maggie stood. "Can I help you?"

"Nope." Mark set some silverware and a napkin in front of her. "You relax."

Maggie appreciated a man that was handy in the kitchen. Cooking looked good on Mark.

"How often do you go home?" Maggie would love to see Mark in jeans with a cowboy hat riding a horse towards her with his devilish grin.

"Definitely once at Christmas, but sometimes I try to go in the summer." Mark took the broccoli out of the microwave and added butter before putting it in a bowl next to Maggie.

"Do you have any siblings?" Maggie drank more water hoping it would cool her down from her sexy vision of Mark.

"I have a younger brother named Steve. My mom and dad are Janice and Frank. And to answer your next question, we are close. But I didn't want to be a rancher, so Steve runs the ranch with my dad." Mark put a plate in front of her with a thin chicken breast.

"How did you know I was going to ask that?" Maggie smiled.

"I know how you think, Nancy Drew." Mark tapped his temple and smiled back. Then he grabbed his plate, came around the island, and sat next to Maggie.

Maggie took a bite of her chicken. "This is fantastic. What did you season it with?"

"Balsamic Vinaigrette." Mark lightly shoulder bumped her. "Did you think all I could cook was steak on the grill?"

"Maybe." Maggie bumped him back. "But now that I know you can cook other things, I may just have you cook for me all the time."

Mark chuckled. "I can do that. Have you spoken to your brother?"

"No." Maggie sighed and put her fork down. "I'm worried about how they will retaliate. I don't want him to get hurt."

"Can you tell me why they took you?" Mark took a sip of water and turned to Maggie. "Please."

Maggie released a deep breath. She owed Mark an explanation. "When my parents were shot and killed, José went crazy and rode to the LR's clubhouse alone. He did a drive by shooting that killed three of their members. Los Lobos immediately patched him in and congratulated him for his bravery and craziness. That was the day they gave him his club name 'El Loco'. Both clubs continued this rivalry for the last eleven years. José was always afraid they would come after me. That's why I changed my name to Maggie and started using my aunt's married last name, Walker. I guess it worked until I forgot to tell José that I no longer worked at Teramar. That's when he got worried and showed up at the center."

"Do you think they followed him there?"

"I'm not sure." Maggie took a sip of water. "But he's beating himself up over that visit because he thinks that's what led them to me. And maybe it was, but according to what they said when they were hitting me, it was just a matter of time before they found out where I was. Apparently, the main guy beating me was the only survivor from José's drive by shooting."

"I'm so sorry, Mags." Mark reached for her hand and squeezed it. "I promise to keep you safe."

"I know you will try, but my brother said the same thing and look at me." Maggie pulled her hand away and motioned toward her face and body. "I'm not blaming him, it's just that the LR's are crazy scary."

"I hate to tell you this, but Los Lobos are just as scary. Hell, I wouldn't want to cross your brother or Machete." Mark sat back down.

"You're right." Maggie appreciated Mark lightening the mood. "I lived with them for about a week after my parents died and they are wild. Pretty sure I watched a drunken orgy until one of his brothers saw me and escorted me back into my brother's room." Maggie laughed.

"Drunken orgy, huh?" Mark raised his eyebrow. "I bet that was interesting."

"More like shocking. But even with everything I saw, they were all nice to me and tried to protect me from harm. I mean, I know they are into illegal shit, but at least they don't traffic women and children. I've always heard the LR's are heavy into human trafficking." Maggie's hand was shaking.

"Hey." Mark reached for her hand again and turned her toward him. "I won't let anyone take you again. You have my word. Let's finish eating and we can watch anything you want."

"Thank you." Maggie pulled her hand away and finished eating. She had to talk about sleeping arrangements now that they had a semblance of a truce. "I can't sleep with you."

"I didn't ask you to." Mark stood and carried his plate around the island and placed it in the sink.

"I mean, I'd rather sleep in one of your guest rooms." Maggie set down her fork and stared at Mark.

"No." Mark braced his hands on the sink and glared at Maggie. "I want to lay next to you in case you need something. I won't touch you, if that's what you want, but it will make me feel better if we are in the same room."

"You can't tell me what to do. I want another room." Maggie stood and carried her plate to the sink.

Mark stepped back. "I'm sorry Maggie, but it's still a no."

"I knew you were being too nice to me." Maggie pointed her finger in his face. She could not sleep next to him. She didn't have that much self-control. "I don't want you near me."

Mark flinched and dropped his head. "Okay, I'll sleep on the floor in the bedroom."

"Mark."

Mark held up his hand and left the kitchen. "I'm gonna take a shower. Watch whatever the hell you want on TV. Sky, stay with Maggie."

"Wait, Mark." Maggie felt like such a bitch. Here Mark was trying to help her and she kept giving him shit. *What the hell is wrong with me?* Did he want to touch her?

This was for the best if she wanted to keep him safe. If he hated her, he wouldn't make a move on her. She was bad news and would always have the LR's after her. Mark didn't deserve that. He deserved a woman who didn't carry as much baggage as she did. Really, she was doing him a favor—even if he didn't know it.

*** Mark ***

What the fuck am I doing? Being nice to Maggie isn't working. I'm not an asshole and I hate forcing her to sleep in my room, but I need to make sure she's safe. I can't do that from another room because all my other rooms are upstairs. The master bedroom was the only one downstairs. If Maggie had to climb stairs, it might hurt her ribs. He'd just sleep on the floor. It's not like he hadn't slept on the hard ground during cattle drives.

Mark undressed and stepped into the shower. The water was still cold, but that was good because his cock was so hard he could pound nails into the wall. *Fuck.* He had to find release so he could fall asleep tonight. Seeing Maggie in his shirt had turned him on like nothing he ever expected. He never lent his clothes to girls. One because he'd never get it back and two because of what it represented. Letting a girl wear your clothes screamed of girlfriend and forever. But somehow when he saw Maggie in his shirt, a calm feeling came over him. Totally opposite than when he saw Maggie in Barrett's shirt. The only reason he didn't rip it off her the minute he saw it was because he didn't want Barrett seeing her breasts.

What nice breasts she had. Mark grabbed his cock and began stroking it while he pictured Maggie's rosy, perky nipples on her perfect tits. Mark groaned. He would love to suck her tits and play with her nipples. Mark slapped a hand against the tile wall of his shower while his fingers spread his pre-cum down and around his cock. Increasing momentum, Mark knew he wasn't going to last long. A topless Maggie was a teenager's wet dream and like a teenager, he shot his stream against the wall as he growled during his release. *Fuck, that was intense.*

Mark cleaned his shower wall and finished soaping up. He prayed that would hold him over until tomorrow morning's shower. Mark usually slept naked, but not wanting to make Maggie mad again, he opted for a pair of sweatpants and a t-shirt.

"Maggie, did you take your medicine?" Mark said on his way to the living room.

Maggie was curled up on the couch with Sky. Her arms wrapped around Sky's neck. Sky lifted her head and looked at Mark, tilting her head. "It's okay girl. You can stay with her, but I'll carry her into the bedroom."

When Mark picked up Maggie, Sky jumped off and ran into the bedroom.

"What time is it?" Maggie mumbled.

"Time to go back to sleep." Mark whispered before he placed Maggie in his bed and covered her with his blankets. "Sky, stay."

Mark left the girls in the bedroom and went into the kitchen. He expected to find all the dirty dishes piled up in the sink, but the sink was empty. Opening the dishwasher, he saw them rinsed and ready to be washed. Huh, he had not expected that. Not that he thought Maggie was a taker and not a giver, he figured since she was mad at him, she wouldn't lift a finger to help him. But he was wrong because Maggie had done his dishes while he was in the shower. Maybe she didn't hate him so much. Mark grabbed a beer from the fridge and went to lay on the couch. A couple of hours on the couch had to be better than a couple extra hours on the floor.

He watched sports late into the night before he grabbed a pillow and blanket from his spare room and made his bed on his bedroom floor. Maggie and Sky were sleeping soundly. Mark was frustratingly awake, and it wasn't because he was sleeping on the floor instead of beside her. He couldn't forget the horrifying image of Maggie lying unconscious on the floor where the LR had abandoned her. He wanted to see if her cuts had healed, but if she was still mad at him, she would kick him in the balls if he lifted her shirt to check.

Mark kept tossing and turning on the floor to get comfortable. He quickly realized it was a stupid idea to sleep on the floor. There was no way to get comfortable. The last time he slept on the ground during a cattle drive, he'd found a patch of grass that somewhat cushioned his body. *What the hell was I thinking?* It's not like when he was a teenager and sleeping on the floor was fun. Especially when there was plenty of room on his comfy, king size bed.

Maybe he could slide in and stay on his side without Maggie noticing he was there. Hell, he'd even put Sky between them if it meant he could sleep in comfort. As thoughts of sneaking into the bed began to motivate him, he heard whimpering. Was that Maggie or Sky? It sounded like Maggie. Mark stood, walked to the side of the bed and waited to see who it was.

He didn't have to wait long. Maggie's body jerked as if she was trying to get away from someone. A strained, murmured plea escaped her. Sky whimpered, her gaze bouncing between Mark and Maggie like a spectator at a tennis match. It was as if Sky was telling him to help her.

Mark sat on the side of the bed.

"Maggie?" he whispered, gently running his fingers over her face and pushing her hair back. The sounds Maggie made were tearing his heart apart.

Thrashing her head from side to side, tears ran down her cheeks as she continued to murmur, "Please don't. Let me go. I'll do whatever you ask just don't hurt me."

Every word was like a knife piercing his heart. He had to wake her up slowly because Maggie was a fighter, and he didn't want to end up having to restrain her. The last thing he wanted to do was hurt her. Wrapping her arms around her abdomen, she rolled into the fetal position.

Mark went with his gut and slid in bed behind her, wrapping her up in his arms. Her head tucked under his chin. He ran his hand down her arm. Resting his head on hers, he whispered near her ear, "Shhh, I got you. You're safe." He said it a few times before her body tensed and she released a deep breath.

"Are you okay?" Mark murmured and kissed the side of her head.

"What are you doing?"

"I'm holding you. What does it look like I'm doing?" Mark smiled. "You were having a nightmare, and I wanted to wake you up slowly so I could someday have children, Killer." Mark hoped if he made a joke out of it, she would begin to feel like herself. Sure, she would be all snappy with him, but a snappy Maggie was better than the pain he'd witnessed on her face just a few moments ago. He didn't like to see her suffering.

Maggie took another deep breath and wiped her eyes. "Thank you."

Mark liked this Maggie. She was all soft and sweet. Afraid it wouldn't last long, Mark sat up and began to unwrap himself from around her before she found a new move to incapacitate him. "I'll leave you alone."

"No, wait." Maggie gripped his arms and turned her head to look at him. "Please, stay with me."

Mark would never say no to this Maggie. She looked so scared and helpless as she stared at him.

"If you're sure?" Mark lifted an eyebrow. "You're gonna remember this was your idea in the light of day, right?"

Maggie finally smiled and Mark felt the clamp around his lungs release. He could breathe again. "I'll remember you were only holding me to help me feel safe, Surfer Smurf."

Mark wanted to tell her he was also holding her because he cared about her, but she seemed so fragile and having a truce meant he got to hold her. This was a moment he wasn't going to pass up.

"Okay." Mark laid back down, pulled her tightly into his chest, and spooned her. Their bodies touched from her head to her toes. Who knew it would feel so right with Maggie in his arms? She fit perfectly. "Do you want to talk about it?" Sky was not to be left out. She curled up behind Mark's back and rested her head on his waist.

"Yes and no." Maggie sighed. "I feel like I should so I can release it into the universe and let it go, but it's hard to relive."

"I get that." Mark continued stroking her arm while his other arm was under her, holding her against him. "Do you want to try? I'm a good listener."

"First, I want to say I'm sorry for the horrible things I've said and done to you. I know you're trying to help me, but sometimes you know just the right button to push." Maggie squeezed his forearm.

"It's a gift." Mark chuckled before he kissed the crown of her head.

Chapter 37

Releasing My Night

Maggie

Lying with Mark in the dark and being held in his arms gave Maggie a deep sense of comfort. She hadn't felt like that since she was a little girl in her mother's arms. There was nothing sexual about his hug, just a sense of peace. She knew she needed to talk to someone about her fears and now seemed like the right time.

"I feel so stupid for letting my guard down."

"Darlin', you did nothing wrong." Mark rested his head on top of hers. "No one can live through their life always looking behind them. I'm proud of you for staying safe for so long."

"All I did was change my name. The LR's aren't that bright if they couldn't find me for eleven years."

"Let's be glad they're not the brightest bulbs on the tree." Mark chuckled. "But I'm grateful to the woman who came into the room and was smart enough to keep them from raping you. I would thank her if I could."

"Why?" Maggie was shocked by Mark's comment. "She let them carve and beat the shit out of me."

"I wish she had stopped that too, but you gotta know it could've been so much worse."

Maggie sighed, "You're right."

"Speaking of the beating, your face looks better. Not as black and blue, but more on the yellowish side." Mark's hand that had rubbed her arm glided over her face. "Does it still hurt?"

"Only if I press on it." Maggie grabbed his hand and held it. "Are you saying I looked like shit?"

"No, Darlin'. You could never look like shit." Mark pressed their joined hands against her chest.

"I like this gentle side of you, Surfer Smurf. Maybe I should get beat up more often." Maggie grinned.

"Fuck! Don't even joke about that." Mark tightened his hold on her. "I think I died a million deaths seeing you like that. I wanted to go out and beat the shit out of whoever did it to you."

"You'll have to stand in line behind José for that quest." Maggie exhaled and in a low whisper said, "I'm worried about him."

"I know. Believe it or not, I like your brother. Not that I want to be a member of Los Lobos, but I can respect how they took care of you." Mark's thumb stroked her finger.

Maggie turned her head to look at Mark. "Do you think they'll declare war on the LR's?"

"Yeah, Darlin'. I think they will. They've been rivals for a long time. They're not going to let this go." Mark released her hand and cupped her chin. "This isn't your fault. Whatever happens is the result of what started years ago."

Maggie blinked and turned to face Mark. "I know, but I don't want anyone hurt. I'm tired of this vendetta."

Mark held her face in his hand and stroked her cheek. His eyes roamed over Maggie's face, finally lingering on her mouth like he wanted to kiss her. If Maggie was being honest with herself, she craved his kiss. Gazing into his eyes, she whispered, "Mark?"

Mark's gaze rose to her eyes. Maggie could see his hazel eyes were more green than light brown and filled with what she hoped was love and a lot of lust.

"Yeah?" Mark released his breath.

"Will you kiss me?" Maggie reached out and touched his bicep. She wanted Mark. Only Mark could make her feel whole and safe.

"Are you sure that's what you want?" Mark closed his eyes. "If I kiss you, I don't know if I can stop from taking you and making you mine."

"Mark" –Maggie stroked his hair back– "I want that too."

Mark's eyes popped open, and he stared at her. "Be absolutely sure this is what you want, Darlin'. We will be exclusive, and I can be demanding in bed. Once I have you, I'll fuck you all the time."

Maggie clenched her thighs, attempting to ease the ache between her legs. "I can live with that."

Mark's hand that was behind her cupped her ass. His other hand released her face and lightly ran across her ribs. "Does it hurt here?"

Maggie knew Mark didn't want to hurt her ribs, but right now, somewhere else needed his attention.

"No," Maggie grabbed his hand and pushed it down to her pussy. "It hurts here. Will you help me and ease my pain?"

"Oh, Jessica Rabbit, I would love nothing more than to ease that pain. But first I need to taste those lips and your sexy mouth again." Mark leaned down and ran his lips over Maggie's. The tip of his tongue ran over her bottom lip before sucking it into his mouth. Maggie gasped, giving him the opening he needed to enter her mouth. His tongue possessed hers, licking and sucking every part of her mouth. His hand travelled from her ass to the back of her head to hold her in place while he dominated their kiss. Just when Maggie wondered what other tricks he could perform with his magical tongue, his hand slid under her pajama pants and panties until his thick finger entered her pussy.

"Darlin'," Mark groaned, "you are so fuckin' wet." Mark released her mouth, and Maggie took a much needed breath. Mark licked and sucked his way to her neck. "You're wearing too many clothes." Mark murmured against her neck and Maggie agreed. She wanted nothing between her and Mark.

Mark straddled Maggie and ran his hand to the bottom of her t-shirt, slowly pulling it up over her head. Maggie stared at him the whole time. She wanted him to know she was with him all the way.

"Did that hurt? Are you okay?" Mark threw the shirt to the side of the bed and cupped her face, waiting for her answer.

"I'm okay, Surfer Smurf. Ready to ride your wave." Maggie grinned at him.

Mark smiled. "Oh, you're gonna ride a fuckin' Tsunami, Surfer Smurfette." Mark's gaze followed his hands as his fingertips glided over her collarbone, down to her breasts. With his pointer fingers he drew circles around her areolas.

Maggie sucked in a breath and pushed her chest out. "I need more."

"Oh, yeah?" Mark twirled his fingernail around the tip of her nipple. "Like this?"

"More." Maggie grasped his forearms and attempted to push his arms toward her, but he was stronger than her and he was determined to work on his timeline, not hers. But she needed him to take her breast into his mouth and feel the roughness of his tongue on her nipple. "Please."

"Tell me what you want." Mark leaned down and whispered in her ear. "I'll give you anything you want."

"Kiss my breasts like you did my mouth." Maggie placed her hands on the back of his head, pushing it towards her achy breasts. They were throbbing for his attention.

"At your service," Mark said before he latched onto one of her breasts. He lavished it with his tongue and teeth before taking as much as he could in his mouth and sucking the hell out of it.

"Oh my God, how are you so good at that?" Maggie's body jerked. "No, don't answer that. I don't want to know how many tits you've had in your mouth."

Mark froze and let her tit pop out of his mouth. Raising his head, he stared at her. "Darlin', when we're in bed together, there is only you and me." The other hand on her other breast twisted her nipple. It was painful, but in a good way. She knew he did it to get her attention. "Look at me." Maggie opened her eyes and looked at his face. He was so serious and a little angry. "You hear me? It's just us. Got that?"

Maggie nodded. "Yes, I got it." He softened his fingers on her nipple and began stroking it. Maggie licked her lips.

"Good." Mark nodded before he lowered his head to the breast he'd been toying with, sucking it into his mouth. While he gave that breast as much attention as the other, he ran his hands under her pants and panties, pushing them down. Releasing her breast, he ran kisses over her ribs on his way down to her mound.

Maggie quickly placed her hands over her abdomen covering her wounds. She didn't want Mark to see where they cut her. *What if he found her ugly?*

"Darlin'." Mark looked into Maggie's eyes as he gently removed her hands. "Nothing on your beautiful body will ever make me think less of you. You should not be ashamed of what those cowardly assholes did to you. You didn't do anything wrong." Mark kissed Maggie on the lips.

"Please, skip over that area tonight." Maggie's eyes pleaded with him.

"Okay." Mark kept his gaze on her eyes. "Do you want me to continue, or do you want to stop?"

Maggie gave Mark a slight nod.

"I need words, Darlin'."

"You can continue." Maggie gave him a crooked grin. "I'm okay."

Mark scooted down and gave her several kisses from one side of her abdomen to the other, continuing down to her thighs, knees, and ankles. Giving each part of her body equal attention. Cupping the heels of her feet, he pulled her pants off and threw them toward the shirt on the floor. Holding her calves, he spread her legs and licked his way up one leg to her pussy. Maggie gripped the sheets. The anticipation of having his mouth on her pussy was driving her crazy. She craved his tongue.

Maggie felt him blow a breath on her open pussy before he widened her legs and laid down, holding them open with his shoulders. *Oh Shit! That was hot.* She could feel herself leaking out. He slid his hands under her ass, lifting it up to his face, his thumbs spreading her open at the same time his mouth sucked her clit. Maggie's body trembled and her back bucked up.

"Oh, God!" Maggie screamed out before she came.

"Not God, just me Darlin'," Mark groaned before spearing his tongue into her pussy and lapping up her juices. "Damn, you taste so fuckin' good. Shit, I need another one."

Maggie didn't think she could take another orgasm like the last one, but shit, his mouth was magical, and the pressure to explode was building up again. When she didn't think she could take it anymore, he slid his finger into her while his tongue applied pressure to her clit. "Mark, I've never come twice." Maggie was panting. Could she come again?

"Oh, Darlin', you can, and you will." Mark inserted another finger and reached her special spot as he curled his fingers, applying pressure. "Now."

Maggie's body spasmed and just like Mark promised, she came again harder than the first time. She heard Mark chuckle. Maggie felt like her body was run through the ringer. She felt the bed dip. Was he leaving her? No, not now when she wanted to feel him inside her. Maggie opened her eyes and saw Mark take off his clothes and put on a rubber. *Oh, thank fuck, he isn't leaving. Damn, he looks good naked.*

"Ready for me?" Mark licked her breast and laid his body over hers holding himself up by his forearms. "Darlin', you good?" Mark had a very cocky smile on his face.

All Maggie could move now was her head and she nodded.

"I think it's best if you're on top. I don't want to put pressure on your ribs." Mark rolled them over and moved her thighs around his hips. "Up you go." Mark pushed her upright on his hips. "Let's see what you got. It's your turn to ride the wave, Darlin'." Mark smiled.

"You mean this monster wave?" Maggie lifted her eyebrow and smirked. Reaching behind her, she grabbed him and positioned him at her entrance. At first Maggie was going to slide down onto him slowly, but seeing his cocky smile, she shocked some sense into him and rammed herself onto him.

"Oh, fuck!" Mark grabbed her hips and gritted his teeth.

Oh, yeah, that was the right call. Gone was his cocky smile, his eyes filled with lust and surprise. This was going to be fun. She was going to drive him crazy just like he did to her. Sitting up straight and throwing her shoulders back, she kept her eyes focused on his face, wanting to see his reaction. She ran her hands over her breasts, playing with her nipples as she rotated her hips, grinding her pussy onto him.

"Fuck, Darlin' you are so hot." Mark grunted and pushed up into her.

Maggie dropped down, placing her hands on his abs and lightly dragged her nipples over his chest while she kissed the shit out of him. Mark was gripping her hips while he thrust into her.

"Fuck. Maggie. Fuck me. Take my cock and get yourself off again. I want us to come together and I'm fuckin' close." Mark was panting underneath her.

Maggie wanted to keep torturing him, but she was craving him again. Sitting up, she grabbed his waist and rode him like a true cowgirl. She chased her orgasm, wanting it so bad, but not quite reaching it. Luckily, Mark could read her body, and he placed fingers over her clit and applied pressure. Maggie held on tightly and ground down on Mark as her body released the best orgasm of her life.

"Fuck!" Mark's body tensed before she felt him grip her hips and explode inside her. Pulling her body on top of his, one of his hands held her head against his neck and the other ran up and down her spine.

"Damn, Miss Rabbit." Mark rumbled. "I think you killed me. But what a way to go."

Maggie laughed with the last bit of energy she had left. "Ditto."

"Are you okay? Do your ribs hurt?" Mark massaged the back of her head.

"Nope. But I am sleepy now." Maggie scooted to Mark's side, but kept her leg draped over his thighs and her arm around his waist.

"Darlin', let me up for a second." Mark kissed her forehead and sat up. "I'll be right back."

"Mmkay." Maggie mumbled.

"Darlin', roll over." Maggie rolled onto her back and felt a warm washcloth between her legs. Mark gently cleaned her up. No one had ever done that for her. He was a keeper. She felt the bed dip next to her. Maggie automatically rolled into him, laying her head on his shoulder and draping herself over him.

"Good night, Darlin'," Mark murmured into her temple before he kissed her.

"Good night." Maggie squeezed him and melted into his body. She was safe with Mark and, if she was being honest with herself, beginning to fall in love with him.

Chapter 38

Man of Many Talents

Mark

Mark got up early and went for his morning run. He left Sky with Maggie which didn't make Sky happy at all, but he needed her to watch over Maggie while she slept. Mark knew Maggie liked to go on fun adventures. He wanted to get her mind off everything, but he couldn't do anything that would hurt her ribs now that they were finally feeling better. He needed to take her away from here to some place where they could blend in, and she could relax. Mark knew just the place.

After his run, he went into his bedroom and noticed Maggie was still sleeping. Sky raised her head and stared at him. If he didn't know better, he would think she was mad at him. Mark mouthed "sorry." Sky blinked and dropped her head back onto the bed. Well, maybe one of his girls would wake up happy with him. Mark undressed and got in the shower. Tilting his head back, he ran his hands over his hair and let the water run over his body for a few minutes.

Fuck, he couldn't get Maggie out of his mind. Last night had turned out better than he'd hoped. Never did he think Maggie would give in and become his. He could see her vividly in his mind laying on her back naked on his bed or touching herself as she rode him. Fuck, his girl was sexy as hell and giving him a hard on. Mark soaped up in a futile attempt to stop thinking about Maggie and calm his throbbing cock. He knew after having Maggie only she could relieve him, but he didn't want to wake her up. He could use his hand, but had a feeling that would only last a few minutes. What he really needed was Maggie. *Fuck!*

He tried thinking about the ranch, but an image of Maggie on a bed of hay popped into his mind. Law enforcement rules might work, but then he pictured a naked Maggie cuffed to his headboard. *Shit!* Mark rubbed his hand over his face. He needed something stronger–ice cold water. Leaning back, he shut off the hot water and gritted his teeth as cold water ran over his head.

"Oh shit, that's cold." Mark's eyes popped open and saw a naked Maggie trying to get out of the shower.

"Wait!" Mark's one hand turned the hot water back on while the other grasped Maggie's wrist.

"Why are you taking a cold shower?" Maggie shivered.

Mark felt the hot water pouring over his shoulders. "Do you really need to ask me that?" Mark raised his eyebrow and pointed to his hard on.

"How can it still be up and ready when you've been in here for a while in cold water?" Maggie gasped.

Mark was not superman and hated to burst her bubble, but he had to tell her the truth. "I was taking a hot shower and daydreaming about fucking you, because I didn't want to wake you up. I just switched it to cold, hoping to calm the fuck down." Mark adjusted the water temperature. "Come here. It's hot now and you're shivering."

Maggie let him pull her into his arms. Damn, she felt good. "Better?"

"For me yes, but that feels painful for you." Maggie reached between them and stroked him.

"Well, that's not helping." Mark closed his eyes. Her hand felt so damn good, but her mouth would feel better. As if she was reading his mind, she released him. Mark opened his eyes and watched her. Maggie winked and dropped to her knees.

"You don't have to." Mark said, but he hoped she would.

"I love your cock." Maggie smirked at him while she stroked him.

"I'm glad, Sexy Smurfette, because it loves you." Mark held his breath, hoping he didn't say too much. He didn't know if he loved Maggie, but his dick sure did.

"That's because I give it special attention," Maggie murmured as she licked his dick from top to bottom. The clincher was when she gripped the bottom and played with his balls.

"Oh, fuck, Darlin'." Mark leaned against the tile wall.

"What do you want?" Maggie grinned up at him.

"You really want to play this game?" Mark looked down at her.

Maggie nodded.

"I want you to place your sexy lips around my cock and let me fuck your mouth. I want my cock deep in your throat even if it gags you. Then I want you to suck me off until the last drop." Mark placed one hand behind her head, pushing her mouth onto him. Maggie was staring at him with her mouth hanging open.

"Too much?" Mark grinned.

Maggie shook her head, and she surprised him when she inserted two fingers into her pussy before lifting her hand to his face. His nostrils flared when he smelled the salty, tangy smell of her secretion on her fingers. His girl was turned on and ready for him. Gripping her hand, he licked her fingers and groaned. "Do not touch yourself. I promise to take care of you when you're done."

Maggie nodded and returned her hand to his cock. Mark's body jolted in pleasure the minute her lips took his cock into her wet mouth. With one hand on the wall and the other on the back of her head, he fucked her mouth until cum was dripping from the sides of her mouth and he was empty. *Oh, Fuck!* His girl really was going to kill him.

Mark helped her up and held her tight while he controlled his breathing. Now it was her turn. Mark turned them around, so the water ran over her hair and shoulders. First, he shampooed and conditioned her hair. Then he used the soap to arouse her, gliding his soapy hands all over her responsive body. Her nipples were so hard, it looked painful. Mark grinned and rinsed her body, then he dropped to his knees and relieved her throbbing breasts by sucking them greedily. He needed to taste her again. Mark licked his way down, but stopped when he reached her hands.

"Mark wait." Maggie had covered her belly with her hands.

"Darlin', I skipped over it last night, but you have to understand, I don't want you to hide any part of your body from me." Mark looked up into her eyes. "You're perfect for me just the way you are."

Maggie dropped her head and closed her eyes.

"Maggie." Mark reached up and cupped her face. "Those scars tell me you're a survivor, not a victim. Please, let me see?" Mark wanted to make sure they weren't deep because she needed to heal her mind as much as her body. He slowly reached for her hands and pulled them away from her abdomen. Maggie didn't fight him, which he took as a good sign.

Mark saw faint lines where the letters were, but the lines weren't raised or puffy. If, someday, she wanted it, he would gladly pay for her plastic surgery. Since he received monthly checks from his family's ranch, he had a lofty nest egg in the bank. He would gladly invest it in Maggie. As far as he was concerned, all the scars did was make him mad that someone had hurt her. Realizing Maggie was holding her breath, he had to let her know how he felt.

"Darlin', breathe. I'm more worried about your mental scars. You know you can talk to me anytime, right?" Maggie nodded. Mark was trying to help her heal. "These scars just make me mad at the LR's. They don't turn me off. I see them as a warrior tattoo my strong woman wears with pride because she is alive and with me." Maggie released her breath and smiled at him with watery eyes.

"Can I continue?" Mark was relieved when she nodded. Mark kissed every cut on her skin, his eyes focused on her face. He wanted her to see how much she turned him on. Once her eyes filled with lust instead of embarrassment, he continued.

Smiling sinfully, Mark pinned her to the shower wall and placed his hands on her ass, sliding her up the wall until her pussy was at his mouth. "Put your legs over my shoulders and hold on Darlin'."

"Oh, Shit!" Maggie screamed out before Mark felt her hands pushing his head into her pussy. *That's it*, he thought, *fuck my face Darlin'*. Maggie's thrusts into his face were coming faster and faster. She was so fucking close. "Darlin', squeeze your nipples. I got you." Mark said between licking and sucking her pussy.

"Oh, Fuck!" Maggie released her nipples. Her hands slapping the tile wall while her hips bucked into Mark so hard he was glad he had a good hold on her. She came all over his face and continued to undulate on him until her body finally gave out. Mark felt her body go limp. *Did she pass out?* Mark moved her legs off his shoulders and stood. Maggie was smiling and licking her lips like the cat that ate the canary. Except he's the one that ate her.

Mark couldn't help himself, he leaned down and kissed her. She didn't even flinch when she tasted herself on his tongue. Maggie was definitely the girl for him. Still kissing her, he turned them both and stood under the water.

"Are you good?" Mark smiled and brushed her hair away from her face.

"Couldn't be better." Maggie blinked and ran her hands over his face. "You have razor stubble."

"You don't like it? I'll shave it." Mark tilted his head. "I usually only shave on workdays."

"No, I like it. Don't shave it." Maggie leaned up and kissed his cheek.

"Done." Mark nodded. "I would like for us to get out of town for a couple of days. We could go to Wally World. What do you think?"

"I would love that." Maggie threw her arms up around his neck. "I've only been once, and it was a long time ago."

Mark loved seeing that gleam of happiness in her eyes. By damn, he was going to do his best to keep it there for a very long time. She deserved some joy in her life. Mark kissed her, then stepped out to get towels.

Chapter 39

Workday Nerves

Maggie

After two days of fun with Mark, Maggie was ready to get back to work. They had ridden only the rides that wouldn't put a strain on her ribs. Mostly they walked and enjoyed getting to know each other. They had come home late last night, but Mark still went for his morning run.

"Hey, you're up," Mark said when he came into the bedroom, dropping his shirt in the hamper.

"Nicc abs." Maggie wiggled her eyebrows.

"Thanks." Mark dropped his drawers and walked naked into the bathroom. "You know we don't have time for whatever dirty thought is running through your mind, Sexy Smurfette."

"Why?" Maggie got up and followed him into the bathroom. Now that they were making love several times a night, there was no reason to wear pajamas. They just got in the way. Lying next to his hard body was a temptation that was too hard to resist.

Mark was already under the spray, facing the water spicket when she entered the shower. "Because I like to be at work before we have to open. I like to be the first one there to check everything out."

"I can be quick." Maggie pressed her breasts against his back, reached around him, and stroked his cock, which hardened quickly. "See, he's happy to see me." Maggie kissed his back while she stroked him.

"He's always happy to see you, Naughty Girl." Mark groaned.

"Aren't you happy to see me?" Maggie dragged her breasts around his body and dropped to her knees in front of him, replacing her hands with her mouth.

"Fuck, Darlin'. I'm always happy to see you." Mark stepped forward so she wouldn't get a spray of water all over her face while she gave him head.

"Show me." His moans drowned Maggie's last words until he let his orgasm explode out of his body. Maggie loved to see him out of control. It was why she enjoyed sucking him off and riding him in bed.

Mark pulled her up and held her. "Thank you. I'll repay you tonight because we really need to go."

"Okay," Maggie chuckled. "Who knew you were such a stickler about getting to work on time?"

Mark released her and rinsed himself off. "You're right, I'm anal about not being late. But now I'm even more motivated to make sure the center is safe. I will not let anyone hurt you ever again." Mark faced Maggie. Cupping her face, he bent down, gazed into her eyes, and said, "You are too important to me." With a quick kiss, Mark released her and left the shower. Maggie put her hand over her heart.

Did that mean he loved her? Because she wasn't just falling for him, she'd fallen. Could they make it work? Alex and Tori were co-workers who lived together. They didn't work in the same area, but it was still the same place.

"Maggie, stop daydreaming, we gotta go." Mark stood outside the shower with a towel in his hand, shaking it at Maggie.

"Sorry, Surfer Smurf." Maggie rolled her eyes, turned off the shower, and grabbed the towel he offered.

"Am I ever going to get a new nickname?" Mark sighed.

"What do you want me to start calling you? Sexy Smurf? Eight Pack Smurf? Overprotective Smurf? Security Smurf?" Maggie dried off while Mark brushed his teeth, giving her a dirty look in the mirror. "Ooh, I know. Big Cock Smurf?"

Mark spit and wiped his mouth. "Never mind," Mark grumbled and left the bathroom to get dressed.

"You don't like any of my names?" Maggie hollered. She was met with silence, so she brushed her teeth and blowdried her hair. Maggie turned to leave and jumped when she saw Mark leaning against the doorframe with his arms and ankles crossed.

"Do I look like a short, big bellied blue man?" Mark quirked an eyebrow. "Now that I'm fucking you several times a night" –Mark pointed toward his manhood– "not even blue balls here. Can we just forget about Lucy's blue hairstyle?"

"Ooh, Snugglepot, are you pouting?" Maggie pressed her lips together in a pout as she walked toward him.

Mark squinted at her. "I'm not pouting. And what the fuck is a Snugglepot?"

"You don't like that one either, huh?" Maggie wrapped her arms around his waist and rested her head on his crossed arms. "How about Big Sexy?"

"Better, but what's wrong with the basics like honey, babe, baby, sweetheart?" Mark uncrossed his arms and pressed her hips against his.

"I'm not basic." Maggie got up on her tippy toes and gave him a quick kiss. "I mean, I don't complain about the names you call me, and some are quite rude, my naughty boy." Maggie grabbed his ass and pressed him into her.

"Do not start something we don't have time to finish," Mark growled.

"Okay." Maggie kissed his chest and pulled out of his arms.

"You're going to be the death of me," Mark murmured.

Maggie glanced down and saw the big bulge in his pants. Smiling, she turned and went into the closet to get dressed. Yep, he'd be thinking about her now.

Maggie finished and found Mark sitting on the island, waiting for her.

"Dude, let's go. I've been waiting for you all morning," Maggie said before grabbing her purse and heading out the door.

"Oh, Wise One?" Mark walked to the door to the garage.

"Yes?" Maggie pivoted to face him. Mark was pointing toward an open door.

"We're going out the garage. My truck is in there, remember?" Mark smirked. "Or were you so out of it from my fingering you on our way home that you didn't know where you were?"

"Jerkface," Maggie rumbled as she walked by him.

"I think I like Surfer Smurf better." Mark slapped her ass as she walked by him.

"Hey!" Maggie jumped and suddenly stopped. "You have a bike?"

"Wow, you really were out of it." Mark pushed her into the garage and opened the door. "Are you glad or mad? I can't tell from your reaction."

"I love bikes. I don't love motorcycle clubs." Maggie hurried toward the black and shiny chrome Harley. "Can I ride it to work?"

"Yeah, no." Mark pulled her away from the bike.

"Why not?" Maggie whined. "I'm a good driver. I won't crash it, I promise."

"No." Mark opened the truck door. "Sky, in". Sky jumped into the back seat and Maggie felt Mark pushing her in.

"Alright, alright. I'm going," Maggie huffed and crossed her arms. "Party pooper."

"Seatbelt." Mark pointed toward the seatbelt.

"Fine!" Maggie belted in and Mark shut the door.

Maggie couldn't understand why he wouldn't let her ride his bike. José let her ride his bike. She could control it and stay between the lines without swaying and falling. She would have to prove it to him one day.

"Why can't I ride it?" Maggie was like a dog with a bone. She wasn't going to let this go.

"One, because people are looking for you right now and, on a bike, you are an easy target." Mark pulled out of the garage and closed the door. "Two, your ribs are not totally healed. And three, that bike is too heavy for you to handle."

"I handle you, don't I?" Maggie loved getting a rise out of Mark.

"Are you saying I'm heavy?" Mark had a look of horror on his face and placed his hand over his heart. "I work hard for these abs. If you remember, one of your pet names for me was eight pack."

Okay so Mark gave as good as he got. "Sorry, I forgot. You'll have to show me again. Are you sure I said eight pack and not one pack?"

"Hmm." Mark tapped his lips with his pointer finger. "I do have a huge one pack underneath the eight pack. Maybe, that's what has your mind jumbled."

Maggie must've been quiet for too long thinking about his one pack because Mark chuckled and said, "Cat got your tongue, Captain Snark?"

"Your cock is going to have my tongue in a minute just to get you to shut up," Maggie mumbled.

"Promises, promises," Mark sighed.

"Surfer Smurf, you're turning into Full of Shit Smurf." Maggie shoved his shoulder. Their banter stopped as soon as he pulled into the parking lot at the cultural center and saw a police car parked there. His demeanor switched from funny boyfriend to security officer in the blink of an eye.

"I'm gonna go check this out with Sky. When I get out, move over to the driver's side and leave the truck running, but lock the doors. If you see anything strange, pull out, and get to safety." Mark got out and pulled out his gun while he waited for Sky.

Maggie scooted into the driver's seat. "I want to come with you."

"Absolutely not." Mark checked the gun chamber. "Stay. Here." Mark glared at her and slammed the truck door.

Maggie watched Mark and Sky carefully walk toward the entrance. The thought of abandoning Mark if things went south churned her stomach and sent a shiver of anxiety down her spine. Looking around, she spotted a brightly lit grocery store across the street. She could drive there and call the police. But wait, they were already there. Ugh, she hated waiting and not knowing what the hell was going on.

Chapter 40

Police Help

Mark

Mark and Sky cautiously entered the cultural center. That was weird—the alarm was still set. Once they entered, Mark looked around and it looked just like it did every morning when he came to work. Nothing was out of place or broken.

"Sky, search." Mark gave her the command to check every room. Sky was much faster than him, although he did run behind her. Had they parked a cop car outside as a deterrent? Was there a cop inside needing assistance? They cleared the exhibit room, warehouse, storytelling room, Thunder's office, gift shop, and the bathrooms. The only place left to check was the kitchen at the back left of the restaurant.

As they approached the kitchen, Mark heard a noise and signaled Sky to be quiet. Mark crouched and Sky went ahead of him. Taking a deep breath, Mark entered the doorway to the kitchen and screamed "Freeze!" At the same time, he heard someone else say "Freeze!" *What the fuck?*

Deputy George was shirtless, standing in the kitchen, pointing a gun at him. Both dropped their guns when they saw each other.

"Oh, Fuck!" Mark placed his gun on the counter and leaned against it, taking deep breaths. He'd used a gun before, but not to shoot an intruder. "What the fuck are you doing here? Was there a problem? Shit, I almost shot you, man."

Sky ran up to George, waiting in a seated position in front of him, ready to be petted.

"Hey, girl. I've missed you, too." George had already set his gun down before Sky reached him and was now hugging her and giving her kisses. "You wouldn't have shot me. You're too good of a guy." George chuckled. "You would've talked me to death before shooting at me. Anyway, I'm living here now. Where's Maggie? I thought she was coming with you?"

"Oh Shit! She's in my truck." Mark re-holstered his gun. "I told her to stay there while I checked everything out. Seeing the cop car in the parking lot put me on edge." Mark rubbed his face and stared at George. "Put a shirt on, would you. I don't want her walking in and seeing another naked man."

"I'm hardly naked, but I see how it is." George smiled at him. "How the bachelor hath fallen." George shook his head.

"Put a fucking shirt on," Mark grumbled before he left the kitchen to get Maggie. Mark heard George laughing. *Asshole.* Of course, he didn't want Maggie checking out another man's chest. Mark was secure in his own manhood, but he did recognize that George was good looking and very fit. Fucker better come downstairs dressed in the mornings or Mark would beat his ass. He didn't care that George was a cop.

Mark saw Maggie sitting in his truck with her hands braced on the steering wheel. Her knuckles looked white, and she was panting. Shit, he should've texted her when he saw George to let her know everything was okay. Mark opened the door, and Maggie lunged at him in a tight hug.

"Hey." Mark rubbed her back and helped her out. "It's okay. Everything's okay."

"Oh my God, I was so scared that something happened to you. You were gone a long time." Maggie's grip was not loosening around his neck.

"Darlin'." Mark put one hand behind her head and massaged it. "I'm okay." He lightly gripped her hair and pulled her face back to look at her. "The car belongs to Deputy George."

"Oh." Maggie relaxed her breathing and loosened her grip on his neck. "What is he doing here?"

"He said he's living here now." Mark kissed her temple.

"What?" Maggie's brow furrowed.

"I don't know the whole story. I wanted to come out and let you know it was all clear." Mark released her and got in his truck to turn it off and shut the door. "Let's go talk to him and find out what's going on."

Mark led Maggie inside. Sky was sitting by the front door.

"Good girl." Mark patted her on his way to the lobby desk.

"Where is he?" Maggie looked around before booting up her computer.

"In the apartment upstairs getting dressed, I hope," Mark grumbled.

"Was he naked when you saw him?" Maggie wiggled her eyebrows at him.

"Don't start that with me." Mark pointed at her. "The only man you are allowed to see naked is me. Got that?"

"I got it, Big Sexy Smurf." Maggie winked at him.

"Again, with the fucking Smurf," Mark sighed.

"Big Sexy, huh?" George said from behind them.

Turning around, Mark saw George fully dressed in his uniform—Thank Fuck.

"Well, he is big and sexy." Maggie grinned at Mark. "How are you, Deputy George?"

Mark watched Maggie get up and hug George. He didn't realize he'd growled until Maggie turned around and said, "Down boy." Then she walked to Mark and sat on his lap, surprising the shit out of him. Mark quickly recovered and put his arms around her. Maggie wrapped her arms around his neck and whispered in his ear. "I only want your big, sexy cock so don't be getting all jealous on me." Then she nipped his earlobe.

Fuck! His big sexy cock was about to bust through his pants seeking his favorite haven.

"I think it's time for me to leave. It's getting really hot in here." George cleared his throat. "Right, Mark?"

Mark grunted– "Behave" –to Maggie and positioned her on his lap to cover his hard on.

"I thought you liked me naughty," Maggie whispered in his ear. Mark covered her mouth with his hand, closed his eyes, and took a couple of deep breaths. When he thought he was under control, he opened his eyes and glared at George.

George had a grin on his face and was leaning against the desk.

"What did you mean by you're living here?" Mark finally had his brain back in gear, even though Maggie was trying her damnedest to derail him. If she fucking shifted her ass one more time, he was dragging her to the warehouse, bending her over a table, and fucking her senseless.

"My lease is running out at the end of the month, and I asked Thunder if I could move into the apartment upstairs. With all the problems he's had, I want to keep this place safe for him. He's worked too hard to make this cultural center succeed, and I would hate for him to lose it. Thunder's done so much for me over the years, I wanted to do something for him. I thought between me and you, we can do that for him." George rubbed the back of his neck. "Thunder's the dad I never had."

Mark knew George was the first shelter kid Thunder mentored. When they met, George was almost eighteen and had to leave the shelter the day after his birthday. Thunder opened his home to George and let him live in his spare bedroom, rent free. He also got George a job as a waiter at a restaurant near his house. George worked there for a few years, becoming a bartender as soon as he turned twenty-one. That was when he moved out. George always said he wanted to help people, to give back, and being a police officer gave him the chance to protect and serve. He applied to the police academy and passed with flying colors. Now he was a full-time deputy and he and his partner Sean always looked out for the American Indian Cultural Center and the Rock 'n' Roll Resort & Casino.

"I'm glad you're here at night." Mark nodded. "Thunder must be thrilled."

"I am." Thunder beamed from the front door. "Good to see you, George." Thunder walked to George for a hug. "I see you two aren't fighting anymore," Thunder said to Mark.

"Sorry," Maggie murmured and bolted off of Mark's lap.

Mark felt the loss and wished she'd sit back down, but he knew they had to work.

Thunder waved his hand. "No worries. As long as you do your work and keep it clean in the lobby...it's all good."

"Well, this has been fun, but I have to get to work and start my shift." George waved. "See you all later."

"Bye." Maggie waved.

"Stay safe." Thunder pointed at him.

"Always." George turned and smiled.

"Wait up. I'll go with you." Mark stood and tapped his thigh, signaling Sky to go with him. "I'm gonna do a quick perimeter check."

"Let's do it." George raised his arm vertically to the full extent, closed his fist with his pointer finger up and waved his forearm in large horizontal circles. Mark smiled because he knew that hand move meant 'Assemble' and all he could think of was 'Avengers Assemble.' "I'll go one way, you go the other. We'll meet back here."

"Sounds good." Mark loved superhero movies.

They went around and met in the front, then George waved and left for work. Mark went back in with Sky and sat at his desk.

Chapter 41

I Can Be Fun

Mark

"What are you working on?" Mark saw a slide show up on Maggie's computer.

"I take night classes. I only have a couple of classes left, and I can graduate with my bachelor's degree in marketing." Maggie was taking notes.

"That's great, Hermione. Ugh, wait, I can't call you that, it sounds like you're a teenager. I mean, you would look fucking sexy in a plaid, pleated, short skirt with knee-high socks." Mark adjusted himself because that was quite the image of Maggie. *Shit, down boy.* "Which nights? I'll drive you."

"Tuesday and Thursday." Maggie flipped to the next slide. "I missed last Thursday, so I have to go tonight. You don't have to drive me."

"I want to drive you. Besides" –Mark rolled next to her and whispered in her ear– "if you're a good girl, I'll even carry your books to class." Then he kissed her cheek.

"Aww." Maggie turned and kissed him. "You're such a good boyfriend."

Mark stiffened, hearing Maggie call him her boyfriend surprised him.

"What?" Maggie turned to face him. "Did I say something wrong? We are dating, right?"

"Yes."

"And we are exclusive, yes?" Maggie placed her hand over his on his armrest.

"I don't share...ever!" Mark grunted.

"Then why did you freak out when I called you my boyfriend?" Maggie shook his forearm.

"I guess I just hadn't thought of it." Mark turned his palm over on his armrest and wound his fingers with hers. "But I like it." Watching the weary look on her face turn into a bright smile melted the walls around his heart a little more. Hell, if he kept feeling this way about her, those walls would just be a puddle around his heart. Mark leaned forward and captured her mouth with his.

"This is different." Alex had his arm around Tori's shoulder, and he was pointing his finger between Mark and Maggie. Mark released Maggie and faced the front entrance.

"Hi, lovebirds." Tori smiled. "I knew your fighting was a sign of pent-up sexual aggression."

"Who are you and what have you done with my fiancée?" Alex turned to Tori.

"What do you mean?" Tori tilted her head, looking at Alex.

"Those are not words you would normally say." Alex shook his head, and they walked up to the desk. "Never mind, it's Frey Talk."

"What's Frey talk?" Mark was glad that Maggie asked because if she hadn't, he would have.

"My innocent, sweet fiancée has been spending a lot of time with my crazy potty-mouth sister."

"Hey, it's not like you're a choir boy." Tori elbowed him and whispered something in his ear.

Mark saw Alex grin at Tori. Clearly, he liked her naughty talk because he whispered something in her ear that made her blush.

"See you all later," Alex grabbed Tori's hand and pulled a giggling Tori to the kitchen.

"They are so cute." Maggie sighed. "I wish we could go to another room and go at it like bunnies."

"Stop, Sexy Smurfette." Mark adjusted himself yet again and rolled back to his computer. "Finish your schoolwork, so you'll be ready for your class tonight." A sexually charged Maggie was much harder to resist than a snarky Maggie. *Fuck!* If she didn't stop, he was going to have to take her into the warehouse for a quickie.

"Fine." Maggie flipped to the next slide. "You're no fun."

"I'll show you fun." Mark bolted out of his chair and grabbed Maggie's hand, pulling her out of her chair. Mark stormed toward the warehouse, stopping in front of Thunder's office for a second to tell him that he and Maggie had to check some inventory. Mark opened the warehouse door and swung Maggie inside.

"Sky, stay." Mark followed Maggie inside.

"What are we checking?" Maggie turned around to face him.

"How fun I am." Mark lunged at her and wrapped her up in his arms as his mouth ravaged hers. Walking her backwards, he moved her into the far back corner behind several boxes that were stacked in front of a table. Mark walked her behind the table and spun her around. Grabbing her hands, he placed her palms on the table.

"Keep them there." Mark reached under her skirt and felt her wet panties. Groaning, he slipped his fingers inside her. She was drenched. Just the way he liked her. He pushed her panties down to her thighs with one hand while his other pulled his gun out of his holster. He didn't need to have an accident with the gun while he was fucking her.

Once Maggie was undulating her ass into him, he removed his fingers and dropped his pants. One hand continued to play with her clit while the other released her tits from her bra so he could play.

"I would love to take my time, Darlin', but we gotta get back to work." Mark released her breasts and pushed her forward, laying her face first on the table. Moving his hand to her shoulder, he held her in place while he rammed into her with his hard cock. Maggie gasped and pushed back against him with every thrust. He wasn't going to last long, and he wanted, no needed, her to come first. He released the hand on her hip and glided it toward her clit, stroking and rubbing it in circles. Maggie went off so loud, the hand on her shoulder quickly covered her mouth. Mark had closed the warehouse door, but damn that scream had been loud.

Mark pumped harder and faster into her until he came with such force, his legs nearly gave out. Leaning over her, he kissed her neck.

"Okay, you're fun." Maggie mumbled.

Mark chuckled. "I told you." Mark got off her before his weight hurt her. Stepping back, he got dressed.

"I prefer the show over the tell." Maggie used her arms to lift herself off the table slowly. "What are you doing? You're going the wrong way."

Mark was sliding her panties down her legs. Mark tapped her left leg. "Lift." Maggie lifted her left and then he repeated the action on the right leg. Once her panties were free, he tucked them into his pocket.

"Uh." Maggie pointed to her panties with one hand while the other cupped her pussy. "I need those. I'm dripping."

"Stay here." Mark left her behind the table, blocked by the boxes. He went into the men's room and took several wads of toilet paper and paper towels. She could clean herself off, but he was keeping her panties. This would teach her not to tempt him at work. *Pfft, telling me I'm no fun. Who's the fun one now?* Mark found her exactly like he left her. One hand braced on the table and the other under her skirt.

"I brought you these so you can clean yourself off." Mark handed her the toilet paper and paper towels.

"Gee, thanks." Maggie used everything he brought her. When she finished, she reached out her hand. "My panties?"

"Nope." Mark shook his head. "This will make you think twice about seducing me at work."

"What if I get horny and wet?" Maggie quirked her eyebrow. "I won't have my panties to stop it from dripping down my legs."

"I'll bring your ass back here and lick you dry." Mark shrugged. Mark watched Maggie open her mouth to say something, but nothing came out. He'd left her speechless. Grinning, he gave himself a mental point for winning this battle. Maggie squinted at him and stormed out. Damn, that's the first verbal sparring match he'd ever won against her, and it felt fantastic.

Puffing his chest out, he strolled back to his desk, finally calm and ready to get back to work. Sky sat next to him and sniffed his pocket. Mark pushed her head away, but Sky was persistent.

"Sky, stop. Sit." Dammit, Sky was female. Why the hell was she wanting to sniff the hell out of Maggie's panties? If she was a boy, he'd understand. He loved smelling Maggie.

"Serves you right, Panty Stealing Smurf," Maggie said before she threw a rolled-up piece of paper at his head.

Mark saw it out of the corner of his eye and caught it before it hit his head.

"I can't believe you caught that. You weren't even looking at me. Do you have eyes on the back of your head?" Maggie sounded frustrated.

"I played baseball. I'm used to seeing flying objects coming at me from different directions." Mark smiled and heard Maggie mumbling to herself. "What was that?"

"At least you don't have supersonic hearing," Maggie said sarcastically.

Chapter 42

What's the Plan?

Reaper

"How did it go? Is he staying away from our shit?" Reaper asked Numbers. Numbers was still pretending to be one of Reaper's lawyers so he could visit Reaper in jail and give him updates.

"For now, but I think they're gearing up for something. I sent over the proposal you wanted." Reaper wanted part of the drug trafficking pipeline that Los Lobos ran with the Colombia cartel. Machete was not giving in, and it was pissing him off. In Reaper's mind, they owed him for the death of Tools and two other brothers. Tools had been the best mechanic he'd ever seen. Over the past eleven years, they'd had other mechanics, but none of them had his talent or charm. When Tools ran the business, people trusted him. The brothers that replaced Tools threatened the customers, which caused them to go somewhere else. Once word spread, their garage was like a ghost town. Now, they only serviced their own cars and bikes.

El Loco owed him for killing Tools and losing him money. But money wasn't the only thing he lost after Tools' death. He also lost his daughter, Angel. He was slowly endearing himself to his grandson, but his daughter was a lost cause. She would never forgive him. In her mind, Tools died because of Reaper. Which technically, was true. Had he not gunned down El Loco's parents, Tools would be alive. Then again, had El Loco not stolen one of their shipments, Reaper wouldn't have killed his parents. It was turning into a vicious cycle that he wanted to win, even though he was in fucking jail.

Reaper thought taking and hurting Maggie would do the trick. He knew how much Los Lobos loved José's sister. She was a little sister to all of them.

"Let me guess. They said no." Reaper crossed his arms.

"Yep."

"Where's the girl?" Reaper never thought they would find her, and if his daughter hadn't stepped in, they could've made a better example of her. Yet Reaper needed to restrain his men to win his daughter over. *How fucked up was that?* If he were out of jail, he'd slap the shit out of Angel and put her in her place. He knew Tools had never hit Angel, and he couldn't discipline her while they were married. But now, she didn't have his protection. The only thing saving her from Reaper's wrath was a jail cell and her son, Steele.

"Don't know. But our friend has a girlfriend." Numbers leaned back in his chair and crossed his arms.

"Interesting." Reaper sat up and leaned forward. Things were looking up. "Are you sure? Do you know her name?" After they threw Maggie at the Los Lobos doorstep, Reaper told Numbers to find someone who could be a hang-around at the Los Lobos club. A hang-around wasn't a prospect, just someone who hung around the club hoping to be asked to prospect for them. Reaper didn't know who it was, but his plan had worked if they knew who José was dating.

"I do. What do you want me to do?"

"Show her the same hospitality you showed the other girl but give her a deeper, more intense experience." Reaper smiled wickedly.

"You got it." Numbers stood.

"And Numbers?" Reaper stood and walked to the door. "Make sure my daughter is not around. I don't want her interrupting the new girl's experience." Reaper knocked on the door to let the guard know to let him out. "Do it before this weekend. We need to get this situation resolved. I want that pipeline."

Numbers nodded.

Chapter 43

Waiting for the Other Shoe to Drop

Maggie

Maggie was on edge with a feeling of impending doom. Not because of work or Mark. Everything was great on those fronts. She saw no one from LR's near the office, and each day was much like the last. She continued to stay with Mark. They went to work together, and they had sex multiple times a day and night. This past week, Mark drove her to her classes, carried her backpack, and was always outside her classroom door when she walked out.

She hated seeing the college girl's eye fucking her man, but Mark never acknowledged them. He would only keep eye contact with her. He made her feel safe and loved, although he still hadn't told her he loved her. Then again, she hadn't told him either.

Just after lunch on Saturday, she was sitting at her desk after finishing a tour for a sweet family visiting from North Carolina when Mark ran in with Sky. He pocketed his phone before he reached her. His face looked worried.

"What's wrong?" Maggie stood.

"Get all your shit," Mark said as he ran past her.

"Mark?" –Maggie turned around– "What's happening?" But Mark was already sliding into Thunder's office. Maggie grabbed her purse and stuffed school notebooks and pens into her backpack.

"Go, go!" Maggie heard Thunder come out of his office with Mark. "I'll sit out here. Tori, get Alex and get the hell out of here!"

"What's going on?" Maggie was shaking. Tori ran into the restaurant, Thunder was enraged, and Mark gathered his belongings and logged out of his computer.

"Maggie, log out of your computer," Mark ordered as his fingers flew over the keyboard.

Maggie froze to the spot, her mouth opening and closing like a fish.

"Maggie." Thunder grabbed her shoulders and shook her out of her stupor. "I need you to listen to Mark. He'll keep you safe. Do as he says...okay?"

"Okay." Maggie shook her head to clear it.

"We're leaving" –Alex shouted as he ran out of the restaurant– "you good?" Alex pointed at them.

Who was he talking to? Maggie didn't know what the hell was going on.

"I'm good, just go, get her to safety," Thunder yelled.

"Okay, let's go, Darlin'." Maggie saw Mark log her out of her computer while she stood like a deer caught in headlights.

"Will someone please tell me what the fuck is going on?" Her eyes ping-ponged between everyone.

Mark grabbed her backpack and put it on, took her hand, and patted his leg for Sky.

"Call me when you get home." Thunder followed them out the door and locked it, turning the sign to closed. *Why was Thunder closing two hours early? And why the hell was Mark dragging her ass out to the car?*

"Okay, stop!" Maggie screamed and pulled her hand out of Mark's when they reached his truck. "I'm not going anywhere until you tell me what the hell is going on."

Mark unlocked the truck and opened the door. Sky jumped in. "Not here, not now. Get in the fucking truck Maggie before I throw you in there."

"What?" Maggie was dumbfounded. *Why was he mad at her? Why was everyone scrambling?*

"Sorry." Mark gave her a quick peck on the lips and looked around. "I'll explain as soon as you get in the truck, please."

"Okay." Maggie got in and buckled up. Mark tossed her backpack on the floor next to her feet and slammed the door.

"Mark," Maggie said when he got in, "you're scaring me. Please tell me what's going on."

"I just got a call from Machete because your brother is losing his shit."

Maggie turned in her seat and covered her mouth. "What happened?"

"The LR's kidnapped his girlfriend Lola and dropped her off at the clubhouse this morning." Maggie noticed he was speeding and scanning his surroundings like never before. There had to be more to this story.

"What aren't you telling me?" Maggie whispered, but Mark wasn't looking at her. "Mark! Dammit, tell me! Is she dead?"

"No." Mark reached out and grabbed her hand. "She's not dead. But they raped her multiple times in her front and back entrances."

"Oh My God," Maggie whispered releasing his hand and covering her face as the tears came hard and fast. "Lola. No. No. No!"

*** Mark ***

Mark felt helpless listening to Maggie' heart wrenching cries. He was almost home when he heard her scream before she started slapping and punching the glove compartment.

"I hate them!" Maggie screamed between punches. "Why do they have to hurt women? Fuckers!"

"Maggie, stop." Mark did not expect this reaction, or he would've told her before they got in the car. He tried to grab her hands with one of his and keeping the car from swerving with the other. Thank fuck, they were almost home. "You're hurting yourself."

Pulling into his driveway, he came to an abrupt halt and put the truck in park. He hauled Maggie into his lap and held her tightly against him. Maggie fought for a couple minutes, but then stopped and gripped his shirt while she bawled into his neck. Mark opened the garage door and drove the truck in. Turning the truck off and closing the garage door, he checked the rearview mirror to make sure no one followed him.

"Shhh, Darlin'. She's in the hospital now. Deb went with her," Mark murmured into her hair. Mark massaged the back of her head. Sky jumped in the passenger front seat and tilted her head, whimpering as she watched Maggie.

"I need to go see her," Maggie whispered into Mark's neck.

Mark cupped her face and lifted it up. "Maggie, look at me." Mark waited until her gaze collided with his. "I can't take you there now. I need to get you out of town. Let's pack a bag, we need to go."

Mark grabbed his stuff and Sky's while Maggie packed up her bag. They were out the door in twenty minutes. Driving like a bat out of hell and praying he didn't get pulled over, Mark pulled into a private hanger on the other side of the Ft. Lauderdale Airport.

"You missed the parking for the airport? What are we doing here?"

"We're leaving on a private jet." Mark parked and got out before Maggie could ask any more questions.

"Who's private jet?" Maggie asked as soon as he opened her door.

"Mine." Mark waited for Maggie and Sky to get out, then slammed the door. He'd already called Chris, their family pilot, and asked him to be ready to fly out today.

"Wait" –Maggie's arm shot out and grabbed his wrist– "you have a private jet?"

"My family does, and I use it to go home for the holidays." Mark wasn't stopping and Maggie had to run to keep up with him. "I'm leaving a little sooner than planned, but Chris won't mind since he's already here."

"Who the hell is Chris?" Maggie saw Sky run ahead and jump up on an older man wearing khakis and a polo.

Mark pointed. "That's Chris, our pilot." Mark knew he had a lot of explaining to do, but right now, he just wanted to get on the fucking plane and get the hell out of dodge.

"Hey, Chris. I'm sorry for the quick call." Mark shook his hand.

"No worries, man. Me and the fam just got back from the beach." Chris smiled and extended his hand to Maggie. "I'm Chris, your pilot for our flight."

"Hi. I'm Maggie and very confused right now."

"No need to worry." Chris slapped Mark's back. "This guy will take care of you, and I've been flying since I was in the Air Force, so you're in good hands. I've checked everything out and filed my flight plan. We're ready to go. I'll see you guys inside."

"Mark?" Maggie braced her hands on her hips and faced Mark with an angry scowl on her face. "I am not moving until you tell me where the hell we are going."

Sky laid down and whined. Yep, even she knew Maggie was mad.

"Darlin', we don't have time right now." Mark pointed to the plane. "Please get on the plane so we can get the fuck out of here before all hell breaks loose."

Maggie wasn't moving and now she had cocked her hip and was tapping her foot. If she was a cartoon character, steam would be coming out of her ears and her face would be cherry apple red. Mark didn't have time for this. He didn't think he'd been followed, but the last thing he needed was someone knowing he had a jet and where it was kept. The easy way hadn't helped so now he was going to get her on the plane the hard fucking way.

"Get your ass on that plane," Mark said through gritted teeth. He was slowly losing patience. Why couldn't she just listen to him?

"No." Did he hear right? Did she just say no? Oh, hell no. Mark bent down and tackled her, lifting up once his shoulder was at her waist. He gripped her ass and held her in place as he climbed the steps of the plane. Maggie wasn't one to go down easy. She pounded on his back and ass screaming to let her go. Yeah, that wasn't happening until he had her in a seat and buckled.

Sky followed him and Chris closed the door, locking it. Mark dropped Maggie in a seat and tried to buckle her in, but she was fighting him every step of the way. Mark ducked his head so her slaps wouldn't hit his face. He'd had enough of this shit.

Finally grabbing her hands, Mark shoved his face in front of hers and growled. "Settle down, Hothead. I'm trying to help you."

"Then tell me what the fuck is going on," Maggie screamed in his face.

She could be so infuriating. He needed her to shut up and follow orders for once in her damn life. A life that would be cut short if the LR's got ahold of her. Mark was sure that if they took her again, she would be dropped off at the Los Lobos clubhouse dead. And that was not going to happen on his watch. But he had to stop her from fighting him. Even though he had her hands, they were still pushing and pulling against him while her feet kicked him. Fuck, she almost got his balls again. Mark braced his legs outside of hers and quickly squeezed them shut, stopping them from moving around. Bending down, he knew of only one way to shut Maggie up and calm her down—he kissed her. If you can call it a kiss, really it was an assault. He plundered and ravaged her mouth until they were both breathing heavy. She loosened her arms just long enough for Mark to buckle her in. The plane was not in motion, yet. Mark knew he had to buckle Sky in before it increased speed and lifted off. Releasing her lips, he patted the chair next to Maggie and Sky jumped up. Mark buckled her in and sat in a chair across from them. Dogs were good at comforting people, so he knew Sky would help Maggie feel more at ease. Although after that kiss, he wasn't thinking about Maggie being scared or mad—he was thinking about how he wanted to fuck her. They stared at each other, panting. Had it not been for the seatbelts, they would be in each other's arms, tearing off their clothes.

Chapter 44

Mark Owned a Plane?

Maggie

Maggie licked her lips and braced her arms on the armrests. Closing her eyes, she tried to take deep breaths to calm down. Although Maggie was all in for an adventure, flying on a small plane was not on her bucket list. The last time she took a connecting flight on a puddle jumper, she ended up using the barf bag when they hit a lot of turbulence. Since then, she preferred to travel by car.

"Are you okay?"

"No," Maggie panted. "I don't like flying on small planes and I've never gone backwards."

"Switch with me." Maggie heard him unbuckle and felt his breath on her cheek before his hands undid hers. Then he swiftly grabbed her by the hips moving her to his seat and buckling her in.

"Sky, switch." Maggie heard Sky jump on the seat next to her before Sky licked her hand.

"Sorry, I should've sat you there to begin with." Mark stared at her. "Better?"

"Yes." Maggie took a deep breath. She needed to talk to Mark and distract herself from the view outside the window. Besides, he had a lot of explaining to do. "Now, I want answers."

Maggie opened her eyes and watched him buckle Sky in next to her. "Thank you. I like having her next to me." Maggie reached out to pet Sky. "Start talking."

"Okay." Mark gave Maggie a curt nod. "What are the questions?"

"Not funny, Surfer Smurf," Maggie retorted and crossed her arms.

"I see we're back to where we started," Mark sighed and rubbed his face.

"Where are we going?' Maggie began her interrogation.

"Montana."

"Why, Montana?" Maggie pointed her finger at him and leaned forward. "Do not give me one-word answers or I'll...I'll—" Sky lowered her head and laid down, whining.

"You'll what?" Mark grinned at her.

Why the hell was he amused by her anger? She had to come up with something good. "I'll tie you to a bed and tease you for hours before I suck you off." Maggie watched his eyes dilate with lust as he stared at her mouth.

"Let's go." Mark pointed behind her.

That didn't get the reaction she was hoping for. "I'll...I'll spank your ass hard before I tie to you the bed and tease you." Nope, now his cock was creating a huge bulge in his pants.

"Like I said, let's go." Mark moved his hands to unbuckle his seatbelt.

Maggie screamed out, "I won't let you fuck me or touch me for weeks!" Yup, that got him. He released his breath and dropped his hands to his armrest, closing his eyes, he took a deep breath.

Opening one eye to look at her he said, "You wouldn't."

"Oh, yes I would Big Sexy." Maggie crossed her legs and pointed at her pussy. "There would be a closed for business sign right there." *Hah! Take that.*

"Then you wouldn't be getting any either?"

"I'll get it from somewhere else." Maggie shrugged. *Oh shit!* Clearly, she went too far because right after Mark growled, he unbuckled himself and her, dragging her to the door at the back of the plane. *Oh, hell no!* She was not doing it in a cramped bathroom. Mile high club be damned.

"Think again, Mouthy Girl. If you don't get it from me, you're not getting it at all."

Mark opened the door and pushed her inside a room with an enormous bed. Before she could look around, he cupped her face and attacked her mouth. He walked her backwards until her knees hit the bed, then Mark's hand pushed her chest, and she fell onto the bed. While her back bounced on the bed, he stripped her of her panties, pants, and shoes in one smooth movement. Before Maggie had a chance to say anything, he was between her legs, sucking her clit. His fingers reached her favorite spot and just as she was ready to come, he removed his fingers and tongue.

"Why did you stop?" Maggie grabbed his hair, pushing his face toward her.

"Why did you threaten to keep me from you?" Mark swiped his tongue over her clit.

"I didn't mean it." Maggie bucked her hips toward his face. He couldn't possibly leave her like this...could he? She did threaten to leave him like that. Crap, her plan royally backfired.

"Are you sure?" Mark swiped his tongue again, this time pinning her down with his hands on her belly and breasts.

"Yes," Maggie moaned when Mark scraped his teeth over her clit before he slipped his tongue inside. She was relieved he was going to continue. "Yes. Yes." Maggie was almost there and then he stopped...again! "No. Don't stop or I'll cut your cock off and use it as a dildo anytime I want!"

"Damn, Lorena Bobbitt," Mark chuckled. "That's just mean." Sliding his hand around her ass, he pressed the tip of his middle finger inside her puckered hole, Maggie bucked and pressed into his hand. "I think my girl would like a dildo up the ass while I fuck her." Those were the last words Maggie heard before he dove into her pussy with his mouth and other hand while his other finger entered her backside at the same time. *Oh Shit!* Maggie's orgasm exploded out of her body, her mind going blank. No one had ever entered her from behind.

But damn, her body loved it. She heard rustling, but couldn't find the energy to open her eyes.

Mark pulled her legs up and fucked her with his cock in her pussy and his fingertip still in her ass. Maggie didn't think she had any orgasms left, but he proved her wrong. Her body spasmed and she came again, with him this time. Mark lowered her legs and a few minutes later, she felt him cleaning her up and moving her up on the bed. Was he leaving her? She wanted to cuddle. She still wanted to know why they were going to Montana.

Maggie had just enough energy to roll onto her side and mumble into the pillow. "Mark?"

"I'll be right back." She heard Mark say before she fell asleep.

*** Mark ***

Mark wanted to explain everything to her, but when she mentioned getting it from somewhere else, he saw red. Before he knew it, he was dragging her into the bedroom cabin and fucking her. Looking down at her as she drifted off to sleep, she looked relaxed. The frown lines on her face were finally gone. Mark tucked her in and went to check on Sky and Chris.

Sky was lying on her side on the couch. She opened one eye when Mark walked by her. Mark crouched down on his knees and pet her head. "All good, girl. You can go back to sleep." Sky closed her eye and exhaled.

Mark continued into the cockpit, sat in the co-pilot seat, and grabbed the headset. "How's it going up here?"

"Clear skies." Chris glanced at Mark and pointed behind him. "How's it going back there?"

"Good now. She's sleeping." Mark checked all the controls. He had his pilot's license and could've flown them home, but then he wouldn't have been able to spend time with Maggie. Besides, Chris had come down with his family on vacation to the beach. "I'm sorry to take you away from Jenny and the girls."

"It's all good. My body is so pale, I can't take too much sun. I'll drop you off at the ranch and go back." Chris shrugged. "A couple of days away from the sun will do me some good."

Mark touched his arm and saw the red go to white in an instant. "Yeah, that's gonna hurt."

Chris chuckled. "I have aloe to put on it, but that doesn't hurt as much as the top of my feet."

"Oh, shit. You forgot to put sunscreen on the top of your feet?" Mark laughed.

"Rookie mistake," Chris sighed.

"If you were a rookie, I'd agree. But you've been bringing the family down here every year the week before Christmas for the past four years, so you can fly me home for the holidays." Mark relaxed in the seat. He was just there for backup.

"Yeah, yeah, yeah." Chris pointed behind him. "What's going on with the hot girl in the cabin back there?"

"I don't think your wife would appreciate you noticing the hot girl." Mark smirked at Chris.

"She knows I don't stray." Chris shrugged. "Who else is gonna put up with my shit?"

Chris met a good woman while he was in the Air Force and found a way to make it work. They'd been married for twenty-five years and going strong. Mark hoped to find a good one, but in Montana, everyone knew his family. Hence, they knew he had money, and the girls would do just about anything to catch the wealthy bachelor, even though they hated ranch work and living several miles away from neighbors. Yet another reason Mark moved to Florida and told no one about his family ranch.

Everyone in Florida, except Thunder, thought he was just a receptionist and now a security officer. What they didn't know was that he was rich beyond his means and didn't need to work. He received a family allowance every month, which he put in the bank. He lived on his income from the cultural center. The only things he used his allowance on were his truck, down payment on his house, and education. He'd become close to Thunder over the past couple of years and confided in him, mostly because Thunder was family.

He would have to tell Maggie the truth about his family when she woke up or she would be in for a shock when they reached the Big H Ranch. They still had the small house his great grandparents had lived in, but his dad bought his mom a two-story custom built log cabin and stone house of her dreams with a wraparound porch soon after they married.

"Hey, Romeo." Chris snapped his fingers in Mark's face. "The girl?"

"Oh, sorry." Mark shook his head, dislodging his daydreaming. "Long story short, I work with her and she's in danger from a bad motorcycle club who's fighting with their rival. Her brother is a member. Lucifer's Renegades already took her once and beat the shit out of her. I'm not giving them a second chance. So, I'm taking her out of town until Christmas and hopefully, the two clubs will figure their shit out."

"Not likely if they're rivals," Chris sighed. "That's quite the hornet's nest she shook."

"Yep, and they're not stinging her again on my watch."

"What about when you get back?" Chris glanced at Mark. "I know you're not moving back to Montana, so what are you going to do then?"

Mark let out a huge breath. Chris was right, he was not moving back to Montana. "I think she and I can stay at our friend's resort. They have a lot of security and it's near impossible to breach their family floor."

"Gotcha. I'm gonna go use the restroom since you're up here." Chris took off the headset when Mark nodded.

Mark hadn't talked to the Panthers, but he was sure they would let him and Maggie use the room she had used for the past few days. At least until the wedding. He knew Maggie would want to help Tori and Frey. Between Holt, Alex, Barrett, and him, surely they could keep the girls safe. Chris came back a few minutes later and they flew in silence, enjoying the view from above. Flying was a hobby Mark had taken up at a young age. Being up above the clouds, seeing the never-ending sky gave him a sense of peace.

Chapter 45

Mark is Loaded

Maggie

"**H**ey, Sleeping Beauty." Maggie heard a soft voice in her ear and felt light kisses on her neck. "Time to rise and shine."

"Do I have to?" Maggie groaned. She was so comfy, wrapped up in the nice bed with a cushiony pillow under her head.

"Yes." Mark pulled her up. "We are going to land in about five minutes, and I need you seat-belted in."

"I thought your pilot had experience." Maggie refused to open her eyes while Mark sat her up in bed like a rag doll.

"He does, but sometimes things can go wrong." Mark chuckled.

Maggie's eyes shot open. "Like what?" –she raised her hand– "Stop, don't tell me. I'm getting up." Mark grabbed her clothes, placing them on the bed for her to put on. "Can I use the bathroom?"

"Yeah." Mark checked his watch. "You got a couple minutes."

Maggie ran to the potty and emptied her bladder. Mark was waiting for her with an amused look on his face. He'd sat Sky next to her.

"What's so funny?" Maggie barked at Mark while she snapped her seatbelt on and draped her arm around Sky.

"You." Mark pointed at her. "Running around like a chicken with her head cut off to get in your seat."

"Well, if we crash, I have a better chance of survival if I'm seatbelted, right?" Maggie pointed at Mark and braced herself. "Buckle up, Surfer Smurf." Then she closed her eyes and petted Sky.

"Darlin', we're not going to crash. I just needed you to get up and seated as a precaution, Scaredy Cat." Mark attached his seatbelt and watched her with a smile on his face.

"Stop smiling at me," Maggie snapped. "I don't know how Sky puts up with you." Sky whined. Sky always seemed to whine when she and Mark were being snarky with each other.

"How do you know I'm smiling at you?" Mark chuckled. "Your eyes are closed."

"I can hear the laughter in your voice." Maggie knew he was laughing at her, but flying in this jet was not like a regular airplane. She was holding on, waiting for the jolt of the landing.

"Relax." Maggie felt Mark's hand squeeze her thigh as the plane hit the ground and applied the brakes. "See, we've landed, and everything is okay. Take some slow, deep breaths before you hyperventilate."

Maggie followed his instructions and opened her eyes when her nerves calmed down and the plane was traveling at a slower speed.

"When Chris stops, I'll unbuckle Sky and get our bags."

"Where are we going in Montana?" Maggie looked out the window, but it was nighttime and all she could see were the beams of lights on the runway.

"My family's ranch." Mark unbuckled.

"How far are we from your family's ranch?" Maggie watched Mark walk toward the front closet to get their bags and place them near the door.

"A little over an hour at this time of night." The plane stopped and Mark came back to unbuckle Sky.

Maggie followed Mark to the front of the plane. The cockpit door opened, and Chris came out.

"Thank you." Maggie hadn't been crazy about flying on a small plane, but Chris had made it a smooth ride. Not that she remembered most of it since Mark had distracted her in the bedroom and then she slept the rest of the way to Montana.

"You're welcome." Chris nodded.

"Are you spending the night before you head back?" Mark opened the cabin door with steps so Sky could run out and potty.

"Yeah, I'm gonna stay here and leave early in the morning. When am I coming back to get you?"

"Let me see what's going on this week and I'll text you." Mark shook Chris' hand. "Thank you for uprooting your plans for us."

"Anything for you." Chris pulled Mark's hand toward him for a hug and back slap.

Maggie bent down to grab her bag, but Mark pushed it away.

"Go on down. I got your bag."

"I can carry my own bag, Surfer Smurf." Maggie pushed his hand away and grabbed her bag storming down the stairs.

"Surfer Smurf?" Chris grinned at him. "Do I even want to know?"

"Nope."

"She's a live one." Chris followed Mark down the stairs. "Have fun with that, Surfer Smurf." Maggie heard their conversation but pretended not to. Smiling to herself she walked away from them to look for Sky.

"Sky, where are you girl?" Two seconds later, Sky came running at her full speed. Maggie held up her bag to cover her face. Which didn't make any sense because if Sky jumped at her to give her kisses, she would fall back on her ass. She should've dropped the bag, so she had full use of her hands to brace her fall. But she didn't need to worry, because she heard Mark yell.

"Sky, no!"

Sky skidded to a stop before Maggie and sat down on her haunches with her tongue sticking out.

"You are one crazy girl." Maggie laughed, dropped her bag, and gave her a kiss on the top of her head.

"Maggie?" Mark called out to her. "There's no place to stop, so if you need to use the restroom use the one here."

"You said an hour, right?" Mark nodded. "I'll be fine."

"Okay ladies, let's go home." Mark picked up Maggie's bag on his way to the hangar's exit door. Stopping at the wall of keys, Mark snatched a set. Once they stepped outside, there was a truck parked in the lot.

"Well, this is convenient." Maggie waited by the passenger door while Mark tossed the bags into the covered trunk.

"I asked my brother and dad to drop off my old truck so I could drive home when I got here." Mark opened the back door and Sky jumped in. "I knew we'd be getting in late. They get up at the ass crack of dawn, so I didn't want them to have to come get us so late at night." Once everyone was seated, Mark pulled out.

On the drive home from the airport, everything was dark except for what was highlighted by Mark's headlights. Not that there was anything to see. It all looked like land with a few scattered houses along the way. What really stuck out were the stars in the sky. No wonder they called this state 'Big Sky Country'. Maggie couldn't wait to see all this beautiful scenery in the daytime. Growing up in South Florida, her family had told her about how it was when they first moved there, but all she ever saw was overcrowded areas and bumper to bumper traffic. Mark had been driving for about thirty minutes and she rarely saw a car come from the opposite direction. Between the darkness, the low country music playing in the car, and the movement of the truck, Maggie leaned her head against the window and fell asleep.

***

"Come on Sleepy." Mark unbuckled her seat. "We're here."

"Why am I so tired?" Maggie yawned.

"You've had quite a week, and your body needs rest." Mark helped her down. Sky followed Maggie out and ran to the front door.

Maggie's eyes followed Sky, and she saw an older woman illuminated by the indoor light, standing in the doorway with a shawl over her shoulders. Maggie assumed it was Mark's mom, Janice. The woman bent down to give Sky a hug when she reached her.

"She doesn't jump on your mom." Maggie wrinkled her forehead in thought.

"She knows better." Mark came from the back of the truck with their bags.

Maggie reached out for hers and Mark pulled it away.

"Don't even think about taking your bag," Mark grumbled. "Especially in front of my mom. She'd kick my ass if she thought I wasn't treating my girlfriend right."

"Your girlfriend, huh?" Maggie shoulder bumped him.

"That's what I told her." Mark glanced at Maggie. "Am I wrong?"

"No, Big Sexy, you are so right." Maggie winked at him. "Do you think we'll be in the same room?"

"I don't know, but probably. I mean shit, I'm twenty-seven, not sixteen." Maggie tugged on Mark's arm before they reached his mom, who was still loving on Sky.

"I am not having sex with you in your mom's house," Maggie whispered in his ear.

"Noted." Mark nodded.

Maggie walked beside Mark to the front door.

"Hi, I'm Janice." Mark's mom reached out to Maggie for a hug. "Come inside dear, it's pretty chilly out there."

Maggie hadn't even noticed the chill in the air, she was too busy being in awe of their home. Maggie had never seen such a beautiful two-story log cabin home before. She couldn't wait to see the inside.

"Hi, mom." Mark hugged his mom after Maggie. "Is everyone asleep?"

"Yes, busy day tomorrow." Mark's mom shut the door.

"Always a busy day here." Mark dropped the bags and introduced them. "Maggie, this is my mom, Janice. Mom, this is my girlfriend, Maggie."

"So good to meet you, Maggie." Janice had kind eyes similar in color to Mark's.

"It's a pleasure to meet you as well." Maggie shook her hand. "You have a beautiful home. Thank you for opening your doors to me."

Maggie glanced at Mark and saw the stunned look on his face. When his mom turned around, Maggie shoved his chin up to shut his mouth. "Why are you looking at me like that?" Maggie whispered as they followed his mom to a bedroom.

"I've never seen you so...so...nice and formal." Mark shrugged.

"I'm full of surprises." Maggie grinned over her shoulder at him.

"No, shit," Mark whispered.

"Here is your room." Janice pushed the door open and stepped inside. "Since you're together, there's no sense in separating you. Besides, it's one less bed I have to make." Janice laughed.

"Thank you." Maggie spun around. "This is lovely." The logs from the outside were visible through their window. The headboard and bed were wooden, topped with a beautiful, homemade-looking quilt. There was a dresser and rocking chair, both also made from wood. "This is a beautiful quilt. Did you make it?"

"No," Janice chuckled. "My mom made this one. My quilt is in the other room. I'll show it to you tomorrow. This was Mark's room. But when he moved out, I took down the half-naked model posters and feminized it. Is that a word?"

"I like that word." Maggie smiled at Janice.

"Really, mom?" Mark set the bags on the floor. "You make it sound like I had tons of posters. I only had two."

"They were half naked, and it was two too many." Janice huffed. "Anyway, I'll let you guys get settled in." Janice gave Mark and Maggie a kiss on the cheek and headed out. "See you in the morning."

Mark shut the door behind his mom.

"I like her. She doesn't let you get away with shit." Maggie pointed toward the door.

"Never has." Mark grabbed Maggie and hugged her. "I told you I liked strong women," Mark whispered and ran his hands over her body while he kissed her neck.

"Yeah, no, Surfer Smurf." Maggie pushed him away from her. "No sex while we're here."

Mark stared at her. "You do realize we might be here for a week."

"I am absolutely not having sex with you in your parent's house." Maggie cocked out her hip and crossed her arms. She had to stay strong.

"We'll see." Mark winked at her and grabbed his duffle, putting it on the bed.

Maggie looked around. "Where's Sky going to sleep?"

Mark bent down and pulled out a doggie bed. "Mom keeps it under the bed."

"That's really sweet." Maggie pointed toward the dresser. "Can I have the top two drawers?" Maggie opened the top drawer.

"Sure, Darlin'," Mark chuckled. "Anything you want."

"I like Montana Mark." Maggie lightly tapped his cheek. "He's so nice."

"Yeah, well, don't get used to it. Unless of course, you want to see Big Sexy?" Mark came up behind her and thrust into her backside.

Maggie laughed. "Big Sexy needs to put on PJ's and go to bed." Maggie pulled out shorts and a tank and turned to face him, holding her clothes up. "Show me where the bathroom is so I can change."

"Uh, Mags." Mark rubbed the back of his neck. "I hate to tell you this, but we need to get you some flannel pj's tomorrow or you're going to freeze at night."

"Why? I have you to keep me warm."

"What about when you go down for breakfast?" Mark opened the door to leave the room.

"Valid point. Okay," –Maggie sighed and dramatically draped her hand over her forehead– "take me shopping."

"Funny Girl, here's the bathroom." Mark pushed the door open. "I'll take you tomorrow."

Mark swatted her ass before she got through the door. Maggie giggled, then stuck her tongue out at him before closing and locking it.

"Don't give me that tongue unless you're going to use it," Mark grunted right before the door shut in his face.

Maggie realized this was going to be a fun week driving Mark crazy.

Chapter 46

Why I Left Montana

Mark

"Darlin'," Mark whispered in Maggie's ear and kissed her cheek the next morning. "I'm gonna go help my dad and brother."

"What time is it?" Maggie mumbled.

"Too early for you." Mark kissed her temple and tucked her in. "Go back to sleep."

"Okay." Maggie grabbed the pillow to hug and went back to sleep.

Mark brushed her hair away from her face. She looked like an angel laying in his bed. His young self would never have imagined such a beautiful girl in his bed when he was older. So many crappy relationships and heartaches he could have saved himself from if he'd just waited for Maggie. Then again, without those experiences, he might have stayed in Montana and never met her. That would've been a damn shame.

Mark went into the kitchen to get coffee and wait for his dad.

"Mornin'," Janice looked up and poured his coffee in a tall thermos. "I knew you'd get up early to help your father. Him and Steve already headed to the barn."

"Thanks, Mom." Mark grabbed his thermos and gave his mom a kiss on the cheek. "Maggie's pretty tired, but I'm sure she'll come down when she wakes up."

"Sit for a minute and tell me what's going on?" Janice sat at her kitchen table and patted the empty seat next to her.

Mark knew he wasn't going to get off easy with his mom. His dad was more the silent type, but his mom wanted to know everything that was going on with Mark and Steve since they were little kids. They didn't get anything past her. Mark sat and gave her the condensed version, letting her know they would be safe here. No one knew where Maggie was, not even her brother.

"That poor girl." Janice got up to refill their coffees. "No wonder she's exhausted. When she gets up, I'll make her a big breakfast."

"Thanks, Mom." Mark closed the thermos lid and got up. "I'm gonna go, but text me when she gets up. I'll come back and eat with her. I don't want her to feel uncomfortable in an unfamiliar place."

"Mark Anthony Holmes" –Janice braced her hands on her hips and stared at him with a look of horror– "are you saying I can't make someone feel at home?"

Mark knew not to mess with her when that middle name came out. Janice loved everything to do with romance. When he was born, she was torn between naming him after Cleopatra's legendary lover 'Mark Antony' or the popular Puerto Rican singer 'Mark Anthony'. Janice didn't speak a lick of Spanish but loved listening to his music. Even though she had no clue what he was saying. Ultimately, "Anthony" (with the "h") won because she insisted on correct grammar and pronunciation. It didn't matter that it was his middle name or that he would rarely use it. She wanted everyone to pronounce it correctly.

"Absolutely, not. You are the kindest, most loving, wonderful–"

Janice interrupted him. "Stop with the bullshit and just go." Janice chuckled and pushed him out the kitchen door that led outside while Mark continued with his compliments– "sweetest, best mom ever!"

Janice slammed the door after him to shut him up. He knew his mom would take care of Maggie. He just wanted to see her and find out when she wanted to go to the store. Mark strolled into the barn and saw his dad and Steve saddling up.

"'Bout time you got here."

"Mornin' to you too, pops." Mark walked to his horse to get him ready to ride.

"See you boys out there." Frank mounted his horse and rode off.

"I see he's as talkative as ever." Mark petted Daisy. He'd named her that because she had a white marking below the hair on her forehead that looked like a daisy. Beside her daisy, she had a shiny chestnut coat with black hair. Daisy was neighing and happy to see him.

"I've missed you too, girl." Mark went into her stall and ran his hands over her neck and side. Daisy had been a birthday present from his parents when he turned fifteen. Mark rode Daisy every day until he moved to Florida. He'd thought about bringing her with him, but, at the time, he didn't know where to board her. Now, he would board her with Grayhorse if he ever decided to drive her to Florida.

"Yup, not much changes around here." Steve led his horse out. "I'll meet you outside. We're working in the south pasture barn. Dad bought some calves and they're ready to be tagged."

"Great," Mark snorted. "My favorite." There were many things on the ranch Mark loved to do, but tagging calves was not one of them. Through his studies, he'd learned that ear tagging caused them pain-associated physiological and behavioral responses. Unfortunately, it had to be done to ensure traceability. Losing cattle meant losing money and even though his family had money, they still had to pay all their employees and ranch hands. At least they'd be working in the barn because it was fucking cold outside.

Mark mounted up and followed Steve, ready to get it over with.

*** Maggie ***

Maggie was woken up by a muffled ringing phone. It was the burner phone in her purse. It must be José. "José?"

"*Sí* Margarita. *¿Cómo estás?*"

Maggie scooted up on the bed. She was so glad to hear from her brother. Mark had told her he was angry with what they did to Lola. Sky must have sensed her anxiety, because she jumped up on the bed and laid next to her. "How are you? How's Lola?"

"Lola is going to be okay physically, but mentally..." José sighed. "I'm not sure. They gang raped her, Margarita." José's voice choked up.

"I'm so sorry." Maggie was terrified when they had her they would do that to her. She felt horrible about the terror Lola went through. "Is she still in the hospital? I wanted to go see her, but they wouldn't let me."

"They did the right thing. Lola is with me. Deb is helping me take care of her." Maggie loved Deb. She always took care of all the girls. "Stay where you are for now. Don't tell me where you are—no one needs to know. I just wanted to hear your voice."

"Please take care of yourself." Maggie knew better than to ask him if they were retaliating. Of course they would retaliate. José wouldn't let what they did go unpunished. But she didn't need to know their plan, just that her brother would be safe. "I love you."

"Tell them thank you for keeping you safe. *Te quiero mucho también,* Margarita." Maggie was ready to say goodbye, but José had already hung up. Maggie hugged her knees and rested her head on them. She was so worried about everyone, not just José. What if the LR's attacked the Los Lobos clubhouse or vice versa? Was Tori okay? She hadn't talked to her since Mark whisked her away. She decided to call right now.

"Hello?" Tori answered on the first ring. "Who is this?"

"It's me, Maggie. I'm on a burner phone. Mark was afraid the LR's had my number. Are you okay?" Maggie's heart was racing. What if they hurt Tori?

"Yeah, ever since what happened with Winston, the resort has more security. Have you heard from your brother?"

"He just called." Maggie got up and walked to the bedroom window. "He can't tell me much, but at least Lola is out of the hospital."

"Mark talked to Thunder before he left, and Thunder gave Alex all the details. I feel horrible for her."

"Me too. How are you?" Maggie pushed the curtain aside. It must have snowed overnight because the view outside was breathtaking.

"Wow." Maggie could see the mountains in the distance covered in snow. It looked like a postcard.

"Maggie, what's wrong? Are you okay?"

"It snowed." Maggie grinned. She was in awe of the beauty before her. She'd heard about freshly fallen snow and seen it on TV, but never had the pleasure of being surrounded by it. An urgency to go outside and make a snow angel or snowman overwhelmed her. "It's so beautiful. I can't wait to go out there and play in it."

"Snow is beautiful until you have to shovel it or watch it turn into brown slush." Tori giggled.

"Ohh, maybe I'll volunteer to shovel it for them." Maggie's excitement grew at the thought of being out in the snow.

"Now I know you are a snow virgin. No one, and I mean no one, who has lived in the snow, loves to volunteer to shovel it. Back home in South Dakota, my sister and I took turns. Although Lizzy would pretend to be asleep, and it would be me shoveling." Tori sighed.

"Well, I can't wait to get out there. But now for the real reason I called, how are you?" Maggie worried about Tori because she had been through so much and was a gentle soul. Tori tended to want to isolate herself. She didn't play the victim; she just didn't want to be a burden. Whereas Maggie tended to get mad and continue with her regular schedule. That's not to say the LR's didn't scare her, she just hid it better from everyone.

"I'm okay," Tori sighed. "Tired of feeling scared. I just want all this to end."

Maggie heard Alex's voice in the background.

"I'm talking to Maggie." Tori said.

"I'll let you go. Tell Alex I said hello." Maggie released the curtain. "Call me at this number if you want to talk."

"Sounds good. I'll tell him. Take care of yourself."

"You, too. Bye."

"Bye, Maggie."

Maggie saw a robe draped over the dresser. It hadn't been there last night. Mark must have borrowed it from his mom for her. Maggie put it on and sat next to Sky on the bed. Sky whined and placed her head on Maggie's lap.

"How are you, Sky?" Sky rolled onto her back. "Are you missing Daddy?" Maggie ran one hand over her head and the other over her belly. "I miss your daddy, too." Staring into Sky's eyes was quite calming. "Let's get up. I gotta go potty. Then you can go potty while I help Janice in the kitchen. I'm in serious need of coffee." Sky tilted her head from side to side.

Maggie thought Sky would head downstairs when she went into the bathroom, but she waited for her outside the bathroom door. "You are such a good girl, Sky. Let's go downstairs and find your grandma. Lead the way to the kitchen."

Maggie followed Sky. She'd been tired when they arrived. All she remembered was how grand the house was. Thank goodness the house was an open concept downstairs with the kitchen connecting to the living room. It made it easy to see Janice sitting at the kitchen table reading the newspaper.

"Good morning." Maggie watched Sky make a beeline for Janice.

"Hi, Sky." Janice put down the paper to hug Sky before looking up at Maggie. "Good morning, honey. How did you sleep?"

"Really good, thank you." Maggie looked around for the coffeepot. "Do you, by chance, have any coffee?"

"Of course." Janice stood up, grabbed a mug, and poured her a cup. "Come sit with me. The boys will be in soon to eat their breakfast."

"They haven't eaten yet?" Maggie looked at her watch and knew Mark had been gone for at least a couple of hours. It had been dark when he left.

"They go out and do some work, then come in to eat before heading back out again." Janice smiled at Maggie and sat.

"Oh." Maggie took a sip. "I guess I'm not familiar with ranch life. I've always lived in the city."

"It is different out here." Janice folded her hands and laid them on the table. "Mark told me about what happened to you and why you guys left so quickly."

Maggie's panic-stricken face and grip on her coffee mug must have told Janice she didn't want to talk about it because when she started to say something, Janice held up her hand, cutting her off.

"It's okay, honey. We don't have to talk about it." Janice placed her hand over Maggie's. "I just wanted you to know I spoke with Mark. If you need a shoulder to lean on or an ear to listen, I'm here for you." Janice patted Maggie's hand before grabbing her coffee.

"Thank you, Mrs. Holmes."

Maggie saw the sour look on Janice's face. Had she said something wrong already? Mark's mom was being so nice, she didn't want to insult her.

"None of that Mrs. Holmes crap. Call me Janice." Janice smiled at her.

Whew, for a minute there Maggie thought she fucked up. "Thank you, Janice."

"Here's my girls!" Mark hollered as soon as he walked into the kitchen, stomping the snow off his boots. Sky ran to him with her tail wagging a mile a minute. "Have you guys eaten?"

"No, honey." Janice stood. "We were waiting for you. I'll have it ready in a jiffy. Are your dad and brother coming?"

"Yes, but I left before them." Mark walked to Maggie and kissed the crown of her head. "I'm gonna let Sky out. Are you good?" Mark rubbed her back while he waited for her answer.

"Yeah." Maggie held up her coffee mug. "I'm good."

"Okay. Sky, outside." Mark followed her to the door and let her out. "I'll be back. As a puppy, she hated running around in the snow–definite Florida dog. But now, she loves it."

"Wait!" Maggie screamed and came around the table. "Can I come?" Maggie was about ready to run out the door.

"Maggie!" Janice shouted. "Wait, you need a proper jacket, or you'll freeze out there. Why don't you take a shower and get dressed while Mark walks Sky. Then you can both play in the snow after breakfast."

"Yes ma'am." Maggie smiled and turned to head back upstairs. Janice had just made her feel like a daughter. That was something her mom would have said to her if she were alive. She could get used to this. That was the quickest shower Maggie had ever taken. She was so excited to play in the snow. Hell, she was excited to see the snow.

Chapter 47

Snow Virgin

Maggie

"**I**'m back," Maggie announced when she ran down the stairs and tried to continue to the kitchen door.

"Just a minute, young lady." Janice stepped in front of her and pointed behind Maggie. "You need proper shoes and a jacket. Follow me."

Janice handed her a pair of boots from the closet and gave her one of her jackets. Maggie ran out before zipping it up. She planned to make a snow angel and a snowman and have a snowball fight. Running, she came across a patch of untouched snow, perfect for a snow angel. With a backward twist, she landed on her back, a scene straight out of a Christmas film.

"Mark!" Maggie screamed. *Where was he?* "Help me up so I can see my snow angel."

Mark appeared in front of her, grabbed both her hands, and pulled her up. Maggie spun around and stared at her angel in awe. It was so beautiful. Turning to Mark, she grabbed his hand. "Let's make a snowman." Excitement was coursing through her veins. She felt invigorated. Well, except for that slight twinge in her ribs from when she dropped to the ground.

"You're killing me, Sunshine." Mark grabbed her and kissed the life out of her. "I would love to put this smile on your face every day for the rest of my life" –Maggie's smile froze at the same time Mark's eyes widened and he turned away– "or until you get sick of me."

"I'm not sick of you. You're too much fun to pester, Surfer Smurf." Maggie bent down and made a snowball while his back was turned. "Mark!" Maggie yelled and he turned to face her. That's when Maggie threw the snowball at his chest. "Gotcha!" Maggie pointed at him and ran to make another snowball.

"I thought you wanted to make a snowman?" Mark braced his arms on his hips.

"I changed my mind." Maggie threw another snowball that landed on his thigh. "I want to make you a snowman from my snowballs, Big Sexy." Maggie giggled as she bent down to get more snow. This time, her aim was true, and it hit Mark right in the face. Maggie was laughing so hard, it was infectious. Mark grinned and Sky jumped around her in the snow. Maggie knew if Sky could make a snowball, she would. For this next snowball, she would aim for his arms. Maggie bent down and grabbed a handful of snow. As she was rolling it into a ball, Mark tackled her into the snow, turning both of them mid-air, so she landed on top of him.

"Oof, ouch," Maggie shouted and closed her eyes. It really didn't hurt, but she was going to play it off until she could smash the snowball she made over his head.

"Fuck, Darlin'. Did I hurt you?" Mark ran his hands over her face.

"Nope." Maggie opened her eyes and slammed the snowball on his head. The snow broke apart and ran down his face.

"Little Faker." Mark rolled her over and tickled her.

"Oh, no. Stop. Stop." Maggie tried to get away from him. She was very ticklish and if she didn't stop laughing, she'd pee herself.

"Okay, you two." Janice screamed from the kitchen door. "Come in for breakfast."

"Come on." Mark kissed Maggie and helped her up. "I've worked up an appetite."

"You always have an appetite." Maggie walked around him to the house.

Mark swatted her ass. "Smarty Pants."

"Hey." Maggie turned and walked backwards. "Don't swat it unless you plan to tap it?"

"What?" Mark laughed and pointed at her. "You're the one putting a halt to that Darlin'."

"Damn, you're right." Mark wrapped his arm around her waist and pulled her toward the house. Maggie turned around in his arms and walked in coming to a dead stop. "Where did you guys come from?"

Frank and Steve were already sitting at the table, eating.

Steve pointed at Maggie with his fork and chuckled. "We walked right by you guys while you were turning Big Sexy into a snowman."

Maggie busted out laughing.

"Thanks, Darlin'. I'm never living that one down." Mark pulled out a chair for her and sat next to her.

They continued with their breakfast conversation about ranch life, Florida, and how Maggie and Mark met.

"Gotta get back to work." Frank gave his wife a kiss on the cheek and got up with his plate.

"Me too." Steve took his plate to the sink. "Are you coming, Big Sexy?"

"Fuck me," Mark sighed.

"Uh, no thanks." Steve walked behind Mark and slapped his back.

"Do you want to get some warmer clothes?" Mark turned to Maggie.

"Yes, please." Maggie beamed at him.

"I'll help you guys tomorrow after I get Maggie Montana appropriate clothing." Mark got up and cleared his plate and Maggie's.

Maggie cupped her mouth and looked at Janice. "You've trained them well."

Janice grinned. "Of course. We all pitch in on the farm."

"See you ladies later," Frank opened the door for Steve and right before he walked out, he hollered. "See you later too, Big Sexy."

Maggie heard his loud laughter even after he closed the door. When she turned back to see Mark, he was gripping the sink with his head bent. Oops.

"Mark?" Janice cleared her plate and rubbed his back, sliding her plate into the sink. "What's your pet name for Maggie?"

Maggie held her breath because he had so many names, some not so nice. She wondered which one he was going to say.

"Darlin'. I call her Darlin'." Mark put his arm around his mom.

Maggie was shocked by Mark's answer. Then again, it's not like he was going to tell his mom he called her Sexy Smurfette, Naughty Girl, or Little Faker. Those were just some of the ones she remembered because he was constantly coming up with new ones.

"That's so sweet." Janice rested her head on her son's chest. A sweet mother-son moment.

"Janice, can I do those for you before we leave?" Maggie put all the other dishes on the counter and wiped the table.

"No, honey. You kids go to the store and get whatever you need."

"Thanks, Mom." Mark bent down and kissed her temple.

Mark grabbed Maggie's hand and pulled her away from the table. "Come on, Trouble," Mark whispered in her ear.

"Oh, Maggie?" Janice yelled from the sink since her hands were in the sudsy water.

"Yes." Maggie stopped and faced Janice.

"Take my coat. And Mark...buy her one."

"Yes, ma'am." Mark pulled her toward the door. Sky was whining to go with them. "Sky, stay with grandma."

Sky plopped down and dropped her head on her paws in a pathetic attempt to convince Mark to take her.

"No moping, Sky. When we come back, we'll go for a run."

Sky raised her head and barked, her tail wagging on the floor.

Maggie walked out and headed to the truck. "I hope you're planning on going for a run, because Sky will be very upset if you cancel on her."

"Yeah, I know. I'll take her even if it's dark out."

"You're such a good doggie daddy, Big Sexy." Maggie buckled in.

Mark chuckled and shook his head.

They had to drive almost an hour to get to town. There, they walked to several small local shops. Maggie bought a couple small items, but most were overpriced. Mark offered to buy her some clothes, but she refused to spend his money. She preferred going to a superstore where she could get more for less. Her budget was tight.

"How about this coat?" Mark pulled out a beautiful, hooded coat that was lined with fur.

Maggie immediately looked for the tag and almost passed out when she saw it was almost two thousand dollars. *Who pays that kind of money for a coat?*

"Uh, absolutely not." Maggie left him holding the coat.

"Maggie?" Mark held it out to her. "Try it on."

"Nope." Maggie ignored him and continued to look through the racks.

"I promised my mom I'd get you a coat." Mark sounded frustrated by her rejection of the coat.

"Okay, but not that one." Maggie pointed to the coat still in his hand. "Chose another more reasonably priced coat."

"Fine." Mark sighed and returned the overpriced coat. "How about this one?"

It was like the previous one, but when Maggie checked the tag, she saw it was a quarter of the price.

"That's still a lot," Maggie wrinkled her nose. "Can't we just try at a supercenter store?"

"Look, Warren Buffett." Mark draped the coat over his arms and crossed them. "Please try this on. If it fits—and I want to see it on you—then I'm buying it. We can get anything else you want at the supercenter store, deal?"

Maggie bit her lip and thought about her choices. On the one hand, if the coat fit, they could leave, get the rest of her stuff, and go home. But if she said no, they would continue to stand there and argue until she said yes. She wasn't going to win this one. At least she convinced him not to buy the expensive one.

Mark grabbed her wrist and pulled her against his chest. "Deal?"

"Deal," Maggie consented, and Mark sealed the deal with a kiss before shoving the coat at her.

"Try it on."

Maggie took off his mom's coat and put the new one on. She had to admit it was soft and comfy. She turned from side to side. "What do you think?"

"Perfect. Let's take it." Mark spun her around and pushed her toward the register. "Anything else you want from here? Oh wait, shit, you need boots."

Mark changed direction and pulled her toward the shoes area. "What size are you?"

"Seven and a half." Maggie dreaded looking for shoes in this store.

"Try these." Mark dropped boots on the floor in front of her. "They're waterproof and fur lined on the inside."

Maggie grabbed the box to see the price, but before she could find it, Mark tore it out of her hands.

"Nope, no price checking," Mark said before he put the box behind him.

Maggie made a grab for it, but he gave her a quick kiss and lifted the box above his head. Since he was at least a foot taller than her, she couldn't even reach it with a good jump.

"Come on Ornery Girl. Try them on."

He was insufferably stubborn when he set his mind to it. Then again, he would probably say she was too. Maggie sat on a bench and put both boots on. They felt like she was walking on a cloud.

"Wow, these are really nice." Maggie walked around.

"Perfect. Give me the coat and boots." Mark put the boots in the box but kept her on the other side of him so she couldn't see the price. When Maggie saw the total price for both items, she just about had a heart attack. Before she moved in with Nancy, Maggie had checked the prices for one-bedroom apartments. That bill was the same as a month's rent for an expensive one bedroom in Miami.

"Can you please cut the tags off? She's going to wear the coat and boots out." Mark asked the cashier. "But we'll still need a bag, please."

"Of course, Mark."

"I'm sorry, do we know each other?" Mark looked confused.

"You dated my older sister." The girl snickered before she handed the coat and boots to Maggie.

"Oh. Okay." Mark turned to Maggie, his eyes pleading with her to help him out.

"Thank you so much for your help" –Maggie read her nametag– "Katie. Have a great day." Maggie grabbed the receipt and pushed Mark out of the store. *Fuck the bag, she could carry Janice's coat and shoes to the car.*

"Do you remember her sister?" Maggie asked when they got outside.

"Yeah, I dated her in high school." Mark rubbed the back of his neck. "But I haven't seen Katie in over eight years. I'm sorry about that."

"Listen, Romeo. I knew you had a past." Maggie shrugged and walked to the truck. "That was before me. As long as you don't cheat on me—we're good."

"Maggie." Mark grabbed her elbow and turned her around. "I would never cheat on you. Here, give me those." Mark took the coat and shoes. "Let's go to the supercenter store so you can get anything else you need."

"Okay, Cowboy." Maggie winked at him.

"I see I'm rubbing off on you." Mark draped his arm around her.

"Well, if you can come up with names for me, two can play at that game, Surfer Smurf."

"Ahhh, my Maggie is back with my favorite name." Mark placed his hand over his heart and sighed.

"Come on, Big Sexy Cowboy. Take me to my kind of store."

"At your service, Foxy Cowgirl." Mark took a bow.

Maggie found everything she needed at the superstore, including flannel pajamas and a velour robe.

Chapter 48

The Shit Hits the Fan

Mark

The next week went by quickly. While Mark helped his brother and dad, Maggie helped Janice around the house. As much as Mark couldn't wait to leave Montana when he was young, he enjoyed coming back for visits. Maggie learned how to make homemade biscuits and Janice's homemade mac 'n' cheese. Mark wasn't surprised his mom taught Maggie how to make those two things, since they were his favorites. On days where Mark would come home from school tired from baseball practice, his mom always had a fresh pan of mac 'n' cheese. It was his comfort food, but she'd never given him the recipe. His mom must love Maggie, because she gave her both recipes.

Mark had returned from mending a portion of the fence around the house and was brushing Daisy when his cell phone rang. He looked at the caller ID and froze.

"José, what's up?" Mark was hoping Maggie's brother wasn't calling to tell him he was hurt.

"We got them back, but now they're pissed."

"What did you do?" Mark pinched the bridge of his nose. "Or should I not ask?"

"Nothing bloody. We derailed their shipment of women to the port and drove them to the police station." That was not what Mark was expecting to hear. They actually did a good thing instead of killing someone.

"Wow, I didn't expect that."

"No one did. That's why it worked." José chuckled. "We're trying to keep our hands clean because the police and feds are sniffing around. A bloodbath wouldn't bode well for us. Besides, this hit them where it hurts. I'm fucking tired of them hurting and trafficking women. *Hijo de putas.*"

"You know they're going to retaliate, right?" All Mark could think about were the consequences and how it would affect Maggie. She wanted to go home for Christmas, and she had promised Tori and Frey that she would help them with their wedding.

"Yeah, I know." Mark heard José sigh. "That's why I'm calling you. When are you guys coming back?"

"On the twenty-third. Maggie wants to be home for Christmas Eve and Day."

"Are you going to be staying at your house? I can send some brothers over there to watch over her."

"No need." Mark had spoken to Alex and Thunder a couple of days ago and they had a plan. "She and I will be living at the Rock 'n' Roll Resort & Casino in the room she had after the accident. There's no way anyone can get on the family floor without a key card, and they've stationed an officer by the downstairs elevator twenty-four seven."

"Okay. What about work?"

"Thunder always closes the cultural center the week between Christmas and New Year, so that won't be a problem." Mark finished brushing Daisy while he talked to José. He couldn't wait to let Maggie know her brother was okay. "Plus, Deputy George lives there now in the apartment upstairs. I've got her, I promise."

"Thank you, Mark. Let me know if you need our help."

"I will. Please stay safe. It would kill your sister if anything happened to you." Mark put the brush away.

"I'll do my best, always. I gotta go."

"Yeah, see ya." Mark hung up. Pocketing his phone, he went into the house in search of Maggie.

"Hey." Mark found her in the kitchen, making cookies with his mom.

"Hi, Big Sexy." That had now become his name at home.

"Can I talk to you alone for a second?" Mark pointed toward the staircase.

"Sure." Maggie wiped her hands. "I'll be back, Janice."

"It's okay, honey. I'll finish up here."

Maggie took off her apron and walked toward him. When she was close, she asked, "What's wrong? Is my brother okay?"

"Let's talk in our room." Mark followed her upstairs and locked the door when she sat on the bed.

"Tell me, please." Maggie fidgeted with her hands on her lap.

"It's not as bad as you think, I just didn't know how much you wanted my mom to know about your brother." Mark sat next to her and held her hands. "I just talked to your brother. He wanted to let me know his club just riled the LR's by intercepting one of their shipments."

"A drug shipment?"

"No, a human trafficking shipment filled with women." Mark saw Maggie's eyes widen and her mouth drop open.

"I always thought they trafficked women and children, but I wasn't sure." Maggie pulled her hands away and stood, pacing the room. "They are going to hit back."

"Yep." Mark stood and put his hands in his front jeans pocket. "That's why he called. He wanted to know when we are going back and where we're going to live."

"I know we're leaving the twenty-third so Chris can fly back before Christmas, but where are we going?" Maggie stopped in front of him.

"I spoke to Thunder and Alex. We're going to live in the room where you stayed at the resort." Mark grabbed her hips to stop her from pacing again.

"And work?"

"Thunder closes from Christmas to New Year, so you can help Tori and Frey with wedding things. I'm sure Isa will join you ladies, too."

Maggie wrapped her arms around him. "Thank you for helping me with all this."

"I will do whatever I can to keep you safe." Mark held her tightly against his body. In hindsight, that wasn't such a good idea because she fit him so damn perfectly, he hardened within seconds. He was going to miss home, but he couldn't fucking wait to leave so he could fuck his girlfriend again.

"Ooh, someone's happy to see me." Maggie squeezed his ass.

"Don't mess with me, woman. I'm two seconds away from throwing you down on that bed and fucking the hell out of you," Mark moaned.

"Just a few more days, Big Sexy." Maggie kissed his chest and stepped back.

"Don't remind me." Mark rubbed his eyes. "I think I need a cold shower, again."

"I'm gonna finish helping your mom. See you downstairs?"

"Yep, I'll be down after my shower." Mark grabbed clothes and headed toward the bathroom. Even though it was freezing outside, he was turning that water as fucking cold as he possibly could.

Chapter 49

His Wounded Dove

José

José felt better now that they had fucked with Lucifer's Renegades and not only ruined their cash payment, but alerted the police to their human trafficking ring. Fuckers deserved it. José knew he had blood on his hands and would someday have to answer for his sins, but he never hurt women, children, or the elderly. Some of his brothers sold drugs and guns to minors. Whenever he heard those stories, he tried to stop them. Children were off limits—he didn't do that shit.

"Hey, babe." José laid down next to Lola. She still didn't want anyone touching her, which he totally understood. He loved her and would wait until she felt comfortable around him again. José had fallen for Lola from the first day she entered the clubhouse with her friend. She had borrowed her friend's clothes. José stayed close because she seemed like a fish out of water. While her friend flirted with the guys, Lola kept pulling down her short, black leather skirt and adjusting her top to cover her cleavage. Whenever a brother approached her, José made eye contact and shook his head.

The news got around and soon no one was talking to Lola. José made his move and won her over. He would've made her his old lady long before now, but was afraid of putting a target on her back. A lot of good that did. They still found out she was his girl. They had to have a mole because Lola knew better than to tell anyone outside the club about José.

Lola didn't even acknowledge him when he spoke to her. She would just lay still on her side and stare at the wall. The only person who could get through to her was Deb. So, José would lay quietly next to her, and he prayed for the day she turned to him and smiled or hugged him. He didn't expect her to want sex, but he would love to just hold her and comfort her. José and Deb had tried to get her to see a professional and seek help, but she wasn't ready yet.

"I called Mark, Maggie's boyfriend, and told him about the women we saved. They're going to come back before Christmas. Maybe I can find a way for you and Maggie to see each other. I know she's thinking about you and wanted to visit you at the hospital. I can't tell you where they are, because I don't know, but I do know Mark is keeping her safe." José sighed. He talked to Lola even though she never answered. "They're going to be staying at that resort where Maggie stayed after her...incident." José didn't know what to call it, but he was afraid if he said kidnapping, it would upset Lola. José felt the bed shaking and he turned toward Lola.

"Babe, are you okay?" José touched her shoulder to lean over and see her face.

Lola screamed and bolted out of the bed, scrambling to the corner of the room where she drew up her knees. Wrapping her arms around herself, she rocked her body and mumbled. "Please don't touch me."

"I'm so sorry." José jumped out of the bed and backed up toward the door. "I'll go downstairs and send Deb up here. I'm so sorry."

José left the room. *What an idiot!* He knew better than to touch her. *Fuck!* When he found Deb, he told her what happened and asked her to sit with Lola until she calmed down. José knew he would be spending another uncomfortable night on the disgusting couch in the living room, unless he could bunk in the downstairs bedroom.

Chapter 50

Last Day in Montana

Maggie

Mark had just left to work on the ranch with Sky. Maggie couldn't fall back asleep. Her brain was too loud thinking about this past week at the ranch. It was the best week of her life, being surrounded by Mark's awesome family. Janice took her in, treating her like a daughter from the first day and they set up a daily routine that comforted Maggie. Every day was an adventure. Mark always left at the crack of dawn, but came back for breakfast, lunch, and dinner. Several times, he took her out on a horse. Maggie remembered the first day when he thought it would be a good idea for her to ride in front of him on Daisy. He'd pressed her up against his chest with his thighs holding her in place.

"What are you doing?" Maggie startled when she felt Mark's cold hand.

"Helping you relax." Mark held the reins in his right hand while his left hand slipped under her sweatshirt and coat to caress her breast. His lips licked and sucked her neck and collarbone.

"Are you sure that's what you're doing?" Maggie released the horn on the saddle, grabbed his thighs, and tilted her head back, giving him better access to her neck. They hadn't been together in several days and her body was ready for his attention. Why had she told him 'no sex at your mom's house'?

"Mmhmm."

"That feels so good." Maggie moaned when Mark released the front clasp on her bra, peeling it away to play with her nipples. "Can we go somewhere, please?"

"I thought you insisted on no sex at my mom's house." Mark squeezed her breast and pulled her closer to his hard on. Oh, yeah, he was just as turned on as she was. Maggie pushed her chest out into his hand.

"We're not in the house." Maggie turned her head, searching for his mouth.

"I am not fucking you in the snow," Mark groaned and captured her mouth.

Daisy couldn't go any slower and the rhythm was a huge turn on. Maggie was ready to mount him and ride him reverse, cowgirl style.

"Then fuck me on Daisy." Maggie's right hand squeezed his thigh while her left hand ran up his neck and grasped his hair. "Don't you guys have a shack out here somewhere?"

"Yes, we do, Miss Impatient." Mark lowered his hand into her pants and dove into her pussy. "You're so wet for me."

"I know," Maggie growled. "Do something about it."

Mark slipped his finger inside and stroked her clit with his thumb. Maggie couldn't stop her pussy from fucking his hand. She needed release. Between his tongue and fingers, she was about to come.

"No, no, no. What are you doing?" Maggie groaned when he pulled out of her pants and pressed her belly against him with his spread hand. "Go back, dammit! It's not nice to leave your girl needy."

"Shh. My dad is riding up on us and I don't think you want him to catch us with my hand down your pants," Mark whispered in her ear. "I'm sorry."

Sure as shit, Maggie had heard Frank's voice a few seconds later. After that, Mark taught her how to ride her own horse. He'd told her if they were on the same horse again, he was going to find a spot and throw her down to fuck her thoroughly and he didn't give a shit if it was on the snow or in front of his parents. It was good to see Mark was just as sexually frustrated as she was. It was going to be an interesting plane ride home.

Maggie got up and went down to help Janice prepare their special holiday meal. She couldn't wait to find out what they ate for Christmas Eve. When she went to her aunt's house, they always ate *lechon asado, arroz blanco con frijoles, yuca, and platanitos (tostones and maduros)*. Aunt Inez always made *tostones* in memory of her father because everyone else liked the *maduros*. Maggie always had a couple of each because her mom had loved the maduros and she always made both on Christmas Eve. One of the best things about Christmas Eve was her aunt bringing an assortment of Cuban pastries from her favorite Cuban bakery, Vicky Bakery, in Miami. Her favorite pastry was the *pastelito de guayaba*. She needed to talk to Mark and see if they could go to her aunt's house tomorrow night.

"Good morning. I didn't realize you were going to start so early. You should've woken me up." Maggie walked into the kitchen, grabbed her apron, and stood next to Janice. "Is that gingerbread? It smells so good. What can I help you with?"

"You need your rest." Janice plopped the brown dough on the counter and separated half. "You take this half, roll it out, use these cookie cutters, and place them on this cookie tray. The oven is ready."

"I've never made gingerbread cookies." Maggie grabbed a roller and got to work. Janice was ready, she had gingerbread men and women in all different sizes. "Can I have your recipe for when I go home?"

"Absolutely." Janice was rolling her dough. "You can do the next batch so you can practice."

"Why so many?" Maggie thought they had enough for the four of them.

"Some of my friends and I always donate gingerbread cookies to the church for the kids who attend Christmas Day Mass. Some of us make the cookies and others provide snack size baggies with icing for them to decorate them at home." Janice grabbed their finished tray and placed it in the oven.

"That's so sweet of you guys." Maggie leaned against the counter and placed her hand on her heart. "I love that. I would be honored to make more cookies with you."

"Good" –Janice hugged Maggie and smiled– "because we have to make a total of 150. Joannie is sick and I'm covering her batch since I have a helper."

"Gotcha." Maggie chuckled. She was going to miss Janice. During this last week, she made her feel wanted and loved. Her mom and Janice would've gotten along so well. "Let's do this."

Maggie and Janice worked all day finishing the cookies and telling each other stories about their previous Christmases. They put out the trimmings for the boys to make their own sandwiches for lunch.

"What time should we start dinner?" Maggie asked Janice after the last tray went into the oven.

"We'll start the mashed potatoes now, because I have a special recipe my aunt gave me and after we make a pan, it goes into the oven for an hour. Then you can make the biscuits since you're becoming a pro." Janice winked at Maggie. "We'll cook the Prime Rib when the boys come in to wash up since it only takes about thirty-five minutes to cook. Oh dear, I didn't even ask if you liked Prime Rib. We tend to cook it medium. Is that okay?"

"I've never had it, but I'll try it." Maggie shrugged and began washing the dirty dishes and pans from the gingerbread cookies while Janice dried them before putting them away.

"If you don't like it, I can make you something else."

"No, you don't have to do that." Maggie placed the clean measuring cup on the drying rack. "I'll have plenty to eat with the sides."

"We'll see." Janice shoulder bumped her and grabbed the cup to dry it. "If I don't see you eating enough, I will make you something else. This is my house and I will not let anyone go hungry."

Janice was a hoot. Now she knew where Mark got his bossiness from.

*** Mark ***

"I'll meet you guys inside." Mark put his horse back in her stall and waved his hand at his brother and dad. "Sky, come." Sky loved running around the ranch.

"I've never seen you put Daisy up as fast as you have this week, Big Sexy." Steve shouted from his horse's stall. "I wonder why?"

"Ignore him, son." Frank hollered from the tack room. "One day he too will find a good woman that he can't wait to get home to. We'll meet you up there."

That's exactly how Mark felt. If he could come home to Maggie every night for the rest of his life, he'd be a happy man. Tonight, they were celebrating Christmas, and he couldn't wait for Maggie to see what he got her. This trip home had been great. He was glad he brought Maggie home to meet his family instead of going somewhere else. His mom had already pulled him aside and told him to treat her right and not let this one get away. Yeah, that wasn't happening. Maggie was stuck with him forever.

Mark was in heaven the minute he stepped into the kitchen. The smell of fresh gingerbread cookies assaulted his senses and reminded him of his childhood. His mom always made these cookies, and they decorated them on Christmas Day. One year, he ate so many his stomach ached well into the night. Those were also the cookies they left out with a glass of milk for Santa. Watching Maggie laughing with his mom in the kitchen made him realize that he loved her. Mark stood frozen in the doorway until his brother pushed him from behind into the room.

"Come on, Big Sexy." Steve smirked at him as he walked around him. "Stop drooling over your girl. We need to get ready for dinner."

Maggie turned around when she heard Steve's voice.

"Hi." Mark had never seen her glowing like she was. Happiness looked good on her. Maggie walked up to him and gave him a peck on his lips. Yeah, that wasn't going to work. Mark opened his mouth and pushed his tongue against her lips until she let him in. Maggie tried to push him away.

"Mark, your parents." Maggie murmured against his lips, but Mark wasn't having it. He grabbed her around the waist and held her tightly against his chest. When she gasped, he entered her sweet mouth and kissed her senseless. When he released her mouth, she swayed and gripped his shirt. Oh yeah, his girl loved that kiss as much as he did. Mark gave her his best cocky grin. Maggie blinked several times, then smacked him.

"What was that for?" Mark laughed. He knew why she smacked him, but he wanted to tease her. Plus, he knew his parents weren't going to get upset. They already loved her too.

"For embarrassing me, Surfer Smurf." Maggie dropped her head onto his chest.

"They weren't even looking." Mark hugged her. Maggie turned around and realized Mark had lied. His parents had seen the kiss. His dad had his arm around his mom and they were grinning from ear to ear at Mark and Maggie.

"Mark!" Maggie smacked his stomach, causing him to laugh harder and Sky to bark.

"Oh, honey." Janice had tears in her eyes. "Don't be embarrassed. We're glad Mark found you and brought you to us. I'm so happy for you both." Janice stepped forward and hugged Maggie.

"Can I have my girl back now?" Mark asked his mom.

"Don't you sass me, Mark Anthony Holmes. I will smack you and it will be harder than her slaps, Big Sexy." Janice winked at him.

Mark busted out laughing and hugged his mom. "I love you, mom. I'm gonna go take a shower. I'll be quick cause I'm starving, and it smells great in here." Mark attempted to grab a cookie on his way out, but his mom's hand came out of nowhere and smacked his hand.

"Not before dinner you don't." Janice shooed him. "Now, go."

Mark turned and lifted his arms in defeat. "I'm going. I'm going. Maggie, are you coming?" He hollered on his way out.

"She's staying with me, so you don't dilly dally." Mark heard his mom say when his foot landed on the first step.

Damn, cock blocked again by his mom. At this rate, Big Sexy was going to blow just from looking at Maggie naked. And he planned on getting her naked as soon as they boarded that fucking plane to go home. Mark washed up in record time and headed back downstairs.

Dinner was delicious. They decided to move into the living room and open presents before decorating and eating the gingerbread cookies because everyone was so full.

Mark, Maggie, and Steve sat on the couch. Mark's dad sat in his recliner and his mom played Santa.

"First gift is for my granddaughter, Sky." Janice tossed Sky a toy filled with treats.

Mark rolled his eyes. "She's gonna love that."

Maggie started crying when Janice handed her a gift. Mark gave her a side hug and kissed her temple.

"You didn't have to get me anything." Maggie looked from Janice to Frank. "Letting me stay with you was gift enough."

"Don't be silly." Janice waved her off. "We loved having you here with us. That's just a little something so you remember your time here."

Maggie opened her box and pulled the tissue paper aside. Janice had written all the recipes they made together this week on individual recipe cards. She even included a new apron like the one Maggie wore this week.

"I don't know what to say," Maggie whispered. "This is...I love it. Thank you." Maggie handed Mark the box and ran to Janice for a hug. Then she hugged his dad and kissed his cheek. "Thank you both."

"I didn't give you the one you wore while you were here because you're gonna need it when you come back to visit." Janice winked. "Deal?"

"Deal."

"This is from Maggie and me for you both." Mark grabbed a box from under the tree. Maggie walked to him and quirked an eyebrow. He should've told her, but he totally forgot he got his parents a gift from both of them.

Janice opened the box and pulled out sunscreen, two books (a romance and a mystery), a beach hat, a baseball cap, and two tickets. She dropped the box and covered her mouth as tears ran down her face. Mark knew she'd always wanted to go on a cruise, but dad never wanted to take two weeks off.

"What is it?" Frank stood and held his wife.

"Mark and Maggie bought us a fourteen-day cruise in the U.S. Virgin Islands." Mark watched his father glare at him, then smile. Janice turned around, wiped her tears, and ran to Mark and Maggie for a hug.

"Now you have to take time off." Mark walked to his dad and hugged him before handing Steve an envelope.

"Did you buy me a cruise too?" Steve joked.

"Open it." Mark motioned with his chin at the envelope.

"Well, hell, bro. You remembered." Steve couldn't stop looking at his gift. This past summer when he'd been home, Steve told him he always wanted to go to Ireland and see where their ancestors came from.

"What is it?" Janice turned to Steve.

"Airfare for a round-trip ticket to Ireland through a travel agency. I can pick whichever package I want." Steve gave Mark a huge hug. "Guess I get a vacation next year, too."

"You don't go on vacation?" Maggie sounded confused.

"Not usually." Steve hugged her. "Too much to do on a ranch. But I'm taking this one. Thanks bro."

Mark grabbed a wrapped long box and handed it to Maggie.

"Mark?" Maggie held it and stared at him. "I didn't get you anything."

"All I need is you." Mark kissed her and heard a chorus of aww's behind him.

Mark watched Maggie's face when she pulled out a charm bracelet with three charms on it. He had a fourth one that he was going to give her on Christmas Day.

"I didn't fill it because we have a lot more adventures ahead of us. So, I started it with a surfer for your favorite nickname for me and Florida. The BBQ grill represents our first kiss, and the horse is for your first horseback riding lesson and Montana."

"I love it." Maggie smiled through glassy eyes. "Will you put it on me?"

"With pleasure." Mark fastened it on her wrist and kissed it before he pulled her in for a real kiss.

"Okay, you two. Mom has your gifts from me." Steve pointed to Janice holding two boxes.

Mark opened his and busted out laughing. He held up red boxers with white hearts that said "Big Sexy" in bold block white letters on the ass.

Steve got Maggie a beautiful cashmere scarf that Maggie rubbed against her cheek. "This is so soft and beautiful. Thank you so much." Maggie hugged Steve.

Not to be outdone, his dad stood up and grabbed his mom's hands, putting a small black box in them.

"Janice," –his dad cupped her face in his hands and gazed into her eyes– "I have loved you since we were kids, you are the love of my life–my soulmate. You are the best wife, mom, and woman I know. My life would be nothing without you. When we got married, I couldn't afford the style of ring I wanted to get you."

Mark whispered in Maggie's ear. "Our family has money, but my grandfather wanted my dad to start at the bottom and paid him the same wages as his other ranch hands."

"Honey, you deserve better." Frank kissed her and released her, pointing to the box. "Open it."

Mark's eyes bulged out of his head. *Damn, Pops.* That had to be at least two carats.

"This is too much," Janice cried.

"Nothing is too much for my soulmate." Frank took off the old ring and put the new one on. Janice covered her mouth with one hand while she turned her hand in all different directions.

"Wow," Maggie murmured.

"I'll give you the rest of your gifts on Christmas," Frank told Janice.

"There's more?" His mom deserved more. She kept everything running smoothly while his father worked the ranch.

"Yup."

"Yeah, I only got Maggie's. I gotta go shopping for you guys tomorrow."

"Tomorrow," Maggie glanced at Steve and tilted her head. "That's Christmas Eve."

"That's when he goes." Mark laughed. "He likes to get good deals."

"I'll mail you yours Big Sexy." Steve winked.

"Are you sure the postage price isn't gonna break your savings?" Mark teased.

They moved into the kitchen for cookies and then watched Christmas movies until they went to bed.

Chapter 51

Not the Massage I was Expecting...but Better

Maggie

Frank, Janice, and Steve drove Mark and Maggie to the airport. Chris was waiting for them by the plane. Maggie hugged everyone and promised to come back to visit.

"Ya'll ready?" Chris grabbed Maggie's bag.

"Yeah." Mark slapped his back. "The faster we leave, the quicker you can get back home." Sky ran up the stairs before them.

"It's all good. I left them in Florida. We'll celebrate Christmas there and then fly home." Chris nodded and followed them up the stairs.

"Good plan." Mark put away their luggage while Chris pulled up the stairs.

Maggie stood next to Mark waving at his family out the window. It was a bittersweet feeling. She was happy to go home, but couldn't wait to come back and see Janice, Frank, and Steve. She was going to miss them.

"Come on, Darlin'," Mark pulled her away from the window. "Time to buckle up. Sky, come."

Maggie sat in her usual seat and buckled in while Mark buckled Sky.

"Did you have fun?" Mark smiled at her.

"I did. I love your family." Maggie felt the plane move and draped her arm around Sky. "At least for a week I could forget about the shitshow that is my life. Flying back home is bringing it all back."

"Let's not think about it yet. We don't have to face reality for another eight hours." Mark lightly kicked her foot. He was sitting across from her so she could hold Sky. "Let's stay in our bubble for a little while longer." Mark wiggled his fingers at her. "Slide off your shoes and give me your feet. I'll give you a massage to relax you. I know you don't like when the plane takes off."

"Really?" Maggie quirked her eyebrow. "You're gonna give me a foot massage?"

"Yup, I'll start there." Mark placed one foot between his legs, lifting the other to rub her instep.

"You're spoiling me, Big Sexy." Maggie sighed and scooted down in her seat. If he kept this up, he was going to have to give her foot massages every time they were on a plane. *What was she thinking?* He would have to give her foot massages every day after work. Maggie closed her eyes and focused on his magical fingers. Mark was alternating between her feet and before she knew it, they were up in the sky and the plane had leveled off.

"Come on." Maggie opened her eyes and saw Mark standing in front of her with a bulge in his pants. He must've unbuckled Sky because she walked by Maggie and headed to her favorite spot on the couch. Mark held out his hand.

"Where are we going?" Maggie stood and took his hand.

"I'm gonna give you a full body massage." Mark pulled her into the bedroom.

That sounded fantastic, but how long could Maggie hold out with his hands all over her body? *Minutes? More like seconds.* Didn't matter, she didn't think Mark would last more than a few seconds either if the bulge in his pants was any indication.

Mark pulled her into the room and locked the door. He cupped her face and kissed her, running his hands through her hair and releasing it from her ponytail. "Darlin', I've missed you." Mark leaned down and kissed her neck.

"You've kissed me every day." Maggie leaned her head back to give him better access to her neck. "Besides, you promised me a massage."

"Don't you worry." Mark sucked her neck while his hands massaged the back of her head. "I'm gonna massage every section of your beautiful body."

Mark's hands ran down the collar of her coat unbuttoning it as he went. Pushing it off her shoulders, he let it drop to the ground. He cupped her face and went back to kissing her mouth. Opening his mouth over her lips, he sucked her bottom lip into his mouth. When Maggie gasped, he slipped his tongue into her mouth and stole her breath away. While he was kissing the shit out of her, his hands glided under her sweatshirt, lightly skimming her skin higher and higher until his fingers reached her bra.

Mark released her mouth, and she took a deep breath as he pulled off her sweatshirt. Maggie didn't see where he threw it because she was caught up in his eyes as they glazed over and softened. Maggie had worn draw string sweatpants so she could be comfortable on the plane. Mark didn't break eye contact as his hands pulled the bow on the drawstring, pushed her pants down, and knelt to help her step out of them. Cupping her ass, he pulled her toward his mouth, closed his eyes, and breathed in her essence. When he opened his eyes and stood, a gleam of excitement sparkled within them, eager for the adventure that awaited.

"You are so fucking beautiful." Mark looked her up and down. Maggie could hear his breathing coming out heavier. He grasped her hand and turned her around, stopping her when her back was to his chest. Mark tucked her into his arms. Resting his chin on her shoulder, Mark murmured, "Look down, Maggie. Watch my hands worship your body." Mark's hands drifted up her belly to her bra, unclasped it, and massaged her breasts.

Maggie moaned and arched her back, pressing her breasts into his hands. Each breast rested in the palm of his hands, holding their weight while he drew slow circles around her areola, instantly hardening her nipple. As if that wasn't enough to drench her panties, he captured each nipple between his thumb and pointer finger, slowly alternating between rotating and pulling them.

"So needy, how they stand up for me, begging me to suck them." Mark swirled his tongue down her neck to where it met her shoulder. Slowly, his hands came up to slide the straps of her bra off, letting it drop to the floor. His mouth followed the right strap and found her sensitive spot before he latched on, sucking so hard, she knew she'd have a hickey when he was done. If Mark continued with this slow exploration of her body, he was going to have to do it from the floor because she was about two seconds from losing the ability to stand on her own.

"Mark," Maggie moaned. Mark moved his left hand to her belly and pressed her tightly against his chest. His right-hand glided around her hips and dove into her panties. Seconds later, he plunged his finger into her, ripping a low scream from her mouth. She undulated against his hand. Her hands reached back and grabbed his ass, pulling him toward her so she could feel his shaft while he played with her. She needed more. She needed him–NOW. Maggie's eyes slammed shut as her body shuttered and she came all over his hand.

Mark spun her around to face him. Maggie was panting when she opened her eyes and stared into his. Mark grinned at her while he spread her cum all over her pussy. He lightly ran his fingers over her clit. Maggie's body jolted still sensitive from his touch. Maggie's eyes widened when he pulled his hand up to his mouth and licked every finger while he watched her. Maggie had never met a man that liked to go down on her like Mark. She wasn't complaining. She loved it and was grateful to the powers that be for creating such a man.

"You taste as good as you look. Get on the bed for your massage." Mark motioned with his head toward the bed behind her.

Maggie didn't have to be told twice. She turned around and placed her knee on the bed, ready to crawl to the center, when she felt Mark grab her panties on the sides and slide them off as she crawled away from him. Before she reached the center of the bed, Mark grasped her hips and stopped her.

"Lay your chest and head down, but keep your ass up." Maggie did as instructed, instantly rewarded by his tongue in her pussy, licking her up. One hand gripped her hip while the other came around the front to play with her clit. Maggie gripped the sheets and screamed into the pillow. Her heartbeat soared as euphoria claimed her for a second time and she came in his mouth.

"I want every part of you. I want to fuck every hole." Maggie felt the tip of his finger at her puckered hole creating a stretching sensation, but no pain. She'd never let anyone fuck her up the ass, but for Mark, she would willingly allow it. Thinking he was going to enter her there, she was shocked when she felt him ram into her pussy.

"Not this time, I need to get you properly ready. I don't want to hurt you. You mean too much to me." Mark grumbled before he pounded into her a few more times. "Fuck. I need to see you when you come."

Mark flipped her over and entered her slowly this time. He braced his elbows next to her head. His hands pushing her hair off her face, he bent down and kissed her lips gently. His tongue mimicked the motion of his cock inside her. Maggie opened her legs wide and wrapped them around his thighs. Her hands gripped his ass trying to keep him pressed against her. She wanted him to go faster, but he was taking his time. He wasn't fucking her–he was making love to her. He released her lips and leaned his forehead against hers. Increasing his speed, he held her head in his hands and opened his eyes.

Clamping down on his cock with her inner muscles, Maggie opened her eyes. Her gaze traveled over his face. She noticed several things at once. His eyes were glazed over with what looked like love, his nostrils were flaring, and sweat rolled down his temple as he gritted his teeth waiting for her to come first. One of his hands slipped down to her clit and rubbed it a few times. "Don't close your eyes. Look at me." Mark rumbled when Maggie's mouth opened, and she came again.

Mark placed his open hands behind her head, his thumbs on her cheeks, holding her in place. "You are mine. Say it."

Maggie stared at his intense gaze as he pleaded with her to agree with him. He didn't need to plead; she didn't want anyone else. "I'm yours and you're mine." Maggie rubbed his back, never breaking eye contact. She felt Mark's body grow taught, his cock growing even bigger before he growled, finally letting go of his self-control, and emptying himself inside her. His body relaxed into her as soon as he finished.

"I love you, Maggie." His eyes went from having storm clouds to frightened. She heard him suck in a breath and hold it.

Maggie cupped his face. "I love you, Mark."

Mark's eyes closed for a second before he released his breath. A smile spread over his face. His hand stroked her cheek while he looked at her with love-filled eyes.

"You've made me the happiest man on earth." Mark kissed her. "Let's shower and hold each other before we have to face the shitstorm waiting for us."

"I'd like that." Maggie smiled. "Besides, you still owe me a massage."

"I gave you a massage." Mark pulled her out of bed.

"You massaged all my pleasure points, but I don't recall you massaging my shoulders, my arms or my legs, Big Sexy." Maggie followed him into the bathroom.

"True, Miss Unsatisfied." Mark turned on the water and got it nice and hot.

"Whoa, I didn't say I was unsatisfied." Maggie pinched his ass. Mark jumped and swatted her hand. "I just said I wanted a massage."

"Keep pinching my ass and you'll get a massage and then some." Mark slapped her ass and pulled her into the shower.

"Promises, promises," Maggie mumbled against his mouth.

*** Mark ***

"I need to go talk to Chris and make some calls," Mark announced after he got dressed. "Go ahead and get dressed. I'll be back in a few minutes."

"What calls? Is something wrong?" Maggie peeked around the shower curtain.

"No." Mark leaned his back against the sink and crossed his arms. "I just want to make sure the room at the resort is ready for us."

"Okay." Maggie dried herself and wrapped the towel around her before stepping out.

"I'm gonna let Sky come in." Mark helped her step out of the shower and headed for the door. "Is that okay?"

"Always. I love Sky." Maggie smiled at him.

As soon as Mark opened the bedroom door, Sky jumped off the couch and ran inside. "I'm sorry, girl." Mark bent down to pet and hug her. "Go ahead, you can get on the bed and wait for Maggie." Sky barked and got on the bed, sitting on her hind legs and facing the bathroom door.

Mark chuckled and shook his head. He knocked once before entering the cockpit.

"Everything good back there?" Chris said once he put on the headset.

"Yeah," Mark sighed. "All good up here?"

"Yep." Chris nodded. "We should land in around four to five hours."

"Great. I need to make some calls." Mark rubbed the back of his neck.

"Sounds good."

Mark left the cockpit and sat on the couch. His first call was to Alex.

"Hey, man," Alex answered on the second ring. "What's up?"

"We're heading back. Should be there in four to five hours." Alex put the phone on speaker and laid it on his lap.

"Sounds good. It'll be easier to watch her and Tori if they're in the same location. I know originally you wanted to take her to your house, but..." Alex never got to finish because Mark interrupted him.

"It's fine. I get it." Mark rubbed his eyes. He'd acted like a possessive cave man when he pulled Maggie out of the resort. The green-eyed monster called jealousy had bit him hard when he saw her with Barrett. Things were different now; he knew Maggie was his and she loved him. The resort was the best place for her to be. "I'm gonna stay with her, that cool?"

"Of course. As long as Maggie's good with that, we're cool."

"Thanks. How's Tori?" Mark should've asked that first, but his mind always went to Maggie first.

"She's good. Wedding preparations are a good distraction."

"I bet." Mark smiled even though he knew Alex couldn't see his face. "Still set for New Year's Eve?"

"Yep. Frey and Tori are in a frenzy, but I think deep down they are loving every minute of it. Holt and I are trying to steer clear and only given our opinions when asked."

"As a good fiancée should," Mark laughed.

"Especially if I want to be able to fuck my fiancée before the wedding. Hey!" Alex shouted. Mark heard Tori mumble something in the background. "I gotta go. I have some groveling to do. See ya tomorrow. Baby..."

Mark laughed when Alex hung up on him. Unless Alex went to great lengths to beg for forgiveness, he wasn't having sex until the wedding.

Mark dialed Thunder's number.

"Hey. Is Maggie okay?" Thunder answered before the phone even stopped ringing. He wasn't surprised. Thunder was a huge protector of women and kids.

"What about me?" Mark teased him.

"Pfft. You're fine. You're calling me and your voice sounds perfectly fine." Add perceptive to Thunder's many talents.

"Then why did you ask about Maggie, if my voice sounds fine?" Mark was messing with him.

"Stop busting my balls. What's up?"

Mark laughed. "Maggie's fine. I just wanted to let you know we should be landing in about four hours, and we are going to stay at the resort. I spoke to Alex and he said you both thought that was the best idea."

"We do. I'm glad you agree." Mark heard a hesitation in his voice. "Are you guys good?"

"Yeah, we're good. We're together and we love each other." Mark leaned back and placed the phone on his chest.

"Yay! I knew it!" Mark heard Isa yell.

"Sorry," Thunder grumbled. "Isa saw it was you and pushed the speakerphone button. She's worried about Maggie."

"No worries," Mark chuckled. He was glad Maggie had Isa as her friend.

"Can I talk to her?" Isa's voice came over the phone louder. She must have taken the phone from Thunder.

"Honey, they'll be home in four hours." Mark heard Thunder tell her. "We can meet them at the resort and you guys can leave us to go discuss the double wedding."

"Fine," Isa sighed. "But you owe me a foot massage until they get here."

"Sure, honey. Mark I gotta go. I've been given my orders from my beautiful and very pregnant wife. We'll see you at the resort."

"Sounds good." Mark smiled and hung up. Maggie would be happy to find out Isa would be at the resort when they arrived. He didn't know about Tori, it all depended on how well Alex groveled. Mark sat up and headed to the bedroom. Maggie was lying on her back with Sky's head on her abdomen. Mark laid next to her and pulled her into his arms. Later, when Mark told Maggie to roll over for her massage, Sky grumbled and jumped down, leaving them to their foreplay and lovemaking–smart dog.

Chapter 52

Home Shitshow Home

Mark

When they got home, Isa and Maggie ran into Maggie's bedroom and shut the door, leaving Thunder and Mark in the living room until late at night. Mark figured Maggie was telling Isa all about her time in Montana. Mark and Thunder watched sports until the girls came out. Mark had a beer, but Thunder didn't drink since he was driving Isa home. He always said he was carrying precious cargo and wasn't taking any chances. After they left, Mark and Maggie enjoyed a night of passion, making up for their week of celibacy.

Glancing over at Maggie, he saw she was still sleeping. Good, she needed her rest after their marathon sex. Plus, he wanted to set up some surprises for Maggie. His goals for today and tomorrow were to give her the best Christmas Eve and Day she's ever had. Sliding out of bed, he took a quick shower, and quietly slipped out of the bedroom.

"Sky, come." Mark patted his leg and put Sky's K-9 officer vest on before they left the room. Dogs weren't allowed in the resort, but since Sky was a K-9 officer, the Panthers had let him keep Sky in the room. He decided, since he had to take Sky out to do her business, he would order breakfast in bed for him and Maggie. On his way downstairs to get it, he made a couple of phone calls to set up Maggie's surprise.

The last phone call he made was to José.

"Hey. Everything okay?" José sounded tired.

"Yeah, we're good." Mark stopped in the lobby and sat in front of the fountain. "We got in last night. How are you?"

"Alive." José coughed. "Those fuckers tried to burn down our clubhouse, but we stopped it in time and returned the favor. It was a late night."

"Did your attempt work?" Mark wished they would stay out of it and let the police take care of the LR's.

"Yep, but now they've scattered. Not sure where they all are. Things are tense, to say the least." José sighed. "Not gonna lie, I wish you guys were still gone, but I get it."

"How's Lola?" Mark wished they were still in Montana too after hearing that. But for how long could they hide out? They had lives to live, and those lives were here.

"Same."

"Sorry, man." Mark told him about his surprise for Maggie before he hung up. José was on board.

Mark walked into Savor and recognized Tiffany, one of the servers.

"Hi, Mark. Alex isn't here yet. Do you want to have a seat?"

Mark smirked at Tiffany. He knew why Alex wasn't here yet–still groveling–but he wasn't about to tell Tiffany. "I actually didn't come to see Alex. I came to place a to go order."

"Oh, of course. Have a seat. I'll give you a few minutes to look over the menu. Do you want anything to drink while you wait? Coffee?"

"Coffee would be great. Thank you." Mark opened the menu and looked at his choices. After spending a week with Maggie, he knew what she liked. When Tiffany placed the coffee in front of him, he was ready to order. Sky whined, he needed to take her out.

"I'm ready." Mark smiled at Tiffany.

"Great." Tiffany took out her pad. "What can I get you?"

"Can I get a veggie omelet with wheat toast and two eggs scrambled with cheese. Please add a side of bacon and fruit. Oh, and two coffees to go. I'm gonna take Sky out. I'll be right back." Mark stood and handed her the menu when she stopped writing.

Tiffany ripped the sheet off her pad and looked at Mark. "I'll give this to Bernie and tell him it's to go."

"I'll take that." Alex pulled the sheet out of Tiffany's hand and smiled at her.

"Good morning. I thought you might be delayed longer." Mark covered his smile with the mug and took a sip.

"Nope. Hey, girl." Alex smirked and petted Sky. "I did my best grovel, worked hard, and won the best fiancée award ever by this morning."

Mark burst out laughing almost spewing his coffee out of his mouth. "Oh, yeah?"

"Yep." Alex looked around, probably making sure Tori didn't hear his bullshit before he leaned in and whispered. "I'm that good. No doghouse for me."

"Yet." Mark quirked an eyebrow at him.

"True, my friend, true." Alex slapped him on the back and walked away with his order.

Mark grabbed his coffee and walked Sky outside. Everyone admired Sky, luckily people knew not to pet her when she had on her working vest. Mark walked her around while she sniffed the grass to find a good spot. Mark scanned the parking lot looking for any trouble. When Sky finished, she sat next him, and people watched. Mark felt bad keeping her cooped up inside, so he sat on a bench and let her take in some fresh air. He took out his phone to call his mom and let her know they were good. He texted her last night, but he wanted to talk to her and thank her for everything.

*** Maggie ***

Maggie woke up to an empty bed. Where were Mark and Sky? Maggie did a full body stretch and felt a twinge in parts of her body she didn't know existed. Last night had been a better workout than going to the gym. She grabbed her phone to check the time and saw the bracelet Mark gave her as an early Christmas present. She wanted to give him something just as special, but she only had one day to go shopping.

Her mind was racing with ideas like a shirt, sweater, or watch, but none seemed personal enough. Plus, he didn't want her strolling around the mall. *That's it!* Maggie snapped her fingers and called Isa.

"Mornin' Mags. How are you feeling?"

"I'm good. Really good." Maggie rolled to the side and grabbed Mark's pillow. She could still smell his woodsy scent.

"I bet," Isa laughed.

"Can you do me a favor?"

"Of course. What do you need?"

"Can you go to my room at my cousin's apartment and get a black box that's stashed in the back corner of the bottom drawer in my dresser under my shorts?" Maggie knew what Isa was bringing her would make a great gift for Mark.

"Why can't your cousin bring it tonight?"

"Why would she? She doesn't even know I'm home." Maggie was confused by Isa's question.

"Ah...right." Isa sounded weird. "Never mind, just ignore me, I'm losing track of my days. Yes, I'll bring it over today around lunchtime. I'll call Nancy now. Can you text me those directions in case I forget by the time I get there? Pregnancy brain and all that."

"Okay, sure. I'll text it now." Maggie swiped up and texted the instructions. "Don't tell Mark. It's a surprise."

"Okay. See you later," Isa said and hung up. Maggie looked at her phone. That was a strange call. Isa never hung up that quickly on her. This pregnancy must really be getting to her.

Maggie pulled the covers off and swung her legs over the side, ready to stand up when she heard Mark's voice.

"Hey, Darlin' where you goin'?" Mark was carrying a big bag and two coffees. His eyes traveled all over her naked body. Maggie noticed when he let his guard down, his Montana southern drawl was more prominent. "Sit back. I got you breakfast. Let me get it ready for you and I'll be back. Sky, come," Mark croaked.

"She can sit with me." Maggie tugged the sheet back up securing it tightly under her arms. Sky had been sitting at attention, but left the room when Mark gave her the command.

"Let me take the vest off and then I'm sure she'll run into the bed with you." Mark left and Maggie ran into the bathroom to empty her bladder and put on a robe. She came back and sat when a ball of fur ran to her and leapt onto the bed, pushing Maggie back while she licked her face.

"Sky, you're crazy." Maggie was laughing, petting any part of Sky's body that she could reach.

"Sky, really?" Mark stood in the doorway, holding two plates.

Sky backed up and laid down, placing her paws over her face. Maggie covered her mouth to stifle her laughter.

"You're no better," Mark mumbled and handed her a plate.

Maggie took the plate and patted Sky. "I think we're both in trouble." Sky howled and put her head on Maggie's abdomen, her favorite place.

Mark shook his head and placed his plate on his nightstand. "I'm gonna go get your coffee. Sky?" Mark pointed to his food. "Do not touch."

"I'll make sure she doesn't eat your food."

"Make sure she doesn't eat yours either. You need your energy for tonight." With those parting words and the sexy look on his face, Maggie clenched her thighs, her breasts tingling.

Mark put her coffee on her nightstand and kissed the top of her head.

"I talked to your brother." Mark dropped that bomb as soon as he sat next to her.

"Is he okay?"

"Yes, but both clubs are stirring up trouble. I need you to stay inside for the next few days." Mark forked some omelet into his mouth.

"What kind of trouble?" Maggie lost her appetite and the few bites she'd eaten were swirling around in her stomach, making her sick. She pushed her food around her plate, but couldn't bring herself to take another bite.

"Maybe I should tell you after you eat." Mark motioned to her plate with his fork.

"I'm not hungry." Maggie put the plate back on the nightstand and Sky cried, licking her chops.

"Sexy Girl, I need you to eat." Mark turned his body and cupped her face in his palm. "Please."

Maggie grabbed her plate and ate a few more bites before setting it aside again. "I can't stomach the bacon. Do you want it? Or can I give it to Sky?"

"You can give it to Sky." Mark smiled as Sky waited patiently for Maggie to give her the two strips. "She'll love you forever now."

"Please tell me what you meant?" Maggie put the plate back on the nightstand and laid back down, curling up under the covers.

"Okay."

Maggie watched Mark cut up the rest of his omelet and put the plate on the floor. "Sky, eat."

Facing her, he crawled under the covers and pulled her into his arms. Was it that bad? Was her brother okay?

"You're scaring me." Maggie whispered as she laid her head on his chest and wrapped her leg and arm around his body. She needed to his warmth.

"Darlin' your brother is okay." Mark placed one hand behind his head while the other ran soothingly down her back. "The LR's tried to burn their clubhouse..."

"What?" Maggie bolted upright bracing herself with a hand on his abs as she stared into his eyes. "Is everyone okay?"

"They put it out quick, but they retaliated and burned down the LR's clubhouse. The LR's weren't so lucky and now they've scattered. No one knows where they are. So, we need to be careful."

"Oh, shit." Maggie dropped back onto his chest. "That's not good."

"No," Mark sighed. "I need to talk to everybody and let them know to stay alert."

"Do you think they would come here?" Maggie snuggled closer.

"I don't know, but neither Sky nor I are leaving your side." Mark removed his hand from behind his head and held her tightly. "I got you."

"Can we just lay here, watch something on TV, and keep the world away for a little while longer?"

"Of course we can, Darlin'." Mark reached over for the remote and turned on the TV. "What do you want to watch?"

"A Christmas movie?" Maggie didn't care it if was a romance or a children's movie. Christmas was her favorite holiday and she wanted to be in the moment.

"This channel is playing all those animated ones back-to-back. Do you want to watch these?" Mark was still on the guide.

"Oh, yes, please. I love those." Maggie used to watch them with her family growing up. They reminded her of happier times.

"Okay. Let me take these plates into the kitchen. I'll be back." Mark cleaned up and came back to lie with Maggie.

Around lunchtime, Isa stopped by with Thunder. They brought them burgers because Isa had a craving for a bacon cheeseburger with fries. Isa secretly gave Maggie the box and they left after lunch. They were headed to Aurora's house for their Christmas Eve. Mark walked them out so Sky could go outside. Maggie went back into the bedroom and laid down. Maggie would love to see her aunt and uncle, eat some Cuban food, and visit with her cousin. Some years, José would sneak into her room and visit with her for a little while. She wasn't going to get to see him either. The enormous sense of loss overwhelmed her, and she wailed into the pillow.

Chapter 53

Turn That Frown Upside Down

Mark

As soon as he stepped into the room, Mark heard loud wailing sounds coming from the bedroom. What the hell was going on? Was Maggie hurt? Did someone get in the room? Mark ran into the room after Sky and froze in the doorway. His beautiful girl was in the fetal position, sobbing into the pillow. Her body shook so hard, his heart shattered just watching her. He wanted to tell her everything was going to be okay, but that was a promise he couldn't keep. If the two rival clubs kept fighting, he couldn't guarantee José's safety.

Sky sat at the foot of the bed, crying. Mark walked up to the bed and spooned Maggie. Wrapping his arms around her, he stroked her hair away from her face. "I wish I could take all this pain away from you. Let it all out, Darlin'. I'm here for you."

Maggie didn't say a word, she just cried harder while Mark held her and tucked her head under his chin. It seemed like they laid there forever. Eventually, all the crying must've tired her out, because Maggie fell asleep. Mark checked the time and saw his surprise would arrive in an hour. He had some cleaning to do. Slowly, so as not to disturb Maggie, he got up and closed the bedroom door.

He called Sehoy.

"Good afternoon, Rock 'n' Roll Resort & Casino, how may I help you?'

"Hi, Mrs. Panther. It's Mark. Did Alex, ask you for some items for me?" Mark crossed his fingers, hoping Alex had come through for him.

"Hi, Mark. Call me Sehoy. Yes, he did. Are you ready for them?"

"Yes, ma'am."

"Perfect. I'll have one of our bellhops bring them to you."

"Thank you so much." Mark released his breath, not realizing he'd been holding it.

"Not a problem. Anything for you and Maggie. I hope you don't mind, Alex and Tori told me what happened. If there is anything else either of you need, please call me."

"I will. Thank you again." Mark said goodbye and hung up. Part one of his plan was coming together. Part two would come into play as soon as the bellhop brought him the items he requested. Then the grand finale would happen in forty-five minutes. Maggie's nap couldn't have come at a better time. Unfortunately, the reason for her being so tired was not ideal.

Mark stood in the doorway with his foot propping the door open. He didn't want the bellhop to knock and wake her up. When the elevator doors opened, his mouth dropped in awe of all the boxes the bellhop had on a cart rolling toward him. He thought Sehoy could only spare a box, but this...this was fantastic. Mark helped him unload them in the foyer of their room and tipped him. Time to get to work organizing everything and making it look good.

Forty-five minutes later, he put on the final touch, spinning around when he heard Maggie gasp from the bedroom doorway.

"Oh, my God! Mark?" Maggie walked slowly into the room, looking all around. "It looks like a winter wonderland in here. Where did you get all this?"

Mark spread out his arms. "Do you like it? Sehoy Panther hooked me up."

"It's so beautiful." Maggie touched every strand of green leafy garland adorned with white flowers that were dipped in silver glitter. Twinkling white lights, wrapped garland-style and draped across the room, cast a warm glow across their living room. The scent of pine filled the air as the candle inside the glass globe on the cocktail table flickered, its light dancing on the festive garland of pinecones. When she approached the dining room table, he watched her count out the seven place settings with Christmas dishes and glasses.

"Why seven?" Maggie tilted her head, staring at the table.

"Because we have seven guests, including us." Mark walked up behind her and spun her around. "I have another surprise for you."

Knock, knock.

Mark checked his watch and kissed her forehead. "Right on time."

"We're here and we brought everything you asked." Aunt Inez came through the door and walked up to Maggie for a hug.

"*Tía*, you're here." Mark turned around to see Maggie openly crying while she hugged her aunt.

"*Mi niña*, we're all here." Aunt Inez stepped back and looked around. "Wow, *qué lindo*. You did a good job, Mark." Uncle Thomas, Nancy, and Kevin all came through the door pulling another cart filled with items.

"What is all this?" Maggie walked to the cart after hugging everyone.

"We brought Christmas Eve to you!" Nancy shouted. "Per your boyfriend's instructions."

"You did all this for me?" Maggie looked at Mark, tears in her eyes.

"We" –Mark pointed to all of them– "did all of this for you."

"I don't know what to say," Maggie whispered as the tears rolled down her face.

"Darlin', just to see you happy is all the thanks we need." Mark wiped her tears and kissed both cheeks.

"We even brought you a real tree to decorate," Nancy announced. "Although it already looks pretty festive in here."

"Where is it?" Maggie looked at the cart. Kevin stepped out and came back in with a six-foot Douglas Fir Christmas Tree.

"It's so beautiful. Can we put the tree in front of that window in the corner?" Maggie pointed to the corner to the left of the TV.

"Darlin', we can put the tree anywhere you want." Mark helped Kevin set up the tree in the stand. They spun it around several times until Maggie found the side she liked best.

"Let's let it sit for a while and have dinner." Aunt Inez, Maggie, and Nancy took the food into the kitchen to sort it out while the boys carried the boxes with ornaments and more garlands next to the tree. They set up the food buffet style, so everyone grabbed their plate, walked into the kitchen, and served themselves.

"Maggie, I'm gonna take this cart down in case someone needs it. I'll be right back." Mark hollered before he pulled the cart out.

Chapter 54

Guess Who?

Mark

Mark didn't wait for Maggie's reply. José had just texted him that he was just pulling into the parking lot. Mark was going to sneak him in for Maggie. He only hoped he hadn't ridden his motorcycle and worn his MC kutte. Arriving in the lobby, he didn't see José until a man in a suit stood directly in front of him. Holy Shit! It was José with his hair slicked back and all dressed up.

"Fuck, man. You clean up well." Mark gave him a slap on the back and led him toward the elevator.

"Thanks. I must've done a good job if you didn't recognize me."

"Did you ride your bike in that suit?" Mark pointed at him.

"Nah, I borrowed a Mercedes." José grinned at Mark through the glass interior of the elevator.

Mark groaned. "Shit, did you steal it? Do I even want to know?"

"Let's just say I borrowed it and will be returning it as soon as I leave here. No harm, no foul." José shoulder bumped Mark. "Thanks for helping me out. How's my sister?"

"Scared for you, mainly. But doing good. Having her family here is making her very happy." Mark walked out ahead of José and led him to their room. "She's gonna love seeing you. Lola couldn't come?"

"She's struggling. Maybe some other time." José buttoned up his suit jacket, ready for his reveal.

"Sounds good." Mark swiped his card and held the door open for José.

"*¡Feliz Noche Buena!*" José yelled as soon as he cleared the door.

"¡José!" Maggie screamed and came barreling toward him. "Oh my God, it is you! You look so handsome. Are you hurt anywhere?" Maggie turned him around in every direction possible, checking for injuries. Mark leaned against the wall, watching them.

"Margarita, I'm fine." José hugged her. "Happy to see you, *mi hermanita*."

"*Hola, tía, tío,* Nancy, Kevin." José greeted each one respectively with handshakes.

Mark was so busy watching Maggie's family's cool reception of José, he missed Maggie hurling herself at him. It was a good thing he was already leaning against the wall. If he hadn't been, they would've crashed to the floor.

"I love you." Maggie continued to say thank you at least ten times in between kisses.

"I love you too, Darlin'." Mark gave her a quick peck and eased her into the dining room. Her brother needed saving, and Maggie was the perfect one to step in and make conversation, since it was all about making Maggie happy tonight. No one was going to rock the boat. Mark filled his plate with food and made no comment when the only empty chair was between José and Kevin.

Looking around, he saw the tension in Aunt Inez and Uncle Thomas' faces, but they remained respectful and cordial during the meal. Mark hadn't told the rest of Maggie's family José was coming. He was afraid, they would bail on him if they knew. Uncle Thomas glared at him a couple of times during the meal, but Mark ignored it. They could talk later. Right now, Maggie needed all her family to surround her with their love and that included her brother.

When dinner was over, they put on Christmas music and decorated the tree. Mark offered to clean up so she could spend quality time with them. He hadn't seen Maggie this happy since they left Montana.

"Why didn't you tell us you invited him?" Uncle Thomas stood next to Mark, holding a plate by the sink.

"Because I wasn't sure if you would come," Mark murmured.

"Everything that has happened to that sweet girl has been his fault." Uncle Thomas raised his voice, but not loud enough for Maggie to hear over the Christmas music.

"Lower your voice," Mark growled as he continued to wash the dishes. "Don't do this here, tonight. Look at her." Mark pointed at Maggie. "She's so happy having all of you together in this room. Please, for tonight, just be civil. You don't have to like each other, just tolerate each other. You can pick up your fight tomorrow."

"Fine." Uncle Thomas shoved his plate at Mark. "But I'm only doing this for her."

"I understand." Mark looked at him. "Thank you."

Uncle Thomas took a deep breath and left the kitchen, heading over to sit with his wife while the kids decorated the tree. Mark finished up in the kitchen just in time for the tree topper.

"What are we going to put on the top?" Mark saw Maggie looking around in all the boxes. "They're all empty." Seeing her dejected look made Mark feel like shit for not thinking of a tree topper. He should've bought her an angel in Montana or gone to his house and brought his.

"I have something." Aunt Inez stood and grabbed her purse which looked to be the size of a mini suitcase. Aunt Inez pulled out a beautiful Angel dressed in white.

"Oh my God." Maggie covered her mouth, tears coming quickly. José hugged her before Mark could reach her. "Where did you find it?"

"In a box in our garage. When Mark asked me to bring some decorations, I began looking through all the boxes and came across a couple from your parent's house. Several had Christmas decorations. My brother loved

Christmas, and I couldn't bring myself to throw out any of their decorations. One box even has all the Christmas crafts you and José made for your parents from school. I didn't know how much room you had here, so I only brought the angel. When you're ready, you can come get those boxes and sort through them." Aunt Inez walked toward Maggie with the angel.

"Thank you," Maggie whispered before she hugged her tight. "This means so much to me."

"*Gracias, tía.*" José murmured and hugged them both. At first, Aunt Inez's body stiffened, but then she relaxed, and they all held each other. Aunt Inez held her hand out and Nancy and Uncle Thomas joined in the hug. Even Mark had to wipe a tear from his eye. Kevin walked toward him.

"Thank you for this," Kevin said loud enough only for Mark's ears. "They needed to forgive each other. José's never been welcomed in Aunt Inez's house which is why he would sneak in to see Maggie. But this family needed to heal. They may not agree with his life choices, but he's always tried to protect them, along with Nancy and Maggie."

"I'll be honest, I wasn't sure how tonight was going to go, but I'm glad you all came." Mark put his arm around Kevin, and they toasted with their glasses.

"Mark," Maggie called him over after the family hug. "Can you help me put the angel on top?"

"I would be honored." Mark set his glass down and walked to Maggie. Gazing into her eyes, he bent down and picked her up under her thighs. Maggie held onto his head with one hand and leaned into the tree with the other. Setting the angel on top, she pulled the cord down the center of the tree until she found a lights outlet to plug into. Mark held her up until the angel lit up.

Mark heard her suck in a breath.

"Good job, Darlin'." Mark let her body slide down his.

"It's just like I remember," Maggie whispered. Mark looked around and watched everyone, faces glued to the special angel. He wrapped her up in his arms from behind and rested his chin on her head. "It's beautiful."

"Yes, it is." Maggie wrapped her arms around his. "Thank you."

After a few minutes, José cleared his throat and approached Maggie. "Margarita, I have to go. Lola is not feeling well, and I don't want to be gone too long."

"I understand. Please give her a hug for me." Maggie hugged José. "I love you. Please be careful."

"I will." José stepped back and looked at Mark. "Thank you for this. I'll never forget it. We haven't had a night like this in a long time. I will treasure this memory forever."

"I'm glad we could make it work." Mark went to shake his hand, but José pulled him in for a hug. "We're huggers, you know that."

"Yeah. I'll walk you out." Mark moved to step around him, but José stopped him.

"No need. It'll be better if I slip out on my own." José turned to Nancy. "*Prima,* always good to see you and your husband." José hugged them both. "*Tía, tío,* forgive me, please. I never meant for any of this to happen. I'm truly sorry." Mark watched José, waiting to see if his aunt and uncle would say something.

It was a tense few seconds before José turned around, shoulders slumped and headed to the door. Mark followed him.

"José," Mark called out, catching the door before it shut. "Please, keep me updated. Maggie and I need to know you are okay."

"You are good for her, gringo." José smiled. "Please, keep her safe. She means the world to me."

"*Gringo*, huh?" Mark smirked. "I guess I've been called worse." Mark laughed then turned serious. "She means the world to me too. You have my word." This time they shook hands, sealing the promise between them.

"*¡José, espera!*"

Mark heard shuffling behind him. The door was pulled open, and Aunt Inez squeezed by him. "Your father accepted your decision to join that club. He loved you very much and would never have turned his back on you. I will honor my brother's decision. I forgive you. Please be careful." Aunt Inez pulled him into a hug and Mark heard her whisper. "*Te quiero mucho, mi sobrino.*"

"*Yo también, José*," Uncle Thomas came out and hugged José.

"Gracias." José stepped back and walked to the elevator. When it arrived and the doors opened, he turned and waved. "Thank you all for giving me the best Christmas present I could ever have. The gift of the family I'd lost." José blew a kiss to them all as the doors closed.

*** Maggie ***

Never in her wildest dreams had she ever imagined her aunt and uncle forgiving her brother. For years, they called him every name in the book and didn't want Maggie to associate with him. But today, thanks to Mark, that all changed. Unbeknownst to him, he closed the gaping hole of pain her family had lived in for the past eleven years. Now more than ever, she knew he was her soulmate, the man she would love and cherish for all the days on this earth and the ever after.

"*Mi niña*," Aunt Inez touched her arm. "We need to go too. Keep the leftovers and enjoy your pastries. We left gifts for you and Mark under the tree. Come for dinner soon, okay?"

"*Sí, tía.* We'll come soon and I'll bring your presents then. With everything going on, I never went to the store." Maggie side hugged Mark.

"We don't need anything except to see you." Aunt Inez hugged her.

"*Gracias por todo.*" Maggie hugged her uncle. "I love you both."

"We love you too," Uncle Thomas responded.

"Well, I left you a present too and I expect one in return, so you'll have to come back to the apartment at some point or I'll hold your stuff hostage." Nancy nodded before turning to her husband. "Right, honey?"

"Yes, dear." Kevin shook his head. When he hugged Maggie, he said, "Come when she's not there, you can take anything you want."

"I heard that," Nancy hollered on her way to the elevator.

Kevin rolled his eyes. "Of course you did," he mumbled.

After they entered the elevator, they turned and waved before the doors closed.

Maggie leaned back into Mark, who was leaning against the doorframe with his hand on her hip.

Maggie waved back and turned to Mark. "Thank you for tonight. Big Sexy, you are going to be rewarded handsomely tonight." Maggie stood on her tippy toes to reach his mouth.

"Oh, yeah?" Mark murmured against her lips.

"Oh, yeah." Maggie winked and walked into the living room. She waited until Mark came in and began to strip for him. Okay, it was a little strange stripping to slow Christmas songs, but from the look on Mark's face, he was enjoying it. After several new positions and multiple orgasms, they crashed onto the couch, naked.

Chapter 55

Christmas Day

Mark

T hey woke up the same way they fell asleep, with the love of their lives in their arms, all the Christmas lights on, and the Christmas music blaring out of the TV. *How did we sleep through that?* Exhaustion and contentment could do that to someone. Right now, Mark felt a heavy dose of both. Maggie stirred and kissed his neck.

"Merry Christmas, Darlin'." Mark rolled on top of her and kissed her.

"Mm, Merry Christmas." Maggie tapped his chest. "I need to go potty and get your gift."

"Okay, meet you back here in ten?" Mark got up and pointed at her. "Stay naked. I like you like that. We can consider it another Christmas gift to me." Mark held his hand out to help her up.

"You're crazy, Surfer Smurf." Maggie put her hand in his and he pulled so hard, she crashed into him.

"I love when you call me those sweet names." Mark ran his hands down to her ass and squeezed.

"Okay, Big Sexy, settle down." Maggie giggled and pushed him back to walk around him. "I gotta pee."

Mark held up his hands. "Okay, okay. Run while you can."

As soon as Maggie left, Mark put on a pair of sweatpants and pulled out the charm he'd hidden in the closet. He placed the box under the tree.

"Darlin'," Mark hollered from the bedroom doorway. "I need to take Sky outside. I'll be back."

"Okay."

Mark took her out and rushed her back in as soon as she finished. He'd take her for a long walk later, but right now he wanted to give Maggie her next charm.

Sky ran in ahead of him and Mark heard Maggie yell. "Sky, no!"

Mark walked into the living room to find Maggie draped naked on the couch with her hand out to ward off Sky. Yep, that would've hurt.

"Just what I like to see, my obedient girls waiting for me." Mark smiled.

"You're lucky she stopped, or you'd be seeing me crying out in pain if she scratched my boobs with her paws." Maggie snorted.

"Sky, you can't maim those beautiful breasts. Go to the other couch." Mark pointed and Sky lowered her head before jumping onto the other couch.

"Now, are you going to drop your pants?" Maggie winked.

"Yes, ma'am. Miss Bossy." Mark kicked off his shoes and let his pants drop to the ground. Stepping out of them he walked to the Christmas Tree.

"Where are you going?" Maggie sat up, dropping her legs to the floor as she watched him.

"Easy there my Little Miss Impatient." Mark bent down and grabbed the box. "I'm coming back."

Mark sat next to her and pulled her onto his lap. "I have a couple more gifts for you."

"I wanna give you mine first." Maggie gave him a wooden mini treasure chest that was no bigger than the palm of his hand. "Open it." She hadn't wrapped it, but that was okay because he hadn't wrapped hers either.

"This is a really cool box." Mark looked at all the sides before opening it and pulling out a necklace. "This is nice. St. Michael, right?"

"Yes. That gift has several special meanings. My dad made that mini treasure chest. It's one of the only crafty pieces I have that he made. He loved to craft things from wood with his hands. Not sure if there's more in those boxes my aunt was talking about, but before I left the wreckage that was my home, I grabbed that box off my dad's dresser. My mom bought him that necklace when he worked the night shift at one of his jobs. She wanted him to stay safe. Ironically, he wasn't wearing it the night of the shooting. I didn't know that until I got to the Los Lobos clubhouse and opened the box." Maggie draped it over his head, placing her hand over the charm on his chest. "I want you to have it so it can keep you safe."

"Oh, Darlin'," Mark pulled her into his arms, one arm wrapped around her waist as the other pressed her head to his chest. "I love it. Thank you."

They stayed like that for a moment. Mark was so used to worrying about Maggie, he hadn't thought about anything happening to him. Knowing how much Maggie wanted him to stay safe was humbling. He would treasure the necklace and vowed to himself to do everything in his power to keep them both safe from the LR's.

"Your turn." Mark held her biceps and pushed her upright.

"You already gave me my gift, my charm bracelet." Maggie lifted her wrist and wiggled it.

Last night, in between lovemaking sessions, Mark had gotten up and slipped the bracelet onto her wrist. He'd wanted her to wake up Christmas morning with his gift of love for her.

"I have something else for you." Mark motioned for Sky, holding up one finger and pointing at the boxes sitting in front of her. Sky picked up the first one with her mouth and brought it to him. Mark said, "Drop." Sky opened her mouth and dropped it into his open hand.

"Open this one first." Mark handed it to Maggie.

"This is perfect for my charm bracelet." Maggie leaned forward and gave him a kiss. It was two silver hearts bound together by a bead. Each heart was engraved with their names. Maggie took off her bracelet and opened it, sliding on the new charm. "Can you put it back on?"

Mark smiled and snapped the lock closed.

Maggie murmured, "It's perfect."

"Not yet, you still have room to add more." Mark chuckled. "Sky." Mark motioned to the other box which Sky brought to him.

"You have something else for me? Mark" –Maggie widened her eyes– "that's too much. You shouldn't have. Wait. When did you?"

"In Montana while you were helping my mom." Mark grinned.

Mark dropped the box in her hand and watched Maggie open the box.

"Oh, wow. They're so beautiful." Maggie's eyes watered as she ran her fingers over the gift. Mark had gotten her a matching set of earrings and a necklace with two twined hearts. In the center where they interlocked was the shape of the infinity symbol with diamonds down one side. Mark took it out and clasped the necklace around her neck. She put the earrings on.

"What do you think?" Maggie twisted and turned her head.

"Beautiful, just beautiful." Mark made the right choice. They were the perfect size, and her face glowed with joy. "I wanted you to know you're mine forever. Pull up that bottom piece in the box, there's something else in there."

*** Maggie ***

Giddy with excitement, Maggie pulled the inside out and covered her mouth. *Oh my God, Oh my God, Oh my God. That's an engagement ring. Holy Shit!* Maggie couldn't stop staring at it. "Is that what I think it is?"

"Yes, my Smart Smurfette." Mark chuckled and took the ring out of the box, holding it up between them. Maggie couldn't stop looking at it. It was stunning. A huge diamond surrounded by smaller diamonds that all shined brilliantly as it moved.

"Look at me," Mark spoke softly. Maggie glanced up from the ring. "Maggie, I know we haven't been together that long and if you want a long engagement, I'm okay with that. I'm old enough to know when the right woman has come into my life and knocked me on my ass. You are smart, beautiful, funny, sexy, driven, and have enough sass to keep me on my toes for the rest of my life. I can't imagine my life without you. I promise to love you with all my heart and protect you always until the day I die. Will you marry me?"

Maggie was still frozen, sitting on his lap with her mouth open. Sky was nudging her leg, probably urging her to answer, so her daddy could relax. She couldn't believe he was proposing to her. They hadn't been together that long, but when you know, you know. He was the perfect man for her. She had already fallen deeply in love with him.

"Oh Shit!" Mark's eyes bugged out. "I'm doing this all wrong. Stand up and I'll get on one knee?" Mark scooted to the edge of the couch, ready to stand up, but Maggie stopped him.

"No, this is perfect, Surfer Smurf." Maggie smiled at him. "Perfectly crazy for us. I would love to marry you and be your wife, forever. I only have one request."

"Name it" –Mark slid the ring onto her finger– "anything I can give you is yours."

"Scoot back and let your fiancée fuck you," Maggie murmured against his lips.

Mark groaned and scooted back, holding her in place. "You can use me any time, any place, any day, any way. I'll be your boy toy...forever."

Chapter 56

Christmas Day...Much Later

Maggie

After making love to seal the deal, it was time to clean up and go downstairs for Christmas Breakfast in Savor with the Panther family. They celebrated the meal like Thanksgiving. Frey with her seating chart, Alex with his cooking, and all the usual attendees. Maggie didn't get two steps into the restaurant before Tori squealed and ran to her, grabbing her hand and congratulating her. Maggie had debated taking the ring off until after Tori and Frey's wedding. She didn't want to take anything away from their day, but in the end, she loved Mark and couldn't wait to show her friends. Maggie told everyone they hadn't set a date. They were taking it one day at a time. Congratulatory hugs spread like wildfire before they all sat down to eat.

This time Deputies George and Sean got to stay throughout the entire meal. Instead of heading to the pool after their meal, they went upstairs to the family floor to open presents.

The best gift was watching the shelter boys open their gifts from everyone. Everyone pitched in and bought Tim a Honda Civic since he was turning eighteen in a couple months and the car he was driving was falling apart. George got him a job at Giovanni's, the restaurant George worked at when he turned eighteen. Holt and Frey got Luke a Kinetic Building Set. They got Kenny and Jimmy each their own Magnetic Dart Game. Bryce raked it in with a Train Table, complete with extra trains and accessories. Alex and Tori gave the kids eShop Gift Cards because Matteo and Gaby gave them Nintendo Switch Lite devices. Barrett was all about the fun and bought them each their own Nerf Gun. Plus, one for himself for a surprise attack after they all opened theirs.

Mark and Maggie got them Remote Control Stunt Cars for indoor play. Grayhorse and Sarah went with sports stuff like Spike Ball for Luke, a glow in the dark basketball for Kenny, an indoor basketball hoop for Jimmy, and Legos for Bryce. Osceola and Sehoy thought to make their home experience more personal and got Luke a mini personal fridge stocked with sodas and water, nightlight Bluetooth speakers for Kenny and Jimmy, and a big bean bag chair and book for Bryce. Thunder and Isa were the practical ones, which made sense since Thunder spent the most time with them at the cultural center and at the shelter. He knew they didn't own many clothes and the ones they had were hand-me-downs from previous boys at the shelter. Thunder wanted them to have their own outfit and duffel in case they went to visit Bryce at the resort for a sleepover. Each child got a duffel bag filled with joggers, a long sleeve hoodie, a T-Shirt (with funny sayings that pertained to each one), and a pair of Vans.

After the presents were all opened, the kids played until everyone left.

Happy Christmas to all, and to all a good night!

Chapter 57

Special Thanks

Neri

Thank you to my wonderful friend Michelle, who listens to me about all my trials and tribulations as I write these stories. Your input is invaluable to me.

My wonderful and patient friend K-9 Deputy Bryan Wright, for answering all my endless texts about law enforcement. Now your name will forever be in print, which you deserve because you are not only an outstanding person, but a caring officer. For this book, I also contacted Sergeant T.J. Williams of our local law enforcement agency. Not only did he answer some questions for this book, but offered to help me in future books. You guys are amazing. Please stay safe out there. If I got anything wrong or applied creative license, it is my doing.

I was writing this book while I was in Alessandra Torre's Boot Camp Workshop thru Inkers Con (see more info on inkerscon.com if you are interested). Alessandra is a New York Times, USA Today, Wall Street Journal and Amazon International bestselling novelist. If you are an up-and-coming author, I would highly recommend taking any of her workshops. In this workshop, I sent parts of my book to three other editors besides my usual editor. This book is a compilation of all four editors who helped me: McKenzie Gibel, Tenesha L. Curtis, Whitney Morsillo, and Michelle Rosquillo. Any mistakes are mine.

Thank you to my readers. I love you guys and am truly grateful for your support. If you have the time, please write a review for me on Amazon or Goodreads.

Chapter 58
About the Author

Neri Lopez has worn many hats as a stay-at-home mom of triplets, graphic designer, and high school teacher (Spanish, Art, and Graphic Design). She lives in Florida with her husband, grown kids, and their fur babies, Mocha and Chewy. She is a crafter of all trades, including crocheting (several craft shows a year), jewelry making, scrapbooking, knitting, sewing, and painting.

Neri loves to hear from her readers, contact her at:

website: sirenbookandcraft.com

(When you sign up for her newsletter, you will receive a FREE downloadable bookmark of Red Path.)

Or follow her on:

facebook: Neri Lopez - Author

instagram: Neri_Lopez_Author

(She is most active on facebook)

The Path Series
Book 1: Red Path (available on Amazon)
Book 2: Unconquered Path (available on Amazon)
Book 3: Wagering Path (available on Amazon)
Book 4: Unexpected Path (available on Amazon)
Novella Book 4.5: Double Trouble Path (2025 – *This novella will be free to anyone on her mailing list.)*
Book 5: Twisted Path (2025)
Book 6: Blue Path (2025)

www.ingramcontent.com/pod-product-compliance
Lightning Source LLC
Chambersburg PA
CBHW061345310726
48974CB00001B/209